Pamela Jooste spent a number of years in publishing and in Public Relations with BP Southern Africa and has written radio and film scripts and award-winning short stories. She has always lived in Cape Town. *Dance with a Poor Man's Daughter* is her first novel, her second, *Frieda and Min*, is now available in Doubleday hardback.

DANCE WITH A POOR MAN'S DAUGHTER

Pamela Jooste

BLACK SWAN

DANCE WITH A POOR MAN'S DAUGHTER
A BLACK SWAN BOOK : 0 552 99757 9

Originally published in Great Britain by Doubleday,
a division of Transworld Publishers Ltd

PRINTING HISTORY
Doubleday edition published 1998
Black Swan edition published 1999
Black Swan edition reprinted 1999

Set in 10/12pt Melior by Kestrel Data, Exeter, Devon.

Black Swan Books are published by Transworld Publishers Ltd,
61–63 Uxbridge Road, London W5 5SA,
in Australia by Transworld Publishers (Australia) Pty Ltd,
15–25 Helles Avenue, Moorebank, NSW 2170,
and in New Zealand by Transworld Publishers (NZ) Ltd,
3 William Pickering Drive, Albany, Auckland.

Reproduced, printed and bound in Great Britain by
Cox & Wyman Ltd, Reading, Berkshire.

For Bernard, a memory

Mother behold
your wilful daughter

Yes the one who ventured
beyond our village is back

I is a long memoried woman

Drum Spell
GRACE NICHOLS

I wonder if a memory is something you
have or something you've lost

Another woman
WOODY ALLEN

The facts are always less than what really happens . . .
If you get a law, like Group Areas, under which various
population groups are . . . uprooted from their homes
and so on, well, somebody may give you the figures,
how many people are moved, how many jobs were lost.
But, to me it doesn't tell you nearly as much as the
story of one individual who lived through that.

Nadine Gordimer, *The Listener*, 21 October, 1970

Author's Note

Some stories insist on being told and *Dance With A Poor Man's Daughter* is one of them but because the events in the story are of a deeply sensitive nature and outside my direct personal experience my being the one to tell it requires some qualification.

I am aware that there may be some people who feel it is the height of impertinence for a white South African to write about the suffering of so-called 'coloured' people: but stories come to writers in many and various ways and are no respecters of person. If a writer feels strongly enough about a subject then that writer must go ahead and say what he has to say, however misguided and however criticized he may be for it.

What happens in these pages did happen. It happened to many black and brown South Africans whose lives were irreparably damaged by the harsh laws put in place to enforce racial segregation.

One cannot catalogue these laws in order of severity and I make no attempt to do so but there is little doubt that the Population Registration Act of 1950, which classified people according to racial group, and the Group Areas Act, which designated certain areas for exclusive use by nominated racial groups, were the most hated and among the most cruel.

Like many other white South African children I was raised by a nanny and like many South African nannies her skin was a different colour from mine and my sorties into her life, a life very different from my own, seemed to me endlessly fascinating.

I had my place at the table in her home which was in the

traditional Muslim quarter of Cape Town. We went together on shopping trips to Hanover Street which was the heart of 'coloured' Cape Town. I was taken by her to watch the 'Coons' and together we did many of the things Lily and her family do in this book.

It was inescapable that her attitudes and view of life should play a large part in shaping my own but I was a white child and my life was different. Perhaps it was this difference that fascinated me and made me such a keen observer of what life was like across the colour line.

It is difficult telling a story of this time without lapsing back into racial epithets. So the people in my story are 'Coloured, Native and White'. I mean no disrespect by this. At the time of which I write, this is how things were and newspaper reports of the day reflect these common usages. Nor do I mean to cause offence by using the terms 'Coon' and 'Coon Carnival'. There has been long and hard debate about these anachronistic terms but in my recall this was a term in common usage in those days and used simply to describe an event and not in any derogatory way.

For people who know Cape Town it will be clear that the Valley of the story incorporates in its geography a bit of the Valley in Mowbray and also something of District Six. Constitution Street exists and the houses there still stand although they stand in a wasteland. Constitution Street in District Six stretches along the contour of Devil's Peak and is not on a hill. Constitution Street in the book is a fiction just as the people who lived in No. 48 are.

Perhaps I should have used a different street name but I could not resist the bitter irony of such a street name in such a place at such a time.

There was another circumstance also that made my life different from the average white Cape Town child. I did not grow up in 'Whites Only' suburbia. I grew up in the docklands where my parents managed a small hotel. This is where we lived and this is where I learned some things about street life and dock life and bars and gangsters and Union Castle liners that come and go and colourful characters like Gus-Seep and Jack Hoxie and Mr Asher.

Mine was a special childhood largely because it was peopled by the same kind of characters I have tried to recreate on these pages but it was not my lot to suffer the pain of discrimination, to have my family broken apart and my home taken from me as a result of the Group Areas Act and the forced removals that came in its wake.

I am sure there will be others who will tell this story differently and more ably and draw on more intimate experience than mine, but stories niggle away in a writer's mind and demand to be told. It is then that we find ourselves compelled to put pen to paper.

I have done my best to tell what I felt needed to be told and to tell it with tenderness and respect for those people who endured such great suffering.

As this is a book mainly about women I ask no pardon for recording here my high regard for the endurance of the so-called 'Coloured' women of the Cape. Many of them suffered the displacement chronicled in this story and strove to keep their families together in the face of almost impossible odds. Some succeeded and some did not but all showed the most remarkable fortitude and courage.

When I was checking the background accuracy of this story in the SA Library I found a cutting from the *Cape Argus* dated 6 August, 1986. This is what it said and in many ways this is what this story is about.

Celebration of Women's Courage

[In 1956] Women of all races and from all over the country gathered in front of the Union buildings and raised their voices to warn the [then] prime minister, Mr J.G. Strijdom, 'You have tampered with the women. You have struck a rock.'

Cape Argus, 6 August, 1986

Dance With a Poor Man's Daughter

Three Wise Men of Gotham

1

Dear Carole-Amelia

Carole-Amelia is my best friend. We live in the same town but we haven't met yet and although it won't be easy we've made plans in this direction which we've decided not to tell anyone else.

Carole-Amelia lives with her mother and father in a house with a garden in Rosedale Garden Village.

'If you ask about us, the first thing our neighbours will say is about the cars standing outside our house. A different one every night.'

This is what she writes.

Their neighbours think something fishy is going on. They think her mother is getting funny visitors. The maid says the neighbours talk about them behind their backs all the time.

They lift their eyebrows when they see the cars and think Carole-Amelia's father is in the crime business. They expect the police to arrive any day to take him away but they're wrong about him, so if the police do come they'll be wasting their time.

That is what she says and then it is my turn.

I tell her my name is Lily Daniels. I live at No. 48 Constitution Street. It is in the Valley and no white people really live here any more so perhaps she has never heard of it before. I don't know.

What I do know is that neither of us is old enough to have done much yet, so I don't think she will mind me asking what exactly she knows and what she doesn't know. I had never heard of Rosedale Garden Village before either.

I tell her that this is the house where I was born and because I still live here she can work out for herself that I haven't been around the world much yet and there are probably a lot of things I still have to find out about.

We're all women in our house, my grandmother, my Aunt Stella and me. This is what I write and then I think a little bit before I put down the next bit which is that the men in our family are not worth much.

Perhaps you shouldn't say that about your own relations but in our case it happens to be true and no-one around here can call me a liar for saying it.

'This includes my aunty's husband, my dead Uncle Maxie. He was a gangster but never blood family of ours, so you needn't worry on that score.'

Gangsters aren't everyone's cup of tea and I don't want Carole-Amelia to get the wrong idea about us.

'We got Maxie through a marriage mistake and he died with a knife in his ribs. Good riddance is what we said when that happened because he was good for nothing and broke my aunty's heart.'

The other men in our family aren't as bad as Maxie but it's no secret they're the cross we have to bear. We accepted this a long time ago. My grandmother says life's like that. You can pick your friends but you can't choose your family and it's no good complaining about it.

Life will make up its own mind what it feels like dishing out to us and whatever it is we must accept our portion without complaint and with a good heart.

So we have our life and as far as men are concerned, we have our own stories to tell.

My uncle, Gus-Seep, for example. He doesn't live with us but sometimes when we get up in the morning we find him drunk asleep on the floor of our front room. This is because when he gets a few down his neck he gets homesick. It doesn't matter where he is. It happens even if he's just around the corner and practically on our doorstep.

When he's like this, his heart gets sore and he wants to come back to his mother's house which he says he can find even if he's blindfold and with a skinful under his belt. So this is what he does and never mind how often he does it and despite what people say, drink is not my uncle's whole life.

He is also keen on the horses. Especially racehorses. In that department, his favourite is a filly called Flora Dora. He had so much to say about this horse I felt as if she was a real person and I knew her.

In the end he cut a picture out of the newspaper so I could see for myself what she looks like. He gave it to me to look at, but at the same time he told me he was having second thoughts about letting me see it at all. Then he decided I could see it after all, although I must say he seemed a bit nervous while I made up my mind about his darling.

All the time I was looking at her picture Gus-Seep was looking over my shoulder, mumbling in his boots and making excuses because the picture doesn't really do Flora Dora justice and he doesn't want me to get any wrong ideas.

He needn't have worried. She's a beautiful horse, smooth as satin and dark as night and although she's not an odds-on favourite she's still his favourite, and I'd already decided to like her even before I saw her, no matter what she looked like.

Gus-Seep says Flora Dora will be his favourite for as long as God spares her but we don't know how long that will be, because horses don't live as long as people do.

In any case, in the meantime, while she's still with us, he has a soft spot for Flora Dora. He can't help it. It's because there was a time she was very good to him. Good in the way you feel in your back pocket and anyone will tell you Gus-Seep is not a man to forget a favour.

Gus-Seep is very tender-hearted when it comes to animals, especially horses. If things had been different, he might have been a jockey himself but it didn't turn out like that, so now he has to wait while the horses whisper their money-making secrets to his friends down at the stables and ask them to pass these along to him.

He had great hopes once upon a time but after what

19

happened Gus-Seep had to put his ideas about riding racehorses behind him. Flora Dora will never go past the winning post with Gus-Seep sitting on her back, but life takes away with one hand and gives back with the other and in the end things turned out for the best.

Gus-Seep got his horse even though it wasn't the horse of his dreams, but then not all horses are racehorses and get their picture in the newspaper. Some horses are like some people. They have to work for a living and this is what Gus-Seep's horse does. Gus-Seep is very proud of him. He says people can say what they like. Looks aren't everything and when it comes to work this is a horse who knows what he's doing.

During the week he and Gus-Seep go down to the Grand Parade and the horse stands still as a soldier and patient as a saint while Gus-Seep sells fruit and vegetables off the cart at his back.

Gus-Seep is a twenty-cents-a-bag man and he's got plenty of customers. People down at the Parade know him and look out for him because he always has a story to tell and a laugh and his horse always has a little something too, that makes him special, like flowers or a few feathers stuck into his bridle or anything else Gus-Seep can get his hands on and likes the look of.

On Saturday mornings when his horse goes out in the field for a rest Gus-Seep comes walking to our house to give my grandmother her share of the week's money and the fruit and vegetables that are left over, because it's waste not want not at our house and there's always something we can do with food. On Saturdays I help him pick the winners because it's on their backs his share of the week's money will go and usually we do it with my grandmother's hatpin.

There's nothing to it really, although Gus-Seep says that's fine for me to say because I'm so good at it.

He doesn't know if he should tell me because it's a mixed blessing but I have what people call 'the touch'. This is something very few people have and that's why he always makes a point of asking me to tell him who the winners will be.

It would be no good asking anyone else. Either you have 'the touch' or you don't and my touch is more than good enough for Gus-Seep. It's our little secret and he wants us to keep it that way just in case the day should come when he hits a winning streak. Then our secret must stay where it belongs which is between ourselves and in the family.

That's what he says but I'm not so sure. If what Gus-Seep says about 'the touch' is true he would be a rich man today and he isn't.

What you do is close your eyes and wave the hatpin over the horse bible with all the horses' names in it. Then with your eyes closed you circle the pin around three times as if it was a magic wand and when Gus-Seep says, 'Now Is The Hour,' you jab it down on the book as hard as you like so it sticks in a horse's name, then you open your eyes and shout out the name of the horse and that's that. It's easy when you know how.

This is the way I picked Carole-Amelia although Carole-Amelia is not a horse even if she sounds like one and I used a pencil instead of the hatpin because that's what I had in my hand when the choose-list came in my direction.

I think this is where I went wrong. This and Carole-Amelia being a person not a horse. I think maybe this kind of thing doesn't work so well for people.

Anyway, I did it. I know it's a funny way to choose a best friend but funnier things have happened in the history of the world.

When it suits him, Stella's son, whose real name is Royston, sometimes comes back to our house for a day or two at a time to lie low and then he sleeps in his old cellar room under the house.

Royston has gone bad and become a gangster like his late father and sometimes the police or other gangsters are looking for him. They come rattling on our gate, shouting out his name and asking if he's inside and you can see just by looking at them, they have murder on their minds.

'You tell him we know all about him and we're waiting for him,' they say and you can smell the wine from where you're standing half behind the front door and as far away from the gate as you can get.

When we know it's them at the gate it's always Stella or me who runs quick to the door to shout at them to get away because if my grandmother gets there ahead of us, she'll have a heart attack and go right outside to chase after them.

If she can get there fast enough she'll throw a bucket of water over them as if they are mongrel dogs and they can shout knives and murder at her as much as they like, it won't worry her. She'll still call them cheap Jacks and no-good rubbish and she doesn't care who hears her.

'You tell him we're waiting for him,' they say and it's Royston lying under the bed in the cellar room they mean. 'You just be sure and give him the message and tell him to watch his step.'

'You watch your step yourself,' Stella says. 'We've said all we have to say to the likes of you so you're wasting your time hanging around here trying to cause trouble.'

We won't step right outside the door but we hold our ground and give them hands-on-the-hips, flash-eye, don't-care looks.

They say if Royston is hiding somewhere inside, we better send him out and make it quick if we know what's good for us and they're very nasty about it.

We're supposed to be frightened but it doesn't worry us the way it used to at first. We just stand in the door and look right back at them while they're having their say and we say we're sorry but we don't know anyone named Royston, which is a big lie in one way but, in another way, is also the truth.

Carole-Amelia says she's never heard anything like it in her life before, especially about Royston.

'I wouldn't mind meeting him,' she says. 'But don't get funny ideas. I know I can't have him for a boyfriend or anything like that and in any case, my father says the day he catches me chasing after boys he'll kill me.'

She's never actually come face to face with a gangster. She only knows the ones she's seen on the screen down at the bioscope and she doesn't know any personally. That's why she'd like to have a look at Royston.

It costs nothing to look but I wouldn't build my hopes up about Royston if I was her because he has turned out like all the other men in our family and is a lost cause.

I have another uncle besides Gus-Seep. His name is Errol and he used to be a teacher of Beginner's Classes at the Dorothy Dyamond School of Dance. He taught people to dance their troubles away and everyone liked him. Then something happened, no-one will say what, and he went away in a hurry to be a steward on the Union Castle Line.

You can't say Errol's name in our house without my grandmother having to sit down for a minute or two to talk about him and say how he could make people laugh and how he could dance.

'Some people are born with dancing in their bones,' she says. 'And although he's my own child that's something you can say about Errol.'

We all know about Errol by now. Gone but definitely not forgotten Stella says and she gives me a big wink just for the two of us when my grandmother takes a walk down memory lane and starts counting out on her fingers all the dances he was the champion at.

He could rhumba and samba and cha-cha with the best of them. He could quickstep and foxtrot and Charleston and tango and he could do the waltz as well. The waltz was his speciality.

'He waltzed like a real gentleman,' my grandmother says and you can hear by the way she says it, with a sigh in her voice, that in her mind's eye she can still see him waltzing away and it counts for a lot with her.

'Mr Strauss could get him going. All he was short of was the first few bars of "The Blue Danube" and he was on his feet and not love or money could have kept him in his chair. Everyone knew it.'

Before he left, Errol was the apple of my grandmother's eye because he was her eldest and the one who always looked on the bright side and that's how she remembers him.

When life gets her down and she's feeling tired Stella will say something about Errol to cheer her up and if that doesn't work, she'll go and fetch her snap album and open it up so we can all take a look at snaps of Errol and that will get my grandmother talking.

There's nothing like talking about Errol to put her in a good mood and the subject can't come up without the waltz being mentioned.

'He would be up like lightning and flying across the floor as if he had wings on his feet.'

That's what she says when she looks at a snap of Errol in his tuxedo and bow tie standing behind our kitchen table with all his silver cups and floating trophies for dancing set out in front of him.

She'll turn over the black pages of Stella's album and look for pictures of Errol all dressed up in his dancing days and when she finds them she'll look at them for a while and even stroke her fingers over them as if she hopes she can be like Aladdin and make magic and Errol will come alive like the genie and dance right off the page and back into our lives.

'Never mind what people say behind his back,' she says with a sniff and she looks down and Errol's face smiles up at her from the snap in the album. 'He was no trouble and his heart was in the right place.'

But faraway places got hold of Errol and one day his ship came back without him.

When he didn't come home Gus-Seep went down to the docks to look for him but he wasn't there. His friends said he got off the ship in Southampton same as they all did. They were out for a good time but Errol didn't go with them. He was going to visit some friend or other he had there and after that they don't know what happened to him.

They got worried and looked out for him and reported him gone but he never came back and it isn't only time and tide the Union Castle Line doesn't wait for. It turned out that it wouldn't wait for Errol Daniels either and the ship left without him and that was the end of that.

When people asked why they didn't see Errol around any more, my grandmother made a joke of it and said it looked as if the gentleman waltzer had waltzed right out of our lives but she didn't hold his leaving against him.

'It's ants in the pants,' she said and although her heart was sore she acted as if it didn't matter all that much and was just the kind of thing you expected.

'Boys are like that and you aren't going to change them. They're always on the look out for greener grass. There's nothing we can do about that.'

Errol hasn't forgotten us though, so we can hold our heads up on that score. Every now and then he sends an envelope with a couple of five-pound notes in it and always a nice card, 'Across the Miles at Christmastide' with snow and a robin and a piece of holly which we can show off to the neighbours.

We often talk about him and if she's in the mood Stella will take off the way he used to act. She hops around the room showing how he waved his hands when he talked and the way he had of telling a joke and we all have a good laugh, so although he isn't with us and I can't remember him, I feel as if I know him too.

My grandmother says she's got used to the idea of him being gone now. You must expect boys to leave home. Girls are supposed to be different. It's their job to stay put and be the comfort of a mother's old age but sometimes it doesn't work out like that.

That's because girls are different these modern days and, except for Stella, there are no good, old-fashioned girls left.

When she talks this way, even when no names are mentioned, I know the person she means is my mother.

My mother is in Stella's album the same as the rest of us. You can see her there any day of the week. There is even a picture of her in her white confirmation dress, holding her prayer book in front of her and pulling funny faces at the camera because the sun is in her eyes.

We talk about her sometimes and look at her picture but we don't laugh and Stella doesn't take her off and it's not the same as when we talk about Errol.

Although she's the beauty of the family and was sent to the nuns of the Sacred Heart at a young age because she was so smart no other school knew exactly what to make of her, my mother is a sore point. She started off well but in the end she turned out to be a funny kind of a woman. Everyone says so.

When I was two and a half years old she upped and offed. No-one knows why.

Gus-Seep says sometimes our kind of life gets too much for a person to bear.

He says God gives you one life just like my grandmother always says but the Government have taken it on themselves to give us another one specially made for us and this other one is the one that isn't always to everyone's liking.

It's good enough for some people. They can see straightaway there's not very much you can do about it and they can grin and bear it and turn the other cheek.

They can even make jokes and if anyone asks them they say it suits them and they can live with it and what's the use of complaining because no-one listens to you anyway, but this wasn't the way my mother felt about things.

She had other ideas. She told Gus-Seep long before she left and on the quiet that if you wanted to make what any normal person would call a life you'd have to do it someplace else and in some other way that cut the Government right out of the picture. So this is what she did.

It wasn't as if there was a man waiting for her at the end of the road which was the kind of thing people said you could have expected. It wasn't like that at all.

She got up out of her bed one morning, put on her clothes and tidied her room, then said goodbye to everyone as if she was going to work in the jewellery shop in town just like she always did, except this time, after she closed our front door behind her and went off down the hill she kept on walking and didn't come back.

She left all her belongings, including me, neat and tidy

behind her, although afterwards, when they realized she wasn't coming back and Stella was packing her things away into boxes she found that her portable gramophone and Sarah Vaughan records were gone too.

You can try as hard as you like. It's not easy to understand a thing like that.

Other people took the jobs that were offered to them and were grateful. They could say, 'Yes, boss. No, boss. Three bags full, boss,' and it wasn't the end of the world and it didn't kill them, but not my mother.

When the talk goes this way my grandmother gives a look and shows with her hand to keep quiet and everyone will except Stella. All she'll say is that if you knew my mother you'd know once she got an idea in her head she was capable of doing just about anything even if what she ended up doing was not exactly the kind of thing a decent family wants talked about out on the street.

When they talk about her now this is the only thing everyone agrees about. As far as where she went is concerned, everyone has their own ideas and I don't mind telling Carole-Amelia what they are.

'What people say about my mother is that she took a little trip on the Kimberley train.'

When a person in the Valley says this, it's all they'll ever need to say. Other people will nod their heads and pull their faces because they know all about that story but that's not to say that everyone knows. White people don't know and it just goes to show that they don't know everything.

I knew this before but I know it for a fact now because when I told Carole-Amelia about my mother she asked what was so special about the Kimberley train.

I could have told her if I wanted to.

On ordinary trains you will find suitcases and boxes and parcels with all kinds of worldly goods packed in them. On the Kimberley train, if you know what to look for, you'll find people like us and they'll have no luggage. All they'll be carrying with them are their hopes and dreams.

We all know this but we don't talk about it except behind

our hands and behind people's backs. We never talk out loud about people who leave their families and go to Johannesburg to try and pass for white. The 'try-for-Whites' we call them and because the disgrace is so big we keep what we know about them to ourselves out of respect for the family and the ones who stay behind.

I could tell Carole-Amelia all this if I wanted to but somehow I can't. I'm not sure she'll understand, so all I tell her is that the Kimberley train's secret is that it doesn't go to Kimberley at all. It goes all the way to Johannesburg and Johannesburg is where some people want to be but I don't say why.

In Johannesburg it can suit people to be colour-blind. All you have to do is get there and be light enough to 'pass'. Then you can walk from one world straight into the other. Easy as pie and no questions asked. That's what people say. After that, if anyone asks you to show your ID you look them straight in the eye and say you've lost it, just like a white person would. As if it didn't matter at all. That's all it takes.

People in Johannesburg can't tell by looking and sometimes, if a try-for-white woman catches a man's eye, he will be willing to take a chance and ask her to marry him. Even respectable white men with money do this and sometimes, if the woman is pretty enough, they will do it even if in their hearts they are not quite sure.

It can happen to anyone and if it does happen, then that woman's troubles are over. She can put her family behind her for ever and she need never come back again. Once the ring is on her finger everyone will look up to her and give her respect and the world will be her oyster. Just as long as no-one ever finds out.

It could even happen to a strange woman like my mother. She could have done this and got away with it and got herself an easy life. Gus-Seep told me this himself but he knows for a fact this is a thing she would never do.

'She knows who she is and where she comes from,' he says. 'And she would never-ever lie about it.'

He says she must have had her chances because people

in the Transvaal don't know any better except for the gangsters and the gangsters are the ones who run the show up there and there's one good thing you can say about them. If you get there and things don't turn out the way you planned you can always go to them for a job.

It doesn't matter what colour you are. This type of thing doesn't matter to them as long as you can keep your mouth shut.

They do just what suits them because the law makes no difference to them anyway and they will never slam a door in a person's face or offer slave wages just because they know you're hard up and can't pick and choose what job you'd like to do.

Gus-Seep knows this for a fact.

'You needn't tell your granny,' he says. 'This is between you and me.'

He pulls me to one side so he can whisper in my ear and I like it when he talks grown-up talk like this. I know if my grandmother can see and hear through walls like she says she can, she will have a heart attack to hear whatever Gus-Seep is going to tell me next.

'The gangsters aren't fools,' he says. 'They like a person with brains and it doesn't matter to them if that person happens to be a girl, just as long as she's smart. If she can show them she's got a head on her shoulders and knows how they can make even more money, that's all right with them. For every twenty cents extra she can put in their pocket there's ten cents for her to keep for herself to do what she likes with.'

Our faces are right next to each other cheek to cheek so I don't miss anything but no-one else can hear.

'With money like that in her pocket a girl can dress like a film star and if you and your aunty think you've ever seen anything high class on the screen down at the Gem you can forget about that. You've never seen anyone parade around like the girls who work for the gangsters do. Only the best. And you've never seen the best until you've seen them, so don't let your aunty pull the wool over your eyes. Those girls are covered in jewellery. You can hardly see them for diamonds and the gold the gangsters give them comes straight out of the ground. Fresh every day and plenty more where that comes from.'

'What then?' I want to know and my eyes are big and I sound like a stuck record and Gus-Seep is in full swing and getting carried away and forgetting to whisper and starting to talk loud and I don't want my grandmother to come in and ask what's going on because then he's going to shut up, zip-close and I'll never hear the end of the story.

'What then?' he wants to know and he pulls his cheek away from mine and looks right in my face so I can see for myself he means what he says and every word he's telling me is true.

'Then they jump into fancy cars. Two-tone American gas guzzlers mostly, with no roofs on so everyone can see them and they drive just wherever they want as if they are queens.'

I can't imagine this but Gus-Seep says it's all true and it's a high life while it lasts.

Carole-Amelia's proper name is Carole-Amelia Lombard. She's a Standard Four pupil the same as I am and she's my Rosedale Primary School penfriend, specially chosen by me from the 'Getting to Know You' list that went around our class.

'Getting to Know You' is our class project at St Peter's Primary this year. It's the bright idea of our principal, Mr Randall Christie, who, for our sakes, took it on himself to arrange things with the principal of Rosedale Primary.

Mr Christie told us how important it is for children all over the world to get to know each other better because one day the world will belong to them and they will own it.

I don't know where all the big people will disappear to on that day but that's what he said.

We cannot get to know the entire world yet because the world is a big place but we needn't sit idle while we wait to grow up. We must begin somewhere and we are beginning right now with the Rosedale children because although they are grander than us and in the money, they live in the same town we do.

Mr Christie has great hopes for 'Getting to Know You'. He's so keen on it he says he's willing to forget some of the things we do that make him think knowing us the way he does is not always guaranteed to put anyone in the mood to love us.

He is prepared to put that behind him because we are facing big problems these days and we must all start somewhere to try and put things right.

'Getting to Know You' may be a small thing in the history of the world but it's as good a start as any and worth a try.

Things are not looking too rosy for us in the Valley where we live. The Government says our Valley has had its day and we won't be allowed to stay here for very much longer. Times are changing and they have other plans for us.

There's big trouble coming. People can feel it in their bones and in their water and Mr Christie says, because of this, it can't do any harm for people outside our Valley, like the Rosedale children, to find out for themselves that we are people too and not so very different to anyone else.

He hopes the Rosedale children will take the lead and point this out to their parents because it's with the grown-ups that the actual trouble lies but that's as much as he'll say. After that he gets a lemon mouth and tells our teacher to carry on.

The list of names he leaves behind are the names of children the same age we are, who wouldn't know us if they fell over us on the street, but still say they're willing to be our best friends and Carole-Amelia Lombard is one of them.

If you cut out the Amelia part of her name Carole-Amelia Lombard can also be an actress' name and I take this to be a good sign. Everyone at our house, except my grandmother, is keen on the pictures. When it comes to the pictures you can ask my Aunt Stella any question you like. She knows all the answers.

'If Stella has her way,' my grandmother says, 'she'll spend her whole life sitting in the bioscope. One of these days she'll get so wrapped up in a picture she'll forget to come home altogether and then you and I will have to go down and talk nicely to the doorman at the Gem and ask if we can take a basket of food in to her.'

It's true. It is like that, although no-one in their right mind would want to live their life out at the Gem. It feels nice sitting there in the dark with your monkey nuts in a packet in your lap but when the lights go on you can see it's not really such a wonderful place.

You have to be careful where you sit. Upstairs in the front is where Stella and I go because at least no-one can throw things on your head if you get a place there, although sometimes if there's a cowboy or a cops and robbers show on the gangsters' happy smoke comes floating up at you from downstairs and knocks you almost right out of your seat.

Still, we like it. It doesn't matter if the pictures are old as the hills and jump around on the screen a lot. It's always a treat to us and sometimes I play the fool with Stella.

'Who on the silver screen do you choose to be in love with this week?' I say. It's a question the girls are always asking each other.

Everyone is in love with someone and they don't mind saying who. It doesn't matter if two or three girls are in love with the same film star and are all busy one after another kissing his picture flat in the *Stage and Cinema* magazine.

It's the fashion and it doesn't do anyone any harm and there are some good things about choosing your boyfriends from the screen down at the Gem instead of waiting for real boys to come knocking on your door.

At the Gem you can take your time and pick and choose whoever takes your fancy and most people would pick Clark Gable, although Stella wouldn't. When I ask her who she would take for a boyfriend and is it Clark Gable, she gives me a look as if I'm mad.

'No, thank you very much,' she says and when I say why

not, she says if I know what she knows about 'in love' I wouldn't think it was such a bed of roses.

Whenever I pull her leg and ask her, her answer is always the same. She knows all about 'in love' and doesn't like the look of it and now if she sees it coming down the road towards her she'll run the other way just as fast as she can.

Her days of being in love are behind her and if she never sees them again it will be too soon.

What she enjoys nowadays is a good musical and it doesn't matter if they are a bit long in the tooth by the time they get to us; Fred Astaire and Ginger Rogers are her favourites. Sometimes, if one of their pictures is playing, she'll sit and watch it twice and even three times over, so perhaps there's something in what my grandmother says about Stella putting down roots from her seat upstairs at the Gem although I think the real reason she likes Fred Astaire so much is because we're a dancing family.

If things had turned out differently I don't think Stella would have minded being Ginger Rogers and dancing right along with Fred Astaire but she has a polio leg, so it isn't possible. She wears an iron and leather brace and it gives her a funny walk. When she walks down the street the children limp along behind her pulling faces and taking her off and calling her Hopalong Cassidy.

My grandmother says this is the cross Stella must bear and we all have one, so she mustn't think she's all that special and it's not the end of the world.

She knows this for a fact because she saw the end of the world when polio got hold of Stella and she nearly died. When she talks about it, even now, my grandmother doesn't mince her words.

'Stella was in the iron lung at the Red Cross and the doctors told us straight that it was touch and go with her and I don't mind telling you we were talking in a coffin direction.'

Her face is so serious but we all start to giggle and say we don't believe her, because Stella is standing right in front of us larger than life and twice as ugly, as Gus-Seep always says.

'It wasn't such a big joke then,' my grandmother says. 'Father Marks was spending more time at Stella's hospital bed than at his church and we were all on our knees more than we were on our feet.'

She pulls her mouth and will even wave a spoon at us if she has one in her hand. She doesn't like it when we act as if we're making jokes about this but we don't mean it in that way.

We mean it's funny to talk about Stella being dead when she isn't. She's right there with us and laughing louder than the rest because she's the one who almost died but lived to tell the tale and also because we know this story of my grandmother's. We've heard it so often and we know what the ending is.

Stella isn't going to die so it's all right to laugh. We can't imagine how things would have been if it turned out any other way.

'You think it's funny but it wasn't a joke in those days. In those days, people died of polio and when a doctor told you he had bad news for you, you knew what bad news was all about and you were prepared for the worst.'

But Stella got better and a polio leg is a big improvement on being dead so my grandmother told her she mustn't pay too much attention to the children dancing along behind her and taking her off. They don't mean any harm so she must put up with them with a good heart and this is what she does.

My grandmother says once you've seen life and know it the way she does, you don't think quite so much of the pictures.

If you want to be entertained, all you have to do is put a chair on the pavement outside your gate and sit there for a while and watch the world go by.

This may be poor man's bioscope but you can find out more about life this way than you ever will stuck inside a bioscope looking up at the silver screen, believing what you see there is anything like real life.

'To each his own,' Stella says with a shrug. 'I'm quite happy to pay my money to see how the other half lives.'

The pictures are harmless enough, which is more than you can say for real life. At the pictures, when the show's over the cowboys and crooks and cops and robbers may be dead but you'll still be all in one piece and so will your heart.

It's the 'in love' business that breaks a person's heart. That's why Stella has made up her mind to cut it out in future.

I didn't tell Stella how I came to choose Carole-Amelia's name from all the others on the list. This is because she's always talking to my grandmother about Gus-Seep putting ideas in a child's head.

All I said was that Carole-Amelia is my friend now. She's in Standard Four the same as me and she hasn't got any brothers or sisters and nor have I.

Carole-Amelia told me she wouldn't mind a brother or sister to keep her company but her mother refuses to oblige and her father told her she must grin and bear it because that's part of the trouble with having a beauty queen for a mother.

Before she was married Carole-Amelia's mother used to display herself at the Sea Point Pavilion every summer and anyone who came along could have a good look at her in her bathing costume and she didn't mind at all but when Carole-Amelia's father came along he put a stop to it and she never got over it.

'She says if being married and having a child can take over a person's life like this, then perhaps it's not such a good idea.'

It's too late for tears now. She has Carole-Amelia and she says that's as much as any woman would want because one like her is quite enough thank you and you can take that any way you like. All she'll say is she knows about babies now and she's nobody's fool. She's learned her lesson and from now on she's going to leave the whole thing alone.

We write on the back of our letters S.W.A.N.K. which means 'Sealed With A Nice Kiss' and I.T.A.L.Y. for 'I Trust And Love You', which is exactly how we feel.

Sometimes Carole-Amelia helps herself to her mother's rock and roll pink lipstick and puts a big lipstick kiss on the back of the envelope for me and the postman and the whole world to see.

My grandmother says people will think I have a secret boyfriend and am starting young.

'That's all we're short of,' she says. 'All we need is you landing yourself in the middle of a scandal at such a young age. We've had quite enough of that in our family.'

But this is nonsense and in her heart my grandmother knows it and is just playing the fool with me.

No boys are involved. She knows this and if anyone asks, this is what I'll tell them.

The writing on the back of the letters is to show that my best friendship with Carole-Amelia is a two-way street and we have decided we will always tell each other everything.

When she grows up Carole-Amelia is going to be an air hostess.

When my mother left, our friend James Scheepers was the only one who stood up for her because even if we didn't know for sure that she'd gone on the Kimberley train, after the way she disappeared, there's not very much a family can say to make things look a little bit better.

'But we needn't have worried ourselves about it,' Stella says. 'We didn't have to say a word. James had only just stepped off the boat from England and didn't know anything about it at all but that didn't stand in his way. When he heard what people had to say about Gloria, he jumped in on her side just like he always did and no-one was very surprised.'

I'm not surprised either because he's still doing it today.

It drives his wife, Evie, so crazy she's put her foot down in a big way. The whole Valley knows what she has to say about James and my mother and the rest of our family too. If she had her way, he would never darken our doorstep again but it doesn't make any difference to James.

Almost every second night poor Evie has to send the neighbour's children over to our house to call him back for his supper.

He always says to tell her he's on his way and then he talks a little bit more and takes another cigarette for the road, or he says he'll take a cup of tea with us before he goes home and then he takes his time and only goes when he's ready.

Nothing will keep him away from us and nothing will stop him talking about my mother. He will talk about her to anyone, even to me.

'Your mother didn't abandon you,' he says. 'She left you with people who love you more than anything else in the world.'

When he says this Stella gives my grandmother a look and throws up her eyes but James will always pretend not to see.

'Your mother is a very fine woman and it isn't for us to judge her,' he says. 'She's got her head screwed on the right way. Smart as paint and bright as a button, just like you are and you must never let anyone tell you anything different.'

James doesn't have his own child but it doesn't matter. He has more time for children than a lot of other grown-ups I could mention and a nice way of talking. He always has a hug and a kiss for me when he comes in our front door and something nice in his pockets like a pink Star sweet or some licorice boilings.

James' mother and father were killed in a bus accident when he was young and once upon a time my mother had a lot of time for him and cast her bread on the water and took a chance on him so now, he says, her bread is coming back to her and it's my turn now and he has a lot of time for me.

He says I'm no trouble but there are some other people who don't see it that way.

'That child is the biggest nuisance in the history of the world,' Stella says to anyone who will listen and she gives me a sideways snake look when she says it. She wouldn't dare say it to my face when my grandmother is in the room.

'She won't leave poor James alone for two minutes. He hasn't even got his foot in the door before she's talking nineteen to the dozen and hanging around his neck and asking if he's got sweets in his pocket. The way she carries on, you'd think they were best friends and the same age.'

My grandmother says to leave us alone to get on with our private business. 'They understand each other and she's sitting still for a change and not doing anyone any harm.'

I'm allowed to sit on James' lap and eat one of the sweets he's brought even if it's just before supper and if we don't feel like joining in the conversation we can sit at the kitchen table and talk quietly to each other about anything that suits us, even if it's my mother we're talking about.

We can talk to our hearts' content and no-one minds, even if every now and then Stella looks at us and shakes her head and my grandmother says she's never seen two people with so many secrets to talk about as James and me.

'In the days when I first knew your grandmother she was the biggest tiger you ever saw and now she's like a little lamb,' he says and he's looking at her when he says it to be sure she hears and she's looking into her pots so we can't see her smiling.

'No-one is afraid of her any more and it's all your fault. Your mother would fall on her back if she could see it.'

'She could see it if she'd stayed with us,' I say chewing up and down on my sweet because although my grand-mother says we must keep our ideas about my mother to ourselves, especially in front of James, sometimes the devil gets hold of me a little bit.

This is not the kind of thing I usually say but I'm sitting with my head against James' chest so I don't have to look at him while I wait to hear what he has to say back. But he can find an answer even to this, just like he can for everything else.

'If your mother was here she'd be quick to tell you what a spoiled little madam you'll turn into if you don't watch out. She'd make sure you stayed in your place and didn't get your own way all the time because that's what mothers are for.'

It's not true but I wouldn't want to hurt James' feelings by telling him he's wrong, because although he's the cleverest person we know and has the best education, he doesn't know everything.

He doesn't know about me and my family. Nothing could ever have been different between us no matter who else was there.

My life is the life God saw fit to give me and I'm happy. I've always known I don't need my mother for that and there's nothing she could do to change things now.

When James has gone, Stella lets out a big sigh and we laugh a little bit because it sounds as if that sigh has been sitting inside her the whole evening, just ready to burst.

She sits down hard in her chair and shakes her head. She says, 'The way he goes on about Gloria, I sometimes wonder if we're talking about the same girl.'

My grandmother looks at me sitting quiet in my place listening and she nods towards me with her head and makes 'keep quiet' at Stella with her eyebrows.

'I know you think the sun shines out of James and I like him too,' Stella says even though she's caught the look. 'But sometimes I think he's lost his memory.'

'He remembers what he wants to remember,' my grandmother says. 'We all do that sometimes, even you. It's no good getting into an argument about it. He has his opinions and we have ours and it costs us nothing to listen to him. Let him get things off his chest. It's not easy for him either.'

'Talk about rose-coloured glasses,' says Stella. 'When James is here I spend half the time wanting to chip in and put the record straight and then I bite my tongue for the sake of peace but I can't keep quiet for ever.'

'Then change the subject,' my grandmother says and you can see that's exactly what she's going to do herself before Stella says too much and maybe some things she doesn't want me to hear.

'There's no need to pick a fight about it. It doesn't hurt if he wants to remember things in his own way. It makes him feel better and he's not doing anyone any harm.'

*　　*　　*

'I think you must look for your mother so you can find out for yourself what she's like.'

This is Carole-Amelia's advice to me. 'You must ask the police and the Missing Persons Bureau on Springbok Radio to help you.'

I thought the shows on Springbok Radio were only make-believe stories but from what Carole-Amelia says this is not the case. It just goes to show that what I said in the first place is right. I don't know everything yet. In some ways Carole-Amelia knows much more than I do. She has some bright ideas and I think this is one of them.

Never mind if my grandmother says bright ideas are not always the best kind and can easily get a person into trouble.

I know my mother hasn't forgotten us because every month a postal order with my grandmother's name on it is waiting at the post office, regular as clockwork so, as Gus-Seep says, I'm clean and paid for and that's not a problem but, for all I know, by now my mother may be married to a colour-blind man in Johannesburg and living in a mansion somewhere with the world as her oyster and then she definitely won't want to know about me.

She may even have become a nun like Audrey Hepburn in *The Nun's Story*. That's what I've been thinking lately.

'A nun?' Stella says when I ask her about it. 'Gloria? A nun?'

She's sitting on a stool in our backyard mending some sheets for my grandmother and she looks like a nun or a spook herself with the big white sheet all over her lap and just her head and her hands sticking out.

She thinks about what I've said for a minute and then suddenly, out of the blue, she starts laughing so much she has to put her sewing down and stop working.

'I don't see what's so funny,' I say. 'She went to school with the nuns and they can plant ideas in a person's head.'

I hate it when people laugh loud like Stella's doing and

cut me out and won't tell me what's so funny when I'm only asking.

'I don't think Gloria is a nun,' Stella says. 'It would have to be a very special kind of school that would plant an idea like that into the head of someone who knows her own mind the way Gloria does.'

She tries to stop laughing because she can see I'm getting cross but she can't keep her face straight and under the sheet her shoulders are going up and down.

'Did Gus-Seep say this to you? It sounds just like one of Gus-Seep's nonsense stories to me.'

'It's not Gus-Seep,' I say but my lip is out. If you ask a straight question, you're entitled to expect a straight answer, no matter what age you are.

'I'm sorry, Lily,' Stella says and she's trying hard to pull her face straight but laugh-tears are running down her cheeks and her mouth keeps jumping up.

'I don't think there's any chance of Gloria being a nun,' she says. 'I think you can put that idea right out of your head.'

She starts laughing again and while she's doing it she tells me how sorry she is and she doesn't want to hurt my feelings but she can't help herself.

'Gus-Seep never said it,' I say. 'My best friend Carole-Amelia said it. It's here in her letter that came today.'

I'm happy to show the letter. It's in a pink envelope with blue crayon kisses all over the back and a drawing of a mad-looking stick girl with whirls of yellow hair sticking out all over the place and round glasses on her nose and fat brown freckles all over her face and there's a bright orange sun in the sky with sunglasses and a big smile on its face and blue birds with little black eyes spinning around all over the place.

This girl is supposed to be Carole-Amelia. This is what I tell Stella and she looks at the drawing and she looks at me and she starts laughing all over again.

'Your best friend gets some funny ideas in her head,' she says. 'She must be a crazy little girl, just like you. She certainly looks funny.'

I don't know if Carole-Amelia is crazy. Perhaps she is but

41

I don't mind. I like her letters and the funny pictures she puts on them and the little plastic charm that's always inside the envelope for a surprise.

She says if we put each other's letters under our pillows at night we'll dream about each other and even if we can't play together face to face perhaps we can still have a good time and play together in our dreams and it will be nobody's business but our own.

I can't wait for the postman to bring Carole-Amelia's letters and throw them through our brass front door letter box onto my grandmother's passage lino and my grandmother says she knows exactly when the postman's been because wherever she is in the house, she can hear a certain buffalo running down the passage to see if anything has arrived for her.

Carole-Amelia may be a crazy little girl with a vivid imagination someone should write and tell her mother about but it's through her that I have begun to think about my father again.

Carole-Amelia's father is called Reginald and he's in the used-car business. That's why they have a different car in their driveway every night of the week and that's why it's nothing fishy going on at their house, which Carole-Amelia says is more than she can say about what goes on at No. 48 Constitution Street.

When she asks me about my father and why I never say anything about him I have to say sorry, nobody knows who my father is, including me.

When I was small I used to drive everyone mad asking who my father was and my family always said if they knew they would tell me just for the sake of peace and quiet but they don't know so they can't help me.

When I wouldn't believe them my grandmother took me to one side and said I could pester them until I was blue in the face, I would never get an answer out of them because there was no answer to give.

There are such things as Life's Great Mysteries and who my father is is one of them but I have put my feelers out and started asking questions again and because I haven't said anything about this for a long time, they don't remember they're supposed to tell me this subject is closed.

We like to talk about Life's Great Mysteries at our house just the same as we like to talk about everything else and I can have my say with the others and sometimes when my grandmother's not around we talk about who my father might be because Stella and Gus-Seep are just as interested as I am.

Stella's money is on a man called Frank Adams who used to hang around our house a lot at one time in the old days but Gus-Seep doesn't agree with her.

When she starts her story he gives her a sideways look and makes eyes to me but even he knows better than to try and keep Stella quiet when she starts to talk about Frank Adams.

'She used to fancy him herself,' he whispers quick in my ear so Stella can't catch it. 'But Gloria got in first and she never got over it.'

When Stella looks at us and asks what we're whispering about, we tell her we're pretending to be sweethearts and whispering sweet nothings for our ears only so we can't tell her what they are, but we give her big smiles to show no hard feelings.

We have heard this song of hers before.

She could go on about Frank Adams forever and she doesn't need an audience to do it. But there we are and we're stuck and when we can look quick at each other without her seeing us we smile behind our hands.

'I can swear I have a snap of Frank somewhere,' she says.

This is what she always says and although we know what's coming next, we've stopped pulling her leg about it because talking about the old days and taking out her snap album to show us how they looked is the kind of thing that makes Stella happy.

When she sits down with the snap album on her lap we

say, seeing as how we're there, we may as well have a look at Frank Adams if she can find the snap and she always finds it because that's the page where the album manages to fall open all by itself and, even so, Stella always acts excited as though it's a big surprise.

'You have a look, Lily, and tell me what you think,' she says and she gives the album to me so I can have my look but there isn't much to see.

There's a picture of a man standing with his hands behind his back and an army cap on his head and his face all blurry and before I have a proper look Stella pulls the book back and peers down at the snap herself as if she's never seen it before and the way she's carrying on you'd think it was Errol Flynn or someone like that who was looking back at her.

'Don't you think he's a nice-looking man?' she says with her eyes all dreamy.

The truth is that he's no oil painting but I won't say so and hurt her feelings. She needn't have worried on that score but she doesn't even wait for an answer because the next minute she's asking Gus-Seep the same question and he's asking her what kind of question is that to ask a man about another man but she doesn't expect an answer from him either.

You can see she's in a world of her own and we may just as well not be there at all.

Gus-Seep says it's because of not getting Frank that Stella went off and married her gangster husband. She did it to show the world something and, in the end, all she managed to show anyone was that marrying in a hurry is a very big mistake.

When Stella is back on earth with us she says although Frank wasn't a marrying kind of man, he had a way with the girls that was nobody's business. You could understand how a young girl like my mother could have her head turned by a man as charming as he was.

'I've got my reasons to say what I say about Frank being your daddy,' she says. 'I could never understand why

Gloria wouldn't tell. Mommy was mad as a snake about the whole thing but I would have understood and when you were on the way, I asked Gloria straight, between sisters, to tell me the truth but I might just as well not have wasted my time.'

Stella's told us this often before and we know what my mother said but we say she must tell us again anyway so she can have the pleasure of telling her story herself.

'She said if that's what I wanted to believe it was all right by her and I could suit myself but if I ever talked to Frank about it she'd kill me.'

Despite all this talk if I could pick anyone to be my father it wouldn't be Frank Adams.

I don't know why. I only saw him once and that was long ago when Stella and I were out on the street together waiting to buy snoek from the cart.

We saw him in the fish crowd in Hanover Street and Stella got all excited and pointed him out to me and I know you can't make your mind up after one look, but in this case, one look was quite enough for me.

2

We Shall Overcome

James has been taken to jail. When we heard about it and I asked my grandmother what he'd done she said it's because he can't mind his own business but Carole-Amelia says this is not possible. Respectable people don't get taken into jail just because they don't know how to mind their own business. If this was the case, her father would be down at the local police station every five minutes looking for bail money to get his daughter out.

I have news for her. James Scheepers is the most respectable person I know. Most of the time you can hardly pull him away from his books and newspapers and he's never any trouble to anyone but this is what happened to him.

'I don't know what it's like in Rosedale Gardens but here you don't have to kill anyone or steal. When they take you away the police don't even have to tell you or your family what you've done. You can end up at Caledon Square anyway.'

It looks small when you write it like that in a letter to your best friend but in real life it's a very big thing.

Evie has been crying for days and showing off at the same time. She says she wishes James would learn to mind his own business and just in case people have forgotten she reminds them that James is a man with a university education. He's seen the world and studied in England but it doesn't seem to have done him much good and now they're disgraced.

My grandmother says England is the trouble. You can do

what you like there and no-one bothers about you. They think it's a big joke and let you get on with it. Here it's different. If you try and act English here it doesn't get you very far.

James is finding this out the hard way and we can hardly believe it although he's been saying for a long time that he's had enough of keeping quiet about what's happening to us and our Valley.

Something must be done and if the Government or the Department of Coloured Affairs or the Community Development Board or the Group Areas or whatever those crooks are calling themselves these days think we're all going to sit around quietly while they push us out onto the streets, then they've made a big mistake and can think again.

This is what everyone around here's saying but they're saying it behind closed doors where no-one can hear them. They're acting big stuff behind the Government's back just like they usually do but that isn't good enough for James and it's not his way.

He says the same things as everyone else, only he decided he wanted to say it right out on the street, to the Government's face, in a place he was sure they could hear him.

This is how it started and Gus-Seep saw how it ended because he was there, standing in the street with the others and he saw for himself how James managed to land himself in Caledon Square and in hot water all at the same time.

James and his friends made up their minds about certain things and they went to the Government building to give a letter to tell them this.

They went arms linked together down Plein Street and some of them had big white banners which they held up high and waved around for everyone to see. 'Hands Off The Valley', 'No Forced Removals', 'Respect Human Dignity'.

That's what the banners said and everyone all along the way could read them and knew what it was all about but when they got to the Government building the policemen at the gate said they didn't know what it was about but they didn't like the look of it and they barred their way and wouldn't let them in.

There were too many of them for the police's liking and it was their job to keep troublemakers out of Government buildings, so they told them they'd wasted their own time but they weren't going to allow them to waste everyone else's. They must be off and go about their business and stop making a public disturbance and a nuisance of themselves and when they wouldn't go, the police sent for someone from inside to come out and talk to them out in the street.

A man came out and asked what the problem was and James held up the letter and told him first of all nicely and then in no uncertain terms what it was about and what they'd come for and, before he even finished talking, the man got red in the face and started screaming at him and shaking his fist and saying he was a troublemaker and for sure a communist and then he shouted for the policemen to come and said the people with the letter were causing trouble and James was their ringleader.

James was all worked up by then and wouldn't keep quiet and people in the street were beginning to stop in their tracks to look at him and ask what was going on and saying they couldn't believe schoolteachers would carry on like this and James' friends began to get nervous that things were getting out of hand and they tried to shut him up but James just got redder and redder in the face.

He kept saying putting people out of their houses as if they were cattle and pushing them into holes on the Cape Flats wasn't a coloured affair it was a national disgrace and something must be done to stop it.

Gus-Seep says we should have heard what James had to say about the Government and there he was standing in Parliament Street shouting it out right to their faces for all the world to hear.

His friends tried to stop him and even started saying he didn't mean it and when they said that he turned on them and got even crosser with them than he already was with the police and the Government's man.

He said he meant every single word and was prepared to stand by what he said. He didn't care if, after all they'd had to say, they'd changed their minds about standing up to be counted because that was their business.

He knew some of them hadn't wanted to be there in the first place and were only there because he'd talked them into coming. If they were sorry now and afraid they'd get into trouble they could go back home and no hard feelings.

No matter what happened, he'd never change his mind and no-one could make him and by that time, his friends were hanging around as if they didn't know what to do next and James was waving the letter and suddenly some native messenger boy standing on the pavement, who none of them knew from Adam, came to life and started acting all excited and got it in his head to make a one-fist salute and start singing at the top of his voice and the next thing they were all singing, even the ones who were having second thoughts and had already turned around to go home.

'We Shall, We Shall, We Shall Overcome,' they sang and that song is banned by Government order and absolutely forbidden and you are definitely not allowed to sing it but everyone knows it these days and no-one could stop them singing it because there were too many of them.

The more the policemen tried to stop them the louder they sang and all that happened then was that more policemen came out and no-one was bothering to listen to James any more and there was nothing left for him to do, so he started singing too, flat as a pancake, Gus-Seep says, but singing all the same and when the policeman in charge took a megaphone and shouted at them and said if they didn't shut up that minute and go back where they came from things could turn nasty, they just sang louder and shook their banners at him and, in Gus-Seep's opinion, it was then it was decided that James was not only a troublemaker but the kind of troublemaker the police like to invite to Caledon Square to talk things over with.

*   *   *

49

Evie's nerves have been bad again since James was taken. Even when he came back in one piece and no harm done, she couldn't pull herself together. She spends most of her time lying on her bed with a vinegar rag over her head asking God why He saw fit to give her such a hothead for a husband.

She can't stand it if James is out of her sight for even one minute and she's put her foot down about him spending so much time at our house, so we are not seeing very much of him these days.

She thinks it's high time for him to stay at home where she can keep an eye on him and see he stays out of trouble and so, for that matter, does her mother.

We're all very upset and Stella says she feels sorry for James the way Evie shouts and screams and carries on about her nerves, because when her nerves start it's only five minutes before she's looking for points against him and when she's in that kind of mood she starts digging up history again and our family's name will be mentioned for sure.

'I know all about old times' sake,' Evie says. 'I had a life too, once upon a time before I was married and I wasn't short of gentlemen friends only I knew how to behave myself.'

She's red in the face and her lip is out and their supper is standing cold on the table between them and James is like stone. It's the same old story every night and Evie's pretty face gets uglier and uglier every time she tells it.

'If I put a twenty-cent piece between my knees before I went out with a man, that was where it stayed until I got home to my own bed under my mother's roof and that's more than we can say for some other people we both know.'

She says if James insists on visiting our family there's nothing much she can do about it but he can't expect her to go with him. We aren't the type of people she's used to or would ever want to know.

No matter how much James tells her what's done is done

and why can't we all be friends and enjoy each other's company, not all the sweet talk in the world or a whole pack of wild horses could drag Evie in our direction.

'If I ever hear Gloria Daniels' name said out loud again in my lifetime I'll give the person who says it a piece of my mind and, just for a bargain, I'll tell them a few stories about that little madam that they probably haven't heard before.'

It's the story about the 'shebeen' business in Johannesburg and living the high life off gangsters' money that Evie means and for all we care she can tell it till she's blue in the face. It's a free country and the story's not new.

Some people say my mother is a 'shebeen mama'. That she works in a gangster shop in Sophiatown and sings jazz songs to the Natives to keep them sweet while she's taking their money and selling them liquor, as much as they like, even though it's against the law and they are not allowed to have it and the gangsters look after the police out of one pocket and my mother out of the other pocket so everyone's being looked after and just as happy as can be.

That's the story and Evie acts as if it is gospel.

'The police will catch up with her,' she says. 'Just you wait and see. They'll smash up her place and take away all the money she's made, every single cent and it will serve her right. She won't have so much to sing about then.'

'Have it your own way,' James says. He doesn't even bother to get cross any more. He has heard this story before. We all have.

'So much for your precious Gloria,' Evie says. 'She's a cheap Jack, always was and always will be.' And James pushes his plate of supper away and asks her, if she's quite finished for the evening, if they can please drop the subject.

Stella says worrying about the past all the time the way Evie does is a big waste of time and doesn't get anyone anywhere.

'What's past is past. We can't change it. We can't make it go away and we can't bring it back again, although I wouldn't be surprised if James sometimes wishes he could.'

She's seen a certain look in James' eye and wondered what he's thinking about and she supposes Evie has seen it too and that's what makes her so mad.

'Sometimes, when I hear the way that woman talks about us, I wish I could turn the clock back. I'd like to take her by the hand and show her how James and Gloria were that night down at the Methodist Mission dance.'

Stella puts her hands on her hips and her head in the air and acts as if she's on her high horse and you can really imagine she has Evie by the hand and is showing her a thing or two from the past just the way she always says she'd like to when she gets fed up with Evie.

If it came true, she'd say: 'If you want something to be jealous about, Miss Evie, there you are, take a good look at your husband and my sister and see how you feel about that.'

'You can stop that kind of talk,' my grandmother says. 'It all happened a long time ago and it's not Evie's business. All it is now is water under the bridge and that counts for nothing.'

Stella doesn't care. The Methodist Mission dance was what started off my mother's great friendship with James and if you don't know about that, then you don't know anything at all.

What my grandmother called 'this dancing business' started because of James' first visit to our house and this is how it was.

One day there was a knock at the front door and there stood James nervous on the doorstep hoping my mother would be the one to open the door but he wasn't going to be so lucky. He had to face my grandmother instead.

They all remember it and laugh about it today.

My grandmother says you've never seen such a well-mannered boy in your life, or one who looked as worried as James did when he saw her standing in the passage and heard her asking him who he was and what he wanted.

'I'd like a word with Gloria, please, Mrs Daniels. If she's at home and if you have no objection.'

He knows all about Gloria's mother. Everyone does. He had to take his courage in both his hands to come to the door in the first place but he needn't have worried because my grandmother admitted afterwards that right from the start she didn't mind the look of James.

'He still had a boy's face in those days and I wasn't worried about him. He was the kind of boy who could look a girl's mother in the eye without turning away out of guilty thoughts.'

Stella says how she remembers it is that you'd never have guessed at the beginning that my grandmother had taken a shine to James.

Poor James must have needed hair on his teeth not to turn around and run away when he saw the old dragon who was waiting for him behind the door at No. 48 Constitution but at least Stella was there too. She could hear what was going on on the front doorstep and make a joke of it.

'Who is it, Ma?' she wants to know and her mother tells her it's funny she should ask because just by chance it happens to be Mr Cary Grant.

'He says he's got some time off before the evening show down at the Gem and he wonders why he hasn't seen you down there for two whole days.'

James says that all the time she was saying this my grandmother's hands were folded across her chest and she was standing in the middle of the door with her eyes glued to his face and she had eyes that didn't miss anything.

He said he'd got it in his mind she could see inside his head and knew what was going on there so he was really glad when Stella came out to look who it was and what was going on, because he knew just by looking at her, he'd found a friend.

'Don't be so mad, Ma,' she says and the bead curtains rattle click-click and she's standing in the passage with an apron over her work clothes and her face is floating like an inquisitive pink balloon above her mother's shoulder.

'Don't act stupid and scare our visitor away.' She has a big smile on her face and she's wiping her hands on her apron. 'I know this boy. He may wish he was Cary Grant but it's only James Scheepers. He's the one who lives in the Methodists' back room.'

'He's here after Gloria,' my grandmother says. 'So you needn't get excited and start running to your room for the hairbrush and the rouge pot. You can go down the backyard instead and tell Miss Gloria, if she's finished washing her hair, that she's got a visitor.'

'You better let him come inside, Ma,' says Stella. 'You can't leave him standing on the doorstep. What will he think of us?'

That's how James got in through our front door for the first time and when my mother joined them with her feet in her slippers and her hair still wet from the washing she was giving it outside in the backyard and said it was nice to see him and a really nice surprise, it was too much for James. He jumped up and said straight out, out of nerves, what he'd come for which was to ask if she'd be his partner at a ballroom dance down at the Methodist Mission Hall.

Stella says she'd been waiting to hear what he'd come for and she wasn't one bit impressed when she heard that kind of invitation because the men who came chasing after her sister usually had something better to offer than a church dance in a hall that had seen better days.

'I know that place,' she says pulling up her nose to show what she thinks of it and her sister gives her a sharp look and asks what all the face-pulling is about.

'You'd never get the Methodist Mission mixed up with the City Hall,' Stella says because the City Hall and the Drill Hall were the places where the really grand dances were held and her sister had danced both those halls in her day.

'Why are you so grand all of a sudden?' Gloria wants to know and she gives a look to make James feel at home and put her sister in her place.

'We all know Methodist Mission's not the City Hall but

54

a dance is only a dance. You don't need Edmundo Ros and the Crystal Room at Del Monico's to have a good time.'

She pats at her still wet hair and it lies like licorice twirls on the white towel around her shoulders.

'You have to excuse my sister,' she says to James. 'She can be very stuck up when it suits her. The Methodist Mission may not be good enough for some of us but it's good enough for me.'

She's saying these things to try and make up for Stella being so uppity and to make it a bit better for James and she leans forward and looks at him with a face still damp, gleaming between the dancing snakes of her hair.

'You could put candles around,' she says. 'You could put them all over the place and nobody could see what was wrong with it then. That would make it look really nice.'

'Very smart,' Stella says acting smart herself. 'If you listen to Gloria you'll get a really fine light and you'll burn the place down while you're at it and by the time it comes to the Paul Jones you can all dance with the firemen.'

'But we knew even in those days we'd have to get used to places like the Methodist Mission,' Stella says when she tells the story afterwards.

'I only said what I said and pulled up my nose for a joke. I knew City Hall was too grand for a Methodist dance and even if we really wanted it and asked all the way to Pretoria they would never let us use it and it was "Right of Admission Reserved" at all the smart places which was just another way of telling us it was no Coloureds allowed and we weren't welcome there, even if we had money to go.'

She says even my mother, who had big ideas and didn't like it, had to learn to be grateful for places like the Methodist Mission Hall which were still willing to take us.

*   *   *

55

My grandmother said she could never understand how a boy who'd never danced a ballroom step in his life before could ask a champion dancer like her daughter to step out with him.

He must have known he'd need a few lessons before that could happen and was probably hoping Gloria would be the one to give them to him and it was a big surprise when she said she would without him even asking. It didn't seem to worry her.

She said she was happy to show him how it was done. A boy had to learn about dancing sometime and he might just as well have her for a teacher as anyone else and it was all arranged and in the end my grandmother liked the dancing lessons.

The mat in the front room was pushed aside and Stella put all the records out next to the wind-up gramophone and the two sisters had it all worked out. They knew what they were going to do and they'd made up their minds they were going to enjoy themselves while they were doing it.

'There's a snap of it somewhere,' Stella says. 'Gloria was wearing red pedal-pushers and kid glove shoes on her feet. It was all the fashion in those days and her hair was tied up out of the way in a ponytail so she could get on with the dancing and she'd made up her mind she'd turn James into a champion even if it killed her. But I think she really enjoyed herself at those dancing classes.'

She's giving instructions like a sergeant major and not standing for any mistakes and James is red in the face and Stella and my grandmother are clapping one-two, cha-cha-cha, one-two, cha-cha-cha and my mother is showing how it's done and clapping her hands above her head and moving in time to the music and telling James he has two left feet and making him do things over and over again until he gets it right and then making him do it all over again from the very beginning.

Before that day James was what my grandmother called a street friend, which was someone you knew and greeted and talked to out on the street but didn't ask into your house and there was a big difference between a street friend and a house friend and that was the difference that was put right with those dancing lessons.

After that James could never be just a street friend again. He became the friend of our house and nothing will ever change that.

My grandmother says James must have been doing the one-two cha-cha-cha in his dreams and although they agree he'll never make a great dancer he tries hard and it's difficult to imagine another living soul who would let himself be browbeaten by a woman so much smaller than himself.

Her own mother says Gloria isn't sweet-natured like her sister. She's a born bully and she's been like that from the cradle and she won't give James a minute's peace until he puts Gene Kelly out of a job.

When Gus-Seep puts in his head and talks about cradle-snatching which is the kind of talk that's going on down at The Buildings no-one pays any attention to him. They just give him a look and tell him if he can't think of anything more interesting to say why doesn't he just shut up and they go on dancing but despite all those goings-on and being danced right off his feet, some people might say James was lucky to have been there at all.

My grandmother knew a thing or two about men, and didn't have too much time for them after they got past a certain age and the madness got hold of them but she took a great shine to James.

After her evening wireless show she liked to sit like Queen Mary in a Chesterfield chair they pushed into the corner of the room for her and enjoy the jokes and Gloria telling James off and Stella chipping in and winding her heart out on the gramophone and poor James dancing until he was sweating right through his shirt and Stella hopping out for more ginger beer and biscuits and glasses with no chips out of them and Gloria being told to stop acting like a slave driver, to put her whip away for the evening and let the poor boy have a rest.

I would like to have been there and I would have been welcome. I know that. I think I would have enjoyed it and maybe I would have danced too or taken my turn at the gramophone but I was not born then and so I could not be.

3

Miss Tebaldi Will Now Sing

The way Carole-Amelia was going on I didn't think there was a single thing they didn't have in Rosedale Gardens but I can see now they don't have everything and I'm saving up some of these things to tell her one of these days when I feel like it.

One day I will tell her about Mr Asher who I see most afternoons when I go down late to the bakery to fetch our bread.

The bakery is not far from our house but I go late to buy closing-time bread which is just the same as any other bread except cheaper and I am the one who goes to fetch it to save my grandmother the walk, especially the uphill on the way back and this is a sure sign that I'm growing up.

For a long time my grandmother wouldn't let me go anywhere by myself. She was afraid I'd get lost in the rush and she wouldn't ever see me again. When she thought about this, her nerves went so bad she made a label with my name and our address written on it in big, black letters. She pinned it to my coat and would never let me go out of our house alone unless I had the label pinned on me somewhere and had shown it to her before I left so she could have peace of mind when I was not in her sight.

The bakery is OK because if my grandmother stands at our gate she can see me all the way there and all the way back. When I was smaller she always used to do this and now she's in the habit, she can't stop herself.

I go by myself but if I'm not fast enough or stay away too long she stands outside our gate where the branch of the loquat tree sticks out into the street and calls for me to hurry up and come home and the whole street can hear her.

Stella could die of shame because my grandmother sounds like Mouille Point foghorn and Stella can't understand why she won't realize I'm big enough these days to find my way home without always having a stupid label pinned somewhere on me and anyway, she says, I don't need that kind of loud shouting in the street but I don't mind. I am used to it.

For years Mr Asher was the baker and his wife, Goldie, helped in the shop and they were special people and smart too and we could learn a thing or two from them because out of that little bakery and their own hard work they baked a doctor and a chemist which is what their sons turned into.

The sons have moved away now and the bakery is sold but Mr Asher still lives in his house behind the shop and although his sons are always nagging him to leave and live closer to them where they live now in the Big Time, Mr Asher will not go.

He lives alone since his wife died and has a little maid called Joycie to look after him. Everyone says he's in good hands with Joycie. She keeps his house so clean and tidy you can eat off the floors which is what the late Mrs Asher would have wanted.

People are sorry for Mr Asher. They think he's lonely. When you go up and down the street you can see him sitting in his front window with his head bent down as though he's reading. I've seen him there myself when I go past.

Sometimes I see my friends in the street but we never stop to talk or play a few games outside Mr Asher's house. We all know he doesn't have too much time for children.

There was a time, when he was still in business, when certain children used to steal bread from Mr Asher's shop, then use the bread money their mothers gave them to go back and buy cake for themselves. It was quite hard to catch them out and this is what put Mr Asher off children and I can understand that.

My grandmother says if Mr Asher chases children away from outside his house I must remember that someone started it and it wasn't Mr Asher.

All the same, it's not a nice feeling to be chased away so we don't stop outside Mr Asher's house. We just take a quick look and then we're on our way.

But since I've been older, things have changed.

Something's happened and now I always stop at Mr Asher's on my way home from the bakery. It's nothing to do with Mr Asher who mostly sits in his window keeping himself to himself. It's the music that stops me. I know it's rude but I just can't help myself.

In the afternoon, before supper, round about the time I go to the bakery for our bread, Mr Asher plays his music loud and it's as if the whole house is singing and I've never heard anything like it in my life.

It's as if his house, with him inside it, sitting in his window reading, is floating above the ground in a circle of light and is singing its heart out.

I am late every day now. It's so bad, even when it's raining I can't stop doing it, but when Mr Asher sees me in the pouring rain it's too much for him and he can't take it any more so he comes out of his front door and down his steps with a big black umbrella over his head and he holds it over both of us and asks me, if I don't mind him asking, what exactly am I doing there day after day.

I feel a fool but I tell him I can't walk past his house without stopping when his music is playing and he says I must stop and listen whenever I like and I can listen from wherever I choose to stand.

I tell him my grandmother says she's seen me standing there and I'm like a dog listening to whistles only dogs can hear and he thinks this is very funny and just to see if what I say is really true he goes inside and puts on some more music and then he comes out again and we stand together under his umbrella and listen to the music with the sound of the rain in between.

I have never seen Mr Asher up close before. He's very old and a real gentleman. Even just walking out of his front door he stops to put on his hat. He's always neatly dressed and Joycie says he asks for so much starch in his collars she's surprised they don't jump out of the front door all by themselves.

Mr Asher asks if, in future, I would like to come into the house to listen to his music with him and his music is called opera and seeing as how I like it so much he will even choose some special songs I might like to hear and if I like them, it will be his pleasure to tell me a little bit about them and to play them for me.

I tell him it's a nice idea but I'm not allowed to jump in and out of other people's houses and must stay where my grandmother can see me and then I hear her shouting for me and I know I've stayed too long but Mr Asher is the one who says I should run along and be a good girl and not give my grandmother any cause for worry but I can come back any time I like and I am not a nuisance and so it is a good day.

There is more to opera than meets the eye and Mr Asher and I have a new arrangement. He's moved his gramophone into the part of the front room just below the window and Joycie has put a chair on the stoep right in front of it so I can stop and sit there whenever I like and sometimes Mr Asher comes out and tells me things about opera which is really only stories about life but with people singing.

I think people who write opera should come and visit us, because people are always talking about each other around here and nobody's business is everybody's business. We could tell them some stories they haven't heard before and some of them are real heartsore stories that will keep them singing their hearts out for the rest of their lives and Mr Asher agrees.

I like *Madame Butterfly* the best and Mr Asher likes it too.

It's Japanese and Mr Asher likes it so much he has more than one record of it. One is sung by an Italian lady called Miss Tebaldi and another one by an Italian man called Mr Gigli and it doesn't matter that they aren't Japanese. Those Italians can sing and although Gus-Seep says my mother has a wonderful voice, and when she used to sing in our church in her younger days you couldn't hear a pin drop, I don't believe she could ever sing like Miss Tebaldi does, even if it wasn't in church and she was actually being paid for it.

To my mind, opera is even better than the bioscope. Once you know the story, the way Mr Asher tells it, you can make your own pictures in your head.

Sometimes before he puts the record on, Mr Asher and I talk through the window and I push my head right inside so I can have a good look because I have never seen inside a Jewish house before.

It's true what people say. Joycie keeps his house as neat as a new pin. At least as far as his front room is concerned. Everything is clean and tidy and in its place. There are special shelves for all his records and it looks to me as if there could be hundreds of them and there are books too and more photographs than you have ever seen in your life and, in a way, Mr Asher is like us because this is his life in pictures and he says every single one of them means something to him and he likes to see his people around him when he listens to his music.

I know it's not possible for me and Mr Asher to be true friends. I think it's a pity and I have gone so far as to tell him that this is the way I feel but he says the important thing is that we are both music lovers. That's what brings us together and it's a wise rule in life to think about those things that bring us together instead of those things which prevent us being friends.

When we have finished our little talk he says Miss Tebaldi will now sing for us and for the sake of politeness, we mustn't keep her waiting. Or he'll tell me that Mr Gigli is anxious to begin and because they are both such very great stars it's not up to us to keep them waiting too long.

Then we sit on either side of his window and we listen for a while and I look at my pictures which are in my head and Mr Asher looks at his pictures which are all around him.

4

Life is Not a Bed of Roses

My cousin, Royston, Stella's one and only, is a gangster now and his gangster name is Domingo.

Out on the Flats where he lives, Royston says his mother is dead and at our house Stella says we don't know anyone called Domingo and at least while they're so busy lying it shows they still have something to say and they care about each other, even if it's in a different kind of way to other people.

I don't know about gangsters. If you have one in your family you spend the whole time waiting for someone to come and tell you they're dead and it isn't so easy.

There are always gang wars and the police don't interfere, so it's a free for all and they can kill each other and no-one cares less.

My grandmother has spoken to Revd Rainbird about it and all of us have housemaids' knees from praying, but so far it doesn't seem to have helped.

Royston says he's all right because he knows when to keep his head down and he can run fast and he's not ashamed to admit it.

We may not think his life is all that much but he likes it and it's the only one he has and he's seen what happened to his father. He doesn't want to end up a good-looking corpse, so he'll run while he still can and my grandmother says that's what he better do.

'You better run very, very fast,' she says. 'You better make a very good job of keeping yourself alive because I wouldn't like to be in your boots when you turn up at the

Judgement Throne and God is on the lookout for a boy called Royston and He doesn't know Domingo and He doesn't have such a name on His list.'

Royston says he doesn't care but he won't look my grandmother in the face and I think he's scared. I could have told him my grandmother is not as cross as she sounds. Behind his back she says he's a willing boy at heart and that's part of his trouble. He tries to please everyone. It's his nature and his downfall and all the men in our family are a bit like that, so what chance does poor Royston have?

'If there's a slip-up, you can't blame God,' my grandmother says when she's trying to scare him back onto the straight and narrow.

'It'll be no-one's fault but your own. I happen to know there's a nice little place set aside for someone named Royston so it'll be a big pity if God finds Himself sitting with a wrong soul.'

I know she only does this to frighten him but I wish she wouldn't. Whoever he is makes no difference to me. I've never stopped liking my cousin, Royston.

It's hard to believe, but after his father put Stella to one side for Ramona Gamiet and Stella and Royston came to live with us, Royston used to be in Sunday School with me and I would sit in the junior section and look up at him in the big class and tell people loudly that he was my cousin. It doesn't matter how he turned out in the end, I was proud of him in a way, and that's why I bragged and pointed him out.

I didn't mind when the grown-ups were out and he was the one who had to stay behind at the house to look after me. He always had a lot to say about it but in the end he did it and the minute the grown-ups' backs were turned he was nice to me and didn't mind what I did and I didn't mind either.

I would show off and do concerts for him pretending I was a rock and roll singer or a tap dancer or even a ballerina and I would dance around the kitchen and make myself dizzy trying to impress him and he would say that for a small kid and a show-off with no brains, I wasn't so bad.

When Royston still lived with us, he and I walked to Sunday School together and there was always a big fight about that too because Royston didn't want to go and my grandmother had to help Stella push him into his Sunday clothes and they were both shouting at him and if he would stand still long enough my grandmother would happily have given him a quick clip or two for being so much trouble but once we were around the corner it was all right again.

He would let me hold his hand. If I got a stone in my shoe like I sometimes did when my shoes were still big and I was trying to grow into them, he would never grouse about it. We would stop and he would help me take the stone out.

Sometimes this took a long time but he didn't complain although the shoe buttons got everyone down. They were so big and the button holes were so small but he didn't seem to mind.

He was a patient boy and kind just like Gus-Seep always says whenever Stella complains about him and I liked to be with him and would have sat the whole Sunday School lesson next to him if I could and I even tried but they wouldn't let me.

'Jesus won't mind if I sit next to my cousin.'

I told the teacher that straight out.

'How do you know that?' she wanted to know and I said I just knew and everyone started to laugh and she didn't know what to do, so she gave me a funny look and I didn't care. I gave her a funny look back and pulled my face and we could have gone on like that for a long time but she put a stop to it.

'In this case, it's not up to Jesus,' she said. 'This isn't Jesus' class, it's my class and you can stay right where you are, which is where the superintendent of this Sunday School put you and that's all we want to hear out of your mouth today, thank you very much, Miss Lily Daniels.'

I think she could see Royston was going to turn out no good and a bad influence but I'm sorry now I couldn't get my own way because those were special days and once they were gone they didn't come back again.

Eventually Royston made up his mind and left us altogether. He ran away to join a gang and when Stella saw him on the street he turned his head away from her as if he didn't know who she was but she marched right up to him and took him by the collar and made him talk to her even though she didn't like hearing what he had to say.

He said we wouldn't be seeing him around our house any more. He would live wherever the gang lived and he had taken another name for himself because that was the gang rule and, for her information, these days he called himself Domingo and she would have to call him that too. We all would.

I don't know why he did this. I think it was so that if he was caught by the police they would think he was Portuguese and leave our family out of it. This was a trick his father taught him before he was killed and he was lucky in a way. No-one ever asked him about his father because what happened to him was in the newspaper and in any case it was so terrible that before it even got in the newspaper it was around the streets like wildfire.

His father was stabbed to death in Salt River and the gang's money he was taking from the numbers runner was taken from him and the streets ran red with blood that day and the police couldn't do anything about it.

All they could do was take his body down to the police station and send for Stella.

She had to look at her dead husband in the police fridge and she came home with his watch and a gold ring in a brown paper bag because that's all that was left of him and that was only left because it was the gang's money the other gang wanted and nothing personal.

Stella told us her husband looked quite nice and peaceful

lying there with his eyes closed and the sheet up to his chin and just for a change all by himself underneath the sheet and without any company. She didn't lie about it. She said she was glad he was dead and in peace because now maybe she could get a little bit of peace herself.

She said she would go to his funeral to see him safely six feet under and then she would get on with her life.

I think she thought that with his father dead she had a chance to get Royston back but, by then, it was too late and it didn't work out that way.

Royston has let me look up close at his gang mark. It's a blue dagger with a red snake around it on the side of his hand and I've rubbed my hand over it just as hard as I can to see if I can rub it off but Royston says it can never be rubbed off. It's there for ever and will go with him to his grave.

A life of crime is not a bed of roses and things have changed quite a lot since his father's day but Royston has no regrets. He likes it and it suits him fine. He knows everything there is to know about gangs and gangsters now and some things he can tell and some he can't.

'It all depends what our bosses say.' This is what he says and when he says it in front of my grandmother and Stella they want to have a heart attack.

The rest of the world is trying to put any kind of 'boss' business behind them but the news hasn't got through to Royston yet. He likes having a boss to run his life for him and he'll dance to whatever tune the boss plays and go wherever it leads him.

No-one can get a decent word out of his mouth and every time my grandmother looks at him and sees what he's doing to his life she wants to break his neck but I don't mind listening to him and I don't mind calling him Domingo either.

There's no going back and this is Domingo's life now and I don't mind about his name.

'I think it's a good thing,' I tell him on the side when no-one else can hear us. 'When the gangs come to our house looking for you, to kill you, we can tell them no-one named Royston lives here any more and it isn't a lie.'

He knows me and I know who he is and as far as I'm concerned he can call himself anything he likes. It's all the same to me.

He's in our kitchen waiting for his mother to come home and he expects me to get bread and tea for him while he waits because my grandmother is out too and I'm the only woman in the house right that minute and while there's a woman around he won't do anything for himself because he says it's not men's work.

'If those are your gang rules perhaps you better start seeing if some other gang will take you,' I tell him smart as you like and give him a dagger look to go with it. I don't care. 'We don't mind doing things for each other in this house but we aren't anyone's servants.'

I don't care about gang rules and I bang the bread and jam jar down in front of him just to remind him that we have rules too.

'You're very big for your boots,' he says and I tell him I'm always big for my boots with someone who can't get the word 'thank you' out of his mouth and then I sit down next to him and watch him eat and wait for him to open his mouth and speak to me.

'We don't talk gang stories outside,' he says. 'So you needn't sit there with your eyes big waiting for me to tell you my business.'

'You looked a big fool at your father's funeral,' I say and he says I looked an even bigger fool the way I was carrying on and I needn't think he's forgotten it.

When people asked him about me afterwards he was nearly dead with embarrassment having to say he had such a crazy little kid for a cousin and although it's not the kind of thing you can be thrown out of a gang for, it almost is and when he told me that, I was sorry I hadn't acted even crazier.

'Granny will never call you Domingo,' I say. 'Not to your face or behind your back.'

He doesn't care because he's never coming back here anyway which is something I tell him will suit his mother because she's already packed up all the stuff she bought him when he was a decent boy and given it to the Church.

'The gang looks after me,' he says and I ask him if the gang look after him so wonderfully, why is he forever hanging around our place eating our bread and jam or lying low in his old room and expecting us to lie for him when people come looking for him at our door?

'If the boss says I must come here until they send for me, I have to do it,' he says. 'Otherwise, I wouldn't put my foot here and wild horses wouldn't make me come and in any case it isn't for much longer because you won't be here for much longer. Everyone knows that.'

I ask him who 'everyone' is but he says he's already said too much and at first he won't answer me.

'You act blind,' he says, 'but if you take a walk down the bottom end of the Valley you can see for yourself. All those places are boarded up because money's been talking very sweetly to the old Jews who owned them and who do you think owns them now?'

He gives me a smart know-everything look like he knows all the answers and I'm a stupid fool who never knows anything at all. It makes me so mad I jump right off my chair and put my hands on my hips and although I haven't got an answer I give him a look right back.

'Group Areas owns them now,' he says. 'And one of these days they're going to come with their bulldozers and knock them flat and Constitution Street is going the same way and this house is going with it and all of you will have to find a place on the Flats or sit on your backsides out in the street.'

'Is that what the gang bosses tell you?' I want to know and I'm shouting but he's the only one to hear me and there's no-one there to tell me decently brought up girls don't shout so I don't care.

'If it's your crook bosses, you can take them back a message from me. You can tell them Miss Lily Daniels has news for them and the news is that the Daniels family

71

aren't going anywhere and they can put that in their pipe and smoke it.'

'You watch what you say,' Royston says. 'You don't want to mess with gangsters. I'm warning you for your own good. They won't care how little you are or how crazy in the head. If you start that kind of talk and they hear about it, one night when you're asleep in your bed and don't expect it, they'll come with their knives to get you and no-one will be able to help you then and that will be the end of you.'

'Let them come,' I say. 'I'm not scared. I'm not scared of them and I'm not scared of you. They can come and they can bring Group Areas' bulldozers with them if they like because they don't know us yet. This house belongs to us and no-one is going to push us out of it.'

I can talk to Domingo any way I like. He gives himself airs and graces but he isn't all that much older than me and I'm not afraid of him because although he's a gangster he doesn't know everything and he just stands there and looks at me and smiles like a fool and when he smiles I have to look at his gold teeth, because that is what he has now. All his gang do, so you know who they are when you see them coming.

There are just two of them, where his front teeth used to be, and they cost an arm and a leg and we try not to look at them but sometimes it is hard not to. Like when he's wiping up some apricot jam off the plate and putting it into his mouth with his finger.

'It won't make any difference,' he says. 'And it's not just Constitution Street and it's not just the houses, the shops are going too. Everything is.'

The fish shop and the barber shops, The Gay Life and Personality Plus, The Casbah Café and the tailor shops and Khan's corner shop where the spices smell so sweet and they let us buy on the book and the butcher and the hawkers' stands and the Gem bioscope and St Peter's Primary and even the tattoo artist where the gangs and seamen take all their business. Take your pick, Royston says. The Government is going to knock them all down.

'And what do you think will happen once they've got rid

of all of you?' This is what he asks me but he doesn't expect me to answer because he is the one with all the answers today.

'The bulldozers will come in and push everything down flat,' he says. 'It's happened in other places. I've seen it with my own eyes and they're not going to worry about you and you aren't going to stand in their way so you better put that in your pipe and smoke it.'

I hate Royston when he talks like this and I call him a liar straight to his face. Whether we like it or not, lying is in our family and he's even worse than Gus-Seep. He's the worst liar I ever knew and probably mad. We all know where gangsters get their courage and big talk from and the smoke has gone straight to Royston's brains but I remember him now.

When we were small together, before his father took him away, he used to frighten me with his stories. He told the most horrible stories of anyone I ever knew and when he finished he'd say the policemen were coming to catch us and take us away and he'd make us both so frightened we'd be screaming our heads off so my grandmother or Stella would come and ask what was going on and we'd stop screaming but we wouldn't tell because Royston was showing his gangster ways even then and made me promise to keep quiet with my mouth zip-closed if any grown-up came to ask what kind of stories he'd been filling my head with.

I wished for a change he'd do what he always says and stop hanging around our house with his shiny little smoke eyes and his gold teeth and I don't care if I lied to him about his mother packing up his clothes and giving them to the Church and saying she didn't care if he never came back. We can live without his type of talk here.

He just sits there, as full of himself as ever, mopping at his plate with the last piece of bread and waiting for his mother to come back and I get so wild I pull the plate away from him just to be spiteful and then I'm sorry for what I've done because I remember something else about his stories.

It was always the same. When he told them he always frightened himself more than he frightened anyone else.

*   *   *

We're having a heatwave. It's so hot the Government says if it gets any hotter they will close down all the schools in case the children's brains boil.

It's so hot the newspaper doesn't even bother to write about the Government any more and on the front page there's a picture of a man smiling like mad and frying an egg on the top of his car just to show how hot it is, which my grandmother says is just silly and if you take the trouble to think about it, not such a joke as they're making it out to be. Besides which it's a waste of an egg and when you think that there are children without food in the native locations, it's not funny at all.

During the day the water boils in the outside pipes. It comes out of the tap like steam and will burn your hand if you aren't careful. So these days it's my job to see that I'm up before the sun, so I can go into the yard and tap off some water from the outside tap and get it into buckets while it's still cool and we can keep the buckets under the table in the kitchen, and at least have cool water to drink and to wash our faces in.

Children without shoes have to run up and down on the white lines in the road because that's the only place they won't get their feet burned off and in the middle of the day, we all look for cool places to sit or to lie down.

When it's hot like this I like to go to the old graveyard, because once you're over the wall it's lovely and cool under the gum trees. When you get there you can sit in their roots as if they're armchairs and look at the world around you and once you're settled, if you don't mind about the spooks, it's the coolest place in the Valley.

That's where I'm sitting when Portia Elias and her gang come along and I know when she sees me sitting like a queen in the old lady gum trees I'll be in for trouble because she's been looking for me for a long time and I've seen that slit-eye look of hers before, on the days I take my grandmother's food to Mrs Elias.

*   *   *

74

Flora Dora doesn't look after Gus-Seep well enough for us to be rich but we're not as poor as some of the people in the Valley. That's because we all pull together even the ones who aren't here. Every little helps and there's the money my mother sends for me every month like clockwork and that helps the most of all.

Poor people like Mrs Elias live in a row of houses called Kitchener Terrace right near the river where the mosquitoes are and we're always having to run down there, to Mrs Elias' house, to take food.

My grandmother sends me with soup and says I must say she's cooked too much because of Gus-Seep always bringing his end-of-the-week vegetables or she sends me with jam and then I have to say we have so many figs from our tree she's made jam and a nice little loaf to go with it and would Mrs Elias do us the favour of taking these things from us because, just for a change, we have too much and to spare.

Mrs Elias always says thank you, like a real lady, and whatever we take, she never says 'no' and never looks us straight in the eye when her hands come out.

We're never invited into her house and she's always saying how sorry she is about it and she doesn't speak to us in the same way she speaks to the grown-ups. When grown-ups are around she hardly says a word but where children are concerned, she's not shy to speak her heart out.

'One of these days I'm going to have a big party.' That's what she tells me and while she's telling me, she hangs onto our dish for dear life and I can see she isn't going to give it back to me until she's finished what she wants to say, so I stand in front of her with my hands behind my back waiting for her to have her say.

'You'll see if I don't do it,' she says. 'I know you wouldn't think it to see me these days but in our younger days Mr Elias and I liked to entertain and our circle of friends was very wide, very wide indeed and you and your granny are my friends now and you're on top of the list because I'm a person who knows how to show her gratitude but you'll see that too.'

Mrs Elias is thin and pale and her hair is fine and flies out in all directions as if it has electricity in it. She looks like a little bird and talks in whispers as if words make her scared and she thinks if she talks any louder the world will be listening to her and waiting to catch her out.

'Just as soon as the wheel turns and things come right I'll be sending Portia over to your house to set the date. And the wheel does turn, it always does. That's something we can depend on, don't you think so, Lily?'

I don't know what to think and when I get home this is what I tell my grandmother and she says she doesn't think we must hold our breath while we wait for the wheel to turn so that Mrs Elias can give us a party and in the meantime I mustn't spread this kind of talk all over the show because what Mrs Elias told me were only her good intentions and when someone tells you their good intentions it's always on the understanding you keep them to yourself in case of accidents.

I suppose she's right because despite Mrs Elias' good intentions nothing changes and I keep on going down to Kitchener Terrace when I am sent, the same as the other children, each of us singing the same song to a different tune and standing in the door like we always do, holding our food and Mrs Elias standing inside the doorway in her overall like she always does smiling and making a long story out of her good intentions and inside we can see Portia.

She stands on the other side of the door with her hands on her hips and look at us from behind her mother and listens to every mad word her mother says about how they've known better days and about the party she's going to give and her nice things and how nothing can ever be too good for people as kind as we are and when she finishes we hand over our food and Mrs Elias takes it and says thank you and will not look at us but Portia looks.

She looks right at us and from the way that she looked we could see she hates us.

*   *   *

Portia's gang are mostly from Kitchener Terrace so they come and go like the people there do and, although they're not my friends, I know who they are and they look very funny pulling their knees up and jumping up and down off the pebbles with their bare feet and every two minutes sitting down by the sides of the graves and holding their feet up so they can get a bit cool before they go on.

I can hear Portia from where I'm sitting. The whole world could hear her if they wanted to. She's got a voice like a sergeant major and it's the water trough she's after.

She's telling the others that old Andries always keeps it full because he looks after the graveyard and that's his job and no matter how hot it is the water will be cold there and they can have a splash fight to get cool and make as much noise as they like because that's always good for frightening spooks away and old Andries is just a good-for-nothing kaffir and there's nothing he or anyone else can do to stop them.

That's the way she is these days and that's why people cross over the road when they see her coming, but you can't always get away from Portia Elias so easily and once she's seen me and pointed at me and called me a pig and a spy and said I must come down and stand in front of them, I know I'm in for big trouble.

I pretend not to hear but that doesn't work either and she asks if I'm deaf or something and I pretend I am. I pick up my sandals and make up my mind to walk away and out of trouble if I can, but Portia and her gang are standing between me and the gate and Portia has her hands on her hips and her eyes are like fire and I can see she's been waiting for me for a very long time.

'I'm with a gang now,' she says swinging her bent elbows from one side to the other and never taking her eyes off my face. 'And we know what to do about spies.'

Then she turns to the other children and asks them what they would like to do to me and have they got any bright ideas.

'We can do anything we like,' she says. 'No-one can stop us. We can cut out her tongue so she can never tell on us or we can chop off her head and what do you think about that, Lily Daniels? We can chop off your head and send it around to your grandmother's house in a white dish and say it's food for the needy or we can put it in butcher paper and get someone to tell her it's a pig's head from the butcher shop.'

It's happened before. It's a story everyone knows. A man called Lester September went against the gangs and told on them and although he tried to hide away they found him and cut his head off and sent it to his wife in butcher's paper and said it was a pig's head and when everyone got over screaming and shouting, there sat his wife with only his head and she had to ask the police when they were going to find the rest of his body so she could give all of him a decent Christian burial.

Only the police haven't found anything yet, so he isn't buried and his head is in the fridge at the police station still waiting for the rest of him to join it so they can all be buried together. That's what people say.

'Do you know what I'm going to do?' Portia asks me and when I say I don't she says she'll tell me.

'I'm going to teach you a lesson for always holding yourself so high and mighty.'

Her sharp little eyes are on me and it's murder I see in them, just the same as I've seen before in the eyes of the gangsters who come banging on our front door looking for Royston.

Portia tells one of the boys to run over to the trough and fill up one of the glass jars Andries keeps there for carrying water to the graves and you can see he's scared of her because although the pebbles must have burned his feet, he is quick as lightning and when he gives her the full jar and water is splashing all over the place she throws it all over me so my dress is soaking wet and she laughs and says it's only water and it won't kill me and everyone thinks it's a big joke.

She knows I can't get away and I know it too and so I stand quite still while they move closer to me until they can reach out and touch me whenever they like and my

78

heart is beating so hard you can see it pushing up and down right through my dress.

Then Portia makes up her mind and says they should push me right into the trough and they start pushing me, so that one of my sandals falls off my foot and one of the boys is tugging at my shoulders and it feels as if they're pulling almost out of their sockets and that hurts and it's not funny and then I'm sitting on the edge of the trough and kicking out with my legs as hard as I can but I can't keep my balance.

I know what's going to happen but I can't do anything about it. I topple backwards and my shoulders hit the water and someone gets hold of me from behind and pushes hard, so that the cold water closes over my head and bangs my eyes closed and tiny, slimy fronds of waterweed swirl around my face.

My nose is blocked and I go under in such a hurry I forget to breathe and I kick as hard as I can but a hundred hands seem to be pulling at me and I can hear them shouting and myself gasping for air before I go under again and I can hear the flap of water in my ears and a rush of bubbles drowns their voices.

I think I am going to drown and my hair floats over my face like tough little snakes and the water pulls at the skirt of my dress and at my school pants under it.

I know them when they get like this. They'll go on and on until they get tired and it isn't fun any more and by that time I'll be dead.

I try to loose my hand so I can pull myself out. I kick back as hard as I can but it's no good because no matter how hard I pull and kick I can't do it hard enough and there are more of them and only one of me.

I want to scream but I am under the water and when I open my mouth air bubbles out of it and dirty water pours in and there's nothing I can do. I'm going to die and all that worries me is that my grandmother will have to fetch my body from the police station fridge and go with my coffin on the train to Maitland Cemetery.

Portia and her gang won't care. They'll leave me there,

heavy as a stone, cool and dead at the bottom of the trough with streamers of slime floating across me, in and out of my hair and my mind is full of these thoughts and how happy they will be to have killed me and that makes me angry.

I don't care that I'm lying under that water and they're pushing me down. I make up my mind they can do anything they like to me but they needn't feel too happy about it because I don't really mind as much as they think I do, so they have no reason to get so excited and full of themselves about it and act as if they are kings of the castle.

They can do what they like to me and if I make up my mind I can tell myself I don't mind at all. It may even suit me. They may even be doing me a favour.

So what if I die? I have never died before and maybe it won't be so bad. At least when I'm dead they will have to stop pushing me around and I won't have to be afraid of them any more and I will have the last laugh.

So I stop kicking and lie still under the water which, at least, is cool and I'm not sure what will happen next, but if so many people have died before now without any problems then it can't be all that difficult to do. Especially once you've made up your mind about it.

Then it's over. I hear shouting and someone pulls at me and there are bubbles and splashes and I am being pulled out of the water and the sun is almost blinding me and old Andries is screaming at Portia and her gang in native because that's all he knows.

'Hamba!' he shouts. 'Suka!' 'Voetsak!' He has me by the shoulders and is trying to pull me up in my wet dress and I'm sitting in the trough and my other sandal has fallen off in the water and he's pulling me up and his hands are rough. They don't feel like hands at all. They feel hard like pieces of plank. They're under my armpits and he's pulling at me and it hurts. My neck feels as if it's broken and then he pulls me out of the trough and my feet feel the ground and I stand there with water splashing off onto the hot gravel and Andries picks up his stick and waves it at Portia and even dances a little, jumping from one foot to the other, and he shouts a little bit more and his old coat flaps, in the way it does when he jumps around shouting and wanting to scare people.

'We don't have to listen to him,' Portia says. 'Kaffirs are filthy rubbish and no-one has to listen to anything they say.'

He shakes his fist at her and she says he's not allowed to shout at them and screams a thousand words at him and every one is more terrible than the one before. About how he's a no-good old kaffir and a piece of rubbish, how they will come back in the night and catch him when he's sleeping and have sticks to beat him and dogs to pull him apart until he's minced meat but old Andries just keeps shouting at them and telling them to get away and I can see the excitement has gone out of the game and they've had enough.

'And you needn't look like that, Lily Daniels,' Portia says turning on me. 'I'm ready for you. I can come back and fix you once and for all just whenever I like and your kaffir friend won't be there to help you then.'

She stands with her hands on her hips and fire in her eyes and her gang stand behind her waiting to see what she will do next.

'Come on,' she says. 'We don't want to hang around here any more. The old kaffir boy can keep his water. Sis!' She holds her stomach as if she's going to be sick. She looks at me and she looks at the trough standing in its square of wet mud. 'She must have peed in it. Sis!' she says and pretends to vomit. 'We don't want to get her pee in our mouth. It's only good for kaffirs now anyway.'

This is very funny and she starts to laugh as if it's the biggest joke in the world and the others join in and everyone thinks it's the funniest thing they ever heard and they pick up their things and go away slowly, stopping between the graves and looking back at old Andries and me and shaking their fists at us and saying we should watch out because they can change their minds any minute if they want to. If they like they can come back and drown us both any time that suits them and they think this is very funny too and they laugh even more and old Andries shakes his stick a little bit and looks at me a little bit and his old eyes are small with worry.

I've never seen Andries up close before. He's very black and old. His face is creased with hundreds of small shiny lines and he doesn't have a single tooth in his head. Just pink shiny gums like a baby.

If they had killed me, his boss would have taken his job away and his shack where he lives that goes with it. If I tell anyone what happened to me they'll probably take his job and his shack away anyway because that's how it is where Natives are concerned.

If a native boy puts even one foot out of line he gets sent straight back into the bush where he came from and no-one is interested in hearing his side of the story and I feel sorry for him because it's not his fault.

He hasn't asked me but I tell him just the same.

'I'll keep quiet,' I say.

I know he can't understand but I show with my hand zip-close on my mouth and I can see he isn't sure, so I show it again.

'I won't tell anyone,' I say.

My thumb and my pointing finger together zip across my mouth and even though I can't speak a single word of his language I can see he understands me because his stick is down and he's nodding his head and holding his plank hands together as if he's going to pray, the way Natives do when you give them pieces of food or something and I can see his old pink gums because he's trying to smile but he doesn't say anything else and in a funny way I'm sorry about that.

No matter what people say, even if we can't understand what's being said, native is nice to listen to and if you watch Natives talking to each other and having a good time, it doesn't matter if you can't understand them, it can even make you laugh.

Native is like a little river running along and jumping over stones and every now and then an English word jumps in right along with it and that makes you want to laugh because it sounds so funny and it must feel funny for the word too, to find itself sitting there between all the clicks and the clucks in the rolling little river that only Natives understand.

I know about Natives because if we get on the bus these days, even though it's mixed and not the 'Whites Only' bus, we can't pick and choose where we sit any more. We have to sit in the back with the native girls because that's the law now, but I don't mind and it doesn't matter if the front of the bus is empty and the back is very full because then we stand pushed up against one another and hold on wherever we can so we don't get thrown over and if the bus goes mad and tips when we go around corners we all scream together and hold onto each other.

The native girls are maids mostly and some of them have little babies tied on their backs with blankets and they talk to each other and shout right across the back of the bus to show it's a free for all and anyone who can understand can join in and no-one minds.

They all have their say and sometimes they tell very long stories and you know if there's a joke in the middle because everyone claps their hands and laughs.

Never mind if old Andries can't understand me properly. I can't understand the native girls on the bus either but they've never held it against me or asked what I'm laughing at when I join in.

'It isn't your fault,' I tell him and I put my face right up close to him so he will understand and he keeps nodding his head and rubbing his hands and looking at me with his worried little eyes and hoping I won't drop down dead after all and let him down and land him in trouble.

I tell him I'll just sit out in the sun for a while until I get dry and then I'll go home and I won't say a word to anyone and he can trust me.

He can see I mean it and some of the creases in his face go away and he nods his head even faster and I sit down by the side of a grave and put my legs out in front of me and he stands there for a little while longer and that's all we have to say to each other.

When he leaves I sit in the hot sun and my dress and my hair go dry and I find my sandals and put them on my feet and I think what Gus-Seep says is quite right. Whichever way you look at it, life is not a bed of roses.

Gus-Seep says before Mr Asher leaves I must ask him about the candle that burns in his window at night. It's quite small but it's bright as a star and it sits in the middle of his front room window, right by the place where Joycie always puts out the chair for me, and you can see it any time you walk past because it burns all through the night.

My grandmother says I should mind my own business and if Mr Asher has something he wants me to know he'll tell me without being asked but I don't mind asking him about his candle and he doesn't mind telling me.

The candle is a special candle. He keeps it burning for a memory, so he won't forget certain special people and will always remember them and when he's finished telling this he tells me he thinks Miss Tebaldi and Mr Gigli can spare us for a few minutes today because he has a few other things on his mind, concerning himself and our Valley which he would like us to talk about but I think I know what he is going to say.

'Gus-Seep says you're going to be on your bicycle one of these days,' I say. 'He says you've made up your mind and it's all arranged. You're going to pack up here and go and live in a flat in Sea Point to be near your children and Joycie is going with you to live in a maid's room on top of the flats, just like you always said.'

'I see you've got it all worked out,' Mr Asher says and we can smile at one another because he knows as well as I do that there are no secrets in the Valley.

He doesn't want to go but his sons got fed up with waiting for God to tell him direct that it's time for him to move on. They took him to a smart lawyer instead and the lawyer couldn't speak on God's behalf but he'd done his homework and he had a few ideas of his own.

He told Mr Asher things don't look good for the Valley and perhaps the time has come for him to think about selling his house for whatever the Community Development Board will give him and moving into a flat in Sea Point just like his children have always wanted.

'So do you know what I'm thinking about when we're listening to our music these days?' Mr Asher wants to know and I get shy and shake my head and he tells me what he's thinking about is me.

'I'm thinking maybe one of these days I'll be looking at my candle and it will be my fellow music lover, Miss Lily Daniels, and our Valley that I'll be thinking about.'

'I know you want to be near your church and your children,' I say. 'But you don't have to go if you don't want to. No-one can make you.'

'It's not about what you or I want or don't want. Not any more,' Mr Asher says. 'You know what they say about beggars can't be choosers? It isn't only the beggars who can't be the choosers any more. It's the rest of us as well.'

He leans forward in his chair and pulls up his shoulders and bends down his head and when he sits like this with his hands folded between his knees looking down at the ground it's different to when he's standing straight with his stick in his hand.

He looks as if he has all the worries of the world on his shoulders and I would like to put my hand through the window and touch the top of his head and tell him not to be so worried.

'You don't know about Jewish people, Miss Lily Daniels,' he says. 'You're too young to know such things. But I know and I can tell you, as far as Jews are concerned this is not a new kind of story. I've seen it before in my life and when I see it happening again it breaks my heart.'

I have never heard Mr Asher talk like this before but I nod my head as if I know what he means and he looks up at me and gives me a nice long look through the window and a little smile as if he believes that I really do know.

He says the trouble is, when you move on you have to leave people behind you because that's how life works and the pictures in his house that he likes to look at when he listens to his music are the pictures of all the people he's left behind and some of them, his own mother and father, he's never had the joy of seeing before his eyes again, although he never knew at the time he left them that would be the case.

He says he thinks we are a very nice family. He's seen for himself the way we look out for each other and the way my grandmother looks after all of us.

'A family is the most important thing,' he says. 'There's nothing God likes more than to see a happy family together. That's more important than money in the bank, believe me. And when trouble comes, like it's coming now, a family must stay together.'

He's been thinking about me and my family in these terrible times and we must do everything we can to make sure that what happened to him will never happen to us.

This is nice of him to say but I've told him he mustn't worry about us. We have our marching orders the same as everyone else, and when we're ready we'll make our plans and decide what we're going to do but in the meantime we're looking on the bright side.

I never knew Mr Asher had such a sad life. I don't know much about Jews except that they wrote the Bible and wandered in the desert and played harps and everyone seems to hold it against them.

But I don't think Jews know much about us either because, if they did, Mr Asher would know that no matter what happens, our family will always be together. Despite what Gus-Seep says there are some things in life you can be certain of and this is one of them.

Now that Mr Asher has made up his mind to go and the arrangements have been made Joycie is simple with excitement. She's running backwards and forwards. Move or no move, all Mr Asher's things must be perfect and in their place just like he likes them and all his family, his sons and their wives and the grandchildren, are down at his house helping him move and everyone is shouting orders at everyone else.

Stella is standing in the street, outside our front gate, looking down the road at everything that's going on in the big move down at Mr Asher's and inside our house my grandmother has finished icing a special cake because it's my birthday and the cake is chocolate with pink candles on it and she's cooking a chicken just the way we like it.

It's nearly ready and its bones are already in the soup pot with Gus-Seep's end-of-the-week vegetables and the smell is making us hungry and I'm surprised people aren't queuing up at our gate with their jars and tins out asking for free samples the way the poor people do at The Service Dining Rooms and Stella calls for me and says when I'm finished in the kitchen I must come and stand with her.

'Come and have a look,' she says and I go outside and we stand together looking down the hill. 'Take a look at Joycie and the way she's going on, giving Mr Asher's daughters-in-law their orders. You can't tell who are the maids and who are the madams these days.'

I think Stella misses Royston and that's why whenever she likes she puts her arms around me and squeezes me, for no special reason, just for nothing.

When I ask her why she does it she says why do I think? But today I think I know why. It's because it's my birthday and also not a work day and we're all together and our house stands open and the weather is warm.

We can smell my grandmother's food and hear Springbok Radio playing nice songs and I don't have to say anything to Stella because she knows what I'm thinking, and she feels the same.

But before we sit down to our food there is a surprise for me. Joycie comes to our door all in a hurry.

'We're on our way,' she says and she's out of breath from running up the hill. 'They're waiting down the road in the cars all ready to go but Mr Asher says they can wait for a few minutes longer because he's in no hurry to go anywhere. He says a little bird told him a certain person in this house is having a birthday today and I must come and give you this.'

There's a brown paper parcel for me and a letter stuck on top of it which says: 'For Miss Lily Daniels, with my grateful thanks for the happy moments we have spent together. From one music lover to another. Mr Asher Levine.'

I'm so excited I can hardly wait to get the paper off and Stella says she must go for her camera and take a snap of me with my grand present and Joycie must be in the snap too for old times' sake so after she's left us we can look at it and show it to people and say we know a friend who's staying in Sea Point and they can see her for themselves if they like.

So we pose with our arms around each other and the camera is waving up and down in front of Stella's face and she says to say cheese to it and I'm smiling all over my face and Joycie is next to me in a smart new maid's uniform and cap for the Sea Point move and we're holding the present up in front of us.

The present is a box with records in it and I know, before I even look, they're my favourites. Some of Miss Tebaldi and some of Mr Gigli. So now I can listen to them whenever I like, although it will not be the same.

But I will look on the bright side. I will not forget opera or Mr Asher just because they're gone.

Mr Asher thinks I will, but I won't and I won't even need a candle to remind me. One day I'll visit Mr Asher in Sea Point which is what I promised him and when that day comes I can just imagine his face. We won't have seen one another for a little while and we'll have a lot to talk about.

5

Special Gifts

We all have special gifts. God sees to it that each of us has something of our own that no-one can ever take away from us and in this department Carole-Amelia's mother has the best legs in Rosedale Garden Suburbs.

This is what all the men in Rosedale Gardens say and now the men in Durban are saying it too because Carole-Amelia's mother was chosen Miss Lucky Legs in the South Beach, Durban, competition.

Carole-Amelia has told me all about it in a letter written on the Union Castle Line's paper.

Her father was so mad he nearly threw her mother into the sea for the sharks to eat because that's what they do there. He said he'd be happy to pay them to do it because they would be doing him a favour but Carole-Amelia says it is not really her mother who is to blame. It is the Rum Cokes.

The trouble is that, despite taking them to Durban for a holiday, Carole-Amelia's father was not with them to keep an eye.

He was playing darts with his friends and he trusted Carole-Amelia's mother to see she had a good time, because after all that's why they paid all the money to the Union Castle Line; so Carole-Amelia could see a bit of the world.

That's what people go to Durban for, although Carole-Amelia's mother does not agree.

She says snakes and the aquarium and the sea jumping with sharks is not her idea of a good time but she'll take

Carole-Amelia to the beach anyway if it'll make her father happy and keep him quiet.

So Carole-Amelia and her mother are sitting on South Beach which is all black sand and terrible and her mother is made up to the nines and drinking Rum Coke out of a thermos.

She's pouring the Rum Coke into the thermos cup and sipping it like a lady so everyone thinks they're respectable people and all she's drinking is coffee when a man comes over and asks if she knows there's a Lucky Legs Competition and he and his friends are taking bets that if she enters she'll be the winner.

Carole-Amelia says she couldn't believe her ears. It didn't seem to matter to him that her mother was as old as the hills.

The man said he and his friends have been talking about it. They've had their eyes on Carole-Amelia's mother and in their opinion she has the best legs on South Beach and the only reason she mustn't enter the competition is if she feels like giving the other girls a chance.

Talk like this is music to Carole-Amelia's mother's ears and it just makes her sick because her mother believes every word of it and laps it up faster than a cat can eat cream and it doesn't suit her to remember that since she became a married woman and had Carole-Amelia, her Sea Point Pavilion days are over for good but Carole-Amelia knows what's going to happen next and wishes the sand would open up and swallow her.

Before you know it, the man has talked her mother's head right around and her mother has her sunglasses off her face and is telling him it's funny he should ask but she's been a beauty queen in her day and he says he can see that. It's exactly what he and his friends have been saying to one another. They knew if they asked her that's what she would say.

She says in case he hasn't noticed she's a mother now and she pushes poor Carole-Amelia forward which Carole-Amelia doesn't like and the man and Carole-Amelia look at one another and he says he would never believe Carole-

Amelia's mother has such a big daughter. He would have taken them for sisters.

Carole-Amelia's mother says that as far as the Lucky Legs Competition is concerned, Carole-Amelia's father will not like it and will kill her but Carole-Amelia says she can hear the Rum Coke talking and the man is saying so what, because Carole-Amelia's father is not there and he must be mad to leave a beauty queen like Carole-Amelia's mother all alone on South Beach because there are sharks and sharks and what he doesn't know won't worry him and if she'll promise not to say anything, he won't say anything either and he's smiling and Carole-Amelia's mother is smiling and they are winking at each other as if they're the best of friends.

Carole-Amelia says the next thing is that her mother is in the competition, for old times' sake, and she's strutting up and down the stage in her satin hot pants and high-heeled shoes and her new friends are shouting and whistling and telling everyone who will listen that their money is on the blonde and anyone with eyes in their head can see that a pair of legs like that can only lead in one direction and that is straight to Heaven.

Carole-Amelia says if she is born again she will definitely be an orphan and by the time her father comes to fetch them to take them back to the boat the whole beach is looking at her mother who is up on the stage smiling like a mad crocodile, walking up and down and wiggling her bottom in her satin hot pants and there has already been a fight about the hot pants that morning because her father says this is not the type of clothing a decent married woman wears in public.

Carole-Amelia says her father was red in the face and madder than she'd ever seen him and if he could have got hold of her mother there and then he would have wrung her neck but he said one of them making a spectacle of themselves was quite enough, thank you very much. He was wearing his Rosedale Darts Club T-shirt and it pays to advertise but not in this way.

What her mother was doing was not the type of thing

that goes down well in the used-car business where people have standards, but he realizes now that he made a big mistake the day he let her mother get her claws into him because she will never change and that is that.

Carole-Amelia has sent me a photograph of herself. She's standing behind a painting of a very fat lady in a striped bathing costume so it looks as if that is her, and she's laughing all over her face and it says 'Durban By The Sea', so I think she must have had a good time anyway and because it's my birthday she's sent me a writing set and a Pendennis Castle pen with a little lavender boat in it that sails up and down in supposed-to-be water when you tip the pen over.

I really like it. I can't stop looking at it.

'I know that look,' Stella says, 'and you better not let your grandmother catch you. We've seen it before and I won't mention names but don't you go falling in love with faraway places like someone else we know, Miss Lily, because we can't spare you just yet.'

Evie has got over her green eye and on my birthday night James is back with us and he's brought a present for me which he says he won't lie about.

He didn't buy this present specially for me but he hopes I'll accept it anyway and he takes a smart black velvet box out of his inside pocket and gives it to me.

'I bought it for another girl,' he says and the way he talks to me and the nice way he gives me the present, as if I'm his friend and grown up already, makes me feel shy and I push myself closer to my grandmother and she smiles and puts her arm around me.

'I don't have any secrets from you,' James says. 'So I'll tell you straight out that I bought this present a long time ago, when I was in England. It was meant for someone I thought was my sweetheart but I made a big mistake because I found out she wasn't.'

'Didn't she want it?' I want to know and my grandmother gives me a pull and a look to mind my own business and be grateful and stop asking questions.

'She never had the chance to say,' he says. 'When I got back home she wasn't around any more. She'd got on her bicycle and gone on her way.'

'She might change her mind and come back,' I say but I don't look at my grandmother when I say this because I know what her face will look like and I'm only asking because I really want to know.

'She might,' James says. 'I kept this for a very long time hoping she would but I don't think she will now so I'm still on the look out for the right girl to be my sweetheart and I wondered if I could offer you the job?'

I go red to the roots of my hair and push my face against my grandmother's shoulder and nearly die from embarrassment and all the others think this is a big joke except me, because I'm thinking of Evie and her green-eye problem where our family is concerned and whatever it is James is giving me, I think if she finds out about it she will have a pink fit.

My grandmother is laughing more than anyone else because I'm so red in the face and my face is in her neck and I'm hanging onto her for dear life.

'Oh, my!' she says and gives me a little push and tells me to stand up straight and she looks at everyone else and is laughing and pulling up her eyes.

'Look at her, James,' she says. 'I haven't raised two girls for nothing. I know what I'm seeing. One of these days our Lily is going to discover boys and I think that day's just around the corner.'

'Don't be such a fool!' I say and my face is boiling.

'I'm not going to go on about it,' my grandmother says pulling me close for a hug. 'You stop being red. It's your birthday and we're not going to tease you. Take James' present and say thank you and I think you can spare him a kiss and a hug, don't you?'

I put out my hand and James puts the present right in it with a big smile and I open up the box and inside it turns

93

out to be a solid-gold heart locket with a little spring that keeps the two halves together.

When you open it up it makes two hearts and you can put a picture of your sweetheart inside each of them and look at it whenever you like.

It's the best present of my birthday so far and I go over to James and put my arms around his neck and give him a big kiss and he says in my ear that I mustn't mind if they tease me. I'm a good girl and a credit to my family and he's as proud of me as anyone could be.

Usually, we aren't allowed to take anything from people who aren't family, and I'm glad this doesn't apply to James because he's good to us.

I don't think Evie knows and I don't think it's her business, but every month James slips an envelope into my grandmother's apron pocket and it's for my school fees and a little bit extra, just in case.

When I asked Stella why my grandmother allows it, she says it's because James is a friend of our house and we've known him for a very long time.

We're the only family he's got and are like his own flesh and blood. So it's all right for us to take things from him. Taking from him is the same as if he was her own brother and my uncle and when I say I'm really pleased Evie has let him off the hook and he's back for my birthday, she agrees. And I would say so even if he hadn't brought me a present.

My birthday is at a good time of year because it's Labarang and the Muslim women's children are all dressed up in satin and bows and new clothes and shoes and running up and down in the street with the little brown '*kadoesie*' packets their mothers send out for the neighbours and we know about these packets.

Inside them are '*lallimallah*' sweets and pink and white coconut ice and cakes like stars and every colour of the rainbow, with hundreds and thousands, mauve, scarlet and emerald colouring and silver balls and chocolate sprinkles on top and they never forget us at Labarang.

The Muslims have their own church at the other end of the Valley from the graveyard. It's painted pink, the colour of roses, a whole garden full, and you can't miss it. It has Christmas lights around it all year round, all colours, and a silver moon and star on top and there are always men in white caps and maroon hajji hats with tassels on them standing down the steps and outside in the street talking to each other, and every day their minister stands on top of the church and screams his heart out so they'll know to come to church and no-one can make the excuse they didn't hear.

Gus-Seep says what he's shouting is that it's better to pray than to sleep which may be the Muslim way of going about things. It isn't his way but to each his own and what the Muslims do is their own business.

Although we aren't Muslim and my grandmother isn't sure about the Allah business we all like Labarang and will say, 'Salaam Alaikom' just to be polite and our neighbours, in their smart clothes, will say, 'W'alaikom salaam' back to us although, on our side, we don't know what we're talking about.

Late in the morning the Muslim women come out onto the street in their Labarang clothes and we all go out just to have a look at them. It's better than a fashion show. You've never seen such embroidered material and such bright colours, peach and apricot and pink like the inside of watermelons and green like frozen ice suckers and blue as the sky and silver thread and satin and pleats and best-quality patent shoes peeping out underneath.

You can never see all of them because it's not allowed and they wear scarves over their heads and faces so all you see in the end are their clothes and their eyes and their shoes and their little hands sticking out.

Muslim women cannot show themselves because their men have put their foot down about it years ago and will not allow it. That's because they're so beautiful that other men take one look at them and it makes them foolish and it's foolish men who get themselves and everyone else into trouble because that's the way men are and not only Muslim men. Stella is the one who told me this and she says she can tell me that for sure.

I feel sorry for the Muslim women but Stella says I can save my sorry for more important things. The Muslim women are the smart ones. They're far smarter than we are. Their men stand in queues halfway round the block to put a ring on their finger and there's no try before you buy going on with them.

People who try before they buy think they're smart, but it usually ends up with an accident and then it's too late for tears, although I can't see how it can be the end of the world. It seems to me that accidents can make very nice people but this isn't the type of thing we talk about on my birthday.

The night is warm and we are sitting out in the backyard under the old fig tree. My grandmother and Stella and Gus-Seep and James and me.

Gus-Seep and James carry a Chesterfield chair from the front room all the way down the back steps for my grandmother, so she can be comfortable because she works hard and is not as young as she used to be and Stella lies on her back in an old deckchair with her supper apron still on and the skirt of her dress pulled up a little bit so her thin leg without its brace is stretched out bare in front of her to catch the moonlight and the warm night air which is good for it.

James sits under the washline with his thoughts locked in his head like they always are and he's smoking a cigarette and blowing the blue smoke upwards in one long curl without it breaking up which is what he wants and we're tired with talking and laughing and it's very quiet where we are but tonight it's a Muslim moon and the moon sparkles like a silver brooch pinned on the sky and over the wall, as if they're far away, we can hear the Muslim houses enjoying themselves.

'Let's get out the old records,' Gus-Seep says. 'I'm in the mood for some music.'

'You've got ants in your pants,' says Stella. 'We're all sitting so nicely now. Why can't you sit still?'

'He feels like some music,' my grandmother says. 'It isn't the end of the world.'

So he brings down the wind-up gramophone and some old records and Stella says if he gives them to her she'll pick a tune or two for us to enjoy and, even though he isn't Errol, perhaps he and my grandmother can have a little dance together on the occasion of my birthday.

'And then I'm going to take Lily for a turn around the yard,' Gus-Seep says. 'Because she's a big girl now and soon the boys will be queuing up at our door for her and we can't send out a Daniels who doesn't know how to dance. It's high time she learned.'

When they were young, on winter nights when it was too cold to go outside and play in the street, my grandmother taught all her children to dance.

'But I'm past that stage now,' she says settling back in her chair. 'You teach Lily. My dancing days are over.'

'You used to enjoy yourself,' Gus-Seep says. 'Don't say you didn't, Ma, and don't think we haven't all heard the story about you and Daddy doing the Charleston.'

'I didn't want to dance my life away like some people these days do. I was too busy looking out for all of you. I only danced on high days and holidays.'

She's very prim and proper in these days of her old age but we would listen to anything she has to say and it's nice to see her there, sitting in the middle of us in her big chair that takes up half the yard, with her feet up for a change.

'You danced at your silver wedding party,' Stella says chipping in from the deckchair with the records still lying in her lap. 'Don't you remember? We cleared the front room in this very house and Gloria bought a record of "The Anniversary Waltz" in your honour and she put it on for a surprise and you and Daddy took to the floor.'

'You danced too,' Gus-Seep says.

'First and only time,' says Stella and she tells me that all the children joined in and despite her leg they made her dance too and she only did it because they all kept saying

97

she was a part of the family and it wouldn't be the same without her.

'I just hopped along next to them brace and all.'

'Poor Daddy,' Gus-Seep says and the backs of his hands are at his eyes again out of tender-heartedness for days gone by.

'Daddy enjoyed himself that night,' Stella says. 'When we stopped dancing he put his arms around me and pushed me forward. Do you remember that? He told everyone that God had been good to Mommy and him in their lives and I was proof of it.'

He said Stella was his treasure and his joy and he thanked the good Lord every day of his life for sparing her from polio, so that in this life they might all have the pleasure of knowing her.

'Everyone clapped then,' my grandmother says. 'And there were some tears and even Daddy looked as if he was going to cry any minute but our Errol would never allow that.'

'He started singing jolly good fellows,' Stella says. 'And everyone joined in and if my memory serves me that's the last time we were all together as a family and I was so busy enjoying myself, I don't even have a snap of it to show you, Lily.'

I wish she did. I am sure it was a lovely time but I can't really imagine it.

James gets up and walks over to the gramophone and turns over the seventy-eights and looks for one that isn't too scratched and when he finds it he puts it on the machine.

'I've found one for you for a surprise,' he says to my grandmother. 'And you needn't worry. It isn't Mr Elvis Presley. It's a nice old song for you to enjoy.'

'Come on, Ma,' Gus-Seep says and offers his hand to pull my grandmother out of her chair and she gets up slowly and tells us please to remember that she's old and her bones hurt and she's not a spring chicken any more.

James winds the gramophone and Gus-Seep holds out his

arms for my grandmother to dance with him and although he's very small and could easily have been a jockey if things had turned out differently, it doesn't matter because my grandmother is small too and it's nice to see two small people together and my grandmother in her red felt slippers dancing in our backyard under the Muslim moon to a sad song called 'The Tennessee Waltz'.

This is not something you see every day of your life and that is why I remember it.

We all danced, except Stella, and later when we'd had enough and got tired of it, we sat there together and the tobacco bush had all its flowers out and they were white in the moonlight and looked like small stars and because it was night we could smell them and it smelled as if someone had sprinkled a bottle of scent all over us and the grown-ups talked about nothing at all in particular and you could see James didn't want to go home although it was late and he knew he would get it in the neck from Evie, and we didn't want him to go because we didn't want to go to bed ourselves and Stella brought out a jug of pineapple ginger beer and I sat on the ground almost on top of my grandmother's slippers and the ground was still warm from the afternoon sun and my grandmother bent down and put her arms around me and held me against her knees and pointed up at the sky.

'Look, Aunty Lillah,' she says, 'it's a shooting star right over our house and if you close your eyes you can have a birthday wish and it will have a double chance of coming true.'

Suddenly I am the centre of attention. They're all looking at me and waiting for me to make my wish and wondering what it will be but I don't know what to wish for.

The whole day I have been thinking that God is a very sensible kind of person to bring people together the way He does.

For instance, how did He know to take all the people I love best in the world and put them in one place on my birthday night so we could all be together?

This is what I'm thinking but the words won't come out of my mouth and even if I wanted to say it I couldn't.

I feel such a fool sitting there on the ground with the skinny old Muslim moon up high in the sky and James' locket around my neck and the end of the record on the wind-up gramophone going scratch-scratch and everyone, all the people I love, sitting under the fig tree, looking at me but, to be honest, this is what I'm thinking and star or no star I can't think of anything else to wish for.

6

An Old Native is Dead

Old Andries who looks after the graveyard is dead. He put his head down on the railway line at Cape Town station and the train went over it and that was the end of the story. I didn't see it with my own eyes but other people did.

There were children from St Peter's Primary waiting for that train and, after it happened, when the brakes stopped screaming and people ran forward and the children with them to have a look at what had happened, the policemen chased them away.

They said it was a serious accident. A Native was dead. Lying down on the tracks, all run over with his head off and covered in blood and it wasn't a sight for children's eyes.

But they didn't chase them away fast enough, so they had a chance for a good look and they saw for themselves what had happened and so did Stella who was on her way home.

She's white as a sheet when she comes through our door and we can see she's been crying her eyes out because her face is puffed up and her eyes are red but she doesn't even look at us.

She throws her shopping bag down on the passage floor and before my grandmother can even wipe her hands dry and step out of the kitchen to see what's going on Stella says she's seen a terrible thing and someone is dead and if she just thinks about it she feels like she's going to be sick and we think, looking at her, that she will be but she isn't and she starts crying all over again.

'Sit down with your head between your knees so you can get some blood back into it,' my grandmother says taking her by the hand and making her sit down in the kitchen.

'I'm going to get you a nice cup of sugar tea and you just sit down quietly and pull yourself together so you can tell us what's happened.'

We sit there waiting and Stella sips her tea and cries a little bit and wipes her nose with her hanky and sips her tea a little bit more and we wait until she's ready to talk and when she is we're sitting on one side of the kitchen table and my grandmother has her early evening tea in front of her and I have my milk and Stella is sitting at the other side of the table with her tea mug shaking in her hands and she says she's just been down at Cape Town railway station and seen the end of old Andries because it's him who's dead.

He's lying on the tracks with his head on one side and the rest of him on the other and there's blood everywhere and people are screaming and a woman fainted and the train driver had his cap off his head and his head in his hands and he's crying his eyes out in case people blame him for what happened and if people want to get home tonight they will have to walk or hope for the best as far as the buses are concerned.

'What was Andries doing at the station?' I want to know. 'He would never want to go anywhere on a train. He never put his foot out of this Valley.'

Stella gives my grandmother a look and my grandmother looks back as if what's happened is a bad thing they were both expecting. As if to say the two of them know something I don't know and they would like to keep it that way.

'He was going back to the native location,' Stella says. 'That's where all the Natives live now. He was going back so he could live with them.'

'He would never do that,' I say. 'He had his place.'

We all know that and I don't know why they're looking at me the way they are and I hate it when they are know-all like this.

'He had his things with him, Lily,' Stella says. 'I saw

102

them with my own eyes. They were in a big bundle tied up with twine.'

'What things?' I want to know.

'His things,' my grandmother says. 'When someone is down at the station going somewhere they always have their things with them. Don't keep yourself such a fool. You know that.'

'Old Andries would never go anywhere,' I say. 'He never leaves the graveyard. That's his place and that's where his things are. He keeps his things in his shed. If he wanted to go to the native location he would have gone a long time ago. He would never go now. He likes his job and he's too old.'

'You don't know anything about old Andries,' Stella says. 'You're like all the other children around here. If you ever saw him you'd run a mile with your mouth wide open screaming that black Andries is after you.'

That's what she says and that's all she knows and I push my lips together and give her a look and pick up my milk glass. She can stare at me and shake her head as much as she likes. She doesn't know everything.

'I wish you wouldn't act so smart all the time,' she says and I drink my milk sip by sip like a real lady and keep what I know to myself. Stella and my grandmother are not the only ones with funny looks and secrets. Certain people who know me know that I can keep my mouth shut too when I have to.

Stella tells my grandmother old Andries was holding his bundle against his chest and hanging onto it for dear life and people were staring at him and pointing, because two policemen were with him and they couldn't help wondering what it was an old man like him could have done to need two policemen to keep an eye on him.

Stella says at first she thought she'd mind her own business for a change and not bother to ask what was going on but then she looked at Andries again and she felt so sorry for him she couldn't bring herself to turn away.

*　　　*　　　*

103

'I know this man,' Stella says going up to the policeman. 'He lives in the Valley.' And the policeman looks her up and down as if he can't make up his mind whether he should take the trouble to speak to her or not.

'He doesn't live in the Valley any more,' he says. 'He had no business being in the Valley in the first place. We're taking him back to the native location where he belongs.'

'Why?' Stella wants to know. 'He's not a troublemaker. Anyone who knows him will tell you that.'

'I'll be sure and ask them,' the policeman says giving his friend a look over old Andries' bent head and then he looks at Stella again and she's standing right where she was before. She hasn't moved an inch. She's still waiting for an answer.

'You needn't stand there with your hands on your hips as if you're looking for a fight,' the policeman says. 'If you're a kaffir lover and you want to go along to the location with your friend, we can arrange that too. That's our job and we can take one or two or ten, it's all the same to us.'

'Does it take two of you to take one old man back to the native location?' Stella wants to know.

The policemen are young and full of themselves but there are plenty of Woodstock and Salt River people on their way home from work standing around on the station platform and if a fight comes she thinks they will chip in on her side so she isn't scared of the police.

'We have to keep an eye on him,' the other policeman tells her. 'Natives are getting very full of themselves these days, thinking they can do just what they please and live wherever suits them and come and go where the fancy takes them and this old man is just like the rest of them and that's what we're here for.'

'It's our job to see he gets to the end of the line,' the first one says. 'And doesn't get any funny ideas in his head about jumping off the train on the way.'

Afterwards, sitting at our kitchen table, Stella says she got really mad. She doesn't know why. She said she hadn't felt so mad since she stood outside Ramona Gamiet's house and screamed for her snake of a husband to pull himself out of her bed and show his face at the door so she could throw her cheapskate fool's-gold wedding ring right in his face.

'I could feel it coming on me,' she says. 'It was racing around inside me and making my head hurt and I thought if I couldn't get it out, I'd just burst.'

'This old Native is old enough to be your grandfather and he has a name,' Stella tells the policemen. 'His name's old Andries. Everyone calls him that and it won't hurt you to show him a bit of respect and call him that too.'

'Excuse me,' the first policeman says, 'and who exactly do you think you are to tell us what we should and shouldn't be calling people? We're talking about a Native here and when he comes into your house to steal your things or tells you to pull your pants off for him so he can have a good time, you'll be the first one to come screaming for the police to help you. So, don't come here on your high horse and tell us what we must and mustn't call him. Would you like us to call him sir and master? Would that suit you better?'

Stella says she knew old Andries could only speak native and didn't understand a word of what was going on but he was looking at her with big eyes because she suddenly had such a lot to say for herself and, even if he couldn't understand her, he could hear she was speaking up on his behalf as if she had come to save him and she says she felt terrible then. It broke her heart when she saw that look on his old face, the way he was looking to her for help, when she knew she couldn't help an ant.

That was the moment she wished she had learned to keep her big mouth shut.

He was hanging onto his bundle even tighter and you could see he was just hoping that, somewhere in between all the talking, and people going for each other and other people standing around and staring and some of them throwing in their two cents' worth, that someone would make up their mind to laugh and say it was all a big joke and a mistake and he could take his things and go back to his shed and to looking after the graves, which must have wondered what had happened to them when the day dawned that old Andries was not at his post.

'What's going to happen to him when he gets to the location?' Stella wants to know. 'Has he got a place there or people of his own who'll come for him and look after him?'

'When we get there we're going to see to it he goes straight into the Carlton Hotel and we're going to tell the manager to make sure he's got silk sheets on his bed and plenty of hot water and a maid to look after him. After all, it's only what he's used to.'

The other policeman makes a move of his head that his friend must get rid of Stella because she's got too much to say for herself and people are beginning to look at them.

'Don't you know the law?' the first policeman asks her. 'You can't have Natives parking themselves wherever they like. It's not allowed. They've got their own place, the same as we all have, the same as God intended in the first place. Lions go with lions and monkeys go with monkeys.'

And he makes it quite plain where he thinks Andries belongs and Stella says, law or no law, job or no job, you could see there wasn't a person alive who could talk any sense into them. It was just a waste of breath and they were still talking when the train came roaring in and when they looked again Andries was gone, quick as lightning for such an old man, and people were screaming and pointing down to the tracks and it was all over.

7

Our Life In Pictures

Every year round about my birthday I go and have my picture taken by old Dollie down at his shop in Sir Lowry Road.

If my mother ever decides to come back, these pictures are all she will get for the money she sends every month. We keep them in an envelope in a kitchen drawer because if she should ever come walking in through our door my grandmother says she will like to see how I've grown over the years.

Stella says I can add in the snaps she keeps in her snap album and then I will have my whole life in pictures and if my mother doesn't turn up it doesn't matter. I can keep them all together anyway and look at them when I'm an old lady, the same age she is now and show them to my children and they can have a good laugh.

Things are going well with us. The horses have been whispering the sweet nothings that are meant for Gus-Seep's ears and he's feeling it in his back pocket and sharing with us like he always does and my grandmother says to make a change and for a bit of a treat, instead of having a straight photograph I can choose a 'special' out of Dollie's dress-ups and fancy scenes. This is something I've wanted to do for a long time and I know without even having to think about it what my special will be and I choose 'By The Seaside'.

*   *   *

'I've never seen a seaside like that,' Stella says while Dollie puts a chair out for me in front of a big painting of this scene. 'No-one ever in their life has seen a sky that colour or a sea with so many red boats in it.'

I give her a look to mind her own business because I don't want my grandmother to listen to what she has to say and maybe have second thoughts but she's not in the mood to keep quiet.

'And what's supposed to be the sea anyway?' she wants to know. 'You can't even see the water.'

She opens up her eyes big as if she's used to better things and is amazed to see what old Dollie is offering us. I think it's because she takes snaps herself and nothing anyone else can do will ever be good enough for her.

'I know it's what you want, Lily,' she says. 'But it's just as well the picture will be in black and white or we'd all need sunglasses to look at them.'

She may think it's funny but I don't care. I like it and it's only for fun anyway and 'By The Seaside' has all those old-fashioned men in women's bathing costumes and women swimming with scarves on their heads and a man on a big-wheel bicycle that only has one wheel and a boy in a sailor suit flying a striped kite.

All you do is stand in front of it and Dollie puts a light on you and it makes you nice and warm and hurts your eyes a bit and then you smile and there you are and Dollie is enjoying himself. You can see that.

'You sit on this chair,' he says. 'And take this nice sunshade to finish the picture.'

He has the sunshade all ready. It's red and white stripes and he opens it out and puts it in my hand so I can put it over my head and whirl it around by its wood handle as if I'm a fashion model in a magazine and I whirl and smile and Dollie stands back and looks at me and I don't stop until it looks just right.

'You look like Shirley Temple,' Dollie says. 'If you ask me I wouldn't be at all surprised if you're not the next person in your family who finds themselves on the front page of the *Cape Times*.'

'Thank you, Mr Dollie,' my grandmother says from the back of the shop. 'You just take Lily's picture and let us get on with our business. We don't need anyone on any page of the *Cape Times*. We've had quite enough of that type of thing in our family. We don't need any more.'

'Don't have the sunshade, Lily,' Stella says but Dollie says I must because it's the finishing touch.

'Open umbrellas inside a building bring bad luck,' she says. 'It's asking for trouble.'

'That's nonsense,' says Dollie and he's neat and smart under the little black cloth behind his camera which everyone says came out of the ark and he's telling me to watch the birdie and smile for the camera and say cheese.

I think Dollie's right and I want the sunshade more than anything, so I turn my head away from Stella as if I've gone deaf and I smile as hard as I can and it's the best picture I ever saw and I have two copies which is what I asked for. One is for my life in pictures and the other one is for Carole-Amelia.

On the back of Carole-Amelia's I write, From your best friend for ever, Miss Lily Daniels, Queen-for-a-Day and S.W.A.N.K. and no matter what Stella says, I think the umbrella is a nice touch and I don't believe it will bring bad luck.

It's afternoon time in the middle of the week and I'm sitting at the kitchen table with my school books set out around me and a pencil in my hand doing my work and minding my own business.

My milk and biscuit are in front of me and my grandmother is sitting in the little bit of sun at our back door taking her tea before she starts our supper and the radio is singing quietly to both of us when our front door flies open and Gus-Seep comes running down the passage and when he comes into the kitchen his eyes are on stalks and he can hardly get the words out.

He's come straightaway to our house to tell my

grandmother what the story down at The Buildings is and the story is that my mother's back and although he hasn't seen her with his own eyes he believes it and this is what he's come to tell us before we hear it from anyone else.

'She's with a man in a two-tone Chevrolet car with white-wall tyres and a Johannesburg number plate. She's got her suitcases with her. She's dressed up like a queen and made up to the nines. There's gold just wherever you look and money's no object and she and her boyfriend are throwing notes around as if there's no tomorrow.'

'What kind of wild stories have you got hold of now?' my grandmother wants to know but she gets up quick out of her chair and gets hold of Gus-Seep by the shoulder to keep him still and make him look in her eyes when he talks.

'You better go down to Khan's shop and phone Stella,' he says. 'You better tell her to come out of her work because Gloria's back and if she doesn't hurry, she'll be too late and miss it all.'

I don't believe it and nor does my grandmother. We know what a liar Gus-Seep is but even so, I'm not sure that even Gus-Seep would lie about a thing like this but he can see we don't believe him.

'People who know her have seen her,' he says. 'They've gone right up to her and asked, "How's tricks, Gloria?" and asked her where did she fall out from after all these years.'

He says she's telling everyone she's fine and just back on a little visit and that, on his word of honour, is the gospel truth but my grandmother is really cross with him by now.

'I don't know where you got hold of this cock and bull story,' she says, 'but that's enough. It's the last I want to hear about it and I don't want you spreading it all over town either.'

'But, Mommy . . .' Gus-Seep says and he's sweating and his cheeks are red and sweating and his poor face is pulled all over the place by the way he wants my grandmother to listen to his story and believe him.

'Do you think your sister wouldn't write or send a message if she took it in her head to come back?' my grandmother wants to know. 'Do you think she would just turn up on our doorstep without a word? Don't you think she would have sent a telegram?'

'I don't know,' Gus-Seep says. 'I'm just telling you that she hasn't been back five minutes and already people are talking about her. The man she's with is a shebeen king from Johannesburg. They say he's made of money and owns half the shops in Sophiatown.'

My grandmother gives Gus-Seep a look and nods with her head in my direction to be careful what he says and I'm sitting there with my eyes big and my pencil on the table in front of me.

'It's true,' Gus-Seep says and he gives me a little look as if to say he's sorry but he can't keep quiet.

'Philander knows who he is. Everyone knows who he is. Philander says he's got fingers in so many pies you can't even count them any more and he's bought off half the police force and he can do just whatever he likes and no-one will stop him.'

'Do you really think it's my mother he's with?' I want to know.

'I know my own sister,' Gus-Seep says and he's talking to me and not my grandmother because he thinks if he talks to me at least there's a chance there's someone in our house who'll believe him.

'When a person tells me that the bossiest woman they ever saw is down at The Cheltenham Hotel with a big-time gang boss from Johannesburg and she's the one who's shouting the orders and it looks to them like it could be my sister, Gloria, I believe them.'

This is what he says and he gives my grandmother a look when he says it and she doesn't say a word. She tells him to stay where he is and wait just a minute and when she's out of the kitchen and down the passage to her own room Gus-Seep whispers to me.

'It's Gloria,' he says quick, in a whisper just for the two of us. 'And the man's definitely her boyfriend and I wouldn't be surprised if they aren't both on the run from the police and have come here to lie low.'

I'm listening with big ears and my mouth is hanging open

111

like a fish and when my grandmother comes back she takes one look at Gus-Seep and one look at me and she gives him that look, which means he should keep his mouth shut, but at the same time she digs in her apron pocket and gives him phone money.

'Go down to Khan's shop and phone Stella at her work,' she says. 'Tell her to come home because her sister is back and tell her I said so and I was the one who told you to phone, because otherwise she won't believe a word that comes out of your mouth.'

She gives Gus-Seep another look and one for me too as if to say I should be listening to what she says because it's meant for me as well.

'You know your uncle,' my grandmother says when Gus-Seep has gone running off to Khan's to get hold of Stella. 'What he says may be true and it may not be. I don't want you building up your hopes and then being let down. You just take it all with a pinch of salt.'

I'm glad it's just the two of us because there is something important I want to say to her. I thought it the minute Gus-Seep said what he said and I started to believe him but I wasn't sure about saying it then but it's boiling up inside me and I have to say it now.

'This isn't her place any more and we don't want her here,' I say. 'You didn't have to worry about sending for Stella. You could have sent Gus-Seep down to The Cheltenham to tell her that right to her face.'

I pick up my pencil and bend over my books with my nose nearly down on the table so that maybe my grandmother hears what I have to say and maybe she doesn't.

'Look at me, Lily,' my grandmother says but even though I feel myself going red in the face I won't look.

I bend down so I can feel the wood of the table on my nose and my grandmother sits down on the chair next to me and bends down to look at my face on the table and she puts her hand under my chin and lifts my face up to look at her because she has something important she wants to say to me too.

'This is your mother's house just as much as it is yours and if she's got it into her head to come home after all these years I want you to remember that.'

'We don't entertain gangsters under our roof,' I say and I'm happy to look at her when I say it because it's what she says herself all the time. She says it every time the gangster story about my mother comes up. She can't change her mind now and I can see on her face she isn't going to.

'That's quite right,' she says. 'And your mother knows me well enough. She knows how I feel without my having to tell her. If what Gus-Seep says is true, she won't bring her friend to this house. I can promise you that.'

'Why has she come?' I want to know and my grandmother tells me she can't answer that question.

'I don't know,' she says. 'I don't know about any of it. I don't know if any of the things people say about her are true or if all of them are true. I don't even know if it is her and if it is, I don't know if we're on her visiting list. For all I know, maybe she won't want to see us.'

She sits back and looks at my sulky face and she doesn't tease me and say the clock will strike and my face will stay like it is forever. She doesn't tell me to cheer up or ask me if I can spare a smile.

'I can't tell you anything because I don't know myself,' she says. 'All I know is that if it is your mother, then she'll have very good reasons for coming back. That's the one thing you can be sure of.'

'Gus-Seep is probably lying again,' I say.

I hope he is and I think my grandmother knows this.

'Maybe he is,' she says. 'But I think while we wait to find out I should take my apron off and tidy myself up and you should go and put on your best clothes, just in case.'

So this is what we do, and when we're ready and Stella is with us, we sit down at the kitchen table, neat and tidy, to wait and every two minutes Stella makes an excuse and jumps up and we hear her hopalong down the passage and out of the front door to look over the gate and up and down the road and then hopalong back again.

My grandmother sits where she always does and I sit in my place next to her and look at her face, because I'm sure she's going to speak to me but she's looking straight in front of her and thinking about something else and she doesn't look my way, not even once, and in a way I'm sorry.

I want to tell her that I don't care whether my mother decides to visit us or not. I'm happy just the way we are and I don't want anything to spoil it but in the end Stella hopalongs back down the passage faster and when she comes into the kitchen she's full of excitement.

'Gus-Seep didn't lie,' she says. 'It is her. She's with a man in a two-tone Chevrolet car with white-wall tyres and a Johannesburg number plate and he's dropped her at the corner at the top of our road.'

'And what are we supposed to do now?' I ask and I look at my grandmother and I look at Stella and she's all excited and flushed in the face and she says she thinks we must come and look for ourselves.

'The man's driven off now,' she says. 'Why don't you come outside and see for yourselves?' My grandmother stands up with a big sigh as though she's got something heavy on her back and it's hard to get out of the chair.

'Hurry up,' Stella says. 'Or she'll be halfway down the road before you even get there.'

'Come on, Lily,' my grandmother says holding out her hand to me but I'm sitting fast in my chair and don't want to go.

'Don't be like that, Lily,' Stella says. 'All these years you've been asking about your mother. You're always asking what she's like and how she looks and if she's really like her pictures and now's your chance to come out and see for yourself.'

'I don't see why I should,' I say and my hands are under the bottom of the chair and I'm hanging onto it as if I'm stuck there and will never move. 'It isn't me she's come to see and I don't see why I should do anything for her. She's never done anything for me.'

'That's not true,' my grandmother says. 'You're a big girl now, Lily, and there's one grown-up thing you need to learn this minute before your mother gets here and I'm going to tell it to you and you're going to remember it for the rest of your life.'

She stands in front of my chair and looks down at me and I know I've done wrong and this time she really is cross with me.

'Your mother brought you into this world,' she says. 'That's what I did for my children and that's what she did for you. It may not be big in your book but believe me, it's the biggest thing anyone will do for you in all of your life and there's nothing you can ever do to make up to her for it. So you can put your lip back and stop acting like a baby. As far as your mother's concerned, that's all you need to know and all you ever have to worry about.'

So I go out with my grandmother and my aunty and I stand outside our gate looking up the road with my eyes in the sun so I have to shield them with my hand and I can hardly see.

This is the first time in my memory I will actually lay eyes on my mother and when my eyes are ready to look she comes shimmering like magic out of the sun and she's not at all how I expected her to be.

She's wearing plain clothes. A grey tight skirt, a jacket to match and a white blouse. She has lots of hair. A whole cloud of it. It's thick and black and very curly and it seems to belong to someone else and want to fly away home all by itself, but it's held back by combs on either side of her head and her face floats in between it like a pale moon.

She's carrying a big leather bag that looks like a shopping bag and it must have things in it and be heavy, but you wouldn't say so because she's holding it as if it doesn't weigh her down at all, and she's walking down our road with her head held high and her hair floating out around her as if she's enjoying the sunshine and doesn't have a care in the world and the two-tone Chevrolet car has gone and the gangster is nowhere in sight.

She's wearing high-heeled shoes, so she's tall, and she walks lightly as if there are springs under her feet and it

115

looks as if she's floating but perhaps that's just the way the dazzle of the sun makes it look and, because nothing is a secret where we live, we aren't the only people out in our street. Other people are also hanging over their gates watching my mother walk down the hill but we don't care.

My grandmother opens the gate and steps out and she stands on the pavement and I'm behind her and the branch of the loquat tree is over our heads and I can see my mother sees her although I don't know if she's seen me yet and they just stare at each other and then Stella steps out and puts up her hand and waves and then puts down her hand and puts it in a little fist over her mouth and then puts it up again to wave some more and I'm not a part of it.

It's as if I'm the stranger there and no-one knows me and I wish the ground would open up and swallow me in one piece but I know it won't oblige and my mother puts down her bag on the pavement and my grandmother opens up her arms and my mother walks right into them and they stand like that, right out in our street rocking backwards and forwards and they don't care who sees them and then Stella puts her arms around both of them and she's crying her eyes out and my grandmother is crying too, with her 'in case' hanky up to her face and that's something I've never seen before in all of my life and I can't believe it. I just stand there like a spare part and look at them and don't feel anything at all except left out.

In the end my grandmother breaks away and pushes me forward and says who I am, as if my mother hasn't already worked that out for herself, and my mother looks at me the way a person who doesn't know someone looks at them and she doesn't say anything to me.

She just keeps looking and not saying anything and after a while I realize it's because she has nothing to say to me. All she's going to do is look and that's all right too. I don't want her there. As far as I'm concerned, she can go right back where she came from and she can't go fast enough to suit me.

116

8

Black Sheep and White Sheep Together

A boy has brought my mother's suitcases from The Cheltenham Hotel and the whole road has had plenty of chance to see him doing it. He had to walk up our hill twice and he looked like a pack donkey both times.

Although she hasn't said it straight out it looks as if my mother is going to stay for a long time and my grandmother hasn't asked any questions or said a single word about it.

All she does is tell the boy to put the suitcases down in the front room and when my mother's back is turned she gives Stella and me a look as if to say if she's not asking any questions then we can't ask questions either.

'I want some peace and quiet,' she says. 'Just for a change, everyone, except Errol, will be sitting down at our table tonight and if none of you have any objections I'd like to enjoy that moment without any interruptions and to give thanks for it.'

Peace and quiet may be what my grandmother wants but she's running around the kitchen in her slippers cooking and shouting instructions at me and Stella and I have run up and down to the shop so many times that Mr Khan is giving me skew looks.

'I've never known your grandmother for a wild spender before,' he says totting up and giving me my slip and putting his pencil back behind his ear. 'I just hope she's keeping a note of what she's putting on the book because I think she'll be in for a shock when add-up day comes.'

He isn't really worried because he knows my grandmother always pays her bills and while he's putting our things into paper bags he gives me three pink Star sweets free, for 'pasella' and thank you for being such a good customer.

'There's no problem with money at our house this month,' I tell him pulling the paper off one of the sweets and putting it into my mouth straightaway so I can chew it on the walk home. 'My mother's back out of the blue and she's brought a whole lot of money with her.'

I've seen her with my own eyes putting a fat roll of notes in my grandmother's apron pocket and my grandmother showing with her hands that she doesn't want to take it but taking it anyway. Only I don't tell Mr Khan this because it is our business and nothing to do with him.

We are having mutton curry and tomato and onion salad and as much rice as you can eat and little grannies-under-the-blanket which are my favourite and when I get back from Khan's my grandmother is running around talking to herself and the oven is going full blast.

The best tablecloth is out and ready for me and my next job is to bring cups and glasses out of the display cabinet in the front room and although they're sparkling clean my grandmother washes each one over again to be quite sure and it's funny how you can know that a person who's carrying on as if the end of the world has arrived is actually happy, and then Gus-Seep arrives.

Although he's supposed to be helping Philander out down at The Buildings like he always does, Gus-Seep is home for supper and he hasn't even had a chance to say two words to his own sister, when he's already in trouble with my grandmother and being ticked off.

'Let's get one thing straight,' my grandmother says, 'we don't want any more wild stories out of you.'

'I didn't lie, Ma,' Gus-Seep says. 'All I did was tell you it was Gloria and it was.'

'What's said in this house, stays in this house,' my grandmother says. 'We don't need it embroidered and then spread all over the streets by you the minute you put your foot outside again.'

'No, Ma,' he says and you can see he wants to push past

her and go and say 'How's tricks?' to his sister but my grandmother is standing right in his way and I'm standing there, watching them and wondering what will happen next and how he'll get away, when my grandmother's eyes fall on me and my heart sinks because I know that although she's busy with Gus-Seep right that moment I am not forgotten.

'Come here and let me look at you, Lily,' she says and she pulls me forward to see that my face and hands are clean and my hair is tidy.

'I want you to behave yourself in front of your mother,' she says taking my hands one at a time and looking at them front and back checking for dirt. 'No wolfing of food or asking to be excused until everyone's plate is clean. No jumping up from the table without an "excuse me" and don't forget "please" and "thank you".'

She talks as if she's cross with me but she doesn't mean it. When she runs out of breath she looks at me standing there like a fool and she puts her arms around me.

'Just you be a good girl in front of your mother,' she says. 'And make us all proud of you.'

If my mother and Stella were not coming out of the bedroom that minute with Stella talking nineteen to the dozen as if she were telling Gus-Seep's horse races on the wireless on a Saturday afternoon I would have told my grandmother what was on my mind.

They can make as much of a song and a dance as they like about my mother being back but, in my opinion, we don't need her in our house and I don't care if she knows I feel this way.

There we sit, black sheep and white sheep together at my grandmother's table at No. 48 Constitution Street. We dish up and pass things to each other like ladies and gentlemen and when our food is steaming on our plates in front of us, my grandmother holds up her hands and offers them, one on each side, like she always does so we can say grace.

I am on one side and my mother is on the other and my head is already down looking at the white polka dots on the blue skirt in my lap and the moment has come for 'Thank You Lord For Thy Bounty', or 'For What We Are About To Receive' but my mother's hands stay out of sight.

'We're about to give thanks, Gloria,' my grandmother says.

'I'm not standing in your way,' my mother says as if she's surprised we should be waiting for her at all and she's as cool as a cucumber and her hair is tied neat in a black velvet ribbon at the back of her neck and she looks my grandmother straight in the eye.

'It's your house. You must do what you always do and don't worry about me.'

'We would like to give thanks as a family,' my grandmother says and she shows her right hand which is the one my mother is supposed to take hold of but my mother just turns her head sideways and doesn't do anything at all.

'I'm sorry, Mommy,' she says. 'But if what I hear is true I don't think anyone in this house has anything very much to give thanks for. That's my opinion and I think it's better for everyone if I just sit here with my mouth closed and keep what I would like to say to God to myself.'

My mouth is open and I think Gus-Seep is going to fall right off his chair. Perhaps she's forgotten but I could have told my mother if she asked me. No-one speaks like this in our house and I can't imagine she would dare say another word until my grandmother has given her a piece of her mind because that is for sure what's going to come next. But I don't know my mother yet.

'Don't you read the newspapers?' she says. 'Haven't you walked around your own streets lately? Can't you see what's happening here?'

'Please, Gloria . . .' Stella says and she's showing with her face and a little wave of her hand for my mother to leave it alone but she can say 'please Gloria' till the cows come home, you can see in my mother's face she's only just begun and no amount of 'please Gloria' is going to keep her quiet now.

'I haven't been living on Mars all this time you know,' she says. 'The Government means business with you people. Don't you understand that? Don't you know what Group Areas is all about? It's about giving you tuppence ha'penny for this house and pushing you out onto the Cape Flats.'

'We know about Group Areas,' Stella says, very quiet and nice and you can see she hopes my mother will get the hint and that will be the end of the story.

'Do you?' my mother wants to know and now it's poor Stella's turn because my mother turns right around in her chair so she can look right at her.

'You could have fooled me. I would have thought anyone who knows what the Government and Group Areas are going to do to them wouldn't be sitting here with their hands together thanking God for what they're about to receive. If they really knew what they were about to receive they'd be out there, trying to do something to stop it.'

I think this kind of talk will give my grandmother a heart attack but she just sits there quietly and lets my mother have her say and we all stare down at our plates and wonder what's going to happen next and I hope my mother hasn't finished unpacking her suitcases yet because if this is the way she's going to carry on she'll need them again in a big hurry.

When my mother's finished my grandmother asks her very quiet and nice if this is the reason she's come back and she says it is.

'It's not right,' she says. 'It just isn't fair,' and she looks from one of us to the other and some of us look back at her and some of us don't and while she's looking at us she shakes her head and she keeps on saying how unfair she thinks it is.

'And who told you life was fair?' my grandmother wants to know and we're all sitting there glued to our chairs and our food is getting cold in front of us.

'No matter what you may think, I never turned my back on you,' my mother says as if it is the answer to some question which my grandmother never even asked her.

'I'm not turning my back on you now,' she says. 'I'm not

going to stand by and see your house taken away from you. I couldn't live with myself if I did that.'

We're all staring at her when we hear this and you could have knocked us right off our chairs with feathers.

'So you don't like what you think the Government has in mind for us,' my grandmother says and she says it as if she's a bit stupid and wants to make quite sure she's getting the story straight.

Then she gives my mother a really hoity-toity look.

'And what do you plan to do about that?' she wants to know. 'Will you write to Pretoria and tell them it doesn't suit you? And what do you imagine they're going to do then? Do you think they're going to say: "Oh, dear. It doesn't suit Miss Gloria Daniels. Everything is going to have to change"?'

I know my grandmother when she's like this and if I was my mother I would say I'm sorry and I spoke out of turn. I'd say I'm really not such a fool as I sound and I'd hope like anything that all my grandmother will do is give me a look that puts me in my place and then change the subject.

I'm not a genius but even I know there is no answer to those questions. People don't even try to make trouble with the Government. It doesn't work like that.

'You can't push decent people out on the street as if they're rubbish,' my mother says and she says it flat out as if it's a well-known fact and we're the only people in the world who haven't heard about it.

'And what would you know about decent people these days?' my grandmother wants to know. 'Are you meeting plenty of decent people in that place you're working in now?'

I've never seen my grandmother like this before. I think my mother being there brings out some kind of devil in her and when she says this Stella puts her hand up to her mouth and Gus-Seep's face is blood-red and his eyes are like saucers but my mother is like ice and she doesn't look away.

'I haven't been living on Mars either,' my grandmother says and she has eyes for no-one but my mother. 'When it comes to my children I make it my business to know what goes on.'

The way she's going on you'd think she and my mother are the only two people sitting at our table.

'Did you make your mind up about decent people while you were standing behind a till in a gangster's shebeen in the townships, taking money for liquor off Natives?'

When she says this there is a really terrible silence but when my mother answers you'd think it didn't worry her at all. She looks straight at my grandmother and my grandmother looks away but I can see my mother isn't finished yet and she's not going to leave it alone.

'I never knew you were so fussy about where my money was coming from,' she says. 'You should have told me before and I wouldn't have made you ashamed by pushing it onto you the way I've been doing.'

'Mommy didn't mean it that way,' Stella says and I think she wants to say more but no-one is listening to her and her voice gets very small and then it goes away altogether and my mother looks at us with quick little darts of her eyes and you can't see what she's thinking and we're not even trying to guess and we're not saying anything.

'If you don't want me to stay in your house, that's fine by me,' my mother says.

She gives my grandmother a look and says she needn't worry about what's been said, everyone's entitled to their opinion and she'll go on keeping the pot boiling in our house just like she's always done.

'I'll find some other place to stay if that's what you want but I'm not leaving here until I've done what I set out to do and made my voice heard and if none of you will stand up with me, then I'll do it alone.'

We may not know much in our house but we know fireworks when we see them and we also know, now that she's back with us, my grandmother wouldn't want my mother to leave again after five minutes just because of a family fall out.

'I can see you haven't changed,' my grandmother says in the end. 'You're still a woman who knows her own mind and if that's what you want to do, then you must do it. I'm sure no-one will dare stand in your way. I know I won't. But if you're going to stay in this house there's one thing we must get straight.'

I know my grandmother. It is her way of changing the subject so the fireworks will go away but the 'one thing' she changes the subject to is about my mother not saying grace with us and about my grandmother and her God.

So, before we only had fireworks but now we will have dynamite as well because there is no-one born yet who is going to come between her and her Maker and it is my grandmother's turn to have her say.

She says she and her Maker have walked too long a path beside each other for anyone to stand in their way and it isn't in her mind to part company from Him now that the end is in sight.

He knows what's in her heart. He's never let her down in the past, and she knows her future is safe in His hands, so it's her plan to keep walking right along next to Him until they come to the Promised Land, because that's the place where they're headed and she's certain that, in faith, they'll get there one day.

'So, if you'll excuse us,' she says and she gives my mother a look and holds out her hands either side of her for any one of us who would like to to take hold of them. 'We'll take hands just like we always do and bend our heads and pray and as it doesn't suit you, it needn't concern you.'

My mother and my grandmother look at one another in a funny way, and I think this is the kind of look they've often looked before and my grandmother looks down first and then we bend our heads and the room is full of the smell of curry and cinnamon pumpkin and my grandmother gives thanks just like she had made up her mind to do, because her family are together again under one roof; black sheep and white sheep together at her table and it hasn't been like that for a very long time.

This is what makes it a special night and this is what we're giving thanks for.

When we open our eyes I look up and my mother is looking right at me and she smiles but I look away long enough so she knows I have no time for her and she doesn't belong here and when I know for sure she understands, I pick up my fork and begin eating my grandmother's food.

When we're finished Gus-Seep makes an excuse to take my mother to see his horse and cart and have a breath of fresh air and my grandmother and Stella put on the radio to do the washing-up and it's just the two of them in the kitchen and they're laughing about the kind of stories Gus-Seep is telling my mother by now and how strange it is to have her back and how she hasn't changed at all.

'I know her when she's like this, with her fighting boots on her feet,' Stella says. 'I can even find it in my heart to feel sorry for the poor Government because she's going to go out and look for trouble with them and she won't rest until someone listens to her.'

'Maybe she's got the right idea,' my grandmother says wiping a best plate and putting it down on the table. 'Maybe it's time someone said we'd had enough of being pushed around and aren't going to take any more.'

'I can't believe you're saying that, Ma,' Stella says. 'You know as well as I do the world's not going to change just because Gloria decides it's high time it did.'

'Then she'll learn the hard way, won't she?' my grandmother says and they bang the plates around and talk about something else.

'Do you think he knows she's back?' Stella wants to know and my grandmother says if he doesn't he soon will because if Gus-Seep knows something it gets around quicker than if you put it in the newspaper.

'As long as he remembers he's a married man,' Stella says. 'We don't want any more trouble.'

I'm sitting quiet listening with big ears and they're talking the kind of talk I like to hear because I think maybe it's my father they're talking about but then they talk some more and I realize it's only James they mean.

*　　*　　*

My grandmother doesn't seem to mind but I don't like the way my mother treats her. She's taken it on herself to march back into our lives and never asked us if we mind. She thinks she can take us over but it doesn't work like that, which is something I would be quite happy to tell her if she asked me.

She throws her education around as if that makes her better than anyone else but I have news for her. She's not as smart as she thinks she is, and when she stops being so full of herself and listens to other people for a change she'll find out that my grandmother can still teach her a thing or two.

It's no good getting cross with my grandmother because she's not a good reader. She has to go slowly because she's old and her eyes aren't good, but she always gets there in the end which Stella and I could have told my mother for nothing if she ever showed she was in a mood to listen to us.

It doesn't cost anything to pretend you don't notice. My grandmother didn't spend all her young days in school hanging around the nuns like someone else we know but she can read as well as anyone else. She must get to things in her own time, that's all, and Stella and I don't mind waiting until she does.

This is because we aren't like my mother, who has made it obvious to all of us that she's a woman in a hurry.

All we hear now is my mother telling my grandmother to go and look for this paper and go and look for that letter and to put her glasses on so they can read house papers and Government letters together and my mother can explain things to her.

My mother sits at our kitchen table as if she owns it, so I suppose the bright side is that at least these days, for a change and the first time in my life, if I got it in my mind to look for her I would always know where to find her.

I can see her whenever I like, standing behind my grandmother like a schoolteacher and no matter what time of day it is, she always has her shoes and stockings on and

126

her hair is combed back and out of the way and she is made up to the nines and smelling like a scent factory.

When she gets down to business there's no stopping her.

Her hands are in and out of the biscuit tin where my grandmother keeps her private things and there are papers all over the show for anyone who walks in our house to see and when my mother starts asking questions if my grandmother doesn't get her glasses out of her overall pocket and onto her nose fast enough and start giving answers like lightning, she moves papers around with a big rustle and sighs a lot and gets a face as if she's chewing lemons.

It gets on my nerves, which my grandmother says is nonsense because I'm far too young to have nerves.

I don't care. I think my mother is very full of herself and has a cheek to come pushing into our life the way she has and carrying on as if there's only one way to do things and that's her way.

She's not like a proper person at all. She hardly has two words to say to anyone. All she says is that she would like to get her facts straight before she goes into town to speak to the Government, because that's what she's here for and the sooner she gets started the better.

I think she's happy sitting at the table with my grandmother's papers out all over the show and her notebook and fountain pen ready and clean writing paper and envelopes right next to her. The way she carries on you'd think she was the Queen of England. You can just look at her face and the way her red mouth sits right in the middle of it and know that she doesn't know how to laugh and joke.

My grandmother isn't like that. When she's in a good mood and is sitting at that very same table peeling her vegetables or cutting out biscuits she doesn't mind if I come in and sit with her to help her, or just to keep her company and if I feel like playing the fool I can do it if I like because it always makes her laugh.

I ask her if she would like a song and a dance from me, and she says she wouldn't mind. Then I stand outside the kitchen door like an actress and when I'm ready I dance in holding my skirt out at the sides. Then I tap dance or do ballet or I sing 'Darling Clementine', and if I want to make my grandmother jump and say if she gets hold of me she'll wash my mouth out with soap I sing 'Two Old Ladies Locked In The Lavatory'. Only I know what she's going to do when she hears it, so before I even begin I'm always laughing so much I can hardly get the words out.

Sometimes she can be silly too. She takes her glasses out of her pocket and puts them on her nose and says, now she can see straight, I must come and stand in front of her so she can have a good look at me and see how many freckles I've grown on my nose since last she looked. Then she pretends to get a big shock when she looks at my face and sees how many freckles I have, and when she's finished pretending to count we both have a good laugh.

She doesn't like to see me with a long face. She says if the clock strikes or the wind changes my face will stay that way and I'll be sorry and so will she, because she depends on my smiles to light up her day and so I'd better hurry up and find a smile very quickly.

This is my grandmother's way and when Stella's there she always laughs with us and says we're two old fools together and a fine pair.

But when my mother's there and we do our nonsense and are hugging and laughing with each other in front of her, she doesn't join in. She doesn't even try. She just sits there with the biscuit tin open on the table and my grandmother's house papers in her hands and looks at us with small eyes as if we're wasting her time and are the biggest fools in the history of the world.

My mother has been down to town. This morning she went off dressed to kill dancing up the road to the bus stop with all my grandmother's papers in an envelope under her arm ready to tell the Government man where he can get off.

This afternoon her face is like thunder and when she walks in the front door and hears all the talking and laughing in our kitchen and comes in to see what it's about, she isn't too pleased to find my supposed-to-be father, Frank Adams, camping out at our kitchen table.

You can take one look at her face and see she's not in the mood for Frank Adams and if she could, she would give him his marching orders or make him disappear in a puff of smoke but we can all see that Stella still has a lot of time for him.

From the minute he knocked, out of the blue, on our door and Stella hopped down the passage on her hopalong leg and saw who it was, she's been carrying on as if it's Lazarus back from the dead, anxious to give us a visit, and she can't wait to get him into our house and sitting at our kitchen table with a cup of tea in front of him.

'And what are you doing these days then, Frank?' Stella wants to know and she's pink in the face and offering him another slice of bread while she's saying it.

'I go wherever the work is,' he says slamming our butter all over his bread. 'I'm down at the docks at the moment, doing tally clerk work. It's not much of a job but beggars can't be choosers and that's what we're down to these days. We take what we can get.'

'I thought the Natives worked the docks,' my mother says. 'That always used to be the way.' It's the first thing she's said to him the whole time he's been there, so we all get a big surprise.

'We're trying to work them out,' Frank says. 'The Government says this isn't their place and they should go back to the bush where they come from and I, for one, go along with that.'

'That's fine for you,' my mother says, 'until the Government decides it's your turn to go back wherever it is they decide you came from. You won't go along with that so easily. And what are the Natives supposed to do in the meantime? They have to eat too. They have families to feed.'

Her food is cold in front of her and all she's done is push it around her plate as if it isn't to her liking and she won't eat it.

'They can be milk boys,' Stella says. 'They can do the

129

rubbish or they can go back to their kraals in the *bundu* just the way Frank says.'

She points to the teapot and asks if Frank would like some more tea and he says he won't say no.

'I didn't make the rules,' Frank says. 'But if I want to get work I stick by them. It's graft down at the docks, just like everywhere else. First come, first served. You queue up and the Natives are welcome to queue with the rest and you wait until someone says he's got a job for you.'

'You're lucky then,' my mother says. 'From what you say, you don't go many days without work and the Natives get sent back all the time. Isn't that lucky?'

'I don't know about lucky,' Frank says. 'Let's just say we have a little arrangement. We've got friends who look out for us and see we get a little nod in our direction.'

'But not the Natives?' my mother wants to know and we're all sitting in the kitchen steam and there's the damp feel of it and the smell of the food and she's tapping at the table top with her knife and she doesn't even know she's doing it.

'The Natives aren't supposed to be here in the first place,' Frank says.

He says every day more and more people wait for work and they can't all be chosen and the Natives are at the end of the queue and are almost certain to be sent home with nothing and if they don't know that by now, then they don't know anything.

'They take their chances. If it comes to the end and the boss is a man short he might be forced to take a Native because there's no-one else left and you should see how they go for each other then. It's a real free for all.'

This kind of talk makes my mother mad. For the sake of peace she shouldn't really show it but you can see she's had enough and too much and she can't help herself.

'Every time you open your mouth it's bosses this and bosses that and how pleased you are with yourself because you're a "*Ja, baas*" man and can push your way to the front of the queue and do some poor Native out of a job.'

'It's the way the world works, Gloria,' Frank says. 'If we

don't look after ourselves, no-one's going to do it for us. If someone is willing to push me to the front of the queue I'm willing to say, "*Ja, baas, nee, baas*" to him until the cows come home if I have to. I'm not going to say no, thank you very much and stand aside so some native boy can take the bread out of my mouth. I'm not that mad yet.'

Stella says Frank's quite right and he always had his head screwed on the right way and to excuse her sister who's come back home with some very funny ideas and she can give my mother dagger looks as much as she likes, nothing will stop her now.

'If no-one speaks up about it, how's it ever going to change?' my mother wants to know. 'You've got a big mouth, why don't you open it and ask for what's right for a change instead of just what's in it for you?'

No-one likes to be talked to like this and I don't know what happened between my mother and the Government but whatever it was it didn't put her in a very good mood.

If I was Frank Adams I would have got up from the table there and then the way she was going on at him. I wouldn't have hung around where I wasn't wanted.

'I'm certainly not going to keep my mouth shut for the sake of keeping the peace with a man like Frank Adams,' my mother told Stella afterwards. 'You needn't make such a performance out of it. He's got a skin like an elephant and he'll be back. You can be sure of that. He knows a good thing when he sees it.'

'Why must you always spoil everything?' Stella wants to know. 'We were having such a nice time until you came home.'

Her face is puffed up and she's so cross with my mother she's nearly crying with crossness.

'All we wanted was to have a nice evening and all you wanted was to spoil things. I don't understand what makes you do things like this.'

'If you'd been down at the Government office standing in queues with me and speaking to the kind of people I've been speaking to all day perhaps you'd understand a bit better,' my mother tells her short and sharp. 'All I'm short of on top of that is Frank Adams.'

Stella isn't interested in the Government office. All she cares about is that her evening has been spoiled and my mother's the one who did it and she's too cross with her to listen to anything else she has to say.

I think if my mother had her life over again Frank Adams wouldn't be a man she would even look at twice, never mind chase after the way Stella says she did. I think if she saw him coming today she would turn around and run in the opposite direction.

My grandmother and Stella wonder how long it'll be before James comes looking for my mother and if he'll come at all or if there's hope for him yet and he's learned his lesson.

But he does come.

He comes at the end of the month with the little something he always brings for my grandmother and he gives it to her in a big hurry and doesn't even ask how we all are the way that he usually does.

He says, if we don't mind, he's heard Gloria's back and it's her he's come to see.

Stella says he looked to her like a man who'd done a lot of thinking and made up his mind about something at long last and there are no prizes for guessing what that something is.

It's Saturday morning and very warm and Stella and my grandmother and I are all dressed up in summer dresses and sandals, ready to go to the shops which is what we always do on a Saturday, so my grandmother can pick and choose all the best bargains, as much as she likes, because Stella and I are there with her to carry the parcels home.

My mother isn't going with us. She's out in the backyard getting ready to wash her hair. There's a table set out under the fig tree and everything she needs is laid out on it. Soap and towels and a big jug of hot water which we've told her won't do the plants any harm once she's finished with it and it's gone cold.

Her hairbrushes are set out and a big comb and the silver-looking hand mirror and Stella has brushed her hair loose ready for the wash and Stella is really nice to her.

'You've got such beautiful hair,' she says stroking away with the silver brush. 'I'd forgotten. It's grown so long but you keep it nice. I'd forgotten how beautiful it is but it's a handful, I can see that.'

I can see them from my back room window while I'm getting ready and Stella looks really smart in her green and white shopping dress, belted tight at the waist and her hair all tidy in a net at the back and waves over her forehead and ears in front and, if you couldn't see her leg brace, all you'd think is how pretty she is. You'd never think she was different to anyone else.

She's brushing my mother's hair with long strokes from the silver brush and the sun is dancing around them and catching on the silver and sparkling up at me flash-flash like cowboy messages and my mother's head sits high on her long neck and her eyes are closed as if she's one of Gus-Seep's racehorses having a Saturday groom before the race, and Stella is brushing smooth and easy and smiling while she's doing it and she's doing all the talking and her voice comes up to me light and sweet and easy with a little trill in it like a bird.

'James is here,' my grandmother shouts down to the yard from the kitchen. 'He's come to see you, Gloria.'

I can hear my mother say she isn't properly dressed to see visitors but she's already pulled away from Stella's brush and jumped up and is doing up her blouse.

'Don't go inside,' Stella says. 'Why don't you stay out here in the sun and I'll tell James we're on our way out and he can come down here if he wants to see you.'

James is standing in our kitchen right near the open door. His Adam's apple is bobbing up and down but his mind is made up and we feel sorry for him.

'She's in the backyard,' Stella says reaching for her shopping bag. 'You know your way by now. You don't need

133

me to show you and I don't suppose you need a written invitation.'

'I'll stay behind with you,' I say because it isn't every Saturday morning James comes to visit us like this but my grandmother says I won't be staying anywhere. I'll be going down to help with the shopping just like I always do on a Saturday and if James will excuse us we have to be on our way and James is already out of the back door and my grandmother and Stella are giving each other one of their looks which I am not supposed to see.

'I suppose it'll be all right,' my grandmother says and we are already in the passage on our way out and it sounds to me as if it's wishful thinking and it's herself that she's telling this to and she's hooking her handbag over her arm and taking my hand.

'Of course it'll be all right,' Stella says. 'Just as long as he knows what he's doing and isn't suffering from loss of memory.'

When we get home you can hardly see us for shopping bargains and the hair water is ice-cold in the jug and the garden could have died of thirst for all my mother cared.

She's lying back in the deckchair with her legs stretched out sideways in the sun and James is sitting on the little bench right in front of the deckchair and he's bending forward towards her and talking his head off as if he hasn't opened his mouth for a thousand years and I'm glad now Evie made such a big thing about saying she'd never be caught dead in our house, because if she was standing where we were standing on the backyard steps and saw what we saw she would have killed James Scheepers right there and then.

9

Letters

Something's happened. I don't know what it is but I'm in trouble. I have a letter from my school principal to take home with me and that's never very good news and when I get home I go straight to the kitchen and put it on the kitchen table in front of my grandmother.

She knows about these things. She looks at it sitting on the table between us and I stand in front of her with my eyes on the ground waiting for her to say whatever it is she's going to say.

'Don't you think you should give that letter to your mother?' she says. 'I've been turning a blind eye to some of the things that have been going on in this house since your mother came back but even my blind eye can see how you've been ignoring her.'

I push out my lip but I don't say anything.

'I'm sorry you feel the way you do, Lily,' my grandmother says and she asks me if I wouldn't like to change my mind and try and be nicer.

'You'll make life a lot easier for yourself and for the rest of us if you do because whether you like it or not, your mother's living in our house now and that letter should be going to her, not to me.'

She picks up the letter and holds it out to me.

'I know it's not what you want to do,' she says. 'But this isn't my job any more and life isn't about what we want to do or what we don't want to do. It's about doing the right thing and the right thing is for you to give this letter to your mother and let her deal with it as she thinks best.'

So that is what I have to do.

Mr Christie, our principal, is ready for us when school comes out the next day. He's expecting to see my grandmother, who he knows, sitting outside his office with me, but it's my mother he sees instead and I don't know what he's heard but you can see it comes as a big surprise to him.

He tells us to come in and sit down and he sits behind his desk opposite us and makes a big thing of putting the papers on his desk straight which is the kind of thing he always does to children in trouble to keep them waiting and put them on their nerves and when he's ready he gives my mother an up and down look and says he'll come straight to the point.

He has a letter from Carole-Amelia's mother. It's right on the desk in front of him and he can see my mother isn't a person who'll just swallow any old story so he turns it around so she can see the name at the bottom of the page, which is Mrs Reginald Lombard.

My mother doesn't even look at it. She looks straight at Mr Christie and there's a certain look on her face that doesn't seem to make him very happy. I think that's because he was expecting my grandmother and got more than he bargained for.

He says Carole-Amelia and I are penfriends and have been for quite a long time now and he tells my mother about 'Getting to Know You' and trying to make people know us and love us and the reasons why we're doing it, which is not to spread our private business around but to show that people in the Valley are no different from anyone else.

'But Lily's been writing the kind of letter that gives the wrong ideas,' Mr Christie says. 'In Mrs Lombard's opinion the letters her daughter's been receiving aren't the kind of letter any decently brought up child would write.'

'And what kind of letter exactly is it that a decently brought up child wouldn't write?' my mother wants to know and it looks as if she's going to let Mr Christie do all the talking and that's a big surprise to me.

He says I've written about cut-off human heads sitting in police fridges and gangster criminals with gold teeth and he has no idea where such stories can possibly come from and his eyes are like two cross little snake eyes shining over the top of his glasses.

There's another matter too, he says and it's a matter of some delicacy.

'Lily says no-one in your family has any idea who her father might be.'

He moves his look from me to my mother as if it's her turn now and his mouth gives a little flick and she looks right back at him and her face doesn't move at all.

'Mrs Lombard says there's a word we all know which would apply to Lily in this situation, but being a decent woman she can't put it in writing.'

He says the sins of the fathers, and the mothers too for that matter, aren't really his department but if my mother asks for his advice he would say it would be a very easy thing for her to drop Carole-Amelia's mother a line to explain and to put things right.

'And what would you suggest I say?' my mother wants to know and she sits very straight with her nylon knees together and her high-heeled shoes neat in front of her on my principal's floral carpet.

'You can say Lily has an overactive imagination. It's not an unknown thing in a child her age. Girls, in particular, are given to that problem.'

He puts his hands into a steeple on the desk in front of him and leans forward to get a better look at my mother and his glasses are busy sliding down his nose but he doesn't seem to notice.

'You can say she sucked everything she wrote out of her thumb and didn't know what she was talking about. You can tell Mrs Lombard she can leave it to you to deal with the matter in the right way.'

Then we're all quiet to hear what my mother will say next and what she says is much more how I know her because although she's sitting very still, her eyes are flashing like fire and she says she'll do no such thing and she

137

says it so quietly I'm not quite sure I heard right and nor is Mr Christie.

My mother says being an educated man Mr Christie will know the word for a person who takes short cuts around the truth and she's been wondering while he's been talking if such a person is the right kind of person to be put in charge of young minds, not yet set in their ways, especially at a Church school and Mr Christie goes as red as a beetroot and his mouth is so tight together you would think it will never open again and in the meantime I have problems of my own.

I've never felt such a fool, because while my mother is talking, Mr Christie has taken my letters out of his drawer and they're sitting in his hand held together with a red elastic band and my stupid picture under Dollie's striped sun umbrella 'By The Seaside' is right on top and smiling away.

'You obviously have ideas of your own,' Mr Christie says and if he gave me the kind of look he gave my mother I would have fallen over dead on the carpet and my troubles would have been over but it makes no difference to her. She's like ice.

'Mrs Lombard has no right to read my daughter's letters and nor have you,' my mother says. 'You have no right whatsoever.'

The way she says it and the dagger look she gives him you wouldn't know who was the school principal and who was in trouble and I don't think anything like this has ever happened in any principal's office anywhere before. It's never happened at our school.

'I think people of any age have a right to privacy and protection. Mrs Lombard evidently doesn't agree.'

My mother stands up and picks up her handbag and I jump up too in a big hurry. I'm not staying alone in that office when my mother's gone because I'm the cause of all this and everyone knows it and I think Mr Christie would like to kill me with his bare hands.

'You can tell Mrs Lombard that as far as Lily's mother is concerned Lily is the injured party in this matter and, if she cares to, Mrs Reginald Lombard can send her a letter of apology and when we receive it we'll decide whether or not we're in the mood to overlook what she's done to us. She knows our address.'

By now Mr Christie is very red and we all stand up and he tries to give my mother the letters with my photograph smiling like a fool on top of them but she says the letters are mine and he should give them straight to me, into my hands, and so that's what he does and my mother doesn't even look at them.

Our school has a cement floor and when we walk out of Mr Christie's office and he closes the door behind us without even a good afternoon to send us on our way, my mother's high heels tap-tap so loudly that Carole-Amelia's mother must have heard them all the way to Rosedale Gardens.

She tap-taps all the way to the open cloakroom where we hang our hats and shoe bags, where there's a long line of basins where we wash our hands and faces.

Usually there's a lot of screaming and banging but that's only in school time and by the time my mother and I get there the whole school is empty and all you can hear is a big quiet and the taps dripping and that's where we stand looking at one another.

'This isn't a very nice thing and I'm sorry it's happened to you,' my mother says and I say it's all right and shrug my shoulders and look all over the place but not at her face and I say it doesn't matter.

'It does matter,' she says looking down at me as if I'm the one she's cross with. 'You may still be a child but that doesn't mean people can treat you without respect. Your letters are between you and the person you address them to. They're your private property.'

What worries me is that I won't be allowed to write to Carole-Amelia any more after this and when I ask my mother she says that's for me to decide.

'I'll never stop you doing anything you want to do. It's up to you. You'll have to think it over but I think you already know what you have to do.'

That's all she has to say. She says she won't mention the subject again and I tell her I'll think things over and I will, but in my heart I know she's right and I am sorry as I can ever be about anything because Carole-Amelia's my best friend and I don't have another one, so it's not so easy.

Carole-Amelia sent me a picture cut out of a magazine once. It was of a red car called a Ford Thunderbird and she says as soon as she's old enough to have a driver's licence, her father is going to buy her one exactly like it.

I've never seen a car like that in my life before and Carole-Amelia has drawn two round faces into the picture, one behind the wheel and one in the passenger seat and put little arrows pointing down at them.

'This is you and this is me,' she wrote and our names are next to the arrows and she's the one who's driving.

'When I get my car, you'll be the first person I take for a drive in it and that's a solemn promise.'

She says we'll drive all over town together and make sure the whole world sees us.

'We'll be the two biggest madams the world has ever seen. We'll be such a sight to see that no-one who ever sees us will forget it in a hurry.'

No-one knows about this except Carole-Amelia and me but it's a hard thing to give up.

If my grandmother had been there she would have called me Aunty Lillah and said it wasn't the end of the world, but my mother isn't like that. She's just like any other grown-up woman. She doesn't know how to act like a mother at all.

So we just stand there for a while listening to the tap dripping and everything smells of sandshoes and wax crayon and children and I wonder how big a sin it is to love my grandmother so much more than I love my mother and whether or not my mother knows this.

It's not my fault and I can't really say it's her fault either but there's nothing we can do about it now, because it's too late.

*   *   *

My mother and I don't talk about the letters again. She's left me to make up my own mind what I should do just like she said she would but I've told everyone what happened at my school and when I tell Gus-Seep he tells me I should listen to my mother because she knows letters can be very dangerous. They are one of the things that have caused such trouble between our house and Evie.

Letters are a big part of the reason why Evie hates my mother so much.

One day Evie was looking through James' things, which her mother told her was the kind of thing a wife should do, and she got hold of my mother's letters to James. Letters she'd written to him when he was in England. Letters which he kept all these years tied together neatly in a packet at the back of a drawer.

Evie read the letters, every single one of them, one after the other and when she'd finished reading them once, she read them again just to be sure and when she'd finished reading them the second time she went mad and packed her bags and went straight back to her mother's house and took the letters with her stuck any old how in her handbag.

The minute she got inside her mother's door she pulled the letters out again and handed them over to her mother and her mother read them and then they read them again together and when they'd finished they went out into the backyard and made a fire and burned them and Evie said after what she'd read, she'd never go back to James.

He was a pig and a liar. She didn't know why she'd married him in the first place. She was sorry now she had let her mother push her into it because he could have the best future in the world ahead of him, it was still a big waste of her time.

Gus-Seep says he doesn't know what Evie expected James to do when he found her gone but if she expected him to go out and look for her and go on his knees when he found her and say how sorry he was for whatever was in the letters and beg her forgiveness, like her mother said he should, she'd made the biggest mistake of her life.

When James heard that Evie and her mother had read his letters and then burned them, he went mad too.

He said as far as he was concerned Evie could stay exactly where she was at her mother's house and never come back and if he ever clapped eyes on her again it would be too soon.

He was sick and tired of all of it, and the day he'd been such a fool as to let her lead him down the aisle was the blackest day of his life.

She always acted so sweet and nice and she could be very nice when she put her mind to it, but the minute anyone mentioned Gloria Daniels' name which, as God is his witness, he would never be so stupid as to do, Evie turned into a mad monster and now she'd done this to his letters and it was the last straw.

He'd had enough and as far as he was concerned she could stay with her mother for ever and they could be two jealous, spiteful old cats together until Hell froze over for all he cared but after a while they all got over it and Evie went home.

Although they're nice, I feel as if everyone is fed up with me and will stay that way until I stop the penfriend business which is a very hard thing for me to do.

I put Carole-Amelia's last, nice letter under my pillow to maybe see her in my dreams, just for old times' sake because this is something we are always trying to do, although it hasn't worked yet.

I thought maybe if it did, we could sort things out face to face but I lay down on my bed and the fig leaves kissed my window and at last I went to sleep and that was the end of the story. I think my dreams were fed up with me too and so they went off in their own directions and by morning they were gone for ever.

10

A Lovely Light

When my grandmother and Stella aren't looking, Gus-Seep gets hold of my mother around the waist and says won't she, for old times' sake, come and have a quick one with him and his friends down at The Buildings.

Philander remembers her from the old days and he would like to do her a favour because he knows who her Johannesburg friends are and they are people who remember a favour and know what it is all about.

He says he will be happy to see her and offer her a little drink, first one on the house because of certain people they both know but the second one for her alone, because he can be very generous where a pretty girl is concerned.

Gus-Seep winks at my mother as if she is his special friend and they have secrets together and she calls him Seepie and has all the time in the world for him.

It's no secret who her favourite in our house is. When Gus-Seep comes in through the front door, no matter how busy she's making out she is, she'll stop whatever she's doing and push her papers away. She'll say they're not important and they're not good news anyway. She would rather go outside and sit in the sun with Gus-Seep for a while, if he'll tell her a naughty story or two that'll cheer her up and they'll sit under the fig tree for hours and Gus-Seep will tell her the most terrible made-up things just to make her laugh.

He thinks she's wonderful and follows her everywhere and tells terrible lies about her behind her back to make out she's more than she is because it's his nature and no matter how hard we pray about it, he can't stop himself.

My mother knows all about it and doesn't mind. She thinks it's a big joke. The way she goes on you'd think there should be a medal for liars and Gus-Seep should win it and we should all be proud of him and pat him on the back and say 'well done' but you can't say a thing like that out loud. In my mother's eyes, her little Seepie can't do a thing wrong.

In the end it's too much for my grandmother and she takes my mother aside and tells her what Revd Rainbird said about Gus-Seep. How he wouldn't know the truth if he fell over it in the road and how he's broken his mother's heart with his drinking and lies and hanging around a place like The Buildings with a crook like Philander.

'You can smile about it if you like,' my grandmother says because maybe Gus-Seep keeping company with Philander is not so terrible to my mother as it is to my grandmother.

She can see my mother has her own ideas and in the matter of Gus-Seep they're not on the same side. My mother doesn't take Gus-Seep's stories to heart the way my grandmother does and she doesn't mind who knows it.

'You think everything's a joke these days,' my grandmother says and she gives a sniff to show what she thinks about that. 'And you seem to think Revd Rainbird's the biggest joke of all.'

'I've never said a word against Sidney Rainbird,' my mother says and, if you know what to listen for, you'd know from the soft, nice way she says it, there's a big fight coming even though what she says is true.

She never says a word against Revd Rainbird. She never even mentions his name but she doesn't have to. Everyone knows how she feels about him. He knows it himself. She can barely bring herself to greet him if she sees him on the street and it makes my grandmother furious.

'I don't see you putting your foot inside a church,' she says. 'But surely by now you must have learned a little bit about the devil.'

This subject is like dynamite and we never talk about it

in our house. When Sunday comes we go our same way as usual and my mother stays at home and on those walks to St Peter's with our church scarves over our heads and our Book of Common Prayer in our hands you can just about see the big black cloud hanging over my grandmother's head and you don't have to be a genius to know what put it there.

When she says this about the devil, my mother puts down her pen and pushes aside what she's doing, which is to do with house papers and lawyers just like it always is and in the same nice quiet voice she says she does for sure believe in the devil.

He's got a lot of faces and he puts on a different one every day just to try and fool her but she sees him anyway. He's doing very well, thank you, and living in all his different faces down at the Government offices with plenty of work to keep him busy.

The way she says it, it's as if it's some kind of joke or something but not the kind anyone would laugh at and right that minute my mother is definitely not in the mood for laughing. It's all the talk about Gus-Seep that's made her so cross.

'Since when does Sidney Rainbird know so much about the truth that he can pass judgement on Gus-Seep?' my mother wants to know and I can see in my grandmother's face that she's sorry now because all this talk has started my mother off again, but now it's too late.

'I'll tell you what the truth is,' my mother says. 'The truth is that Sidney Rainbird's people are looking to him for help in their hour of need but they're wasting their time because he's hiding in his church hoping this cup will pass him by and he's not going to help anyone at all.'

Where was he she wants to know, when the Government men drove into the Valley and put up condemned notices outside houses where whole families had been living very happily the week before?

Where was he when his people were packing up their things and crying like children in the street as they said goodbye to their neighbours?

Where was he the day old Andries put his head right under the train's wheels?

'Why wasn't he right there shouting so loud that even God could hear him if He was in a mood to concern Himself with our troubles just for a change?'

Her face is red and when she stops talking it doesn't end there because the room is still full of what she's said as if someone's been playing drums there and even after they stop you can still hear the banging in your ears.

That's how it is in our house these days. Fights start out of the blue and this time it's all because of poor Seepie, who in my mother's eyes can do no wrong, even when he says on the streets that she's the girlfriend of a well-known gangster and carries a revolver with her which she knows how to use.

You have to watch out for my mother. My grandmother says she's never known a woman get so worked up as my mother does and about such funny things and living in our house these days is like walking on thin ice every day of your life but all the same, my grandmother has never in her life learned not to say exactly what she wants to say to a daughter who gets too big for her boots.

'You've got it all worked out,' she says. 'And a big mouth to tell it with and all the big words inside you that the nuns put there, so everyone will sit up and listen and be impressed.'

'Leave it alone, Ma,' says my mother and she makes as if she's tired and has had enough and is going to get up and go out for a walk but my grandmother says she can sit right where she is and hear her out.

'Perhaps you should be the one who's out on the streets shouting out all your grievances to Heaven because goodness knows, nothing that anyone else has to say is good enough for you.'

I think there'll be another fight but there isn't. My mother just looks at my grandmother and shakes her head.

'What do you think I've been doing?' she says. 'What on

146

earth do you think it is I've been doing from the minute I put my foot back in this house?'

You can see how fed up she is. She pushes her chair back so it nearly falls over and gets up from the table. She looks for her cardigan and purse and says she's had enough for one day, she's going out for a breath of air and she has to make a phone call long distance from Khan's shop to a friend in Johannesburg and she throws her cardigan over her shoulders as if she's going to the front door but I know her by now. She won't leave without having the last word because that isn't her way.

'If no-one will listen to me, then I'll have to talk louder, won't I?' she says and she's ready to go and her eyes are on fire and she looks at both of us as if she hates us because we're standing in her way.

'I'll just have to get ready to shout and you may as well make up your mind and get ready too because I'm going to be shouting very much louder before this particular night is over.'

My mother thinks old Andries is forgotten but she's wrong. I had my own reasons to be sad when he died under the train and although I didn't see it with my own eyes the way Stella did I will never forget him.

My grandmother doesn't like me playing with fire but she says, because I've asked so nicely, she doesn't mind if I use up the last of my pink birthday candles in the way I want although she's never heard of such a thing before.

'I've never known a child get such funny ideas in her head,' she says. 'And I don't care what Mr Asher told you. Jews are all well and good. They have their good points and their bad points the same as everyone else does but we're not Jews in this house.'

She gives me a look as if she's going to say something and then changes her mind.

'What next?' she says. 'I suppose you'll be talking down

147

at the Muslim shop and you'll come home and tell me it's in your head to try the *khalifa* and if I don't put a stop to it you'll be running up and down on hot coals right in our own backyard and what am I going to do then?'

'Don't be silly,' I say.

She's acting cross and tapping at her head as if I'm mad but I can't help laughing. She knows I'll never do anything like that and she knows what I mean about the candle and I know in the end she'll let me have it. I need it for my own good reasons and although my grandmother doesn't know exactly what it's about she doesn't mind because I'm allowed to have my secrets too, as long as they don't hurt anyone.

'You're turning out to be a strange girl,' she says but she opens up the kitchen drawer and takes out what's left of the packet of candles and gives them to me.

'One at a time,' she says shaking the packet at me for a warning before she hands it over.

'And you or Stella will light it for me,' I say with a pulled face and a big sigh. 'And I must put the candle in plasticine to be on the safe side and must never go to sleep with it burning. I know.'

In that way, with all those warnings, the candles pass from her hands into mine.

'You know too much for someone your age,' my grandmother says. 'That's the trouble.'

'You're the funniest child I ever knew,' Stella says. She's in her nightie and dressing-gown and although she can't get old Andries out of her mind her nerves are feeling a little bit better.

That's what she says although we don't know whether or not to believe her because when she tries to smile, her smile has trouble staying on her face and shakes all over the place.

Her hair is brushed neat for the night and she smells of Eau du Lundi.

She's come to say goodnight to me and hear my prayers and check that the candle isn't going to burn our house

148

down and when it comes to this kind of thing, she's nicer than my grandmother.

If Stella comes to hear your prayers and you're already in bed when she gets there she gives a wink and lets you say what you have to say just where you are without getting out of your bed again and getting ice-cold while you kneel before God.

The candle is almost finished by the time she gets there. Soon it will be just a little black spot on the yellow plasticine and then it will flicker out and all that will be left will be a bit of candle smell that will soon go away.

'It's funny,' she says. 'You never actually knew old Andries but I think you're the only person in this world who is lighting a candle for him tonight.'

She puts her arms around me and gives me a last hug for today and I jump right out of the blankets to put my arms around her and hug her back because she's my aunty and I know her and I'm glad she didn't die of polio when she was small so now we have the chance to be in this world together.

'I don't know where we got you from, Lily,' she says. 'I don't know where you get all your funny ideas.'

She bends down to tuck me back deep under the blankets so I'll be safe for the night and she checks that the window is a little bit open and then she sits on my bed.

She doesn't play the fool like she sometimes does. She doesn't say she hopes I sleep tight and the bed bugs don't bite. She doesn't say sweet dreams. She doesn't say see you in the morning, Little Miss Smarty Pants. She doesn't say anything at all. She just sits there for a little while and looks out of the window at the fig tree and the backyard, and at the next door backyard and the little bit of sky we can see from that window and she holds my hand.

The candle is small and meant for a celebration, so it doesn't last long because it's not meant to but that doesn't matter. It burns steady and you can depend on it and it gives a lovely light.

11

A Highly Dangerous Man

There's big police trouble at the Training College and James is in the middle of it and Dudda Dollie is the one to tell us.

Dudda is young Dollie's son, old Dollie's only grandson and Dudda isn't his real name. When he was born, old Dollie got so excited he gave him a long name no-one could say properly, not even his own mother, so in the end everyone gave up and we all call him Dudda.

Although he's nothing to look at, Dudda's a genius, the smartest boy at Trafalgar High School and the apple of old Dollie's eye.

You can't miss Dudda because he's got a skew eye from the days before he became a genius, when he put his eye out playing with a knife.

People still remember how he was taken away in old Dollie's Studebaker car with a towel around his head and his eye poked half out and his mother running behind crying into her apron and how he came home from the hospital with a glass eye that looked like a gobstopper and could only stare in one direction.

Dudda didn't mind. He liked hospital and while he was there, he made up his mind to become a doctor some day because the doctors had been so good to him.

After that he got very clever and we stopped laughing at him and he started carrying off all the Trafalgar prizes so no-one else in that school ever got a look in on prize-giving night and he still wanted to be a doctor and old Dollie said if that was what he wanted he would make it his business to see that was what he got.

But, never mind how clever Dudda was by Trafalgar standards, old Dollie wasn't taking chances about him not making it into the quota system and not being accepted by the university.

Every day after school, Dudda went up our hill and caught the bus to the Training College so James could give him extra lessons just 'in case'.

While James did his own after-school work, he set Dudda work to do and when he'd done it, they had a little talk and then he set Dudda some more work for the next day and it was like that every day in term time.

One eye or not Dudda was not afraid of book work. He couldn't wait to learn things. He didn't do anything else but learn but he never bragged about how much he knew. He didn't have to, because in that department old Dollie was there to blow his trumpet for him and when he got on to the subject of wonderful Dudda, his grandson, there was no holding him back.

The way he carried on Dudda was already a doctor twenty times over and people were bowing and scraping to him and remembering his grandfather who'd set aside money from the day he was born so that Dudda would have his chance.

The gangsters call him Dudda One-Eye, but they like him too and leave him alone, because gangsters need doctors the same as the rest of us do and they'd just as well have old Dudda as anyone else, because Dudda knows them and they know he'll never split on them and they can't imagine him ever asking them for money. So it suits them if Dudda gets on with his books and stays on the right side of the law which there's no doubt he'll always do.

That's why it came as a shock when Dudda came banging on our door, hot and out of breath, as though he'd run all the way, to tell us he was only one step ahead of the law and we mustn't get a surprise if we hear hammering on the door any minute now because the police are right behind him and they have their dogs with them and by the way, James is in terrible trouble too.

*   *   *

151

'What kind of trouble is James in?' I want to know and I'm thinking about the Plein Street march and the story Gus-Seep told us and the little talk at Caledon Square but my grandmother waves her hand at me to keep quiet.

'Wait a minute with your questions, Lily,' she says. 'Can't you see this poor child's nerves are finished? Let him sit down for a minute and pull himself together.'

She says I must fetch lemon water and poor Dudda is sitting on a kitchen chair and he's red in the face and sweating and I'm at the sink splashing water all over the place trying to get it in a glass and my eyes are out of the back window looking for the police vans and the dogs and I'm in a big hurry because I can't wait to hear what's happened to Dudda and when he's had his water, he tells us.

'I went to the college like I always do,' he says and his good eye is nearly as big as his gobstopper. 'But when I got there the gate was closed with a big lock on it and the grounds weren't empty like they usually are. The students never went home from class today. They're still there. There are hundreds of them sitting on the ground behind the gate and there are police all over the place.'

He says he's never seen so many police in his life. They are in and out of their police vans and there are dogs jumping around on leads and dogs in their cages in the back of the vans and sirens going and policemen shouting orders and even while he's telling us Dudda's good eye is filling with tears because he got such a fright.

'You should have run away,' I say and he turns around and gives me a look for chipping in and says thank you for the advice and for my information that's what he wanted to do and he tried but he wasn't quick enough and the police saw him and got hold of him and asked him what he thought he was up to.

'I told them I was going to Mr Scheepers for extra lessons, just like I always do,' Dudda says. 'But you could see on their faces they didn't believe me. They said I looked like a troublemaker to them and if it was trouble I was looking for I'd come to the right place and they'd see I got it.'

When he told us this poor Dudda was shaking all over and drinking down his lemon water as though there was no tomorrow and my grandmother said he must take a minute to pull himself together.

'They were shouting a lot,' Dudda says. 'And screaming into their walkie-talkies and saying they were just waiting for the word from Caledon Square and then they were going in with a vengeance and they'd show those students a thing or two they wouldn't forget in a hurry.'

You could hear the police meant business, Dudda says and he hoped the students didn't get the wrong idea when they saw him there, standing right in the middle of the police with his book bag in his hand but he couldn't get away and he couldn't have got inside the gate even if he wanted to.

There were blue boys all over the place just wherever you looked.

'You can stay where you are until we make up our minds what to do with you,' the police told Dudda. 'Or you can sit in the back of a police van. It's all the same to us.'

Poor Dudda. He says he didn't like the idea of having to keep a police dog company in the back of a van and he kept thinking about his grandfather who would never get over it if the police forgot about him and he got taken away in the back of a van and he kept remembering about people the police took away who were never seen again.

He kept his mouth shut and stayed where he was and the police carried on as if he wasn't there and he says they seemed to be madder than snakes. They kept telling each other what they were going to do to these communists if they just got the word. How they would crack a few heads together and teach them a lesson they'd never forget and how it was the kind of lesson you wouldn't learn on the inside of a classroom.

They were ready, Dudda says and they were going to get stuck in and do it just as soon as the word came.

But the word didn't come.

The students were sitting around waiting for something to happen and acting very quiet for students and he just hoped someone had told them about the word because he could see the police were good and ready for them and when the word eventually came through they were going to go in and get them and blood was going to flow. Dudda says there was no doubt about that.

My grandmother asked about James and Dudda said James was there and the police were calling him a known communist and troublemaker and saying he was a highly dangerous man and the ringleader of the whole thing.

'He was inside the building but while I was standing there he came walking out as cool as a cucumber. Some of the teachers were behind him and they were acting as if there was no problem at all and they were cracking jokes.'

We couldn't believe that but Dudda isn't a liar although he said maybe not jokes exactly but they didn't look worried. They had a word and a smile for everyone as if what they were doing was perfectly all right and more of a picnic and not such a serious business as the police seemed to take it for.

James was talking to the students, group to group, in a quiet way and smiling and when they got to the bottom of the steps, the teachers stayed where they were and James kept on walking and he walked right up to the gate and unlocked it and let it swing open and then he walked right through it.

'He asked for the officer in charge. He said he had something to say to him and when he saw me, he said they should leave me out of it and let me go home because I was only a schoolboy and what was going on had nothing to do with me.'

James said what he had to say but Dudda doesn't know what it was because he couldn't hear but when James went back inside the gate, the students gave him a cheer and then he turned around and sat down right in the middle of the steps in between the groups of students where everyone could see him and the other teachers sat down with him.

What Dudda did hear was one policeman saying to

another one that James needn't act so full of himself. Tomorrow is another day and they'd make it their business to see he got what he was asking for.

Then they remembered Dudda was still there and they asked him what he thought he was doing standing around with his big ears flapping and they pulled his book bag right out of his hands and the books fell on the ground and they picked them up and looked at them and then they looked at Dudda and asked him what communist tricks James was teaching him.

They said they'd have to take his books away and have a proper look at them because that was the law and when Dudda said he needed his books for his exams, they said he should have thought of that before.

Then they told him he could go on his way but he must remember if he didn't behave himself they had a nice little place in Roeland Street for him because they knew about his type with their university ideas. His day would come. It was only a question of time.

'Don't think you can get smart with us,' they said. 'From now on we'll be on the lookout for you and a one-eye boy from the Valley is easy to find, so don't get comfortable because when you do, that's the moment we'll come and get you.'

Then they said he must get out of their sight.

My grandmother says I must run for old Dollie and tell him what's happened and say he must lock up his shop and come in the Stud to fetch Dudda because poor Dudda has had enough for one day.

It isn't every boy from the Valley who gets as far as university. Even James wouldn't have managed it if it hadn't been for my mother. He is the first to say so. He had his dreams but even in those days he had common sense as well.

* * *

'It doesn't matter what I want or don't want,' James tells her. 'I've got to get out and find someone who'll give me a job so I can make my own way.'

'You can't settle for that,' she says. 'You're too smart.' And she gives him a funny look and a smile and it's as though she's thinking of something else and someone else altogether.

He says he's learned what to expect from life. She mustn't mind so much on his account because that just makes things harder and he may be smart just like she says he is but she's smart too.

In some ways she is far smarter than he is.

She's learned a few things too. She knows life is full of surprises, and anything is possible especially if you want it badly enough and there's someone who understands and cares enough to help you get it.

Gus-Seep says poor James got more than he bargained for the day Gloria decided to take over his life because every time she looked at him she made up her mind more firmly about where he was going and every chance she got she gave him an extra little push in the right direction.

Gus-Seep says it's a miracle James put up with it, because he was growing up fast and when you got right down to it, Gloria wasn't any family of his and didn't have any rights over him. He could have told her any time he liked exactly where she could get off. But he never did.

She did a thing James would never do. She spoke to Revd Wallace and asked for help and he spoke to the high-up Methodists and they got together and gave James a loan to pay for his university and then she persuaded Philander to give him a waiter job nights and weekends to help with his books and his pocket money.

It wasn't a thing Philander usually did but he was a man who was prepared to go out of his way for a pretty face and he couldn't say no to Gloria.

James got on fine at The Buildings and everyone liked him but he had to keep on his toes because Gloria still hung around there sometimes with her men friends drinking coffee and talking and she liked to keep her eye on him to check he was still on the straight and narrow with his nose in his books and his hands off the girlies and that's what people had to say against her.

It was all well and good to help James get a start in life but she was taking it too far and the poor boy never knew from one minute to the next where he stood.

One minute she acted as if they were the same age and best friends or as if he was her brother and it was her business to look out for him.

Then there were other times when something he did didn't suit her, and then she carried on like a cross old tiger of a mother who was absolutely fed up and not in the mood to stand for any nonsense from a child who wouldn't do what he was told.

People felt sorry for James because as far as Gloria was concerned he wasn't dealing with only one person. He was dealing with a whole crowd. He never knew who he was going to come up against next and everyone stood on the sidelines watching while he battled to hold his own because Gloria had begun to carry on as if she owned him body and soul and if he didn't come up to scratch he would hear all about it.

Sometimes when they were down at The Buildings Gloria's friends played the fool with James, man to man, and if they felt like it, they'd even take their life in their hands and do it right in front of her.

'Come and join us for a beer,' they'd say. 'We'll get a couple of girlies and make a party.' Or, 'How about a game of dominoes? We'll give you a chance to take some money off us fair and square to help with your university.'

It was James they were talking to, but it was Gloria who answered. James didn't even get a chance to open his mouth. She'd get that beady look in her eye and answer for him as though he didn't have a tongue in his head and couldn't speak for himself.

'You leave him alone,' she'd say. 'This young man's going

places in life and there's plenty of time for drinks and dominoes after he's got there.'

No-one knew why James took it so well and why he let Gloria crack the whip the way she did but he didn't complain and he didn't seem to mind and he never let her down. He just kept on doing well at the university and keeping his nose clean everywhere else. He would never take a drink or look sideways at a girlie.

She drove him too hard, Gus-Seep says. Any jockey will tell you it isn't always pulling on the bit between the teeth that counts. In that way horses are like people. They want a little kindness and appreciation and they aren't fools. They know it when they see it and when they do see it, they'll do anything for you but if James was looking for anything like that from Gloria, then he was looking in the wrong direction.

She liked to say the days of slavery were over. Sometimes she said it as if it was a joke and sometimes she'd come home with her pay envelope and give it to her mother and then she'd get that look in her eye and say it as if it wasn't such a joke after all.

Gus-Seep says when it came to slave-driving she was so busy looking at the mote in her brother's eye she hadn't taken a good look at herself lately and he didn't like to say it, but where James was concerned, what people said about her was true.

Nothing he did by way of his studies was good enough for her. If he was at his books until two o'clock in the morning she would say he could have sat until three if he'd really put his mind to it.

If he said he'd passed a test, the first thing she asked was if he'd passed first class. When he had flu she took time off her work and went to the university herself to fetch his notes so that even if he died, his studies wouldn't suffer.

Gus-Seep says the thing between Gloria and James was funny. He tried as hard as a person could to make her proud of him but it was never enough. There was no pleasing her but it didn't seem to worry him. He just tried harder and got even better results and brought them to her as if they were a present he'd made with his own hands and everyone said she wouldn't rest until she'd turned poor James into Albert Einstein or seen him dead in the process.

There is only one time Gus-Seep can remember when James ever joined a party for a drink and a laugh and that was on Christmas Eve and just the day Gloria got it into her head to walk down to The Buildings to look for him after the midnight service at St Peter's and she wasn't too happy to find him sitting around a table in the basement drinking beer and cracking jokes with Gus-Seep and his friends and one or two of the girlies and someone had put up a big bunch of mistletoe and the girlies were making jokes about it.

'No charge for kisses because it's Christmas,' they say. 'Kisses come free but you have to catch us first and we're on the lookout for you.'

Gus-Seep says luck was with him that night because he saw Gloria coming and long before she caught sight of him he slid quick as lightning round a corner and found a nice little place behind some beer crates where he could keep out of the way and make himself small so there wasn't any chance she would spot him.

He knows his sister. He knows that look on her face and he knows what is going to happen and what is going to happen is fireworks but he thought that night at The Buildings it being Christmas and after knock-off time that at long last Gloria had gone too far where James was concerned and now it was his turn. But it turned out he was wrong.

'The last thing I expected was what came next,' Gus-Seep says. 'She came in with that look on her face as if she was ready to pick a fight with the whole world and I thought James was in trouble again and I felt really sorry for him but then I saw it wasn't him she was cross with.'

*　　　*　　　*

'I thought you were coming off work,' Gloria says pulling her church scarf off her head and pushing her prayer book into her handbag. 'You always tell me you can't wait to get out of here when your shift ends but when I come to see for myself it's a different story. Is this what goes on every night or only at Christmas time?'

He doesn't want her to be cross with him because it's Christmas and everyone's in a good mood and when she's cross, she's like ice and doesn't care whose feelings she hurts.

'Some people asked me to join in for a drink and a beer shandy isn't the end of the world,' he says but you can see just by looking at her face she isn't in a mood to hear his story.

'I thought we had an understanding. When I got you this job I thought we agreed this is only a place where you pick up some extra money. It isn't where you spend your time or make your friends.'

She throws her bag and scarf down on the table right in the middle of all the leftover party things, the glasses and the half-filled ashtrays, right under the kiss-me-quick mistletoe. It is as if she couldn't care less and the men at the table and some of the girlies too shrug their shoulders and make remarks because they aren't in the mood to be part of a fight but she doesn't care about that and when they get up and move away upstairs where people know what it is to enjoy themselves and she's broken up the party once and for all, that is the last thing in the world she worries about.

For all she cares, they could have stayed and listened to what she has to say.

She tells James she's come straight from church looking for him because there are one or two things she has on her mind. Things that need to be cleared up so they can both get on with their lives.

She's been thinking about the two of them and what he's going to be doing when his final university results come out at the end of the year.

'There's been some talk lately I don't like,' she says. 'Now people can see you're going to get your degree they don't think I'm such a monster any more. They're saying you ought to be grateful to me.'

'I am grateful to you,' he says. 'I owe you more than I can say and I'm going to make it up to you.'

He's been wanting to say this for a long time and there are other things he wants to say too but her eyes are like ice and her voice is sharp as razors.

'Do you think I want your gratitude?' she wants to know. 'Do you think that's what I did it for?'

'Just for a change it's not what you or anyone else wants for me,' he says. 'It's what I want for myself.'

Gus-Seep says you can't imagine how she could act so cross with him when he's always so nice to her.

He says James had changed a lot that year. He was more of a man and not so much of a boy and it wasn't only the girlies who were looking at him and giggling behind their hands. Grown-up women who should have known better were looking at him too and you could see on their faces that they liked what they saw.

They could all see the changes in him but although he'd tried to warn her, he wasn't so sure Gloria could.

'You've done a lot for me,' he says. 'Once I've got my degree and get a decent job and have proper money in my pocket I want to do something for you for a change.'

'And what would that be?' she wants to know.

She says she knows what it's like having to be grateful to people all of your life. It starts off very fine but in the end it's like a rope that ties you down and you can pull against it as hard as you like, you never break free. All that happens is that it cuts into you and you get hurt and although he likes her however she is, it's hardest of all to like her when she listens only to what she wants to hear and her tongue gets sharp and her face is cold.

'When you finish university you'll be free and so will I, and if you're wise you'll take the British Council bursary, the one you haven't told me about, and in six months' time you'll be on your way to study in London because that's the way I want it. I don't want you hanging around here or hanging around me for the rest of your life.'

Gus-Seep says you could see on James' face she'd caught him out. The British Council bursary was a big opportunity for him. It meant three years' study in London and after that the chance of a job and maybe a life there and he's kept it to himself because he knows what she'll say when she finds out and that's exactly what she's saying this minute.

He doesn't like it when she acts tough, as if he lives in one world with all the other people who've been at the university with him and she lives in another world where he doesn't belong and where she doesn't want him.

'Did you think I wouldn't find out?' she says and now she's started she's not going to leave it alone. 'Or am I supposed to pat you on the back for being such a fool as to turn this chance down so you can stay here and rot with the rest of us? If I were you and had a chance to study in London I'd take it with both hands.'

'You're not me,' he says and he says it hard and cool and straight out and he has never spoken to her like this before and he looks at her in a way he has not looked at her before and she can see now that he's changed and in which way and she knows men and how it is with them and she is the one who looks away first.

'You're going places in life,' she says and she's nicer now as though she really wants him to understand. 'I'm staying behind and that's the way it has to be. That's what our story's about and if you don't understand that, then you're not nearly so smart as people say you are.'

Gus-Seep says she just kept on talking and James kept on looking at her in a funny way and it wasn't a boy's look he was giving her.

She says she knows about love and the kind of love that comes with a price tag attached to it and the more people love you, the more they tie you down and before you know it, they turn you into a pack donkey and all their hopes and dreams are packed on your back.

It doesn't matter how much it weighs you down. As far as they're concerned there's always room for a little bit more and one day you realize you've got as much as you can carry. You're loaded down with everyone else's wants and needs and there's no room left for even a single dream of your own.

'But there are no strings attached as far as you're concerned,' she says. 'When you finish university, it's over between us. You go your way and I go mine.'

This is a big thing to say to a friend, especially if you mean it and you can see how James feels when she says it because it's written all over his face for the whole world to see.

Maybe he should put her in her place there and then and shout at her and tell her that after the way she's taken over his life and pushed him around for the past three years he can't wait to get rid of her. Another man might have done it but James doesn't.

'I don't want to go to London or anywhere else for that matter,' he says. 'I don't want to be anywhere where I can't be with you. Surely you know that by now?'

Gus-Seep says he felt sorry for James then because it was a big thing to say and he could see he meant it and she looked at him for a long time and then she said, if that's the way he felt it was just as well to hear it then, so that when the time came she'd know what to do.

'Maybe you'll go on feeling this way and maybe you won't. Maybe you'll grow out of it but it doesn't matter. Whichever way it works out you'll go further and faster without me and I'll make it my business to be sure I'm never around to hold you back.'

Gus-Seep says she had that look on her face we all know, so you could see she'd made up her mind.

'If you make up your mind to stay then I'll be the one who leaves,' she says. 'It's as easy as that. So you may just as well go to London because even if you hang around here, you won't be seeing me any more and anyway I've got some plans of my own.'

That's what she said and after she'd said it Gus-Seep says she cheered up. She told James she felt better, as if everything was settled between them and there was nothing

163

more to worry about and if he felt like offering her something to drink she'd take a Coke from him and when she'd finished drinking it if he felt like it she wouldn't mind a walk home and he looked at her for a long time standing under the mistletoe in her Christmas church dress and then he did something he'd never done before. He put his hands on her shoulders and bent down and kissed her quick before she could turn her head and when she didn't move away he kissed her again and still she didn't move. Instead she reached up her hand and touched his face and he said, 'Merry Christmas, Gloria,' and everything was different.

James is not just in big trouble like Dudda said. He's been arrested and taken away, we don't know where, in a grey police van with two boys in blue in the front and a dog in his little cage in the back to keep an eye on him.

Everyone's talking about it. How nowadays it makes no difference who you are, anyone can get arrested. Sometimes you don't even know what for and they don't have to tell you.

One day you're a hero and the next day you're taken down to Caledon Square or to Roeland Street for one of the little police talks we all know about.

You never know who the next one's going to be. You can hardly put your head out of your house in the morning in case a police car is waiting for you and the plain clothes in it have a Government paper with them for someone to be taken away into detention, and when you look again you realize that someone is you.

'What's going to happen now?' I ask my grandmother because no-one I know has ever disappeared before. 'Will we ever see James again?'

She isn't exactly sure because no-one she knows has ever disappeared before either. She says the first thing we must do is find out where they've taken James so we can at least send him some food wherever he is.

'We can forget about Evie and her mother,' she says and

she's looking to see how much bread we have and if there's any tinned bully beef in the cupboard.

'We know what happened the last time, when James was in Caledon Square for a little talk. Evie was crying at her mother's house because she felt so sorry for herself and no-one was worried about James.'

This isn't the way we carry on when one of our family is in trouble and to our mind James is our family because we're the closest thing to his own flesh and blood that he has.

It may take a little while to sort things out, so we must prepare ourselves but in the meantime we can pack a food basket and I can take it down as far as Caledon Square because I know where that is and when I get there I can ask the officer in charge where James is and my grandmother thinks, if I ask nicely, he'll tell me.

'They'll never turn a child away,' she says. 'Most of them are married men with wives with children of their own and if you're polite and look them in the eye and say you're bringing food for someone who's as good as family to you, they'll give you a straight answer.'

I don't mind walking down to Caledon Square because to get there I go all the way down Government Avenue and walk under the oak trees and the weather is getting cool now and once you're out of the Valley there are leaves everywhere, especially if you go that way.

They're all colours and really beautiful and they come fluttering down right in front of you like butterflies and the little grey squirrels run in and out of them looking for acorns to hide away for the winter and we have a game that if you catch a leaf before it touches the ground you can have a wish and, if I had a wish, I would wish James had minded his own business and not ended up where he is now, with me getting dressed to go out and try and find him so I can take him food and my grandmother saying she's sick to her stomach with worry about him, things being what they are these days and she doesn't mind packing food for him but come suppertime the rest of us will have to make do with bread and jam and tea because she's not in a state to face a stove never mind a plate of food of her own.

While she's still busy talking, a little bit to herself and a little bit to me and buttoning up my coat and seeing to my plaits and clipping plastic slides at the end of them, my mother comes into the kitchen and she stands there looking at us as though the dog just dragged us both in.

'Is that a food basket on the table?' she wants to know and my grandmother says it isn't Scotch mist and hasn't she heard what happened to James, because if not she must be the only one who hasn't, the whole Valley is talking about it but my mother isn't interested in what my grandmother has to say.

'Are you sending Lily down to the jail with food?' she wants to know and she's looking at the basket and you can see she's cross and doesn't want to be bothered with things like that and doesn't think it's a good idea.

'It's for James,' I say and because I'm dressed and ready now, I take hold of the basket as if I mean business and am going on my way and no-one is going to stop me.

'I don't care who it's for,' my mother says. 'You can put it down this minute and you can take your coat off and hang it right back in your cupboard because you aren't going anywhere.'

I hate my mother when she's like this. I hate it when we've made up our minds about something and she comes prancing in and thinks she can tell us what we can and can't do and I'm just as cross as she is and think I will do what I want to do anyway.

'While I'm in this house no child of mine is standing outside a police station with little bits of food in a basket begging to be allowed to hand it over for the prisoner. I don't care who's sitting inside.'

My grandmother shows with her hand that I must put the basket back on the table and for a minute I think I won't do it but my mother doesn't take her eyes off me and I think if I don't do what she wants she's going to smack me.

'I'm not having it, Lily,' she says. 'Not now and not ever

and it's got nothing to do with James. We don't beg for favours from monsters who should be behind bars themselves. I won't ever do that and nor will you and believe me, the people in that prison who are worth anything would rather starve than have a food parcel that got to them in that way.'

She's dressed for the street. She has on her black wool coat and black shoes. Her handbag is over her arm. She has gloves on her hands and she doesn't even bother to take them off because she's on her way out again.

'James is in Roeland Street,' she tells us. 'They've got nothing they can charge him with but that's where they've taken him and that's where I'm going.'

My grandmother and I stand there with our mouths open like fish and when my mother looks at us she seems surprised.

'You needn't look at me like that,' she says. 'What did you expect me to do? I'm going to get James out of that place and I'll be there for just as long as it takes, so you needn't keep my supper for me because you may have a very long wait.'

She gets her things together and we can see she's in a hurry and can't be bothered with us any more and then she's gone, tap-tapping down our passage lino on her high-heeled shoes and all that's left in the place where she stood is the smell of her scent and then the front door slams behind her and she's gone. Just like that and she never even said goodbye.

There are songs about Roeland Street. About my darling sitting in jail and dreaming about me and how the hangman must tell my old mother how sorry I am for what I've done.

The Coons sing them sometimes. Roeland Street is not on the main Coon march but on their way home the breakaway groups take a special turn out of their way up Roeland Street and stop for a little while outside the jail. They stand in the street outside and no-one can stop them or chase them away because despite so many people being inside and so few left to stand in the street singing, it's still a free country.

The Coons blow their saxophones loud and strum their banjoes and they sing their hearts out for old times' sake because some of the people inside are their friends and they want them to hear, so they know they haven't been forgotten.

I have known Roeland Street all my life. Everyone has. People say we've had jails in this country even longer than we've had houses and Roeland Street is the oldest one.

It has a big wooden gate in front with steel squares across it. On either side is a stone wall with chips of glass, all shapes and sizes, stuck on top in case the prisoners get any ideas.

We don't know what goes on inside but they keep the gardens very nice. The prisoners do it and you see them sometimes in the daytime in their khaki overalls standing in between the May bushes and the oleanders.

It's no good shouting out to them to ask how they are, even if you know them, or to try and pass on a message to someone inside. They aren't allowed to answer you and the guard is always watching.

We know how it works. You don't go in at the front gate. That's just for show. Gus-Seep says they locked it one day and threw away the key so they couldn't open it even if they tried and that suits them because the prisoners can rot for all they care and it's their job to see they do.

Gus-Seep says so, but it's just his nonsense. If you want to, you can visit there. I've seen people going there myself at visiting time on a Saturday afternoon and they look perfectly respectable to me.

Visitors go in at the side through a normal door and prisoners go in the back, down a side street and then through a metal gate that takes them right underneath so that one minute the police car is there and the next all you see are the red back lights going down and the car is gone and so is the prisoner.

It's no good hanging around there for last look and last

wave because the cars go too fast and it's a wonder anyone ever gets there in one piece. The police drive like lunatics and nobody stops them. Everyone knows that.

We used to make jokes about Roeland Street when we played Monopoly which James taught us. It's one of his favourite games. If the dice are against you the others in the game shout, 'Go straight to jail!' 'Do not pass Go!' 'Do not collect two hundred!' And once the person is in jail he's out of the game until he throws a six. So, in a way, James is out of the game now, except we're not making jokes about it and we don't know where the six will be coming from.

At night the whole place is all lit up like a Christmas tree and my grandmother says, never mind the gramophone or even the oven, this is the biggest waste of electricity she ever saw in her life and what for? We don't need to have the Roeland Street all lit up so we can find it. We know where it is.

Any normal person would think twice about going anywhere near Roeland Street but not my mother. You can't tell her anything.

No matter what she thinks, you can't just walk in there and ask them to let a prisoner out so you can take him home with you. Not unless he's sentenced to hard labour and you need him for a convict gang and then you need the money to pay for it and, as far as we know, this is not the case with James.

We could tell my mother these things if she asked us, but we know by now it's better to save our breath and let her go to Roeland Street and never mind if she comes home disappointed.

My grandmother says she knows what's coming towards my mother and it's going to be a hard knock.

This is what she says to me but it's not what she'll say to my mother.

When my mother walks back through the door my grandmother will ask her what she expected anyway and say it serves her right.

It's my grandmother's way but she doesn't mean it. Her

bark is worse than her bite and after my mother leaves she gets over being sick to her stomach and not able to face the stove and she starts cooking our supper.

She's making curry tripe and rice which is my mother's favourite and my mother's place is set at the table as if we are certain she'll be home by suppertime and the white shop bread is sliced and there's watermelon jam with ginger to eat with it because although some people run to the brandy bottle when things go wrong, my mother is not one of them and food is really the best thing for life's disappointments. Nothing seems so bad on a full stomach.

We are ready for my mother to come back and tell us about her hard knock and to sit down with us at the table and eat her tripe to make it better. But it isn't my mother who comes. Instead the Muslim women send their children to tell us my mother is standing on the steps of Roeland Street in her best black coat. She's holding a board that says the police must charge James Scheepers or release him and the jail people and other police sent up from Caledon Square in case things turn nasty have told her she must move along or there'll be very big trouble coming her way and she's refused to move and do we know about it?

We don't know and my grandmother has to sit down from shock.

This is the last thing we expect but we know it must be true because the Muslim husbands have seen it with their own eyes on their way home from work.

They stopped their cars in Roeland Street and got out and talked to my mother and told people they knew her and what her name is and offered to give her a lift home in their car if she wanted to leave, but she told them she wasn't going anywhere, thank you very much, and she certainly wasn't leaving until she had James Scheepers with her and she didn't mind if she had to sit there forever.

She'd already told the police and the prison people that. She told them she was in no hurry. She had all the time in the world, so if they wanted her to camp out right where she was, with the world going up and down in front of her looking at her sign and asking her what she was doing there, that was all right too.

The Muslim husbands tell us it's home time in town and Roeland Street is full of people. Full buses are going past and people are hanging out of the windows asking what's going on.

People in cars on their way home from work have put their windows up in case of trouble and are pointing and looking at my mother, because no-one has ever seen anything like it before and by the time the Muslim husbands got there, everyone seemed to know what my mother was there for, about James and everything and, if you ask them, they tell you they don't think she will leave in a hurry.

The police have already asked her. First time nicely like they do, but behind her back they say it's clear my mother has no respect for anyone or anything and the Muslim husbands think, if it's a question of respect, then perhaps my grandmother is the one who must go and try and talk some sense into her daughter before things get nasty and if this is what she wants to do they'll be happy to take her.

But Roeland Street is in town and my grandmother doesn't go into town any more. She always says next time town sees her she'll be going past covered in flowers in the back of the funeral car and when that time comes, whatever is going on in town will make no difference to her.

She's said these things at least a million times and everyone knows she's said them but perhaps she's forgotten because she listens to every word the Muslim husbands have to say, then she goes to her room and gets dressed and when she comes out she's wearing her black coat and good shoes, she's putting her hat on her head and she's ready to go and she tells the Muslim husbands she'll be grateful for the lift.

My grandmother has been in a car before but cars make her nervous and she doesn't really trust them. She trusts her own legs which have taken her everywhere she needed to go all her life.

She always says when the day comes that her legs give out, it will be a sign that the Good Lord thinks it's high time for her to stay at home and, from that day onwards, that is exactly what she'll do and she'll never leave her house again.

But that day hasn't come yet and so she gets in the back of the Muslim husbands' car and Stella and I get in with her and we sit on the back seat on either side of her holding her hands, one each, to give her courage because of her nerves and the Muslim husbands are nice to us and make little jokes to make my grandmother feel better and we drive very slowly up the hill and out of the Valley.

It's early evening and we're going the Coon way down to Roeland Street so that my grandmother can talk some sense into the head of my mother, who we know must have gone mad, although everyone is too polite and has too much respect for my grandmother to say so out loud.

What we heard is true. My mother is standing on the steps of the Roeland Street jail, right in the middle at the top, in her black coat with her handbag over her arm and a piece of board on a stick in her hand, 'Charge Or Release James Scheepers'.

When we get out of the car we stand at the bottom with all the other people looking up at her and despite her high heels she looks very small from where we are.

There are policemen in uniform standing behind her looking important and talking to one another but that doesn't seem to worry her. She holds her board up in front of her and looks straight ahead.

There are a lot of people standing on the pavement looking at her and talking about what she's doing and when my grandmother arrives the Muslim husbands push their car forward and park it right up on the pavement and they say who my grandmother is. They say she is this woman's mother and they say what she's come for which is to talk some sense into her daughter's head before she ends up in jail as well.

The people standing on the pavement with us tell us what happened. The police have tried to make my mother leave but she won't go.

'I'm not going anywhere,' she says. 'Not until my friend, James Scheepers, is released and can go with me.'

The police have told her a hundred times that it isn't possible and she's listened very nicely and told them if it isn't possible then they must make it possible and that is all she has to say to them.

'Charge him or let him go.' Every time anyone even looks in her direction that's what she says and you get the idea she won't mind saying it till she's blue in the face and everyone knows they can't charge him because there's nothing to charge him with.

They only took him in to give him a fright and shut him up and now they can't let him go because they'll look like fools and my mother and her banner stay right where they are, where everyone can see her and it looks as if there's nothing on this earth that can make her move.

When they tell her she must move along she says: 'You say it's a free country. If that's true, then surely I can wait for my friend wherever I like.'

There's nothing they can do about it and she knows that very well.

Everyone going up and down Roeland Street can see her. She's stood there all day and when people ask what the problem is, she tells them.

'Mr James Scheepers, a respectable man and a school-teacher, has been unlawfully detained and I'm not going anywhere until he's free to go with me.'

The people standing with us tell us it was warm in the mid-afternoon and when the prisoners working in the prison garden had something cold to drink they offered my mother water from the tap and the officer on duty even said it was all right for her to drink it if she was thirsty and they should fetch a glass for her because he felt worried about her being a woman and all that, but she said, no, thank you.

She wouldn't eat or drink until James was free and the officer in charge said she better watch out what she said, because they didn't take people into Roeland Street for a holiday and in case she didn't know it, her friend was a highly dangerous man and might have to stay in jail for a very long time and if he did, she would die of hunger and thirst and she looked him right in the eyes and said if that was the way it had to be, that was all right also.

The Muslim husbands say the police hope my mother will move away once it gets dark and the street is empty and what does my grandmother think? Does she think that's what will happen?

My grandmother says she doesn't think so.

'The police don't know who they're dealing with,' she says. 'If they asked me, I could tell them that nothing will move my daughter. She'll stay where she is until she gets what she wants and it won't matter how long it takes.'

She says while she's here she has something to say to her daughter anyway and seeing she's come all the way into town to say it, she may as well get it over with even if it means she has to walk up the steps and nobody but Stella and I knows how much her town shoes hurt her feet.

I don't know what my grandmother said to my mother. They didn't talk for very long but while they were talking something funny happened. The lights that light up Roeland Street came on and the two of them stood there like two small black dots for the whole world to see with the light jumping all around them and Roeland Street all lit up like a Christmas tree behind them.

When she'd finished what she had to say and was ready to go down, the officer in charge sent a young policeman to help out of respect for her age and because there are a lot of steps and they're very steep. There's no handrail and the last thing the police need, on top of everything else, is a dead old coloured woman on their hands but my grandmother says she doesn't need help.

She's all right if she goes slowly and when she comes to the bottom she says she's ready to go home whenever the Muslim husbands feel like taking her because her own home is the place where we'll wait for her daughter.

James said afterwards that Roeland Street was no picnic. When he saw my mother and heard she'd sat two days and a night on the steps outside he could hardly believe it.

He said if he lived a million years he would never forget what she'd done for him.

If he wasn't a man you'd have thought he would burst into tears right there and then. You could see just by looking at him that he wouldn't get over it in a hurry and we didn't say anything. We knew it would take a woman as crazy as my mother to do what she'd done and it was a lot more than Evie would ever have done for him.

12

Death, Dancing and Miss Matilda

Now James is back with us and we have other things on our mind again, Gus-Seep has asked me a little favour. It's about Philander's niece, Matilda, who's staying with him down at The Buildings.

At heart Philander is not a bad man. He's always willing to do a good turn and good turns are what he's doing for his nieces who come in from the country every now and then to stay with their Uncle Philander at The Buildings.

These girls come from the north, from the same part of the country Philander comes from, where he stole his IDB diamonds and got his start in life and he's saving their lives because times are very hard there.

When Gus-Seep speaks about Philander's nieces he doesn't speak in front of my grandmother or Stella because there are some things they don't understand. That's why they cross the street rather than go on the same side as The Buildings and why they're so nose-in-the-air when it comes to nice girls like Philander's nieces.

They won't give these girls the time of day if they see them in the street even though they know who they are and that Gus-Seep is their friend every bit as much as Philander is.

Gus-Seep blames the Church for the way my grandmother and Stella carry on and it's not just about Philander's nieces and the other little girls who give sugar for a living.

He says his heart will break if he lives to see the day when I go the same way as my grandmother and my aunt, because if I knew the things he knows about Philander's nieces and the hard life they had before Philander brought them to town, he knows I will take his side and at least have a smile for them when I see them on the streets.

'You needn't smile too big,' he says. 'Especially if your granny's with you. You can just pull your mouth around your teeth quick-smart. Then at least I can hold my head up and say there's one person in our family, besides me, who doesn't think they're too good for everyone else.'

I will do anything in the world for my Uncle Gus-Seep but I can pull my mouth any way I like, if my grandmother catches me making up to any of the girlies who work in the upstairs sugar shop at The Buildings she'll kill me and that will be that.

Even if Gus-Seep hadn't whispered in my ear I would still have smiled at Matilda, because I liked her. I couldn't help it. You can look at Matilda and think, if things had turned out differently she would be just the type of person you'd like for a best friend and because I am short of a best friend these days that is what I am thinking.

She isn't at all like the other nieces. She doesn't shout remarks down into the street from the upstairs balcony. She doesn't stand outside in her dressing-gown for all the world to see and she doesn't sleep all day.

She's out on the street early and she's always neatly dressed.

'She walks as if she hasn't got a care in the world,' Stella says to my grandmother and she says it as if there's something wrong with that. 'She greets everyone.'

It's true. Matilda greets people she doesn't know from Adam as if they've been her friend for life. She says, 'Hello' and 'How's life?' to everyone and if they don't greet her back, she thinks it's a big joke. She just shakes her shoulders and strolls off as if it's you that's in the wrong and she's the one who's right.

When we see Matilda out on the street we can see for ourselves that life doesn't get her down.

She always greets us, even if we make as if we're very

busy talking to one another and haven't got time for anyone else.

'Good morning, Mrs Daniels,' she says to my grand-mother and, 'Good morning, Mrs Davids,' to Stella. 'Hello, Lily,' she says to me. 'And how's the world treating you?'

Once she came right over and stopped in front of us and told us her name was Matilda and she came from round Upington way. She said she was new to our Valley but she was already acquainted with Gus-Seep.

Stella said afterwards Gus-Seep must have told her to come over to us like that because it's just the sort of thing he'd think was a big joke and when she gets hold of him she's going to show him what a real joke is all about and wring his neck.

'If you see me walking down the road you mustn't think twice about calling me over,' Matilda says. 'I haven't got money to spare for shopping myself. I only come out because I like to see what's going on and I'd never mind giving you a hand and helping you carry your shopping home.'

She gives a nice smile and says we must always remember she's a country girl and stronger than she looks.

'I'm strong as an ox and always willing to help,' she says but Stella is red and puffed up in the face and my grand-mother doesn't know what to say and I pull my mouth quickly across my teeth so Gus-Seep won't be embarrassed by his family and Matilda looks right at me and smiles and gives me a little wink to show she knows what I'm trying to do.

Gus-Seep says Philander is big talk but he doesn't really mind what Matilda does. He lets her get away with murder because she's pretty and he's got a soft spot for her.

She's got a good head when it comes to money and she drives a hard bargain which Philander has very good reasons to know from his own experience.

She puts her money in a little green bank book and won't let Philander keep a single cent of it for her the way he does for the other nieces.

Matilda's little book is getting nice and fat. Every Friday morning you can see her going down Hanover Street towards the bank in town and that's something no other girl from The Buildings has ever managed to do.

Matilda's the nicest, smartest girl anyone's seen for a very long time and she knows how to look after herself. Philander doesn't shout at her or hit her or push her out into the street even if she's the most forward type of a girlie that has ever worked for him. He just looks at her with her neat ways and sees how pretty she is and says she's his little Matilda and a clever girl and he doesn't know what he'll do without her.

You can eat off the floors at The Buildings these days and, although she's strict with the Natives, Matilda's fair and she's got a very soft heart. No-one ever goes away from her emptyhanded. Every beggar on the street will tell you that, and it's something Philander can't stand. He says she's throwing money away quicker than a drunk sailor but Matilda doesn't care. She says he can say what he likes. It's her money and she earned it the hard way and she'll spend it how she likes and without any help from him.

She gives food too. Anyone can go to the back door and if they say they're hungry, Matilda will give them bread and sometimes a little bit extra of whatever Philander and the nieces are eating.

'I'll never say "no" to a hungry person.' That's what she tells Gus-Seep. 'If there's only one crust of bread in the house I'll give it to someone if I can see they're hungry and no-one will ever stop me doing that.'

Gus-Seep says he's told her it isn't the one crust Philander is worried about. It's all the rest as well because when it comes to dishing out food Matilda will believe any hard luck story and she's never heard of the word 'no'.

Philander can swear at her until he runs out of words but he can never make her turn a hungry person away.

This is Matilda's point of view and nothing will make her change her mind and Gus-Seep says if she doesn't watch out the fight he sees coming will come sooner than she thinks.

'There are other people in the world besides Mr Kippy Philander,' Matilda says. 'And if he's got anything to say to me, he needn't send you. He can tell me to my face. I do my best. I don't complain and I do extra too, because I know I must be grateful for what he does for me but there's a limit to how much you can ask from a person for the sake of gratitude.'

The fight has come and poor Matilda is black and blue. Gus-Seep says she brought it on herself because women are like children and as long as he lives he will never understand them and now Matilda has had to learn the hard way who's boss and everyone is sorry, even Philander.

He didn't say so but after the fight was over, he took her to a high-class doctor in Athlone but Gus-Seep says, despite being beaten black and blue Matilda will never stop the food business, so he doesn't think she's really learned her lesson at all and he doesn't think that's really the end of the story.

He says Matilda reminds him of someone else he knows who you can talk to till you're blue in the face, who will listen nicely and then go her own sweet way. He says he won't say names but we all know who he means.

At our house we're having second thoughts about Matilda. We're sorry for what's happened to her, because despite being as strong as an ox Matilda is not really a big girl and like Gus-Seep says, she has feelings like everyone else and now her feelings are probably black and blue just like the rest of her.

'Don't think I haven't seen you, Lily,' my grandmother says. 'I know you like Matilda. I've seen you slipping a smile to her when you think I'm not looking.'

'We both saw you,' Stella says and she's not in such a nice mood about it as my grandmother is, because black and blue or not, she still doesn't have very much time for Matilda.

'I don't know if you think we're blind but Mommy and I have seen you and we've said to ourselves we don't know what to expect from you next. We don't know what's wrong with you. Why do you want to suck up to a sugar-house girl in the first place?'

'You made a big fool out of yourself,' my grandmother says looking at me in that way she has and shaking her head. 'I don't know what she must have thought of you either, with all that trying to smile behind your hand so we won't see you and ending up pulling terrible faces as if you're trying to scare the life out of her.'

But my grandmother has been listening to Gus-Seep's stories and she's been thinking about things and she's been changing her mind about Matilda.

'We've crossed to the other side of the street more than enough times and if I'm not mistaken the Bible has something to say about that.' That's what she says to Stella and me and when we see Matilda again we are going to nod our heads in her direction and give her the time of day.

'As for you, Lily,' she says, 'you can stop that pulling faces business. When you see Matilda out on the street you can smile at her and you can greet her if you like, just as long as what you have in your mind when you do it are the good things she's doing for those in need because we can all learn from that.'

Stella says my grandmother is a fine one. She sings one song in the morning and another one in the afternoon and it's no wonder I'm growing up half crazy but one look puts an end to that kind of talk and when I next see Matilda I give her the biggest smile I can manage and she's very nice. She waves to me and smiles back and comes right across the street to me just to say she's glad Gus-Seep was right about me all the time. I'm no snob.

I know Stella is fed up with my grandmother and me about Matilda because she acts all hoity-toity to us but it doesn't last for long.

When she hears Frank Adams is leaving she sits in the kitchen crying into her apron and it's hard to cry and keep your nose in the air at the same time and so she's willing to have us back again and things are just the same as they always are.

Frank Adams has been offered a job on the whalers and he's taking it and getting out. The work's hard but the money's good. He says he's seen the world once at the army's expense and found it to his liking, so he won't mind taking another look.

'When I come back I'll have money in my pocket for a change and I won't forget you,' he says and Stella's eyes are big and I think she's going to burst into tears all over again right in front of him, although she said later she would never have let him see how she felt.

'We'll be seeing each other again. Don't you worry about that,' he says.

My mother couldn't care less and if Frank needed a lift to get him to the docks quicker I think she would find him one. If she never saw him again in her life it would be too soon but Stella believes him and the idea that he'll come back one day has cheered her up, although even Domingo says if she believes that, she'll believe anything and you can tell her anything you like and she'll swallow it whole because we all know it isn't going to be like that.

Frank's given all his medals to Gus-Seep for a goodbye present and Gus-Seep has put them on his horse's bridle to give it a touch of class. Frank says he doesn't know about class, not the way things are these days, but that's all the medals are good for now and Gus-Seep's welcome to them but the way Gus-Seep's going on you would think Frank had given him a bar of pure gold.

Those medals are his pride and joy and he keeps them shined up and at least they have an airing now and don't spend their lives sitting in an envelope in Frank's pocket like they did before. Nowadays people come up and look at them and say how wonderful they are and Gus-Seep tells terrible stories about how he won them in the war and makes out he is a real hero and everyone feels sorry for him and it makes them buy even more of his vegetables.

The one I feel sorry for is Stella. She can hardly bear to see Gus-Seep's horse going past because of the medals jangling and shining in the sun. It's as if that horse carries all her dreams on its back but my mother says mooning after a horse or a man long gone is just a waste of time. If wishes were horses then beggars would ride and Stella can do a lot better than a rolling stone like Frank Adams.

Since my mother's been back I haven't really thought about Matilda very much but one day I'm walking down the road with my mother and for a change we're swinging along nicely together watching the world go by and minding our own business when Gus-Seep comes running up to us in a terrible hurry, pushing people out of the way as he goes and not even looking back when they swear at him and tell him to mind where he's going.

He doesn't even worry about me. He gets hold of my mother by the arm and pulls her to one side and says she must come with him to The Buildings straightaway because there's a terrible fight going on there.

'Philander's gone right off his head,' he says. 'He's got hold of Matilda and the devil's got hold of him and if someone doesn't stop him he's going to kill her. She could be dead already for all I know.'

'What's it about?' I want to know and I'm pushing myself forward and pulling at Gus-Seep's hand for an answer because I'm always interested in my friend Matilda.

'Be quiet, Lily,' my mother says and she takes over and tells Gus-Seep to talk slowly and pull himself together and tell her, one thing at a time, so she can actually understand him, what this is all about and he tells her.

It's about Matilda telling Philander that she's taking her money and leaving with her friend, Mr Julies, because Mr Julies says if she's willing he's going to do the right thing by her and put a ring on her finger and take her away as a married woman and he's going to look after her and she's told him she was never more willing for anything in her life and when exactly are they leaving and this idea has made Philander go right off his head.

My mother is listening to every word, the same way my grandmother listens to her serial on the radio because she's scared she might miss something but I don't have to listen so hard because now I've heard Mr Julies' name I know what's going on because Gus-Seep has already told me all about him.

Mr Julies is not so young any more. More November than May, Gus-Seep says. He comes from the north, the same as Matilda and Philander do. He's got pots of money and he's mad with love for Matilda.

He comes to town once a month to do his business and when that happens, he says the business can wait but he can't. He goes straight to The Buildings and puts his money down on the counter. He says he's come a long way and it's Matilda he wants to see and no-one else will do and someone must go and call her at once and he's willing to pay extra for the pleasure but he can't wait another minute.

Gus-Seep told me long ago that he'd looked into Mr Julies' face and seen a certain simple look there he'd seen on other men's faces in the past and even if Mr Julies didn't know it himself yet, it made him think we'd soon hear wedding bells ringing.

'You must get ready to say your goodbyes to your friend Matilda,' Gus-Seep said to me then. 'Because if Mr Julies pops the question, Matilda will be gone like a shot.'

Now this has happened just like Gus-Seep said it would but Philander says Matilda can put these ideas about Mr Julies and leaving right out of her head because she's not going anywhere.

The only way she's leaving The Buildings is over his dead body and then he changes his mind and says his dead body is too good for her because he knows what she and her boyfriend are up to. They want him dead, so his dead body will suit them very well. He knows her game. She and Mr Julies are trying to upset him so much he'll die of it. They're trying to kill him so they can get their hands on his money but they'll have to be quick because it's his plan to kill them first and he'll start with Matilda.

Philander has Matilda on the ground. He's kicking her and hitting her and screaming and saying Mr Julies can come in his fancy car with the packets of stolen IDB money he used to turn Matilda's head and pick up her corpse and see how much he likes that.

It's a really terrible story Gus-Seep's telling but you can see my mother doesn't know what she's supposed to do about it and when she asks Gus-Seep that question he says she must come to The Buildings at once and tell Philander to stop it.

'No-one else will,' he says. 'Everyone round here's scared of him but you're not afraid of anyone and you're not stuck-up, you've got time for a girl like Matilda.'

He's got my mother by the hand and he's trying to pull her along next to him and you can see he's got plenty of time for Matilda too because his face is small and screwed up with worry and his hand is on his heart and there are tears in his eyes.

'I never ask you anything, although there's nothing in the world I wouldn't do for you and you know it,' he says. 'Now I'm asking you this. I'm begging you. If you don't come in ten minutes Matilda will be dead for sure and she doesn't deserve it.'

My mother grabs hold of my hand and begins to walk fast as if she's made up her mind about something and then she begins to walk even faster and I'm getting pulled along next to her whether I like it or not and I can see what's coming next and I wonder why this kind of thing always happens to me even when I've done nothing to deserve it.

I don't like the sound of all these things Gus-Seep's saying, which are the type of thing my grandmother doesn't even like me listening to, never mind being involved in.

She doesn't like this supposed-to-be friendship between Gus-Seep and Philander because Philander is a hard man and a crook. There are things it's better not to know about that come and go out of The Buildings in the night.

There's hardly a person in the Customs or on the Liquor Force who doesn't get a little something from Philander every now and then which he can put in his back pocket and we would all rather not know what goes on in the upstairs rooms of Philander's famous Buildings when the sailors come to town and have money to burn.

I hope, for a change, my mother won't get involved but she has me by the arm and she's pulling me so hard I think she'll pull my arm right off my shoulder and won't even notice and she's dragging me along and we're going in the direction of The Buildings so I know what's coming next.

My mother is a mad woman who doesn't care about anything and now she's going to risk both our necks and push her nose right into Philander's business, which any-one who knows him will tell her is not such a wonderful idea.

Gus-Seep is in front and my mother's behind him, moving fast and I'm getting pulled along any old how behind and I'm praying my mother doesn't expect me to go into The Buildings and face Philander, because besides anything else I am in my St Peter's uniform and we aren't even allowed to walk past The Buildings, never mind go inside them.

If we have to go past we're supposed to go on the other side of the road and move as fast as we can and say a prayer quickly for the people inside who we all know the devil uses to do his works but my mother is not interested in devils.

She walks right up the front steps pulling me behind her and Gus-Seep is running along next to us showing her where to go and my eyes are on stalks because we are right inside the bar and I have never been in a bar in my life before and it's the middle of the afternoon and there are people everywhere staring at us and I know, if I should die now, I will for sure go straight to Hell and it will be my mother's fault.

Up close Philander is a big man and he's shouting non-stop. He uses up all the air inside himself shouting how he is going to kill Matilda and when he's out of breath and red in the face he breathes in and starts all over again, and poor Matilda is crouching on the floor with her hands over her head and he's standing over her with his eyes like coals, just like Gus-Seep said, and there's a broken bottle in his hand and he's screaming that he's going to carve Matilda up and give her back to her snake of a boyfriend in small pieces bit by bit like mincemeat and he looks to me as if he will do it.

Everyone is standing there with their mouths full of teeth and nothing to say for themselves because they're scared of Philander and no-one can blame them. He may be sweet as a lamb when Gus-Seep plays the harmonica to him in the evenings and tells him what it is the horses are whispering to him but he isn't sweet today. You can see just by looking that the devil has got hold of him in a big way and if you looked at him sideways and he saw you he could change his mind in a second and then it won't be Matilda who's mincemeat but anyone who tries to stop him.

But this doesn't seem to worry my mother.

She lets go of my hand and steps right in front of him and tells him if he knows what's good for him he'll put the bottle down and leave Matilda alone. Just like that. You never in your life saw anyone who got such a surprise as Philander did when he saw her and heard what she had to say and he wasn't the only one.

'Put the bottle down this minute and let that girl stand up on her feet and go on her way, or you'll have me to answer to,' my mother says and no-one else says a single word. It's so quiet you could think you were in church. 'I'm not like the rest of the people here. I'm not impressed with your big mouth or your bully-boy tactics. I know about men like you and you don't frighten me.'

Gus-Seep's eyes are on stalks and my mouth is hanging open and I couldn't close it if I tried.

'I mean it,' my mother says and you can see she really does. 'I can put up with drinking and money changing hands and goods coming and going under the counter but I won't stand for a man who raises his hands to a woman.'

Philander only has eyes for my mother now and he's asking how this has suddenly become her business and what she thinks she's going to do about it and he's waving the broken bottle in her direction, right close to her face and people are screaming out to be careful or he'll cut her. He's done it before and they've seen him do it but she doesn't even move an inch out of his way.

'You want a fight?' she says. 'You looking for someone your own fighting size to have a fight with, then take me on. I may not be as big as you but I'm a lot tougher and if you don't leave her alone this minute I'm going to kill you.'

Philander and his bottle are nearly right on top of her and I'm hanging onto Gus-Seep's coat for dear life and when I hear her say this I get such a fright I nearly sit down flat on the ground out of nerves, as if my legs won't hold me up any more, just in case what Gus-Seep says about her having a revolver in her bag is true and I'm about to see it with my own eyes.

'Don't think the idea of going to jail for killing you worries me because it doesn't,' she says. 'I can take a lot of things in this life but I won't tolerate a man lifting his hand to a woman. I don't mind sitting in jail for the rest of my life if that's what it takes to put a stop to a man like you.'

You can hear a pin drop but she doesn't care because this is between her and Philander and she stands there looking straight into his mad eyes and you can see she's even madder than he is because she means every word she says. Nothing will move her. Everyone can see that. Even Matilda lying black and blue down on the ground puts her hands down from her head and is staring at my mother.

Everyone's staring because they've never seen anything like it in their lives before. They can see she means business and if she pulled a revolver out of her bag that minute and shot Philander stone dead where he stood no-one would have been surprised but it's Philander who makes a move not my mother and what he does is put the bottle down.

'I know about you,' he says and he couldn't care less about Matilda now. 'People around here may not know the type of woman you are but I know about you. You're a mad bitch and you should be locked up.'

Philander says he knows about the big packet of money my mother gave to her mother and he knows exactly where that money comes from and the type of money it is.

He knows she and her friends sell under-the-counter liquor to the Natives and she's the one with the brains and the golden touch who looks after all the money.

'Johannesburg isn't so far away that I don't know what goes on there. I know who your friends are and I'm not looking for trouble with them. Not over a piece of rubbish like Matilda.'

He says my mother and Matilda are two of a kind, sugar sisters under the skin and when Mr Julies is finished with Matilda perhaps my mother's gangster boyfriends, those bursting-with-money Johannesburg shebeen boys who are always in and out of jail, would like to have her because, as far as he's concerned, they're welcome to her. They can have both of them for all he cares because they're both mad bitches who deserve everything they get.

Everyone's staring and Gus-Seep's Adam's apple is jumping up and down in his throat out of nerves and my mother's breathing hard and you'd think she'd been asleep and suddenly woken up because in a minute everything's different and the show's over and she says she thinks I've seen and heard quite enough, thank you, and it's time we went about our business.

Just like that, it's finished and she's the woman we know again and she turns around quietly and tells Gus-Seep to help Matilda on her way and she takes my hand and says it's time we left for home.

We walk out of there slowly but once we're on the street we go faster and faster as if all the devils in Hell are running after us and I have to run along behind my mother and even so, I can't keep up with her and she won't stop so I can catch my breath and I don't know if she knows I'm still there or if she cares.

She's walking so fast she's panting and she's crying too.

She's crying hard and wiping the tears off her face with the back of her hand.

I don't know why she's crying but I know it isn't because she's afraid. Anyone who saw the look on her face and the way she stood up to Philander could have told you that, but by the time we get to our house she's crying so hard she can hardly breathe at all.

When we get into the house she slams the door behind us. My grandmother gets such a fright to see us both, and my mother standing with her back against the door and her head in her hands and in such a state, I think she's going to have a heart attack.

'What's the matter?' she wants to know and she comes down the passage fast wiping her hands on her apron as she goes and she tries to get hold of my mother but my mother's like a mad person. She pulls away and shakes herself so hard my grandmother nearly falls over and she has to put her hand on the wall to stop herself and she keeps asking if one of us will please tell her what's happened and I keep trying to say but I'm in too much of a hurry and I can't get the story out straight and my mother's crying so hard it's as if she's crying up angry stones right out of her heart and will die of it.

'Why do men have to treat women this way?' she wants to know. 'They have no right, no right at all.'

She says men like Philander are bullies and pigs, like scum on the face of the earth and poor excuses for human beings and she wishes she was carrying a gun the way Gus-Seep always says she is, instead of just bluffing him, because she wanted to kill him there and then and she knew she'd never feel sorry about it afterwards and she could actually have done it and enjoyed doing it.

I don't know why she's crying this way, as if there's nothing in the world that can ever make it better.

I don't have much time for my mother but I know there aren't many people who would have stood up to Philander the way she did and although I never have a good word to say to her I would have been willing to tell her that if it would have made her feel better.

I open my mouth but my grandmother gives me a look to close it again and keep it closed and I do, although I don't know why I'm going to be in such big trouble if I say anything.

No-one has laid a finger on my mother. She isn't the one who's been hit but the way she's carrying on you'd never think so. I want to ask why, but my grandmother gives me a look and makes zip-closed with her hand across her mouth and I know what that means. It means no questions.

New Year is the best time because it belongs to us and on the day when we wave the old year goodbye we can put our troubles behind us for a day or two and enjoy ourselves.

The Government can take away anything they like from us and goodness knows they're doing their best but New Year is our time. That's one thing they can't take away from us in a hurry.

Gus-Seep says they better clear out Roeland Street and all the way into town because although this year hasn't been like all the other years it makes no difference. The boys from the Valley will be on the Coon march just like they always are.

It doesn't matter if people say what's the point because the way things are going, next year there'll be no Valley left and we'll all be on the Flats. It doesn't matter if people are asking where we will march to then.

Gus-Seep says next year's troubles are next year's troubles and we haven't got time to worry about them now and my mother says if we all had Seepie's outlook on life the world would be a much better place and things are better at our house now and we are all ready for the Coons.

You have to go early to get a good place to watch and we go to the same spot every year. The people who stand with us know us and they expect to see us there, same as usual and if we're a little bit late it doesn't matter. They keep our spot warm for us and we'll have our same ringside seats we always do and our chance to wait with everyone else.

Stella brings a big brown paper bag with our food in it and some pink sugar peanuts for me and a flask of coffee and we have our jerseys in case it gets cold because it happens sometimes, even in summer, and my grandmother says as long as we have food and a jersey we have everything we need in the world. We can wait until kingdom come if we have to.

We don't mind because we see our friends and there are people to talk to and in any case the Coons are worth waiting for.

It's funny. Every year Coons are the same but at the same time every year they are also a little bit different and that's the way we like it. We like to know what to expect and we don't want too many surprises. What we want is enough surprises to make it exciting but not so many we don't know where we are any more and have to ask ourselves what we've come out for.

The important thing is that there's a place for us to put down my grandmother's stool somewhere in the front so she can sit comfortably and have a good view and people know her after so many years, so they don't mind making a place for her. That's one thing you can say for the Valley. They have respect for old people.

So, there we sit. Ready.

We like to see the new uniforms and to hear the saxophones and the banjoes, the mandolins and all the old songs and we like to see the Queens-for-a-Day in the front swinging their hips, with their faces painted like women and turbans tied around their heads and big earrings sticking out and the pretend pile of fruit on their heads, the pineapples and bananas and apples and oranges and grapes, and the Queens acting as if they are Carmen Miranda.

We love the Queens-for-a-Day and there are always people in the crowd who are willing to join in the fun and march along behind them moving their bottoms and pretending to be women and the Queens don't mind.

They've got the best sense of humour of everyone and nothing gets them down. The rough element shout remarks at them to make them cross and they don't care. They wave their fingers and shout back and no offence.

We like that. Even my grandmother can't stop herself laughing when boys she knows waggle past her like Dorothy Lamour and make kisses at her with their big red mouths and tell her in their rough boy voices that they love their old sweetheart and how about a date tonight?

Gus-Seep says they don't know if they're Arthur or Martha but nobody cares. They're terribly rude boys but we know their story and you have to laugh at them, the way they carry on when people shout out, 'Swing your hips, sugar lips' and this is what they do and my grandmother really enjoys herself and laughs with everyone else and sometimes shouts out too because that's what everyone's doing and she can't stop herself and in the end she's laughing so much she's crying and she has to lift up her apron to wipe her eyes but it doesn't matter. We've all come out for a good time and that's what the Coons give us and my grandmother says as long as we can have a laugh, life isn't so bad after all.

No-one is too grand to enjoy the Coons, except Evie. Since my mother sat for James on the steps of Roeland Street Evie is flat with green-eye and the way she's carrying on Gus-Seep says she could even die from it and these days you can't even say our name in front of her.

That's all she needs to start her off screaming and crying and saying the Valley isn't big enough for all of us and she won't even put her foot out on the street if she knows my mother is going to be there.

It's her loss. She can spend New Year lying in the back room of her mother's house with all the windows closed and a vinegar rag over her head for her nerves if that's what she wants. She doesn't know what she's missing.

My mother and James are there waiting for the Coons with everyone else and I'm there too, right next to my grandmother so she knows where I am in the crowd and can keep an eye on me.

I'm watching my fingers turn pink from the sugar peanuts and out of the corner of my eye I'm watching my mother standing under the streetlamp waiting with everyone else and I think she's the funniest woman anyone could ever know.

She's been away, we don't know where, for almost all my life and now she's back we don't ask anything, not even how she came to be in our family in the first place which Stella says is something she can never understand because whichever way you look at it she's not like the rest of us. Yet, there she is, back with us and waiting for the Coons, as if she's never been anywhere further than the corner shop.

She could be stuck-up if she liked but she's not. She loves the Coons just as much as we do and when they start and you hear the banjoes and the accordions and the harmonicas coming from a long way off and then you hear the sax's wailing down Sir Lowry Road my mother starts to cry. Right there in the street.

Not loudly. Just big tears that she wipes with her hands but so many tears that her hands are like the window wipers in the Muslim husbands' cars and the tears are still there no matter how much she wipes and James doesn't say anything. He just gives her a handkerchief.

I have never seen anyone cry at Coons before. Stella cries in the bioscope when the picture is sad and then we have to sit long after the lights have gone on and everyone else has gone home and the usher offers us more monkey nuts and asks if we're staying for the next show and as far as he's concerned there's no extra charge if we do.

This is because although Stella doesn't believe in 'in love' it still makes her cry and she doesn't want anyone to see how simple she is.

But no-one cries at Coons except my mother and I wish she'd stop because if she goes on long enough people will begin to notice and think there's something wrong with her and we don't need any more attention on our family, thank you very much. Not after what happened at Roeland Street.

In a way, although I don't want to cry myself and would rather dance if I was invited by the Carmen Mirandas, I know how she feels. It's a funny thing about music, how it can make you happy and want to cry at the same time.

'What's the matter with you, Gloria?' Stella wants to know and you can hear in her voice that she thinks she's seen everything now. 'It's only a banjo the man's playing. The way you're carrying on you'd think he was playing on your heartstrings.'

'Maybe it is her heartstrings,' my grandmother says and my mother says maybe she's right and she wipes her face with James' hanky and I think Stella will have something else to say but she's looking somewhere else.

'Stand up quick and have a look, Mommy,' she says. 'It's Royston. He's with the Dark Town Strutters.'

'Jump up on the stool, Lily,' my grandmother says. 'Never mind the people behind. Jump up quick and have a proper look and tell us whether it's Royston or whether it isn't. I haven't got my glasses with me.'

I stand on the stool and my grandmother has hold of my legs and the people behind say, sit down, because I'm not made of glass and I'm blocking the show but I can see even after such a quick look that Stella's right. She knows her own son when she sees him.

There goes Domingo dancing along with the Dark Town Strutters, shaking his tambourine and turning this way and that, showing the yellow and red satin stripes of his suit so that if he turns fast it looks like flames and he's light on his feet and you can say what you like about our family, one thing we can do is dance and he can't fool us with all that Al Jolson paint on his face. We know it's only black Nugget and white ShuShine and after all he's our family and we know him.

I don't care what people say about the Coons, saying that it's just a lot of drunk Coloureds looking for an excuse for a good time, just like they always do. I'll remember Coons and sugar-coated peanuts and the Carmen Miranda Queens-for-a-Day and my grandmother sitting on her stool and the sound of the banjoes and the tambourines all of my life.

I know I will. Whatever happens this will always be my music. I've locked it in my heart and that's where it'll stay and one day when I need it I'll play it back like a music box

195

and Domingo will dance into my mind just like he is that moment.

He can't see me but I can see him and from the way he's dancing with his feet twirling and his eyes closed and his face lifted up in the streetlights I can see he's happy and that makes me happy too.

So I stand clapping to his music and although he can't see me he turns and shakes his tambourine and his satin suit is dancing like flames in the streetlights and it's really funny. I'm happy because of liking my cousin so much and we could be the only two people there and then I see my grandmother looking right at me and out of the blue she says I'm a funny girl and getting just like my mother because although I'm having the best time anyone could ever have I'm clapping in a different time to everyone else, and the beat of the music changes and Domingo dances on in the procession and he's gone towards Roeland Street with the others. But I've seen him and his mouth is slightly open the way he's smiling and his two gold gangster teeth are shining.

Much later, when the Coons are finished and all that's left is the sound of them disappearing down Roeland Street into town, we pack up and go home but we go slowly. Everyone does.

All Stella's food is gone. The pink polony sandwiches and the white bread and apricot jam sandwiches, the coffee and the bananas and we drift along like ghosts because we don't really want to break anything and although it's quiet the music is still in the air and we can feel it in our bones.

People talk quietly as if the words they're giving each other are presents and not everyday and it's a special night. You can smell the docks' smell of petrol and seaweed creeping up towards the town. You can hear car-hooters and ships' horns going off out at sea to remind us it's a new year now. You can hear the church bells chiming all over the town.

There are even some seagulls still awake and jumping around above the streetlights when birds with more sense are fast asleep but my grandmother says seagulls are like some people we know. They don't like to miss anything.

I have my grandmother's hand in mine and my mother's stopped crying but her eyes are still shining and James is walking very close to her and Stella is walking hopalong ahead carrying my grandmother's stool and I want to catch up with her and talk about Domingo but I think it has been too much excitement for my grandmother and I don't mind walking slowly like this, as long as she is next to me and if I give a hop and a skip, which she won't even notice, I can match my steps to hers and we can walk along together nicely with our four feet rhyming on the pavement and we can walk along like that for ever for all I care.

I like to feel my grandmother's hand in mine although I know she doesn't really need me to show her the way home. She's walked up and down that hill so often, she can find her way home without any help from anyone. That's what she always tells me. But not tonight. Tonight she's walking quietly on her red felt slippers and I'm thinking if we go slowly enough perhaps we'll really be able to walk on like this together for ever and will never get to the end of the night at all and that is all right too.

Before we get home we must go past The Buildings and it's so loud with music going and lights shining, you'd think that for those people New Year will never stop. You'd never think it was already a new day.

The people who hang around The Buildings take life as it comes. That's why Gus-Seep likes it there. There's always something going on and any excuse is good for a party.

Music falls right out of the windows and the girls dance all night with sailors who've come into town to have a good time and with anyone else who asks them and New Year is no exception. It's just as special at The Buildings as anywhere else. The girls are all tarted up in spangled dresses with feathers round their necks, shouting, 'Happy New Year' down into the street and I'm eyes everywhere, looking out for Gus-Seep to see if I can see him with his friends before he sees us first.

This is where he'll be tonight keeping company with the rough element and passing around a bottle with newspaper wrapped round it in case the police come, and making a big show of wiping his mouth with the back of his hands when he's finished his turn.

It's nice to be there and see it all right in front of us and to stop for a rest and watch poor man's bioscope and the world go by.

After all it's New Year. It belongs to all of us to do whatever we like with, and when the girls from The Buildings say to James to come up and dance with them they don't mean it badly. I don't know why James is looking at my grandmother and is red in the face and my mother is laughing at him. There's nothing he can do about it.

Gus-Seep says the girls from The Buildings are good girls at heart. They work hard all year and he can whisper to me that, no matter what people say, their life is no bed of roses. There are sometimes tears behind all the jokes and the laughs. In that way they're just the same as we all are.

They don't know about my mother and James and the dancing but they call out to them and say they mustn't be stuck-up. They must come up and have a dance for old times' sake and Stella says why don't they. It's a long time since they first danced together but she can remember it as if it was yesterday.

Gloria's dress is red, chiffon over taffeta, with a sweetheart neckline and see-through back and sleeves. It used to be her favourite, her 'lucky' dress she called it and in its glory days, when she danced competitions with her brother, Errol, it had its fair share of winners' rosettes pinned to it.

There are sequins on the front of the bodice and down the back the skirt is scattered with hundreds of tiny beads that move and shimmer when they catch the light and the skirt, with its beads, floats over layers and layers of red net petticoat and down in the wash-shed petticoats have been soaked in sugar water and hung dancing on the line to dry and the sugar water has done the trick and they dry stiff as Grenadiers and scratchy as a prickly pear.

'You're not going on the stage at the British bioscope,' Stella says but Gloria is in front of the mirror and earrings are on and earrings are off and her hair has been up and her hair has been down. A fringe has been down to her eyebrows and a fringe has been hairsprayed away.

'Ma,' Stella shouts, 'Gus-Seep keeps hanging around and he won't leave us alone and Gloria's getting dressed and sitting here in her brooks and her bust-bodice and Gus-Seep keeps pushing his face in the door and making remarks. Tell him to behave himself.'

'Leave him alone,' Gloria says blotting red lips between blue Kleenex tissue and then finishing them off with a delicate dab of Vaseline from the tip of a blood-red pinky finger. 'Seepie isn't harming anyone. I'm his own sister, for goodness' sake. Not the Queen of Sheba. I haven't got anything to show that he hasn't seen before.'

It isn't only her lips that are crimson. She has Cutex Fire Engine Red fingernails and the air is heavy with the scent of Wellaflex hairspray and 'Evening in Paris' scent and Gus-Seep's face is at the door again in a sour yeast whiff of Virginia sweet wine and it's all smiling teeth and a pulled-up nose and he says his mother sent him to tell them the scent is nearly knocking the whole house over and it's more than enough and far too much already and if Gloria was a fish, she'd be pickled in it.

Stella is going to the dance too, for moral support and in case the gramophone at the Methodist Mission gets it in its head to let them down. If that happens she says she can always play the wind-up for them because she's expert at that after all the practice sessions and all the free advice her sister was always shouting at her and if James decides to dump them Gloria will have to have her for a partner.

But James doesn't dump them. He's on time and polite and has nice things to say about having two pretty girls for the price of one at the Daniels' house and when she asks he shows his wristwatch to their mother and says, since she asks, he knows how to tell the time and he knows when she says twenty past twelve at the latest, that's exactly what she means and then they're on their way and the night air is warm and they scent it softly as they go with James' Lifebuoy Soap and Gloria's 'Evening in Paris'.

'My mother doesn't trust you quite as much as she makes out,' Gloria says as they walk arms linked three abreast down the road. 'That's why she's sending my sister with us. Safety in numbers. That's what she always says. That's what she told us before you arrived. "Watch out for that young man," she said. "He's a real charmer. I know one when I see one and if you're not home straight after twelve when the dance ends and twenty minutes for the walk, I'm sending the police to fetch you." '

'She's pulling your leg,' Stella says and they swing along together with their steps rhyming and when they're quiet you can hear the crisp little scratches of Gloria's red sugar petticoats against her bare brown legs.

There are flat kid glove shoes for the walk to the hall but when they get there, just round the corner and still out of sight, she takes her red satin dancing shoes out of her bag and puts her hand on James' shoulder while she slides them onto her feet and rises up tall where she can look at him properly and he's standing there with her hand, red-nailed on his shoulder, greeting everyone left right and centre and the Methodists, in their finery, on their way to the dance are looking at him and looking at Gloria and looking at each other and wondering who the lady in red is.

'You're mad,' James says looking at the red satin dance shoes as they come out of Gloria's handbag. 'You'll break your neck. No sane person could even walk in shoes like that, never mind dance in them.'

'I can,' Gloria says and she gives a little shake of her shoulders and flexes her feet in their bright little shoes.

'You don't have to worry about me.' She lifts her hand and straightens his bow tie and her Fire Engine fingers fly quick and warm over the lapels of his suit making them flat and burning heat right into his chest.

'I won't let you go wrong. Just don't count out loud like you do at home and we'll be fine,' she says.

There's no-one who can hold a candle to James and Gloria. No-one comes even close. Those red shoes fly across the floor of that old hall, never once missing a beat and James looks very grown-up in his suit and pleased as Punch with himself and not as plain as usual.

There are others who are good but none of them have been champions in their day the way Gloria has and right in the middle of the cha-cha-cha when people are enjoying themselves and clapping their hands on the beat they stop dancing and stand aside, still clapping, so James and Gloria can have the floor to themselves and she's so light and moves so smoothly it seems when the music is inside her there's nothing she can't do and when the dance is over the Methodists go right on clapping and James takes Gloria by the hand and she curtsies to all sides and everyone claps even louder because they know a champion when they see one.

'That should have been the end of the story,' Stella says. 'But enough was never enough for Gloria.'

They said, for a final turn, James and Gloria could choose and dance any dance they liked and Gloria said, if no-one had any objections and because it hadn't been danced before that evening, she and James would quite like to show them a waltz.

James bends down and whispers to Gloria and says to come closer because he has something to say to her and he doesn't want anyone else to hear it and what he says is that he can't do it. Quickstep yes and foxtrot maybe but not the waltz.

'Yes, you can,' Gloria says and she's warm from dancing and her eyes are shining and she's not interested in cowards and she's not going to take 'no' for an answer.

'It's easy,' she says. 'You just hold onto me and pretend we're in the front room at Constitution Street. Forget about these other people. Just keep looking at me and follow

201

where I show you and I'll do everything else. You'll be fine. You'll see. You may even enjoy yourself.'

Poor James. He's red in the face and his forehead is wet with nerves but Gloria has her mind made up and she's not in the mood for the quickstep or the foxtrot.

'If you don't mind,' she says to Revd Wallace, 'I think I saw a record of the "Merry Widow Waltz" in the pile over there. Perhaps someone would spin it for us.'

There they are in the middle of the floor and Gloria is ready and her red dress is standing out like a tea cosy over the sugar petticoats and she holds out her arms to James and her arms and the music and her scent reach out for him all at the same time.

It's a popular choice because although it's difficult to dance, the waltz is a lot more beautiful to watch than the cha-cha but James looks as if he wishes the floor would open up and swallow him.

Stella is standing right near them and can hear what her sister says to James and she could kill her when she sweet-talks him and makes the waltz sound like the easiest thing in the world.

She keeps telling him all he has to do is forget about his feet and not try to count. He must listen to the music and keep his eyes on her face and when the music starts she moves very close to him in that way that would have given Miss Dorothy Dyamond a fit if she'd been there to see it.

But Miss Dyamond isn't there and even though the hall is strung with fairy lights, all different colours, it is only the Methodist Mission Hall after all but even so it's a wonderful night and Gloria and James are the centre of all eyes and they fly across the floor, with Gloria in her red shoes and the music all around them carrying them on and the lights dancing in the beads of her dress and the chiffon flying free like a soft cloud of fire.

She is so light and so fast and something seems to happen to James because, in the beginning, he looked so worried you'd think he was being tortured and then suddenly it's all right.

He smiles and she moves a little bit away from him and smiles back and his smile grows even wider because suddenly it's fine and the music is carrying him along just like she said it would and he isn't just dancing, he is truly dancing and his feet feel as if they have a life of their own. He's never felt such a feeling in his life before and as far as he's concerned it can go on for ever.

All the way home he keeps talking about it.

'You've got nerve,' he says and if she liked Gloria could warm her hands on the admiration in his voice and the way he can't take his eyes off her when he says it and the way his voice sounds.

'I've never got a waltz right before. Not even once and you're lucky, that's what you are. You must have some guardian angel or something watching out for you, that's all I can say. How could you do it? I could have fallen right over my own feet and flat on my face right there in front of everyone and then we'd have looked a big pair of full-of-ourself fools.'

They're walking side by side three of them next to each other and he turns around and walks backwards so he can look at her and the light from the streetlamps falls down on Gloria's face floating free and smiling in a cloud of hair as thick and dark as the night and her sister's soft face bobbing, hopalong next to her.

'I didn't take any chances,' Gloria says and her cardigan is over her shoulders and her red shoes are in her hand and her feet are bare and they are walking down the smooth old cobbles in the middle of the road. 'I knew you could do it.'

'That's what you say now,' he says. 'But how can you know that?' He makes it sound as if he's caught her out in a lie but she keeps her face straight and smiles a little bit and keeps on looking ahead and walking.

'You couldn't have known,' he says. 'I didn't know myself.'

'Just goes to show then, doesn't it?' she says. 'I'm a witch and I know things about you you don't even know yourself, so you just better watch out for me, James Scheepers.'

*   *   *

It was a long time ago but that night is in their minds when they go up onto the front stoep of The Buildings together and because it's such a hot night some people are dancing there in the cool breeze with the moon and the stars over their heads and I know if Gus-Seep sees this he will fall over stone dead and if Evie changes her mind and comes out on the street to look for her husband she won't be too far behind but there is one thing I have to say now I have seen this with my own eyes.

What people say about my mother is true. She may be a show-off but she's a really good dancer. When you look at her you forget about Ginger Rogers and Cyd Charisse and never mind if she is my mother, I'm glad she made up her mind to dance and egged James on because it's nice to look at them and I'm not the only one who thinks so.

Other people have stopped dancing and are standing aside just to look and you'd think if James didn't keep hold of her my mother would float right off the dance floor. I don't know which of Errol's tricks she taught him but you can see he hasn't forgotten a single one.

I've never seen two people dance like that before. The music is swinging them along and James is singing in my mother's ear 'It Had To Be You' and she's smiling and trying to keep her pose and not laugh because he's being silly and he and my mother are quickstepping away like champions and my mother's flared skirt is whirling around her knees and little bits of can-can petticoat all colours of the rainbow are sticking out and her feet in their high heels are tapping away right in time to the music and her hair is flying backwards behind the combs she always puts in to keep it in place and she and James look happy moving around the floor together. To look at them you'd think they didn't have a care in the world and were just two ordinary people dancing the night away.

You'd think they wouldn't mind if all the people in the world stopped to look at them. You've never seen such a thing in your life not even on the screen at the Alhambra bioscope.

It is the first day of the new year and Domingo is dead.

The police have come to knock on our door and tell us and it isn't the way we thought it would be.

We have all said, so many times, that the problem with gangsters is that any moment someone can come and tell you they're dead but we didn't believe it.

We didn't think it would happen in our family. We thought it was just something you say. When it really happens it's supposed to happen to someone else.

When they come and knock on your door and ask your name and who you are and do you know anyone called Domingo and is he family of yours because by the way, he's dead, it's very different and it's hard to believe because up until that minute everything else is just the same as it is every other day and before this happened my mother was in a good mood.

She's been whistling little pieces of songs since she got up this morning. She's been making tea and jokes just like a normal person and talking about last night and what a nice time we had at the Coons and, for a change, she's talking so much and so nicely that not even Stella can get a word in.

My grandmother is sitting under the fig tree and our yard smells of figs and the sun is shining down through the big sticky leaves and making hopscotch patterns on the cement.

My grandmother is plucking a chicken for our first day of the new year lunch and upstairs in the kitchen Stella is in her bare feet peeling potatoes and cutting up vegetables and listening to songs on the radio and the smell of raw vegetables cooking and little bits of the songs are floating down to us and we are in the sun and I am sitting around in my shorts and flip-flops reading my Christmas annual books which are the presents James left in my pillowcase for me.

My grandmother is sitting on the stool Gus-Seep made for her in better days when he was apprentice to a carpenter and her feet in their red slippers are apart so that the skirt of her dress and the green-check overall on top of it fall between her knees in a big fold of material and the sun just keeps shining down.

My mother's hanging up wet washing out of a bucket. She's bending down and then reaching up with a piece of wet washing in her hands and pegging it and then doing it all over again so that the washing, skirts and blouses and petticoats in soft colours, is hanging down from its pegs like flags and you can smell the soap and the clean and there are little drops of wash water splashing down on the hot ground and disappearing in curls of steam in the sun and the radio is playing hymns, 'From the Bell Tower', and when a little bit of hymn floats down even my mother hums along and the light is shining over the white pages of my *School Friend Annual* so it turns to water and the lines of writing on the pages jump around so I don't even know what I'm reading any more but it doesn't seem to matter. It's that kind of day.

My grandmother's turning the chicken over neatly while she plucks, first one side and then the other and if you look at the chicken's face with its little eyes closed and its red comb flopping over from side to side when my grandmother turns it to pluck some more it looks peaceful as if it's fast asleep and dreaming nice things.

My grandmother is humming while she works and suddenly the hymn music comes down to her quite clear and it's her favourite which is 'Rock Of Ages' and at first she hums a little and then she starts to sing along.

When she's happy she often sings 'Rock Of Ages' even when it's not on the radio and she's told all of us, at least a hundred times, that this is the hymn she would like to hear sung at her funeral one day.

She sighs and sings and closes her eyes as if it is between her and her God, who I hope is not hard of hearing because although my grandmother's voice is not bad, she says herself it's a bit thin and old these days, just like the rest of her and sometimes it cracks.

'Rock of Ages, cleft for me, Let me hide myself in thee.'

We all know it and Stella says it's funny but the happier my grandmother is, the sadder the hymns she chooses. I know it's upside down but that's the way she is and I'm sure God understands.

She's sitting on Gus-Seep's stool and the chicken is lying on her lap and her face is lifted to the sun and her eyes are closed which is just as well because you can't look right into the sun anyway. Not unless you want to go blind.

Then suddenly, my mother, who I'd forgotten about, starts to sing too and I get a big shock. I'd forgotten what people said about her. How in her choir days she could sing people right up to Heaven's Door if she put her mind to it.

She's standing by the washing line and she's singing along with my grandmother and the radio, softly at first and then louder so you can't hear the radio and then my grandmother stops singing and you wouldn't have heard her anyway because all you can hear is my mother's voice and it's huge like the sea. It's like a whole choir in one person and my grandmother sits there quietly listening and doesn't open her eyes and my mother goes right on singing as if it's a thing she does every day of her life.

I can't believe what I'm seeing and I can't believe my ears. My mother, who's not on talking terms with God, knows every single word and if you didn't see her breathing you could hardly believe the person singing was a person you knew. You'd want to run behind her to have a look for the gramophone just to catch her out except I know there's no gramophone there. My mother's pulling no tricks. It's she herself who's holding the tune and no-one sings like that in our church or even on our radio.

She breathes in deep and fills herself up with air and when she breathes out, the air comes out with the music right inside it, neat and loud and in tune and she sings every single verse right to the end and doesn't leave anything out. I know she doesn't, because I know that old hymn backwards because of it being my grandmother's favourite and every word of it is exactly right, up to the last verse, 'When you soar to worlds unknown and when you see the Judgement throne.' My mother knows it all and my grandmother loves this old hymn so much she can listen to it till the cows come home, so as far as she's concerned, this is like giving her a present.

'Thank you, Gloria,' my grandmother says when it's finished and she's sat quiet for a few minutes and then she opens her eyes and looks right at my mother and my mother looks back at my grandmother as if she is really seeing her for a change and when she speaks her voice is soft and nice.

'No, Mommy,' she says, 'I'm the one who has to say thank you.' When my grandmother asks what she's getting a thank you for out of the blue like this, my mother says it's for no reason but just because.

Those are the words they spoke but they meant something else and perhaps what they meant was not for Miss Big Ears. It didn't matter because, for a change, they seemed to understand each other and no-one was worried about me and we all went back to what we were doing and five minutes later there was a loud knock on the door and the police came to tell us about Domingo and we weren't ready and the day was spoiled and everything was different again.

Royston has been stabbed to death in his Coon clothes down by the canal where the river runs and his gold teeth have been pulled right out of his head.

It's gang business and although the police tell us straight they would like to wash their hands of it, they can't leave dead people lying around the streets, gangsters or not, so they've taken what's left of Domingo to the police station.

They've got him in their fridge right this minute and we must come and have a look and if he belongs to us we must take him away.

A gang can get you killed but they draw the line at fetching your body. That's for the family to do.

It's funny really. We always wanted Royston to come back to us. We didn't say so all the time but we said so sometimes and in our hearts it's what we wanted. Now the police have come to our door and told us we must come and fetch him, so in a way he's back in our family again.

This is not the way we wanted it to be although in my heart I knew it was the way it would happen. I felt it that day at his father's funeral and I know now that was why I did what I did.

'For goodness' sake, Mommy,' Stella says. 'Stop pulling at Lily like that.'

We're at the Maitland Cemetery, Gate Number 3, Coloured section. My grandmother, Stella and me and every crook, hoodlum and jailbird in town. That's what my grandmother says and there are certainly lots of people there and we don't know any of them.

My grandmother is hanging onto my hand for dear life and pulling me along behind her and pushing people out of our way and saying things about them loud enough for the whole world to hear and Stella is blood-red in the face and people are looking at us again.

My grandmother says if I smile at people or stare at the funny ones or dare to tell anyone even once more that I know the dead man and he is my Uncle Maxie, I will know all about it when we get home.

'Lily's too big for her boots and she's too young for funerals,' she says and she takes it out on Stella as if it's her fault. 'She doesn't know how to behave herself and we should have left her at home. We should all have stayed at home. We shouldn't be here in the first place and if you hadn't made such a performance about coming to this funeral I wouldn't be here right next to you and I wouldn't have to pull at anyone.'

Before the service even starts we are pushed all the way through to the front, nearly right into the open grave, because of Stella having been the lawful wife who went to fetch the body at the police station and if the crooks and hoodlums and jailbirds behind us get it into their heads to push forward to have a last look at their dead friend, the three of us will end up right inside the grave with Maxie and have to be pulled out and then everyone will have a good laugh and the joke will be on us.

The minister isn't even a proper priest but that doesn't

stand in his way. He still has plenty to say and Stella has her eye on him so he won't forget to mention who is the lawful widow and in her opinion just about the only person present who has any idea how a decent person behaves themselves at a funeral.

The gangsters have their own way of doing things.

Before they come to the cemetery they walk through the streets carrying the body on a big tray on their shoulders. The body isn't even in its coffin yet. Just lying on the tray all wrapped up in a nice white shawl with only its little face sticking out so people who see, can see for themselves that no tricks are being pulled.

House to house they go to their gangster friends' houses and when they get there they stand outside, body on the tray and all and stamp the ground hard with their feet and shout and say just as soon as Maxie is safe in the ground they're coming with sticks and knives to get his killers and make the slate square.

This has nothing to do with us, but Stella told me about it anyway and Stella, dressed for the funeral, is very smart. She has a little black hat on her head and it looks like a hajji hat and I have pulled her leg about this. It has a lace veil hanging down to her nose and the veil has spots all over it so it looks as if she's had the measles and just for a cheek she has a big white hanky in her hand for 'in case' and my grandmother has had a few words to say about that too.

My grandmother is in the worst mood in the history of the world, so it isn't a good time to look for trouble with her and every time I look at her old tiger face with its lemon mouth right in the middle of it I want to burst out laughing.

There have been big fights at our house about this funeral.

'I can't not be at my own husband's funeral,' Stella says. 'There's been enough talk already. We don't need any more. He is what he is and he's done what he's done but he was my husband after all and I married him till death us do part.'

'I don't need to be reminded of that,' my grandmother

says and Stella goes bright red and my grandmother doesn't have to say any more. She pulls a straight mouth and gives Stella a look so that anyone with eyes in their heads can see exactly what's on her mind.

The gangsters are the problem. My grandmother isn't interested in smoked-up people with gang tattoos all over their arms. She hasn't got time for anyone who is acquainted with the inside of a jail.

'I have to go for Royston's sake.' This is what Stella says to me. 'For myself I couldn't care less.' But the way she's pulling dresses out of her cupboard and mixing and matching them you'd be surprised to hear it.

In her heart, I think Stella is quite looking forward to the funeral. Gus-Seep says we can be sure of a good time because funerals are nothing new to gangsters and they know how to put on a good show, so I should go and enjoy myself.

Live fast, die young and make a good-looking corpse. That's what they say but it doesn't make any sense to me.

Stella didn't say anything about good-looking when she came back from the police fridge and my grandmother had to give her *buchu* brandy with sugar water in it for her nerves but I don't mind going because I've never been to a funeral before and I don't mind being taken out even if it is only for the airing.

A big black funeral car is coming to fetch us at three o'clock sharp and the neighbours will come out as far as their gates to see us get into it in our funeral clothes and it doesn't matter whether my grandmother likes it or not, they will want to pay their respects to us on our family's loss.

Gangster or no gangster, Maxie Davids had got himself into our family even if it was only by mistake and through the back door. There was nothing we could do about that. But we know how to act. When our neighbours come up to us to say how sorry they are Stella's husband is dead, we mustn't say we're sorry too, because God will be watching us and this is not the type of thing He'll easily miss or turn a blind eye to. What we say is it's nice of them to say so and thank you very much.

I didn't really know Stella's husband. When I was small he was not allowed in our house and the only time I saw him was when he was standing big in the street outside and Stella was in the front door with her hands on her hips shouting at him what a piece of rubbish he was and Royston was lying on the back room bed with his hands over his ears trying not to hear them.

By the time I got big Maxie was already a gangster and I'd been told if anyone mentioned his name to me to remind them that he was not blood family of ours and we were not responsible for his actions.

Now he's dead, it's a different story. Stella is hopping around her room pulling widow dresses out of the cupboard and laying them out on the bed and her hat box is down and standing open and she's going to put black nylon stockings on her legs and never mind the leather and iron brace which will scratch and makes holes in them before we even get out of the front gate.

'A woman's husband doesn't get buried every day,' she says. 'I never had anything to do with his friends when he was alive but I don't mind showing myself to them now and people can look as much as they like. It won't hurt to have a bit of quality at this funeral and for them to see a lady who knows what is expected of her and how to behave herself. You'll have to go a long way to find anyone else like that there, you can take that from me and I know what I'm talking about.'

'If we see Royston we'll have to call him Domingo,' I say and Stella and my grandmother look at each other over my head and give each other one of their looks.

'You won't be calling him anything at all,' my grandmother says. 'Because it's a funeral we're going to, not a picnic and you don't talk to gangsters in public, even your own cousin. No-one in this house does.'

So it's in this spirit that we go to the funeral and there we stand. Us on one side of the grave and Royston on the other side with his father's friends packed tight all around him and he's just lucky my grandmother doesn't have wings because she would have flown right across that open grave and given him something to remember for standing there acting big with all his father's jailbird friends and for the way he's treating his own mother who's there for his sake and who he doesn't even look at.

He doesn't look at me either and when I wave and point to myself and show where I am right in the front with the black band Stella sewed on my coat, my grandmother nearly pulls me right over into the grave and tells me to remember she has eyes in the back of her head and one more trick like that and she's more than ready for me.

I don't care. I like Royston and it's nice to see him again. It's nice standing in the sunshine by the grave and looking at all the flowers and Maxie in his coffin at last and the brass on the coffin handles shining in the sun and Royston right across from me with some big men with Sexy Boy tattoos on their arms.

When we were small if we caught ourselves staring at one another we used to turn it into a game and have staring competitions. We made our eyes big and stared and stared and we weren't allowed to laugh and the first one to blink was out.

I made my eyes as big and wished as hard as I could that Royston would look at me but he wouldn't and so I burst into tears and started crying so loud it gave everyone a big fright.

'What's wrong with that child now?' Stella wants to know from my grandmother out of the corner of her mouth because Ramona Gamiet is in the crowd and when she hears me sobbing and wailing as if my heart will break her eyebrows fly up so high they nearly take her hat right off her head.

'Nothing's wrong with Lily,' my grandmother says and she pulls her handbag open to find a hanky and she's cross because she doesn't want to be at the funeral in the first place and now that I'm standing in the front crying my eyes out, and even the minister has stopped to have a look at me, she's really sorry she came.

She pulls a hanky out of her bag and gives it to me. It is her just-in-case best funeral hanky. It has little blue and red flowers embroidered in the corner and eau de Cologne all over it so it nearly knocks you out when she puts it on your nose.

'You can stop that this minute,' she says taking my shoulder hard and talking right close to my ear. 'You didn't even know Stella's husband. What have you got to cry about for goodness' sake?'

She rubs the hanky over my nose hard, in the way that hurts, and says if I don't keep quiet that minute she won't even wait until we get home and people aren't looking at us and laughing any more, she'll give me something to cry about right there and then, funeral or no funeral.

I don't care. I can't stop and I don't want to and I'm not such a fool as they take me for. I'm not crying about the dead and some stupid man I didn't even know. I'm crying about the living. It's Domingo I'm crying about and every time I look at him and he won't lift up his eyes and look back at me, I cry even harder.

Stella's crying and my mother puts her arms around her and my grandmother says I must give one of the children playing outside in the street five cents to run down to The Buildings and find Gus-Seep and tell him to come home and to wait for us at the house, because we have to go to the police station.

It's terrible to die on New Year's Day because it's a difficult day to forget and after what has happened New Year will never be the same again.

It's not Royston's fault but now instead of eating our New Year lunch we're all going down to the police station together to fetch him out of the fridge.

The police aren't nice about gangsters because of all the trouble they cause. They're not nice to their families either, even if they've never caused any trouble in their life.

They like to keep them sitting around waiting as if they have all the time in the world. As if they are ready to sit there waiting forever and it doesn't worry them at all. As if they don't feel like vomiting all over the police station floor out of nerves every time they think about what they're there for and what they are going to have to do.

'Maybe it's a mistake,' Stella says and she and my mother are sitting next to each other on a wooden police bench and they're holding onto each other's hands. 'They're not perfect,' Stella says. 'They make mistakes.'

'Don't build up your hopes too much,' my mother says.

'If they'd hurry up and let us look at him, then we'd see for ourselves. Perhaps it isn't Royston, after all,' Stella says. 'They certainly know how to take their time.'

The police are in no hurry. They're going backwards and forwards past us, calling out to each other and some of them in an office behind a glass wall are drinking tea and we're sitting four in a row on the bench waiting to be called.

'We have to be patient,' my grandmother says. 'And we mustn't give up hope.'

When she says that my mother gives her a look over Stella's head and although she opens her mouth, she doesn't say anything. She puts her lip in a straight line and Stella pulls at the hanky between her hands in her lap.

'It's true what Stella says. We won't know until we've seen for ourselves,' I say. I'm not my grandmother. My mother can't keep me quiet with a look. 'I want to look with my own eyes. Then I'll believe it.'

I give my mother a flash look as if to say where Domingo is concerned she must watch out for me because whether he liked the idea or not he is my own flesh and blood. There is no getting away from that. He is my own person and what happens to him is my business as much as anyone else's.

My mother can keep the others quiet but not me.

'We won't know until we see,' I say and I won't let anyone tell me different. But we know.

To the police, gangsters are like dogs. That's what they tell us when they come past and ask us why we're there and what we're hanging around for. When they hear it's

215

only gangster business they shrug their shoulders and say dead gangsters should be left on the street to be cleared away by the street cleaners with the rest of the rubbish.

It doesn't matter what they say. Royston was never a very good gangster because his heart wasn't in it. He'd say out straight how fast he would run the minute anyone came after him but in the end it wasn't enough. All they had to do to get him was wait until he was dancing and not looking out for himself and now he's dead and you don't have to be a genius to work out this isn't what he wanted.

'It's a funny old life, isn't it?' my mother says and we're still waiting in the passage outside the charge office and it's very hot.

My grandmother has gone to sit outside for a breath of air and my shorts and the backs of my legs are sticking to the police bench and Stella is wiping the sweat off her face with a hanky but it doesn't help very much. She says it makes her hotter than ever and my mother can say what she said about life again because you never know what's waiting around the next corner.

'You know what I'm thinking about?' my mother says and she's hot like the rest of us and there are drops of sweat standing out on her face like pale little pearls and she keeps having to push her hair out of the way.

'I know what we're here for but all the same, I can't help thinking about some of the good times we've had,' she says. 'I was thinking about how excited we all were when we heard Royston was on the way and what a lovesick fool Maxie Davids was when he was chasing after you.'

Only a mad woman like my mother would start talking such nonsense when a person is lying dead in the next room and I think Stella will turn on her for sure and tell her exactly where to get off and I hope she will but it turns out Stella is as mad as her sister.

'He wouldn't take "no" for an answer,' she says and although she isn't making any noise she's still crying while she's talking and wiping her face with her hanky but she looks across at my mother all the same and my mother puts her arm around her.

'That was a wedding,' she says. 'Maxie is what he is but he did you proud that day and you looked like a queen. The whole Valley came out to have a look at you and they didn't go away disappointed.'

The way she's looking at Stella and talking you'd think all she can see in front of her right that minute is Stella looking beautiful in the wedding dress she made herself.

'No-one could see your leg,' my mother says. 'Just that white shoe sticking out under all the satin and those beads coming down the skirt like a waterfall.'

'Do you remember, Mommy?' Stella wants to know and her handkerchief is still in her hands but it's not up to her face any more and there are still tears in her eyes but for the first time since the police came to our door they're staying put and not falling down her face and I could die from embarrassment for Royston's sake, in case anyone listens to them and hears for themselves the type of people he has for relations.

'She had a face like a lemon,' my mother says and you'd think she was at a party the way she's enjoying the story. 'I can see it in front of me now. She kept asking why you were in such a hurry to tie the knot and wasn't there a little something you wanted to talk to her about.'

'She didn't have any time for Maxie. She didn't trust him an inch.'

'She had Maxie all worked out and he knew when he'd met his match,' my mother says and they smile at each other because they were both there and remember what it was like and then my mother starts to talk about the day Royston came into the world.

She and my grandmother sat one on either side of Stella's hospital bed while Royston took his time about making up his mind whether to come into the world or stay behind.

'The doctor was nice,' Stella says. 'He asked why it was baby time all over the Valley at the same time and had we all been at the same picnic.'

'Do you remember the woman in the bed next to you?'

my mother says and she puts her hand up to her mouth and underneath it is that big smile of hers that everyone thinks is so wonderful.

I don't know what gets into my mother when she carries on like this or why she has to get Stella in on the act but I feel sorry for Royston because Stella and my mother should have been talking about him and not worrying about themselves.

'That woman had the right idea,' Stella says. 'And she told everyone what she thought. She said babies fooled everyone. They went in smooth like bananas but when the time came to come out they came out hard as pineapples.'

When Stella says this my mother starts laughing and I wish the floor would open up and swallow me alive because they're making so much noise a policeman comes to find out what's going on and all he sees are two mad sisters holding onto one another and shouting the way they're laughing.

Never mind that someone of theirs is lying dead in a drawer right next door to them and the policeman's telling them we can come and have our look now because Royston is taking up space that belongs to decent people and if he's ours, they want us to take him away.

Now I've seen inside the police fridge and it's not like a home fridge at all. It's like a steel dressing table with very big cold drawers and you know just by looking that there isn't anything nice inside them.

The policeman who opens for us says he's sorry for our sakes if it is Royston. I think it's part of his job to say this and maybe, while he's saying it, his boss is somewhere watching him to see if he gets it right and if it sounds as though he really means it he'll get paid extra.

We know he doesn't mean a word of it but it doesn't matter. We don't need him to feel sorry for us because no-one can be as sad as we are to see Royston lying cold inside that drawer in his yellow- and red-striped Coon suit with his Al Jolson face still on. We are sorry enough for the whole world and even then there would be no room to spare.

It's a shock to see him still in his Coon suit. We didn't expect it, although I don't know why we shouldn't have.

My grandmother says we will have to clean him up and my mother says yes and Stella doesn't say anything at all. She just looks. Not staring, just looking and while she's looking at Royston, I'm looking at her and wondering what's going on inside her head but that's the kind of thing you can never tell just by looking.

I feel really sad for Stella but at least she doesn't have to say goodbye to Royston just yet. In the Valley, being dead makes no difference. If someone belongs to us we like to keep them with us and look at them for a little while longer before we let them go for the last time.

Royston will be put inside his coffin and brought to our house so everyone can have a look at him one last time. Last look, last touch. Some people don't like it but I don't mind. It's not so terrible.

My grandmother says we must keep ourselves together now. There are things that have to be done and we're going to be very busy.

She has Royston's funeral book and it's paid right up to date so at least we don't have to worry on that score. Things will be properly done and we, who have danced with the Coons one night, will spend the next night with dead Royston lying in his coffin on a table in our front room with candles at his head and feet and flowers all over the place.

At first I wanted to go to the funeral parlour with my mother and Stella but after the way they acted I changed my mind.

They can get Royston cleaned up and put in his Sunday suit, which he always hated, without any help from me because I am really fed up with them for the way they've been carrying on. As far as I'm concerned they can get Royston ready for God without my help.

When people die you're supposed to talk about them and

say how good they've been. It may be a bit hard when it comes to Royston but if they asked me I could have found good things to say about him and, if they really wanted to, so could they.

I think it would have made Stella feel much better than any mad talk of my mother's, but my mother never does what people are supposed to do.

If they'd asked me to go with them I might have gone but they didn't, so I walked home with my grandmother instead and every now and then we stopped on our way up the hill and caught our breath and talked a little bit about Royston and better days. About how he had come to our house when he was a small boy and what I said in Sunday School and how fast he could run when he put his mind to it and how safe I was with him.

So I had a chance to say what I wanted after all and I felt better when I'd said it but there was still something on my mind and I asked my grandmother about it.

'You said God would be on the lookout for Royston,' I say. 'You said his place in Heaven was booked in that name and He didn't know anything about anyone called Domingo. So what's going to happen now? Is God going to miss him?'

When I say this my grandmother stops in her tracks and pulls me around so she can look right in my face.

'Have you turned into a fool, Lily Daniels?' she wants to know. 'Don't you know that God knows exactly who every single one of his children is? It makes no difference what they decide to call themselves and only a fool could think it would.'

I felt better when she said that even if she acted as though she was cross with me and shook her head all the way home. When we were right at the top of the hill she was still shaking her head and asking what on earth had got into me.

'You have to get up very early in the morning to pull the wool over God's eyes,' she says. 'It's only a fool who wouldn't know that and you'd do very well to remember it.'

13

A Blaze of Glory

My grandmother says I mustn't say too much about what happened to Royston in front of Mrs Elias because her nerves are in such a state she can't take in another thing and we must spare her what we can.

This is because of Portia who everyone has washed their hands of.

One day the probation officer went to her school to look for her and she'd gone away to be a gangster just like Royston, so although Mrs Elias thinks she knows the end of Royston's story, she doesn't know exactly how it was because she wasn't there and my grandmother says the little bit she knows is enough. She doesn't need me going around there and making it worse with all the details.

Portia has already done her initiation and been arrested for shoplifting. She told her story in front of a magistrate but she got off for a first offence.

Her gang is called The American Mongrels of Lavender Hill and their sign is the tattoo of a spider which Portia has on her arm.

That's the talk and Mrs Elias is acting madder than ever. In the beginning, right after Portia left, she said the angels came to take Portia because she was one of God's chosen but no-one would swallow that story so she changed her tune and said what she was going to do was talk to Mr Elias about it as soon as he got home.

We all knew Mr Elias wasn't coming home because he was dead and anyway, if he did come home, there would be no-one to talk to because Mrs Elias has not clapped eyes on

Portia since she went away although she keeps sending messages to her.

She stops strangers in the street and tells them if they see Portia to tell her to come home because her mother is going to have to move very soon and after that there'll be no home to come to.

No-one can pretend any more, not even Mrs Elias.

The Government mean business. We expect the bull-dozers any day now and there's nothing we can do about it.

I don't know what Portia is supposed to do to make things better and I don't know if she'll come just because her mother sent for her but Gus-Seep seems to think she will.

He says it doesn't matter what went on between her and Mrs Elias, family is family and Portia will come if she's needed, despite her being a big-time girl gangster on the Flats these days and likely to end up the same way as Royston.

But if Portia is going to get here ahead of the bulldozers she better get a move on because they're already standing on the open ground next to the river. We've seen them there with our own eyes and we're not fools.

Soon the Government will give the word to start pushing houses down and when that happens, Mrs Elias' house and the rest of Kitchener Terrace will be the first to go.

Her house is the only one with a light still burning. It's the only thing you can see at night down the river end of the Valley because all her neighbours have gone and every-thing else is dark. One day there were people there and you could see their children playing kick the tin in the middle of the road and then they were gone and only Mrs Elias was left waiting for we didn't know what.

She's forever telling people she's talking to Mr Elias about things and he'll tell her what to do but that's mad talk because of Mr Elias being dead and for sure not coming back to answer her. At least not until Judgement Day. That's what Stella says. My grandmother says we've seen the bulldozers down by the river and know what they're there for and if that isn't Judgement Day then she'd like to know what is.

My mother's still going backwards and forwards to town every day but she goes out cross and comes back even crosser and locks herself in her room. She won't tell us what's going on, even when we ask her, so we're in the dark and have to guess for ourselves.

At night she and James go off together to talk to people who they think can help us and when they come back it's always the same. They find a quiet place to sit where no-one can hear them or they stand out in the street and when we ask them what's going on they only tell us what they want us to know. We're supposed to guess the rest and from the look on their faces that isn't very hard to do.

I would like it if we could just drop the subject and go back to being like we always were but it's not so easy.

The bulldozers are big and you can hear them coming from a long way away. In that way they're a bit like rhinoceroses or elephants. You can't pretend they're not there, because in the early morning when they start up you can hear them all the way up our hill. When everything else is quiet the sound carries like anything.

You can hear the factory whistle too and most mornings when the sun comes up you can hear their minister calling the Muslims to church and when the wind is right you could swear he was standing right in your backyard.

It's better to pray than to sleep he says but no-one is sleeping the morning the bulldozers begin to move.

The minute we hear them we get ourselves ready to go out onto the street because, good or bad, it's still our Valley and we aren't going to sit in our houses behind closed doors pretending nothing's happening when the bulldozers are rolling around our streets.

We've said my grandmother must come too but she won't go because she doesn't have the heart for it but wild horses couldn't keep my mother away.

She's out of her bed before the sun is up and dressed to kill in a red and white dress that looks like a flag. Her hair is clipped up in combs and she's ready to go long before the rest of us have even washed our faces.

Her mouth is red, her cheeks are rouged, her legs are in nylons with their seams dead straight. There are high heels on her feet and our whole house smells like a scent shop.

'You're looking very fine,' my grandmother says and she gives my mother a sideways look and says it in that sniffy way she has, so you know what she says and what she thinks are two different things.

'You look as if you're going to a party,' Stella says when she comes into the kitchen to find out what's going on and she gives my mother an up and down look and her eyebrows are nearly in Heaven.

'I thought you were going to show your face to the bulldozer men but you didn't say if it was to put them in their place or to ask them for a date.'

My mother is drinking her morning tea and being careful not to drink her lipstick off with it and I'm on my way to school and not saying anything at all.

'She looks like a Christmas tree,' Stella says to my grandmother as though my mother is deaf and my mother puts her cup down and looks at us and shakes her head.

'Would you like it better if I looked as if I was going to a funeral?' my mother wants to know. 'That's what those people would like but I wouldn't give them the pleasure.'

It won't do the bulldozer people any harm to see we're not all quite dead yet. Some of us are still very much alive and have some fight left in us and that's what she wants them to see.

I don't know what she's going to do when she gets there but when she gets up from the table and says do I want to come with her, I jump up and say I don't mind.

I know my grandmother won't like it because it's a school day and I'm not allowed to miss school or be late but she says often enough my mother's the one I must listen to these days now she's home so I don't stop myself saying what I really want because everyone will be on the street and I would rather be there with them than in school at my desk because I don't want to miss anything.

Front doors are standing open all the way down the road. Even the girls at The Buildings are out in their slippers and dressing-gowns and it's funny to see them without their shining dresses and their big eyes and their red mouths and maybe Gus-Seep is right about them. Underneath everything they look just like anyone else and they aren't all that much older than I am and their faces are small and sweet.

The shopkeepers are there, because on this day no-one is worried about opening time, and the Muslim women are at their windows and their children are in the street and the poor women from the Woodstock end of the Valley, near where Mrs Elias lives, are out with their babies on their hips and the little walkers pulling at their skirts.

Some of the more respectable women are in such a hurry to see what's going on and not to miss anything that they're out without their headscarves on their heads and my mother is there in her party clothes and walking fast with her head in the air and her hair flying out and her high heels tap-tapping on the pavement and I'm running along behind trying to keep up and all we see are people and all we hear is the most terrible screaming I've ever heard in my whole life. It tears at the air and my heart jumps into my throat and when we get closer we see that the screaming is coming out of the red mouth of Portia Elias.

Portia Elias is called Jack Hoxie now. That's her name on the Flats and in the files at the police station. That's the way it works. Royston told me.

When you become a gangster you are a new person and you can be anyone you like but I think, in her heart, Portia has always been Jack Hoxie. Even on that day when she did what she did in the graveyard.

But things are different now and I nearly fell on my back when I saw her because Jack Hoxie looks a lot different to what Portia Elias ever did.

She's wearing a satin tiger-skin dress and red snake shoes with thick high heels she can hardly stand on. There are red and yellow and purple beads on a long string around her neck and she's screaming so much and swinging her body around so hard that they keep flying around wildly and you can't get close to her.

Not that you would want to. No-one even tries, not even her own mother who is so small and keeps fluttering around like one of the little birds who come to pick at the windfall figs in the backyard and don't bother anybody.

I never heard any human being shout like Jack Hoxie and what she says is so terrible that some mothers cover their children's ears. It may be the way they talk on the Flats but no-one has heard it right out on the streets in the Valley and only the Government inspectors who are there in case of trouble think it's funny to see a woman carrying on like that.

They don't even try to hide it. They're grinning from ear to ear and that makes Jack Hoxie even madder and Mrs Elias is apologizing all the time to anyone who will listen.

Portia's not herself, she says. She says she and Portia's father always believed in talking nicely to their children and he'll come by in a minute to have a few words with Portia, no screaming just everything quiet and nice, and after that it will be all right because Portia always listens to her father.

She keeps on saying it although she says it as if she doesn't really expect anyone to hear her. Her voice is so small it isn't much more than air with a scatter of words hidden inside it but the mention of her father, who everyone knows will not come, makes Jack Hoxie madder than ever and she forgets about the Government men and begins screaming at her mother and calling her a stupid old cow and saying she's so stupid she deserves people to come and take everything she has away from her.

My grandmother said afterwards that Portia didn't mean it. At times like that words were just words and all they were good for was for carrying people's pain and Jack Hoxie was no exception.

I don't know about that. If it's true, then the pain coming out of Jack Hoxie is like the little rivers that run down the mountain after the rain. They're always in such a hurry to get to the sea they just rush along any way they can and don't care what gets washed away with them as they go.

There is something else. The Elias' things are any old how out on the street. They must have been thrown out. You can see they've just been dumped there and Mrs Elias always had big plans and good intentions about those things.

She never wanted people to see them until she was ready. That's why she never asked us into her house and although she always promised one day she would, that day never came and now this day has come in its place.

I don't want to look at them. It seems such a shame. But I don't know where else to look.

There's a bed with the blankets still on it and sheets with pink roses and a three-piece Chesterfield set with patterns like autumn leaves. There's an old stove and clothes pushed any old how into fruit boxes and even a corset that must have belonged to fat Granny Ida who Mrs Elias looked after all those years until she died.

No wonder Jack Hoxie screams and screams so if you didn't know any better you'd think it was a police siren.

We all stare at the Government inspectors and they just stand there staring back at us with their arms folded and the bulldozers behind them and Jack Hoxie in the middle screaming her heart out.

The Government inspectors always come prepared for trouble but trouble is not what they want. Not really. What they want is to do their job and get their pay packet at the end of the week and not have any trouble at all but they have not reckoned on Jack Hoxie.

It doesn't matter how many times they say Mrs Elias was meant to be out of the house months before, that she's been warned and warned and in any case she doesn't own the house and is not entitled to any say.

It doesn't matter that she went every month to pay her rent to her old landlord out of Mr Elias' compensation money and that her landlord told her a million times he couldn't take the money any more because he'd sold the house to the Government like all sensible owners had and he was sorry but that's the way it was because the Valley

227

was a declared black spot now and very soon it would be bulldozed to the ground and gone for ever.

None of this made any difference at all because there we were among Mrs Elias' cups and saucers and pots and pans, and Jack Hoxie's best blue church dress from the long ago days when she was Portia Elias was lying half spilled out of a plastic grocery packet but with enough of it showing so that people who remembered the dress also remembered how different things had once been.

We were all on our nerves wondering what was going to happen next and the next thing, so quietly we never noticed at first, we saw Revd Rainbird, who my mother has no time for, and old Humphrey coming down the road towards us with a whole lot of dogs running behind them because they know Revd Rainbird from his house visits and they all know old Humphrey, and looking at him today I see what I haven't noticed before and that is that he really is very old and he has a lot of wear and tear on him for a dog.

He walks slowly and pants a lot and today he's panting more than ever and hurrying to keep up but it doesn't matter because he is like the rest of us. He is there where he belongs.

My grandmother always says you can see Humphrey has seen life and you only have to take one look at his dog face to see what he thinks about it.

She never thought she would stand for a dog taking up his place in a church as if he was meant to be there but Humphrey knows the meaning of loyalty and that counts for a lot with her.

He's in his place in St Peter's every Sunday and he listens to the whole sermon and even when the Sunday School classes stand in the vestry door and offer him pieces of sausage to get him away he will give them sad looks but he will never be moved no matter how big the temptation is.

That day poor old Humphrey is moving fast, trotting along as fast as he can on his old dog feet with his tongue hanging out and panting like anything and it's a funny sight to see.

The first breaths of a southeaster are pulling at Revd Rainbird's cassock making it big although inside it he is really just a small man and always very polite.

'Good morning, Portia,' he says to Jack Hoxie as if she's a normal person and he puts his arm around Mrs Elias and says something in her ear and old Humphrey just sits around panting.

'Good morning, nice day,' he says to the Government inspectors and to the bulldozer driver and he nods to them politely and they nod back.

'Good morning, Father,' they say, very respectful because being polite costs nothing and what do they have to worry about? It doesn't matter what Revd Rainbird thinks. We all know that.

He isn't going to do anything and even if he wanted to, there's nothing he can do. It's not his job to stand in the way of the Government. We know that too. We know what happens to us is up to God. There isn't anything Revd Rainbird can do about it.

But next thing, before anyone knows what's happening Revd Rainbird sits down on the ground in the middle of the street as if that's something he does every day of his life and his cassock is all over the pavement like a big splash of black ink and he pulls it straight and tidy and we all stare at him as if our eyes are going to fall out of our heads and then he lies down flat right in front of the bulldozer wheel with his shiny shoe toecaps sticking up and his hands folded across his chest.

'This is all we need,' the Community Development Board inspector says and the bulldozer driver looks at his watch acting as if he's seen this type of thing often before but I bet he hasn't.

'What does he think he's doing?' the man standing next to my mother wants to know. 'This isn't his business. He should worry about Church work and saving souls and keep out of this.'

'He's doing what he thinks is right,' my mother says in that voice she has. 'These people have no right to do what they're doing to us. They have no right at all.'

This is just the kind of thing my mother likes. She's standing there straight as a soldier in her Christmas tree dress, looking at everything that's going on and her eyes are shining like stars.

It's Saturday, shopping day, and my grandmother's ID has come. It's been such a long time we thought they'd forgotten all about us but they hadn't. We fetched it registered at the post office and all the way home we remembered the day we went to old Dollie for my grandmother to have her ID photograph taken and what a good laugh we had.

At first she said it was a lot of nonsense and she didn't care if Gus-Seep and Stella had theirs done. If they didn't know who they were that was their business but she wouldn't do it because she knows exactly who she is and she doesn't need to carry a card around to prove it.

Even after Dollie gave her the pictures she wouldn't make up her mind. For a very long time she wouldn't send off her papers but in the end she had to change her mind because these days everyone asks for ID for everything including pension.

I don't think my grandmother would have allowed anyone but old Dollie to take her ID picture because she doesn't like having her picture taken these days.

Errol often sends a note with his money and asks why she won't send him a snap he can put up in a big gold frame in his lounge and tell people who ask why he isn't married yet that this is the mystery girlfriend he's always talking about and hasn't he caught himself a beauty.

My grandmother shakes her head when she reads this and says this kind of nonsense talk is just like Errol.

'You should do it, Mommy,' Stella says. 'Let Dollie do a nice snap of you and send it off to Errol.'

I agree with her but my grandmother says she won't do it because Errol will fall on his back if he sees what she looks like these days.

She makes a joke of it but when we go to Dollie we tell

him about Errol and he says if we make it worth his while he can touch up my grandmother's picture so she comes out looking like Ava Gardner and she says, no, thank you very much. Looking like herself is quite good enough for her. She'll tidy her hair and get herself together but that's all she'll do. After that she'll draw the line so we needn't bother to nag her any more.

'Look to the front and act natural,' Dollie says once my grandmother has got herself ready and smoothed down her dress and settled herself down and it's nice to be there because, besides anything else, old Dollie knew my Uncle Errol and has a soft spot for him.

He has a photograph he took of Errol one year when he was Carmen Miranda, Queen-for-a-Day in the Coons. This was on the front page of the *Cape Times* and Dollie is very proud of it because it nearly made him famous and he'll show it any time I ask to see it.

He won't part with it in a hurry, but he says he'll be willing to make a deal with me. If I ever go and visit Errol, which is not impossible the way people are flying around the world these days, he will give it to me to show him, because he thinks Errol will have forgotten all about it by now and he knows it would still give him a good laugh.

Dollie has his hands full with the ID business and has to spend all his time sticking to Government rules and regulations and the rules say my grandmother must take off her headscarf so he can photograph her ears with the rest of her head.

She doesn't like that idea one bit. She says it's the stupidest thing she's ever heard in her life but Dollie tells her it's rules and regulations and there are people in Pretoria who do nothing else all day but look out for this type of thing and these days it's the Government way or nothing because the Government isn't in a mood to argue about things.

Stella helps my grandmother take her ears out from under her scarf and my grandmother keeps saying under her breath what a lot of nonsense it is and when, at last, they're ready, there sits my grandmother, and we all have to laugh because she looks like a fool, like Bugs Bunny, and in the end old Dollie laughs too and even my grandmother joins in.

'You can laugh your hearts out,' she says. 'The joke's on Pretoria. It's their rules and regulations that make such a fool out of a person.'

So we have our reasons to know all about ID. We know how terrible people look and my grandmother says she thinks she better have a little check first, just in case and she opens the envelope and looks quick up close to her face so no-one else can see and then she puts her hand over her mouth as if she can't believe what she's seeing and she looks again and shakes her head and then she gives the ID book to Stella to look at.

She says that between old Dollie and the ear inspectors in Pretoria they've made her look a proper old fool. She looks as if she caught a fright in the middle of the night and if she sees old Dollie in the street she'll get hold of him and wring his neck but she says Stella can put the ID down on the kitchen table so we can all have a look at it if we like, because it's good for a laugh just like we thought it would be.

'You needn't make a fool of yourself all by yourself,' Stella says picking up her handbag and taking her ID out. 'I'll show mine too. Then you'll see something.'

'Hasn't Gus-Seep got one?' I want to know and Gus-Seep puts down the Saturday horse bible and says of course he's got one. Did he look to me like a person who would want to be left out? And he comes and stands by the table and joins in the show.

He pulls his ID out of his pocket and slaps it down as if it's the ace of spades and a winning card and my grandmother takes her glasses out of her overall pocket and puts them on her nose and when she sees Gus-Seep she laughs so much she says she better sit down before she falls over and Gus-Seep says he doesn't know what's so funny.

'Come and have a look at your uncle,' my grandmother says. 'You too, Stella. Come and have a look at what your brother looks like. If you ask me he's been hanging around with Philander for too long. He's starting to look like a proper crook.'

It's true and when we look at Gus-Seep's picture we say he better watch out because he's starting to look like a hoodlum and a gangster and we can't stop laughing.

'I'm glad to give you such a good joke,' Gus-Seep says and you can see he's sorry now for joining in and would like to take his ID back.

'I'm sorry,' my grandmother says when she sees the look on Gus-Seep's face. 'You mustn't take it to heart, but you really do look terrible. The way you look in this picture, next to you even Revd Rainbird's old Humphrey looks like Prince Charming and goodness knows, he's no oil painting.'

We're standing there with the three IDs on the table next to the teapot and we hear the front door open and slam closed so hard it's a wonder it stays on its hinges and my grandmother looks at Gus-Seep and then at Stella and then rolls her eyes towards Heaven because there's only one person this can be and that person is always in a bad mood these days so we know what to expect.

'Is that you, Gloria?' my grandmother wants to know. 'All of us are here. We're in the kitchen.'

She says the tea's still hot and she's putting a cup out for her this minute and the cup and saucer are already in her hands and Stella is pouring hot water into the teapot and taking the bead doily off the sugar and the lid off the biscuit tin.

'If you want a good laugh, come and look here,' my grandmother says and when my mother walks into the kitchen she pushes the three ID books forward. 'Come and look at your family, if you can stand it,' she says. 'It looks like a proper rogues' gallery.'

My mother is in her street clothes and before you even see her you can smell her scent coming down the passage reaching out for you, telling you she's right there and never far away and she'll never allow you to forget it.

When she comes into the kitchen she's busy pulling off the scarf around her neck. She's tugging it out from under the wool collar of her jacket as if it's done something to make her cross.

We know her when she's like this. It's as if she has brought the winter cold from outside right into our house with her.

She doesn't greet us. She doesn't even look at us. She's looking down and pushing her hair out of the way, lifting it up heavy in her hands, then letting it fall outside the back of her jacket and her scarf coming loose is full of leaves and flowers, bitter orange and dark green and brown like the bark of trees, so it's like the day outside and her mouth is a thin red line and you can see that even if she was in a mood to try she wouldn't be able to find a smile for us.

She pulls off her red wool gloves and her hands come out like cinnamon with red nails as if little bits of glove have stayed stuck on the ends of her fingers.

She looks at the IDs lying on the table and then she looks away. She sits down and Stella hands her cup to her and she picks it up and breathes in the steam and wraps her hands around it to feel the warmth and then she looks up and she looks at us from one face to the other and we aren't laughing any more and she doesn't have anything to say to us and our day is spoiled even though my grandmother tries to make it better.

'Speaking of pictures. I've got something for you, Gloria. I've been saving it up for a surprise but today's as good a day as any, while we're all here together.'

She goes to the kitchen drawer and takes out an envelope and it's all the pictures old Dollie took of me. What Stella calls My Life In Pictures. The Dollie once-a-year pictures my grandchildren are going to have a good laugh at one day. My grandmother has kept them to one side all these years and now she puts them on the table for my mother to see.

'I've been saving these up for you,' she says. 'We've had one taken once a year since you left. I told Lily one day when you came back you'd like to see them and here you are.'

They're tied together with a blue ribbon and they lie on

the green plastic tablecloth between our finished tea things, right next to the funny IDs and my mother looks at the top one of me in my school uniform in my year without teeth and she puts her teacup down so hard in the saucer that the last of the tea splashes brown all over the place and says no, thank you and pushes her cup away and gets up from the table and she won't even look at them.

'These are your pictures,' she says. 'They've got nothing to do with me.'

'But they're for you,' my grandmother says and she meant it nicely as a surprise to cheer my mother up and you can see she doesn't understand when my mother says thank you all the same but as far as she's concerned the pictures are markers on a long road of lost days and they're not hers to take.

'I know you mean well,' she says. 'That's the trouble. You always mean well but you don't actually understand. You can't give me back those years. No-one can and the pictures can never make up for them.'

She picks up the pictures and gives them back to my grandmother right in her hand and to be sure there's no mistake she closes her hand right over them so you can't even see them any more.

'These belong to you,' she says. 'It's all yours to keep and no-one else has the right to a single minute of it, least of all me.'

We're all looking at her and we must look funnier than any ID ever could. Our teacups are out on the table, our lunch is on the stove and we're thinking my mother must be the strangest woman in the history of the world and we will never be able to do anything right as far as she's concerned but she doesn't care.

She picks up her scarf and walks out of the room and we can hear the door of her own room slam closed behind her.

My family look funny in their ID but my grandmother says we mustn't mind too much about that. It's the way the Good Lord saw fit to make us and handsome is as handsome does and at least we know who we are now because at last the Government has decided to tell us.

She says one day when I get ID, if I promise to carry it on me always, she'll think about letting me go out without my name and address label pinned into my coat somewhere.

But I know what my grandmother's like and I'm not building up my hopes on that score. Stella says she doesn't think any of us will live to see that day. We all know how my grandmother worries about me and doesn't like me wandering around on my own and if I'm two minutes late coming home she is always on her nerves and expecting the worst.

Stella says she thinks when I'm a hundred years old I'll still be walking around with my grandmother's label pinned inside my coat just in case I get lost.

But I don't mind. A person gets used to this kind of thing and I have and after that we all go back to doing what we were before and we are waiting for our lunch and my birthday photographs are back in their drawer and I'm sitting by myself at the table looking at the IDs, my family's names and their numbers and I see that Gus-Seep's real name is Giuseppe Daniels.

This comes as a big surprise to me because I never knew it. I have known my uncle all my life and to me and to all of us he's always been Gus-Seep because that's what we call him and I could have gone to my grave without ever knowing I was wrong.

It took the ID to show me who he really is, so I suppose in that way we must thank the Government and one day if they ask me, I'll tell them that ID is good for something after all.

What happened with the bulldozers brought the whole Valley closer together but in the end Mrs Elias still had to go.

She wasn't the first and it was always the same, so you'd think you would get used to it but you don't.

Those that are moving on always come to say their goodbyes and when they're over they walk away and we stand at our gate and wave to them and shout after them and say good luck and happy landings and all the best.

We say we'll never forget them and they say they'll come back and visit us often and we must watch out for them and keep the teapot on the stove and the biscuit tin ready and be prepared because any minute they'll be walking through our door again, like old times, looking for a cup of tea and the pleasure of our company and sometimes they do come.

They come once or twice but it's a long way and two buses. It costs money and it's not the same. So after once or twice they don't come back again and we don't expect them to, so we stop looking out for them.

It's like bleeding to death little by little my grandmother says. At first you don't notice it and even if you do, it doesn't seem important because there are other things going on at the same time and when at last you wake up, it's too late to do anything about it and the shame of it is that people outside will think people in the Valley don't care. They'll think we're just the same as anyone else and willing to let our Valley die without a murmur.

That's what my grandmother says but dying without a murmur is not what my mother has in mind. She has other plans. She's told us so.

'No-one's going out of here with their tail between their legs like a whipped dog,' she says. 'As if they're leaving because of something they've done. As if it's their fault.'

When we ask what other way there is for a person who's had their roof taken away from them to go, my mother gives us a funny look and says she thinks they must go in a blaze of glory. She thinks they must go in such a way that the world will sit up and take notice and she's going to see to it they do.

So, that's decided and as far as my mother is concerned beggars can't be choosers because although I think in her heart she agrees with Portia that Mrs Elias is a fool who won't speak up for herself and deserves everything she gets, she is still the first one to go, so my mother's blaze of glory has to be for her.

Now her mind is made up my mother is a new woman. She doesn't go to town any more. These days she gets all dressed up in her smart clothes and goes out on the streets in the Valley and talks to whoever she finds there.

She stops women who are doing their shopping or minding their children or just standing at their fences talking to their friends. She doesn't mind. She tells them who she is and what's on her mind. She asks what they think about what's going on and what they're planning to do about it and some time while she's talking to them they get to like her and they can see where she comes from, that she was one of them once and they tell her they agree with her but they don't know what to do about it.

My mother wants to know if they agree that when Mrs Elias leaves she must go off in grand style just to show the world that although what the Government have done to her may have got her down for the moment it hasn't beaten her.

'Let people see that Mrs Elias counts for something,' is what my mother says. 'She lived here once and made her mark, and when she's gone we'll still be here. We'll know what was done to her and we'll miss her.'

That's what my mother says to the women in the Valley. She says if they wait for their men to do anything, they'll wait a very long time and there's no law that says women can't stand up for themselves.

She goes out very early in the morning just after the men have gone to work and she stays out until late and she'll say her same old story over and over again just as long as there's someone who is willing to listen to her.

My grandmother knows what's going on and when it's gone on long enough she gets hold of my mother and tells her she must stop what she's doing because she's causing trouble.

'You're going around talking ideas into people's heads

and if they listen to what you have to say, they're going to pay a price for it.'

'I'm not asking anyone to do anything,' my mother says and she's ice-cold and cross all at the same time because she hates it when anyone tries to stand in her way. 'I'm just asking people what they think and if they wouldn't do something about it if they could. That's all.'

'It's all right for you,' my grandmother says. 'You do what you please and there's no-one to tell you you can't. That's half the trouble.'

You can see my mother is not in the mood to listen to this but when she moves as though she's going to go out of the room, my grandmother tells her she can stay exactly where she is until she's finished what she has to say.

'These women have men to answer to,' she says. 'And it's the men who put food on the table and bread in the children's mouths and mark my words, they'll tell their women to keep out of it and away from you and if they don't listen you know as well as I do what will happen and you'll be the cause of it.'

'Then let these wonderful men do something themselves,' my mother says. 'No-one's stopping them but I don't see them out on the streets. I don't see them asking justice for their families.'

We may not have men in our house but I know what my grandmother means. The men around here say often enough that sometimes the only way a woman can learn a lesson is from the back of the hand and the women have the marks to show that on this at least the men's word is good.

'There's enough trouble in the world without you causing more just because you can't get your own way with the Government.'

'These women get beaten anyway,' my mother says and she's like stone. 'So, just for a change, it may as well be for something they believe in. They're not fools. They know what's happening to Mrs Elias today is going to happen to them tomorrow.'

My grandmother wants to know if the next thing she's

going to hear is that my mother's new friends, the women of our Valley who used to have some sense, are looking to my mother to save them.

She says straight out that if that's what's in their minds, she hopes they know they're putting their trust in a very weak vessel.

My mother doesn't say anything but she seems to think this is very funny because it makes her smile.

'They're not looking to me for anything,' she says. 'What they're looking for is to do something for themselves for a change and it's just as well because no-one else is going to lift a finger to help them.'

My mother's plan is simple.

Mrs Elias' big things are being taken by horse and cart and on the roofs of the Muslim husbands' cars but her small things will be carried by the women who have made up their minds to join in.

'We'll each take one thing,' my mother says. 'Just what we can carry and we'll carry it through the streets with us for the whole world to see and we'll walk with it all the way from the Valley to the Flats and when people on the way ask us what it's about, we'll tell them it's about a respectable woman who's losing her home and these are her things.'

She will walk in the front and lead the way and no-one can lift a finger to stop any of them because there's no law that says a person can't walk down a road carrying another person's odds and ends.

If the men will not stand up for what's right and show that we're sick and tired of being pushed around then it's up to the women and when almost all the women say they agree with her and will do what she says and will be happy to walk with her, my mother is happy again. Which is more than you can say about James.

We can hear James come in at the front door and down the passage lino without shouting a greeting to us like he always does, with men's feet like thunder.

We're in the kitchen sitting at the table. Stella's doing a bit of sewing and my grandmother's listening to her after-supper radio serial. The kitchen is warm from the stove and my mother has a book open in front of her and a shawl over her shoulders to keep her even warmer, as if she's never been so cold in her life before and she looks nice with her head bent down over her book and her shawl all around her and she doesn't even look up when James says he has something to say to her.

He's standing in the kitchen doorway with a big winter coat on. He looks like a cross bear and he asks us to excuse my mother and him but he wants to have a word with her behind closed doors.

My mother stands up from the table and pulls her shawl around her shoulders but she doesn't do it fast enough for James. He takes her arm and pushes her towards the door and we can see whatever he's got to say, he's not in a mood to egg her on this time and although they go into the front room and pull the door closed behind them, James is shouting so loud we can hear every word and if they listen hard enough and are interested, so can the people next door.

'What do you think you're doing?' he wants to know. 'Do you want to end up in jail? Is that what this is all about? Is there nothing else that will suit you?'

You can hear how unhappy he is and how cross.

'Have you gone completely out of your mind?'

'You're angry because I didn't discuss it with you,' she says. 'I almost did. I don't like doing things behind your back but I knew there wasn't any point asking what you thought about it. I knew what you'd say.'

'Then why are you doing it?' he wants to know. 'It's asking for trouble and you know it.'

Does she know every second family in the Valley is having a fight about it right this minute and the police will be talking about it soon too, because once my mother finished talking people's heads around, what looks like a walk to the women in our Valley, who are trusting kind of people and eating out of my mother's hand, will look very

241

much like a protest march to anyone else, not to mention the boys in blue who are more than ready for my mother since she sat on the steps of Roeland Street.

'You know what's going on,' James says. 'You know how things have tightened up lately. The Special Branch are just waiting for someone to do something stupid like this. They're waiting for you, Gloria. They've been waiting for you since Roeland Street.'

'Then that's the way it has to be,' she says and James says when she gets in this kind of mood it makes him absolutely crazy.

'I can't deal with you when you're like this,' he says. 'I can't go down to the Government cap in hand day after day, begging and pleading and trying to make them see sense and at the same time be sick with worry about you and what you're going to do next.'

'Then don't worry about me,' she says. 'You have your way of doing things and I have mine. That's the way it's always been and it's really quite simple. Just let me get on with it.'

There's a terrible argument behind the closed door of our front room. You can hear their voices banging against each other and each of them having their say and in the end when things calm down, all James can think of to say is that twenty miles from our Valley to the Flats is a long way to walk in anyone's language and even harder for any lunatic trying to do it in high-heeled shoes.

James is right about one thing. Twenty miles is a long way but that's what we said we'd do, so now we must do it and when we set out there's a small wind blowing with a winter bite in it and when we get out of the Valley and closer to the Flats it will blow even harder.

For the first part the road goes past factories and waste-land and then through Observatory and Salt River where people are still living although we don't know for how much longer because they are black spots, same as us.

Then it opens up across the sandy Flats past the golf course where the river is broad and flows slowly and there are willow trees and grass banks, where people have picnics in the summer and long-legged birds that walk at their leisure, and then it becomes a highway again and goes past the power station and the sewage farm.

My mother has it all worked out. She knows exactly the way we must go and each of us will carry something of Mrs Elias'.

'If the Government think all Mrs Elias' things are good for is to be thrown out onto the street for everyone to see, then people should at least have a chance to see them properly.'

This is what my mother says and the other women agree. As far as we are concerned we feel the same way we've always felt. Mrs Elias has nothing to be ashamed of as far as her things are concerned.

We will each carry something of hers for all the world to see and the world can look as much as it likes and all it will see is that Mrs Elias' things are no different to anyone else's.

We go down to Kitchener Terrace the day before the walk to pick and choose what we want to take, everyone walking in and out of Mrs Elias' house in ones and twos and threes and not just standing at the front door like they used to, and Mrs Elias is there in her apron and doesn't say anything at all, so, in that way, things have changed.

There's a Spanish dancer with a doll face and a real lace dress and a tablecloth with bunches of flowers embroidered on it. There's a clock, a green glass water jug and an egg-timer that looks like a chicken.

We help ourselves to just what takes our fancy and we do it with Mrs Elias standing right there watching us and it feels very funny to see all the neighbours picking and choosing and helping themselves to a person's things while they're still alive.

The only time I've seen this before is when someone dies. Then you're allowed to go into their house and take a little something away with you for a memory and, in a way, this is also like that, although it's not like that at all because Mrs Elias is standing in the corner watching us with big

243

eyes as if we're taking her things for ourselves, which we are not.

I think she's frightened of us although she doesn't say anything but we're only trying to help her and I'd like to tell her not to worry because tomorrow we'll give all her things back again but I've seen the look in her eyes and I don't think this will help, so I make up my mind and pick up the doll and leave the house quickly without even greeting Mrs Elias and I can see she doesn't even notice.

Even though the Muslim husbands won't let their wives walk with us they don't mind if their children come with messages to say their mommies are with us in spirit and will do what they can to help us on our way.

They have sisters and cousins all along the road and we must watch out at the mosques and the Muslim shops because their children will be there waiting for us with food and drink. They'll give us a place to sit down if we get tired and money for bus fare home if we need it.

They want to see us on our way and we say their children must tell them we'll look up at their windows as we pass by, so they can wave us good luck and goodbye and we will wave back.

There have been big fights at our house about my mother's 'little walk'.

My grandmother says she doesn't believe in this kind of thing and she's far too old for it now. She won't come with us and she doesn't want me to go.

'I don't want a fight about it,' my mother says. 'But Lily's coming whether you like it or not. I've made up my mind and you may just as well make up yours. I'm the best judge of what's right for her when it comes to a thing like this.'

You can see my grandmother's tired and not in the mood for a fight but she's not going to keep quiet either.

'This is your battle and it's grown-up business,' she says. 'It has nothing to do with a child and it isn't right to drag Lily into it. She should be in school doing her lessons, not parading around the streets looking to be locked up.'

'Leave it alone, Mommy,' my mother says but my grandmother won't leave it alone.

She turns around from the sink where she's standing and says my mother's had a very good time throwing her weight around and getting her own way and having people dance to whatever tune she chooses to play.

'No-one likes to open their mouths to you,' she says. 'They may not say it out loud but they know how you live your life. Some of them seem to think you're some kind of hero because of it but that's not my opinion. If they asked me I would have told them.'

'That's enough, Ma,' my mother says. 'You don't know anything about it.'

'I'm not a fool,' my grandmother says. 'I know what's going on. People say you make your money working "posh joints" in the Jo'burg townships. What do you take me for? They can dress it up any way they like, I know what people are talking about when they talk about a shebeen.'

We all know about shebeens. Natives are not allowed to drink so that is where they have to go when they want to have a few. Drink makes them mad and dangerous and puts their minds on murder and if they're caught at it they will find themselves in hot water and very big trouble. But at the happy houses they can take a chance and have a good time and drink as much as they like and no-one minds. Brandy, gin, *mampoer* and even *skokiaan* that goes down like fire and kicks like a mad mule and makes you drunk in ten seconds flat. Just whatever they like. No questions asked.

'I'm not new in this world,' my grandmother says. 'I know all about it. As much liquor as anyone wants and a nice fat envelope of money in the right hands and that's the police taken care of and never mind what the law says. I'm sure you all have a good laugh about that.'

'It's a business, Ma. I didn't make the rules about who can have a little bit of pleasure and who must go without,' my mother says. 'It's just another way of making a living. The same as running the corner café or the bobby shop or standing behind the counter in a jewellery shop and

245

watching as your life goes by and old age comes running to meet you.'

You'd think she'd be cross and shouting but she isn't and you'd think my grandmother would take her chance and leave it alone before the fight gets even bigger but she won't.

'It's a business outside the law,' my grandmother says. 'You think that's so smart? The Good Lord saw fit to put you in the front of the queue when it came to giving out brains but when He sees how you use them He must be thinking He's made a big mistake.'

'You really don't understand, do you?' my mother says.

'You think I'm a stupid old fool,' my grandmother says. 'But I understand one thing that you don't. I understand that God gives the shoulder according to the burden. Life here may have been too hard for you but other people put up with it. They don't take the coward's way.'

'I'm not other people,' my mother says. As if we don't already know all about that.

They have said all they have to say except when it comes to the subject of me.

'Leave Lily out of it,' my grandmother says. 'It isn't her fight and it isn't her time. Her time will come soon enough.'

'If Lily's time isn't now, then when do you think it's going to be?' my mother wants to know. 'If you have your way one day she'll be sitting in a hole out on the Cape Flats somewhere wondering how she got to such a terrible place and why no-one did even the smallest thing to try and stop it.'

That is what she says and that is the end of that.

I know my mother is taking a chance and we can all end up in big trouble and maybe even in jail but that won't stop her and if she says I must walk too, it doesn't matter what my grandmother thinks about it, that's what I will have to do.

I am out of my bed, scrubbed clean and dressed, with a jam sandwich pushed into my hand and being pulled down the road by my mother even before the sun is properly up and my mother is smart as paint. You wouldn't think she'd been in her bed at all.

When we leave my grandmother is in her room with the door closed. She doesn't come out to see me on my way and say goodbye to me and my mother says I can't knock on her door and wake her up because it's early and I mustn't disturb her although, between us, my mother and I have already made enough noise to disturb the dead, never mind my grandmother who we all know is a light sleeper and usually in her kitchen by now with our porridge and a coffee pot on the stove.

I have on a new coat which my mother bought me and good shoes and thick socks in case of blisters and I'm carrying the Spanish doll and when we get to the meeting place on the river road we're not the first there.

You can hear women's voices from a long way off and it sounds like bees buzzing and the sun is going up red and sulky in the sky and taking its time about it, the way it always does in winter and the cold and wet are jumping right up out of the ground and creeping into our shoes.

All the women who have come out are willing to walk for Mrs Elias and each one is carrying something of hers in their hands, so people along the way who see them will know what's happening in our Valley and know that even if we can't stop it we're not the fools people take us for. We know what's being done to us and we know it's not right.

Everyone has something to say and Mrs Elias is there too and she keeps saying thank you, thank you and although she's trying to be nice and is tidy in her best coat and headscarf her feet look thin and small and they're pushed into old shoes stuffed with newspaper.

She smiles all the time and keeps tucking her hair away into her scarf but she doesn't really look at us and even when she does, you can see she doesn't see us. I don't think she really understands what's going on.

My grandmother told me I mustn't be afraid of Mrs Elias and I must never turn away from her, no matter how funny she acts.

She only acts the way she does these days because her

spirit is broken and a broken spirit is not much different from a broken arm or leg. It shows itself in a different way. That's all.

My mother leaves me with some other girls but she hasn't forgotten me even though she's the leader and I'm only small fry at the back because the rule is girls behind grown-ups who walk more slowly and will set the pace.

While we're still getting ready she comes looking for me and, in front of everyone, she pulls the collar of my blouse straight and tucks it under my coat. She bends down and pulls at my shoe laces to see they will stay fastened and then she stands up and checks my plaits with a little pull on each and my Alice-band, to see that it will stay in place, so when the police come and take me to jail, at least I will be tidy and no disgrace to my mother and our house.

I can see people are looking at us sideways because no-one else has a mother like mine and they aren't used to seeing us together and I suppose they wonder what she's telling me, whispering in my ear as if we are old friends and have secrets together.

I could have told them if they asked me. She says I must be a good girl and behave myself and it doesn't matter how long the road is, she wants no complaints.

Having a mad woman for a mother is not the easiest thing in the world.

This is what I'm thinking about while I stand in the river road stamping my feet with the others and blowing steam out on the air and holding Mrs Elias' Spanish doll against my chest and I'm thinking about it so hard that I don't even see Revd Rainbird stepping out of his house next to the church and old Humphrey who is being left behind sitting behind the gate with a long face.

Revd Rainbird is neat and tidy and his hair is combed flat. He has his big cross around his neck hanging down to his waist and his Bible's in his hands and he says if my mother has no objection he would like to give his blessing to our march and say a few words.

'I don't think it will hurt us to bow our heads,' he says.

'And then, if you ladies have no objection, I think I might step out with you.'

It is the last thing anyone expected and we all got a big surprise and I don't know what my grandmother will have to say about it when she hears but in my opinion a person is allowed to change their mind if they want to.

Revd Rainbird says a funny thing has happened to him.

'I was waiting for God to show me the way,' he says. 'Some people may say it's been a long wait but maybe even while you're thinking that you'll find it in your hearts to say better late than never.'

You can see my mother isn't impressed. She asks him if he knows we aren't going to Damascus and is he quite sure the way God showed him was the same road we happen to be taking to the Cape Flats and he doesn't answer her back and start a fight. He holds up his hands and says we should pray and we put our heads down.

The river road where we begin is a nice flat walk and as we come to the first turn in the road there are women with their shopping bags on the ground next to them just standing there waiting to see if we will actually do what we said we would and they're surprised when they see us.

'We came to catch you out,' they say. 'We didn't think you'd do it.'

They thought what they heard was a lot of hooey which is the kind of thing people talk a lot around here when they can't think of anything else to say. But there we are, coming around the corner and so many of us and each one carrying a small thing of Mrs Elias' in front of them and holding it carefully as though it's come straight out of Buckingham Palace.

You can hear the women by the roadside talking about it and calling out names when they see someone they know. It's Marie and Elsie and Hettie and Onica and joking about do our husbands know what we're up to and there'll be plenty of trouble when they get home tonight and find out about it.

They're all laughing and calling out remarks and good

luck to one another. They say if the police come chasing after us we must call them boss and master and say we're decent women out looking for domestic work and they mustn't be afraid of us and everyone laughs and says the blue boys can come if they want to. We'll know what to say to them.

I don't care about any of them. All I hope is that my grandmother will come out on the street to wave us good luck and goodbye.

I hope she's not inside our house in our kitchen, staring at the stove and worrying like she sometimes does and thinking about our walk and my mad mother and imagining that because I am marching along behind her, I am busy turning out the same way as her, because I'm not.

This is what I'm thinking as I walk along that cold road with all the others holding hard onto Mrs Elias' doll.

I know if my grandmother comes out my last chance to see her is when we reach the next turn in the road. If I don't see her then, I won't see her at all and my eyes are everywhere and, because I'm not very tall yet, all I see are the women in front of me and all I can see of them are their half arms and the backs of their coats and their heads like little round balls on top of their shoulders.

That's all I see and then they move a little apart and I see my grandmother.

She's small but I would be able to spot her anywhere. She's standing on the bottom corner of our street with her headscarf tight around her head and her apron still on as though she made up her mind in a hurry.

I don't care. I would like to run to her and throw my arms around her, even if it sends Mrs Elias' Spanish doll flying and it smashes to pieces on the ground, even though my mother will kill me if I do something like that.

So I just hold the doll up high and wave it so she'll be sure to see me and she waves back and makes a sign, as if she's pushing something into the inside pocket of a coat and at first I don't know what she's trying to tell me and then I realize.

I put my hand inside my new coat and feel in the pocket

and deep inside, so I have to dig to find it, is my same old label pinned there, and I know my grandmother has not forgotten me.

She must have come into my room in the night and pinned it there while I was asleep. So it's our secret and I think it's the best secret in the world and I smile from ear to ear and nod my head like mad so she knows I know what she's done and when I begin nodding she nods back and she's smiling too and she waves some more but she's happy now and I am safe.

Now I can walk with my head high and people can look at me if they like and whisper behind their hands who I am and if they want to say I'm my mad mother's daughter that's fine by me because I'm also my grandmother's grand-daughter and they can put that in their pipe and smoke it and I don't care who sees me now.

My grandmother always talks about the day the Lord has made. She says the Lord makes all our days, every single day of every single life and all I can say is He must have been on time and a half when he made this day of our walk because no-one who was there will ever forget it and none of us was expecting it to turn out the way it did.

People came out just to have a quick look to see for themselves, the way people do, but once they'd seen us they could see we meant business and so some of them made up their minds and left their shopping and their children with their friends and said they would walk a little way with us to keep us company and some of them asked if my mother was the woman from the steps of the Roeland Street jail and if she was, she was just the type of woman they would be pleased to walk a little way with because she was a fighter and a woman to be reckoned with and those who didn't walk with us clapped us on.

'There's big trouble coming,' people were saying. 'The Valley women are on the march and their minister's with them, walking ahead with his cross in the air and the police will never stand for it. They'll all be beaten up and in jail before the day's out.'

But all we did was walk along quietly carrying Mrs Elias' things with us and we didn't cause any trouble at all.

I thought about Carole-Amelia as I walked and wished her mother hadn't come between us the way she did because I would like to have told her what that day was like and I would have told her the truth.

I am no hero and I would have said so straight out. I would have asked her if she ever had a letter from anyone in jail before, because if she hasn't I will be happy to oblige.

After all, there is a first time for everything and I have an idea that the people standing by the side of the road watching us are right in what they say. My mother is going to march us all straight into Roeland Street and that will be a first time for me too.

It wouldn't worry my mother. I know that.

In Observatory the police are waiting for us and their cars are blocking the road. They hold up their hands to stop us and they ask what all this is about and Revd Rainbird steps forward to tell them and we all have to stop and I am the only one who isn't interested in the policemen. Everyone else is looking at them and laughing and making remarks. Nothing horrible. Just making fun of them because there are so many of them and we are just a few women and they are so young and stupid-looking and they look such fools.

All I have eyes for are the police dogs who they've brought with them for 'in case' and they don't look like real dogs at all.

They're much bigger and they don't carry on like normal dogs do, barking and running around. They sit like little kings in their wire cages behind the drivers in the police vans and they look down through the grille as if to let you know that someone has given them your name and they've got their eyes on you and are waiting for you and are ready.

I don't like it that they don't bark. It puts me on my nerves because I know that when the police tell them to, they can bark like thunder and give you such a fright you

252

almost jump out of your skin and sometimes the police let them do it just for the fun of seeing you jump because this makes them laugh.

So while Revd Rainbird and my mother are talking to the police, I stand there looking at the dogs and the dogs are looking back at me in the funny way those dogs have, not like a normal dog at all and I have a feeling it's me the dog wants and my heart starts to sink and the dog rolls out his big, wet tongue and his dog mouth lifts up at the sides and you can see the white flash of his teeth and if you didn't know any better you'd think he was smiling at you.

When we get to Salt River the factory girls come out in their work caps and overalls to see what's going on and why there are so many people out on the street and what all the noise and shouting is about and although they're supposed to be hard as nails and so sure of themselves I think they enjoy it more than anyone else.

They say we women can show a few other people a thing or two and they clap and dance and throw their hips and walk a little way with us in their factory clothes and shout at those who aren't walking and are standing by the road just watching us. We know them. If trouble comes they are the type who will say they don't know us.

'Join in for a good cause,' the factory girls say and all along the way when people say why are we doing this, we shout back about Mrs Elias and the bulldozers and it's a funny day and there is a kind of fever in the air.

All we're short of is a dancing band and Carmen Miranda, Queen-for-a-Day, walking in front. But my mother is the queen on this day and in a way Jack Hoxie is too, who is decently dressed for a change and says she doesn't care if she's not on gang business and the girl gangsters see her because they may as well find out the same as everyone else that no-one in this world is going to push her and her family around and get away with it.

Twenty miles is not so bad. The ones who get tired and make up their mind to turn back pass Mrs Elias' things on to the joiners and those who have nothing to hold clap their hands and we sing as we walk just to keep us going, not Coon songs, just simple old songs we all know like 'January, February, March' and 'Emma Salemma' and 'Here Comes The Alabama' and every now and then someone will do a few little steps and twirl around just where she stands and the rest of us will clap and laugh and I wish my grandmother was there because although she says her voice is old and tired she has a really nice way of singing those songs and I think she would have liked to join in.

So it isn't so bad at all and when we get to the Flats there are many old faces there and their eyes are big in their heads. They say they heard about us and were waiting. They couldn't believe it but here we are and we have all that long road behind us and we're still in one piece and no-one could stop us and they take their hats off to us and then it all breaks up because they want to kiss us and touch us and take Mrs Elias' things from us to carry them the last part of the way to the place the Government has given her.

They say it's nice what we have done and even if the Flats can never be the Valley, they are not so bad. After a while you get used to them and we mustn't think we have walked for nothing or that this is the end of the line for Mrs Elias.

Wherever she lives Mrs Elias is still a Valley woman and they know her and Flats or no Flats, in their hearts they are still Valley people too and so this counts for something with them and they will see no harm comes to her. We mustn't worry any more. It is ourselves we must worry about now and everyone is talking at once and no-one takes any notice of me.

My feet are sore and I take off my shoes and sit at the edge of the pavement with my legs stretched out in front of me wiggling my toes, fat and hot in their socks.

I'm not getting in anyone's way and everyone is talking at the same time and shouting questions and pushing themselves forward so you can hardly see my mother or Revd Rainbird and I'm waiting quietly until my mother is ready and we can get the bus and go home and while I'm sitting there I feel the air making little puffs as though someone is blowing in my face just to tease me and make me cross and it's the start of a southeaster.

In the Valley we know that southeaster. It comes down like an express train and roars like a lion over our heads and you can see the tablecloth over the mountain and mothers tell their children that Van Hunks and the devil are smoking their pipes up on Devil's Peak and the smoke is pouring over the mountain.

When it's southeaster time you can walk home in the wind and watch the white horses charging across the bay and it may blow for days so that we hold onto trees to keep ourselves down and the girls' dresses blow over their heads and people hold hands to cross the road and the trees bend and we can laugh about it but it's different here. I can see that for myself.

Here there is sand everywhere and there are no trees. There are no proper houses either, just blocks of flats, three and four floors high with washing hanging out of the windows and children and chickens together in dust gardens behind broken fences.

There are plastic packets blowing in the wind, white and red and green, 'Shop 'n' Save' and 'Andy's Liquors' and 'Goolam Cash and Carry' and they stick to the fences and the dust is everywhere.

But I close my eyes and the wind blows me the voices of the Valley and they are the voices I know, talking nineteen to the dozen about this and that, and when I get home I can tell people I have seen the Flats for myself now and even though it is just like everyone says and no picnic I think I can live there and not complain if that is the way it is going to be.

14

A Poor Man's Daughter

It's only a matter of time now before we go. We know that now. Stella says it's only paperwork left to do and sooner or later our name will come up in the files.

Half the Valley is already flat from bulldozers and every day the small piece of sea we can see from halfway up our road gets bigger and bigger and when the southeaster comes down we don't worry about Van Hunks any more or sit down to tell his story.

All we worry about are the piles of bricks where there used to be buildings and when we go out we have to go carefully and half the time we don't know where we are any more. Every morning when we put our heads over our front gate and look down our hill we see another one of the old places is gone and the bulldozers are already busy knocking down even more and there's dust everywhere.

There is never any good news these days. My grandmother doesn't sing her hymns any more and Stella and my mother are getting on each other's nerves in a big way and making us all suffer for it.

Stella calls her the dancing duck because once when we went to the circus we saw dancing ducks. They looked fine and dandy jumping up and down on a tin sheet in time to the music and going nowhere fast and I thought it was a very funny thing to see but now I know all about those ducks because Gus-Seep told me and I don't think it was a lie. It's the kind of thing Gus-Seep knows.

He says before the show starts the duck man makes the tin hot and it's the hot tin that makes the ducks dance. We think they're happy but in fact they jump up and down because their feet are sore and it's sad really.

I think about it sometimes whether I want to or not. I can't help it because it's stuck in my mind and won't go away and I know now that it's not a good thing to know too much.

My grandmother says we don't have to say anything in front of my mother who is still running backwards and forwards to town but we must quietly make up our minds about what is going to happen to us.

We must start telling ourselves right now that if it comes to a move it won't be the end of the world.

We'll get our compensation money and the Government inspectors say if we put our name down and join the queue and then wait our turn they'll be willing to find us a new place in a building out on the Flats.

My grandmother says my mother's done her best which is all anyone can ever expect of her. She gave us hope in a bad time and in one way she was quite right. You must never insult the future by turning your nose up at hope. It isn't a thing you go out and buy twenty-cents-a-bag on the Grand Parade.

'Life doesn't always pan out the way we want,' she says. 'If this is what God sees fit to put our way, we must accept it and know He'll give us the strength to bear it.'

She is brave to talk like this but when she tries the same story in front of my mother all she gets for her trouble is a really terrible look but that doesn't worry her, she just looks back.

'I know how you feel, Gloria,' she says. 'And God knows I would like to take this cup from all of us. I pray every day that one day you'll learn to accept things instead of making life so hard for yourself.'

'You do what you must, Mommy,' my mother says. 'I can't fight with you and the Government at the same time. If you want to give in now, then that's what you must do but I haven't given in and neither has James and we never will.'

We all hear her say this but even if she doesn't know it things have changed and even she and James are different.

These days their voices are two-tone like the gangster's car that brought her back here in the first place. They're all light and bright when they talk to my grandmother and Stella and me and James even finds it in his heart to crack jokes and we even laugh at them just to be polite but when they talk to each other it's not like that.

They're angry all the time. You can hear it. They whisper a lot when they think no-one's watching them and they have too many secrets.

When James is at our house and the evening is over and it's time to leave, he stands up from our table and says goodnight sleep tight to all of us and gives me a hug and goodnight kiss and puts his hand on my grandmother's shoulder and his face next to hers and my mother jumps up and says she'll walk him as far as the front door and say her goodbyes there but these days she walks with him much further than that.

They walk all the way to the bottom of the hill together and no matter what the weather's like they stand down on the corner talking.

Sometimes they stand there for a very long time and when my grandmother sends me to the gate to see where my mother is and what's happened to her, I look down the road and see them under the streetlight and I can look for as long as I like because they never look up until the talk is over and my mother is ready to walk back.

I've seen them. James stands where he is and looks after her up the road to see she gets home safely and he won't move until she's turned at the gate to wave to him and even then he still goes on standing there. He stands there until she's had enough time to get safe into the house with the front door closed behind her and locked for the night.

I don't know what he thinks will happen to her between the corner and our house. I think he just likes to look at her, last look before she disappears because after that he has to go home and face the music with Evie.

*   *   *

Then one day it changes and my mother is different again and she comes through the door smiling and my grandmother asks her what she's looking so pleased with herself about.

She puts down her handbag and sits down at the table and you can see she's pleased as Punch. She looks as if someone has given her a present and we can't wait to hear what it is.

'I've done something I should have done a long time ago. I didn't go to Coloured Affairs today. I'm just wasting my time there anyway. Today I made up my mind and went down into town and joined the Black Sash.'

It's so quiet you can hear the soup pot bubbling on the stove and my grandmother says she thought my mother had run out of surprises for us but she was wrong and now she's heard everything and if we'll excuse her, she's going to have to sit down for a minute while she gets used to this new idea.

'You must have gone right off your head and they must all have turned colour-blind,' Stella says and my mother sits down at the table and makes herself comfortable and says she'll have a cup of tea, thank you, if anyone's offering and for her sister's information, the Sash have got serious work to do, and haven't got time to worry about what shade of skin you happen to have.

'Their work can't be so serious they didn't nearly fall on their backs when they saw you prancing through the door,' Stella says but she pours out a cup of tea and puts it down hard on the table and shakes her head when she looks at my mother.

The Sash are smart as a row of beans and very good at helping people fight for their rights and getting themselves in the newspaper while they're doing it, but if you look at their pictures they aren't what you would call beauties.

'What have you got to say about it, Mommy?' Stella wants to know and my grandmother says she's given up talking but seeing that Stella's asked her she'll say she doesn't like the idea at all.

'You've got big ideas, Gloria. I'll say that for you,' my

grandmother says. 'But you'll find out soon enough that the Sash isn't for a woman like you.'

'And what kind of woman is that?' my mother wants to know and you know when she asks in that certain way that you have to think twice before you answer and she looks at my grandmother and she looks at Stella as if to say which of them is going to jump in with an answer.

'You know what Mommy means,' Stella says and my mother says she doesn't. These days what their mother means is always different to what she says and you can waste an awful lot of time trying to work it all out. She hasn't got time for grown-up people who don't say once and for all what's on their minds and get it out and over with.

'You want me to say it, then I'll say it,' my grandmother says. 'The Sash is for high-society white women who've got someone to speak up for them and pay their bail when they land themselves in trouble. You're a coloured woman and a poor man's daughter and you'll find out soon enough that you don't belong.'

'And won't that make you happy?' my mother says. 'One thing's sure, anyway, if I didn't have the Government to keep me in my place I'd always have you and no-one can do a better job of it than you do. It must be all the years of practice.'

'That's enough,' Stella says but my grandmother says to be quiet and let them speak this thing out once and for all.

'You think I'm against you,' my grandmother says. 'It's not true. But I've been in this world a whole lot longer than you have. I can see what's coming and when it arrives you're going to find out you've got your place the same as everyone else and it isn't with these people and by the time you realize that, it'll be too late.'

'I can't manage on my own any more,' my mother says. 'I need somebody to help me now. Can't you understand that?'

She looks at us, from face to face to face and we look back and we don't understand. All we understand is that she's always made a big thing about being on our side and

260

sticking up for us but now she's going away from us and taking sides with the Whites.

'It doesn't really matter,' she says and for a minute I think she finds us funny and I wonder if she's going to laugh but she doesn't. She just shakes her head.

'What matters is that the Sash know what's right and they're prepared to stand up and be counted for it, and it makes no difference what colour we are or who's poor and who's rich. We're all going in the same direction and right this minute that's all I care about.'

Stella says that's all well and good but just for a change, before the whole Valley see her go off hobnobbing with whites, she could stop thinking about herself and spare a thought for the rest of us and what people will have to say about us now.

At least one person is happy. James is smiling all over his face and although the Sash wouldn't let any man in the back door, never mind the front, he's so happy when he hears my mother's joined you'd think he was going to offer her a medal.

'James is half the trouble,' Stella says the minute my mother's back is turned. 'Whatever mad idea Gloria comes up with, he'll say it's the best thing he ever heard in his whole life. Especially now. He'll say anything as long as it keeps her here for a little while longer.'

My mother is just as bad. She'll keep showing off as long as the limelight is on her and James is watching and so they make a fine pair. They'll keep egging each other on and they won't be satisfied until one of them lands in Roeland Street and it looks as if my mother's one jump ahead of James in the jail queue, because that's where she's going to end up if she joins in with those crazy Sash women who are forever running around saying nothing going on in this country at the moment suits them and holding up placards in the road for the whole world to see, just to show they mean it.

All of us, except James, think it's high time my mother learned her lesson but she's as stubborn as a mule and even

261

I can see that the only way she'll ever learn anything in this life is the hard way.

When I say this to my grandmother she puts down what she's doing and looks at me and says I'm getting very smart for my age.

'You've never said a truer word,' she says and she puts her hand on my head and looks down into my face. 'And it's breaking my heart to see it.'

My mother and Stella fight all the time now. It never used to be like this but these days they only have to look at each other and a fight starts.

At first I thought it was about the Sash because you only have to say the word Sash in our house and Stella's eyebrows fly up nearly to Heaven.

She says if the Sash women want something to complain about they can come and stay at No. 48 Constitution Street for a while, with the Government inspectors knocking at the door every second day with their papers in their hands asking when exactly we're planning to move along and our friends' and neighbours' houses being pulled down all around us.

That'll give them something to complain about she says and she always says these things when my mother can hear and she does it on purpose to try and make her angry.

We all know how my mother feels about her new friends at the Sash and how it's changed her life but although Stella is against this and we all know it, this isn't the real reason she can hardly turn in my mother's direction without giving her a dagger look and a few sharp words.

The reason she's so fed up with her is nothing to do with the Sash. It's about James and the same old song to a different tune that people are singing about him and my mother these days.

'Do you know Evie's mother is going around saying Gloria's a tart and a marriage breaker, that Evie's a nervous wreck because of the way Gloria's leading her husband around by the nose in public and never happy unless he's dancing to her tune.'

'I don't know and I don't want to know and nor do you,' my grandmother says and she looks at me and gives Stella a look to keep quiet but she won't.

'Lily's a big girl now,' she says. 'She's not deaf and she's not a fool. She knows what people are saying about her mother.'

She says since my mother made such a scene about Matilda at The Buildings, Philander is putting out terrible stories about her. Stories about gangsters and gang bosses who spend more time in jail than out on the street and how even when they're behind bars my mother just runs the show and does what she likes and the money rolls in in truckloads and how she's rich as Croesus and a real shebeen queen and a woman to be reckoned with now.

'I wish you'd stop saying you can't be bothered and you don't care. It makes the rest of us ashamed,' Stella says to my mother. 'I don't care if it's true or it isn't true. I don't see why you can't go out there and say once and for all that it's a great big lie.'

On top of it, my mother joining the Sash and prancing around the streets with a whole lot of high-society white women is the final straw.

People say what she's doing is looking after herself. When the time comes for her to move, it won't be the Flats she'll be going to. Her Sash friends will pull strings and it wouldn't surprise anyone if they saw to it that she moved to Constantia just so she could be close to them.

While Stella's going on, my mother sits quietly and listens and when she can get a word in she asks Stella if she's finished and got it all off her chest and feels better now and Stella says no.

She's finished with the Sash and shebeens but she hasn't even started about James and as far as she's concerned there's a lot to say there too and she can't keep quiet any more.

She says if my mother's got James so tight around her little finger that he doesn't know right from wrong and if he

263

can't think for himself any more then it's up to her to do what's right on his behalf.

'We all laugh at Evie but she's not really a bad person and no-one can blame her for the way she feels about you. James is her husband after all. She's the one he promised before God to love and to cherish, not you.'

'Have you finished now?' my mother wants to know and it's hard to know just by looking at her whether or not she's cross.

'Let him go,' Stella says and she says it nicely as if she knows what she's talking about and isn't being unkind. 'Tell him you can't see him any more and tell him why. It's gone on long enough, Gloria. You're both grown up now and it has to stop sometime.'

I know what my grandmother says is true. What you see at the Saturday matinee at the Gem isn't the end of the story as far as love and romance are concerned but you learn some things up there on the silver screen and I'm not blind.

I saw what I saw on New Year's night at The Buildings and I know my mother hasn't got time for any other man the way she has for James, except Seepie and he's her own brother so he doesn't count and anyway I don't think she would have sat a whole night on the steps of the Roeland Street jail for Seepie.

I know my mother by now. She would have sat there for ever if that's what she had to do and she did it for James.

In the pictures that would be love and romance but I don't know what you call it in real life and my grandmother won't tell me.

All she'll do is give me a funny sideways look and say I'm too big for my boots and she's never known a child with a head so full of funny ideas.

She says although I don't know Evie I must never forget that James is a married man and Evie is his wife and my mother is only an old friend and that's the end of that story and she doesn't want to hear another word about it.

Then she's busy and doesn't have time for my nonsense.

She says she has better things to do than answer my silly questions. But she won't look in my eyes when she says it.

The Black Sash is not as bad as everyone says and although they interfere all the time and upset people they have a special way of doing it.

First they talk to each other and then to anyone else who will listen to them and then they make up their minds and when their minds are made up, they put on their sashes and take their handbags and go and stand in the streets with their placards and make sure they get in people's way.

Stella says for a change my mother's got company and isn't alone. At last she's found a whole lot of troublemaking women who think the same way she does.

She may be right but my mother's happy now. When she comes back from the Sash office at night she closes our front door quietly behind her and calls out hello to us in a nice way and when she's washed her hands and tidied herself she comes to sit at our table and has stories to tell us and although terrible things are happening all the time and some of the stories are really hard lines, some of them are funny too and my mother's face is pink and full of smiles when she tells them and she looks really pretty.

The women at the Sash are nice and although they're white high society and have cars of their own and maids at home to do their work for them, we mustn't be fooled by all that. They know what hard work is and they're not afraid of it.

There's a woman who comes in there sometimes and my mother is very taken with her. Her name's Katy van Breda and the way my mother goes on about her you'd think she was a film star or something. My mother talks about her as if she's Christmas.

Every second word is about her. It seems as though everyone down at the Sash talks about nothing but her all the time and my mother is no exception.

In the end, when we've heard about two hundred stories

about Katy van Breda, we ask my mother what it is that's so wonderful that people can't stop talking about her and my mother says it is because there's nothing in this world that Katy van Breda is afraid of.

She says you can take one look in her face and see she's as fearless as a lion and that's something my mother really admires in a person, especially in a high-society girl like Katy who doesn't have to do the things she does.

Katy's father and mother are well-known people. You can read about them and see their pictures in the newspapers all the time and sometimes there are pictures of Katy too but she isn't interested in that type of thing and if she comes into the Sash office and someone puts a newspaper with her picture in it in front of her she will pull up her shoulders and go on with whatever she's doing and not take any notice at all.

Katy is a lawyer and people always say it's hard to believe, because she's still very young and also because she's so goodlooking.

My mother says she doesn't think Katy even knows how pretty she is and it makes her cross, although she tries not to show it, when people say they can't understand why a girl like her, with looks like hers, who could have the world on a silver plate from her mother and father if that's what she wanted, would want to go around fighting other people's battles for them in the way that Katy does because there are some people who don't think what Katy does is a nice way for a decent young woman to spend her time.

Katy works for Legal Aid and she doesn't get any money for it. It's just something she wants to do. She has a little red sports car and it's no trouble to her to jump in it and go wherever she likes to sort people out and she'll do it any time of the day or night.

No place is too rough for her and she goes where no-one else would dare. Not even the police. Not even with guns. She doesn't care.

My mother says as far as gangsters are concerned she will go right up to them and she's always polite. She acts as if she doesn't see their gang tattoo or hear their rough language.

Things like that just wash over her. It's their story she's interested in and they aren't stupid. They know that, and the word gets around and after a while they will come out when Katy is looking for them and tell her anything she asks them, because they have never seen anyone like her in their lives before.

At first they thought there must be something wrong with her and they asked her out straight if she'd had her head read lately because not even the police carrying guns and driving with dogs in protected vans will go into their territory. Not if their lives are something that's important to them.

They told her they'd had her in their gunsights more than once and could have killed her any time they liked, right there and then if it suited them.

One gangster even said he was quite ready to kill her for hanging around his territory and poking her nose into his gang's business and the only reason he hadn't was because he wanted to know the answer to a question. Was she mad or what?

Katy said she probably was mad and he wasn't the first person to mention it but she'd rather hear it from him than anyone else because at least it meant he was talking to her and that's why she'd come looking for him. She told him she wanted to find out his side of the story and see that he and his gang got a square deal, no matter what they may have done. That's what Katy said.

The gangs are one thing but Katy would also go right into the native locations and that's really mad because everyone knows no-one in their right mind will do such a thing.

There are only Natives there and no-one knows the kind of thing that might go on there. For all we know they could hang around waiting for you and then catch you and cut off pieces of you to use for medicine and *muti* and leave the rest of you to die in your own good time, or they could cook you and eat you for their supper. We aren't sure and we don't know for certain and it's foolish to take chances.

All we know is that a person can go in and never come out and if their family want to take their life in their hands they can go in and look for them but they will have to go by themselves. It's no good asking the police. They won't go with you because they like life as much as the next person.

Katy said it made no difference to her and people seemed to forget the law was meant for all of us and it never changed. It was the same for everyone, Natives included, and it was her job to see that was the way things worked and she wouldn't listen to anyone who tried to stop her.

'There are plenty of stories about Katy,' my mother says. 'And some of them would make your blood run cold.'

'Why does she do it then?' I want to know. 'Why does she do all those mad things?'

'I don't know,' my mother says. 'Some people say she carries on as if she knows for sure God is taking special care of her. As if there's some kind of divine light over her and no matter what she does, no harm will come to her.'

Although we didn't show it, Stella and I nearly fell right off our chairs. Everyone in our house knows my mother and God are not the best of friends, so it is a big surprise to find Him back in the conversation after all these months and I must say you could take your hat off to Katy van Breda for that because she was the one who got Him there.

We thought my grandmother would say something to my mother about this and she did. She said to all of us that this was nothing new. It was the selfsame thing that happened to Daniel when he stepped into the lion's den and I could see my grandmother liked the idea of Katy much better after God and the Bible found their way into the picture.

'She doesn't care whether people like her or not,' my mother says. 'People come up to her on the street and spit at her and call her a kaffir lover.'

My eyes are big when I hear this but my mother won't stop. She says my grandmother can make eyes as much as she likes, it's the way we live these days and it won't hurt me to know such things because I'm going to find out about it sooner or later anyway.

'People have got hold of her and told her that she better watch out because one of these days they're going to see to it she's very sorry for taking sides with gangsters and Natives.'

'What will they do to stop her?' I would like to know but my grandmother says that's quite enough, thank you. We can change the subject right now because we don't need this kind of scare talk in our house but before the subject is changed I ask my mother if Katy isn't frightened when people talk to her like that. I know I would be.

'She doesn't care,' my mother says. 'When people talk like that she says it's just sticks and stones and she acts as if she doesn't hear them. There's one thing you can say about Katy. If she wants to do something she won't put up with any nonsense from anyone who stands in her way. She won't rest until she gets it.'

I put my hand over my mouth because I want to laugh. I can see Stella's face with her mouth open right in the middle of it and my grandmother with her eyebrows up and her lips pushed closed like a lemon as if to stop the words from jumping out all by themselves before she can stop them. We don't say anything at all. We just sit there quiet as mice and think to ourselves that we have heard that song before.

'I suppose it's put your head full of ideas again,' Stella says. 'But you better remember this kind of thing is fine for a person who's rolling in money and can afford to work for nothing. Her father's a judge, for goodness' sake. Do you think anyone's going to do anything to hurt her?'

She says she's heard about charmed lives but she never really knew what that meant before and now she does because she thinks Katy van Breda has been dished out one of them. She can do whatever suits her. It's different for a poor man's daughter.

When Stella talks like this my mother gets so angry with her she can hardly stay in her seat.

'If you think getting nasty phone calls and letters and being spat at in the street by total strangers is having a charmed life then you've got very funny ideas and I hope my life goes on exactly the way it is because if what Katy's got is a charmed life, I can live without it.'

I think what the gangsters say about Katy van Breda is right. She is mad.

If I was beautiful and had all the money in the world and a normal mother and a father as well, I wouldn't be running around native locations fighting other people's battles for them and having gangsters waiting with guns and knives to kill me.

I would be living in the lap of luxury and having a good time and that, as Gus-Seep would say, is a dead cert and something you can put your money on.

Daniel in the lion's den is a nice story but in a way it's like the pictures we see down at the Gem. It isn't a bioscope show but it isn't real life either. I don't want to upset my grandmother by telling her this but I think it's something we should all remember.

The important thing is that at least my mother is happy at the moment. That's because there always seems something to be happy about down at the Black Sash office. There certainly isn't at our house.

I don't mean to listen to other people's conversations but sometimes I can't help myself and then I listen on purpose and hear everything and once you've heard it, you can't pretend you don't know any more and that's what happens the night my mother says what she has to say to James and she says it under the fig tree in our own backyard.

Although I'm already in bed and meant to be asleep I can hear them from the moment my mother's key turns in our front door and the tap-tap of her high heels on the lino in the passage and James' feet in their men's shoes making a thump next to her.

James doesn't always come inside when they're out late because every time he's with my mother, even when they're out on important business trying to save what's left of our Valley, he gets into terrible trouble with Evie.

270

But trouble is in the air anyway. I can hear it in the way they move and talk.

I sit up in my bed with the fig leaves so still they're not even tickling my window and the moon shadows move on my white wall and I can feel trouble creeping up the backstairs and reaching out towards me with cool fingers like sea mist.

There's so much of it around that perhaps when James thinks about Evie and what's waiting for him at home, he decides a little bit more won't make any difference at all and that's why he stays although it's already very late.

They're hardly in the house when they're down the steps into the yard and sitting like they always have from the very first day. My mother in the deckchair and James in front of her on the rickety old stool Gus-Seep made when he was a carpenter's apprentice.

I kneel on my bed in the white princess nightie Stella made for me, safe behind my screen of new leaves and I'm on my soft warm bed of clouds and I lift up my arms like an angel with my white nightie falling down on either side of me and I look down and although James and my mother are close they look small and safe behind my leaves and I feel bigger and stronger than they are and I stretch my arms out wider to take them in as if I will bless them.

My mother is talking in quick, sharp sentences in that way she has when she's already made up her mind about something and James' voice is soft beneath hers, waiting to catch the moments when she stops to take breath, so that he can put something nice into them, in between all her anger, like soft centres into hard chocolate but you can hear from the way she just keeps on talking that he's wasting his time.

One thing about our house. We know trouble when we hear it and James knows it too and that's why he's there, sitting under the fig tree in our backyard listening while my mother talks herself out, when he should be at his own house with Evie.

I can see them under the yellow outside light. It's pouring over them and her face is floating free inside it like the moon and if she wasn't my mother and I didn't know her I could at least understand why people say she's the beauty of our family.

From where I'm kneeling on my bed, I feel so close it's as if I can reach out and touch them. I can see midges dancing in the light's beam and my mother pulling her cardigan closer around her and I suppose they think they're talking softly enough for secrets but they're wrong. Anyone who wants to can hear them. At least they can hear my mother. She's talking in that hard voice she sometimes has as if she doesn't care if the whole world hears what she has to say and every now and then James says 'shush' and puts his fingers to his lips and once he even put his hand over her mouth but I could have told him he was wasting his time.

Once my mother gets in that kind of mood she says what she wants to say and nothing in Heaven or on earth will keep her quiet.

She's half-sitting and half-lying in Stella's old deckchair and her legs are stretched out in front of her. It's late and she's pulled on the old green plain stitch cardigan that hangs behind the kitchen door. It's washed big and has sewn-up holes in it and I don't know why we keep it hanging there, except that sometimes when it's cold or begins to rain we throw it over our shoulders if we run out to fetch in the washing or go down to the wash-shed.

James has moved my grandmother's stool so it's in front of my mother and sometimes his back is between us but mostly I can see her quite clearly and she looks different. She doesn't look like herself at all.

The combs are out of her hair and it's hanging loose around her face, although usually she says her hair is just a nuisance and she doesn't know why she doesn't have it cut off so she doesn't have to worry about it any more.

She's wrapped that old cardigan around herself as if she's going to freeze to death and her arms are folded across her chest and you can see the skirt of her summer dress sticking out. You can see her bare legs and her feet in their high-heeled shoes.

At first they talk so quietly that it sounds like a little river murmuring along. First his voice and then hers. Talk like bees humming that can put you to sleep if you don't watch out and while they're talking like this she laughs once or twice in that way she has. Just enough so he'll know that whatever it is that's made her so angry, it isn't James and she doesn't want him to think maybe it is and be hurt by it.

You can see just by looking at them that it's the whole world she's cross with, but not James and they are happy together.

She bends down to take off her shoes and he bends down too and gets there first and he takes her foot in his hand and takes off her shoe for her, in the way Royston used to do for me when I got stones in my shoes on the way to Sunday School, except it's not in that way at all.

He holds her foot in his hand as though it's a present and then he touches it and puts it back on the ground and she lifts her other foot and he does the same and his head is bent down and she lies back in Stella's deckchair and looks at the top of his head as if she's surprised to see it. As if he's some stranger she's walked home with from the Valley meeting and she's never seen him before in her whole life.

'I knew I'd regret it if I came back here,' she says. 'I should have stayed where I was but I couldn't. Can you understand that? Does it make any sense to you?'

'It doesn't matter to me,' James says. 'I don't ask myself those kind of questions. You're here now. That's what's important. That's what matters.'

'Part of it is because of you,' she says. 'You were on my mind and I couldn't get you out of it. I never told you that and you never asked but you always seem to know everything so I took it for granted you knew that too.'

She tells him that when she left she vowed she'd never come back but she's always felt as if she was tied fast to the Valley by a rope and once trouble came and things started to go wrong it felt as if someone had begun to tug on that rope so that in the end she had no choice but to come back.

'I pulled against it in the beginning. I knew I'd made my choices and there was nothing here for me any more. I knew the wisest thing was to send money and keep as far away as I could but in the end I couldn't keep away at all and I suppose in my heart I knew that right from the beginning.'

She says she came back for my grandmother and Stella and me, to help us in our time of trouble because she thought she was the only one who could do anything to help us and in the end she hadn't been able to help us at all.

'It's funny, isn't it?' she says. 'It could make you laugh to think that the prodigal should be the one to come back thinking she can offer salvation.'

But James isn't laughing and she tells him how tired she is and she wonders if it ever occurs to anyone that she's human just the same as the rest of us. She gets tired just like we all do.

'I don't think I can face them,' she says. 'I don't think I can walk into that kitchen tomorrow morning and tell them it's all been for nothing and there's nothing more to be done. The Government have won after all.'

'You hate being forced to give up,' he says. 'I think that's what worries you more than anything else but it shouldn't because there'll be another day.'

'It's not just that. It's the way they are. Sometimes I look at them and think what they say about me is true. I must be off my head. Why do I get so full of anger because of them, when they won't do a single thing to help themselves?'

She lifts herself a little bit out of her chair and folds her hands in her lap and bends towards James with her face in the light and tells him that our world is like the buildings in the Valley, falling to pieces all around us. It's coming to an end and nothing will ever be the same again and we're too stupid to realize it or so beaten down we no longer care.

My mother is a woman with a thousand voices and I thought I'd heard them all. I've heard her mad with anger. I've heard her soft to James and full of love for Gus-Seep. I've heard the edge on her voice when she's trying to be patient with my grandmother and Stella.

I've even heard her when she's trying to find the right

words so that she can talk to me in the way a proper mother would but I've never heard the voice she speaks in now. It's different. It comes out all in jagged edges as if the breath lifting it is burning like fire and she feels it aching in her chest as if she has bronchitis and it hurts so much she will die of it.

'I've had moments when I've wanted to give up and walk away from it all,' she says. 'I've wanted to go away and leave them to sort it out for themselves.'

James leans forward and shakes his head as if he knows something she doesn't know. He picks her hands up out of her lap and lifts them and holds onto them between his own two hands as if he knows how cold they are and is keeping them warm and then he puts them close to his face and holds them there for a long time and he touches her softly, in a nice way, as if her hands are precious to him. As if he has touched her many times before.

'Do you remember, once, long ago, you asked me to go away with you? Do you remember that?' she wants to know.

She's the one now who draws his hands closer so her face is right against them and her voice gets caught in his fingers and I can hardly hear what she's saying and it is as if it's the secret of secrets that she's telling.

'I remember what you said,' he says and he says it softly and nicely as if it's no hard feelings, just days that are gone and the music and perfume gone with them along with all that water that has flowed under the bridge since then.

'What will you say if I tell you I feel differently now? What will you say if I tell you I want to go back and begin again; that I've changed my mind and it's my turn now and I'm the one who's asking?'

She has it all worked out. She says if they make their minds up nothing can stop them. She has money, enough money for both of them and this is not the only place in the world. There are other places. Whole countries that are colour-blind and if they want it badly enough the world can be their oyster and never mind about Evie. She's thought about that too.

'She's always threatening to leave. She's forever running

275

off, going back to her mother. Next time she goes, let her go and let her stay there. Don't go running after her. You think now she'll never get over it but she will. There are worse things that can happen to a woman than being left by a man. Much, much worse things and strong people survive and it makes them even stronger.'

She says it as if she knows what she's talking about but James says she mustn't talk like this.

'You're tired,' he says. 'You say so yourself. When you've had a good night's sleep, when you've thought about it in the cold light of day you'll be yourself again.'

When he says this it's her turn to pull her hand loose and put it on his mouth to stop him saying any more.

'Myself?' she says and they look at each other and they're more quiet than they've ever been together and the light is falling bright on her face.

'Which is myself, James?' she wants to know. 'Is that what's in your mind when you look at me the way you sometimes do? Are you asking which I am really, the girl who left or the woman who came back? Is that what you're asking yourself when you look at me and then look away again?'

'You'll be cross with yourself tomorrow for saying all these things and you'll be cross with me for hearing them.'

'There are a lot of things I've been sorry about in the cold light of day,' she says. 'More than you'll ever know but this isn't going to be one of them.'

'Being together is dreams,' James says and his voice is the one that's funny now. 'It's not real life. Real life isn't about running away. It's about staying put and making do and getting on with things. It's about learning to live with big compromises and small victories.'

Anyone can see just by looking that this isn't what she wants to hear and James can see it too.

'Don't you know?' he says. 'Haven't you worked it out after all this time? What we have is so much more, so much finer than real life could ever be and I would never have it any other way.'

This is what he says and when she hears it she pulls

away from him and the light is on her face and they sit there for a while looking at one another and not saying another word and in the end James gets up to go and she doesn't move at all.

He stands looking down at her and the light is dancing all around him making him shimmer.

All we hear about these days is trouble so that sometimes I think we're all just sitting around like sitting ducks waiting for it to come and get us.

The problem is that trouble doesn't always come marching along behind a big brass band, so even though we are on the look out we don't know who it will single out or from which direction it will come and when it does come, it comes to my mother and we are not the ones who see it.

It is old Dudda One-Eye Dollie, the first-year medical student, who sees it and his one eye doesn't let him down because he sees everything and goes straightaway to tell James about it and James comes to tell us what's happened and to fetch us in his friend's car and take us to the hospital.

My grandmother and I are sitting in the back of the car together and my grandmother is still in her apron and she's holding onto my hand for dear life because we only have a second-hand story. We don't know what to expect when we get to the hospital but the news isn't good and I'm crying because I don't know what else to do and James keeps on blaming himself which is not what my mother would want him to do.

My mother has been attacked by a policeman and is very badly hurt. All because she was running around in a black sash and not minding her own business and being egged on by James while she was doing it and that's what James is blaming himself for.

Men are funny and I don't mean James.

This thing that has happened to my mother started with

277

a man and when she hears it my grandmother says she isn't surprised. It's a well-known fact that it's usually men who start these things. If men don't get their own way they very often go mad and that's when the trouble begins.

She's seen it so many times in her life she's stopped counting and Dudda says he's in no position to call her a liar although he's a man himself and should stand up for men.

What happened is that some madman attacked his wife outside the Parliament building where the Sash were standing holding up their placards and minding their own business.

'No-one could have seen it coming,' my mother says and that makes my grandmother cry even more because my mother's sitting in a hospital bed with a tube going into her arm and she looks really terrible.

You can see every word is hurting her on its way out, so she has to speak very slow and quiet and we have to listen very hard to find out the story for ourselves.

The woman who was attacked was right next to her standing quietly and holding up her placard with the rest of them and the next thing my mother knew this poor woman was down on the ground and her husband was screaming and shouting and holding her down and bellowing like a bull and kicking her just wherever he could find a good spot to put his boot in.

Part of the trouble was that she knew this woman and she wasn't a woman really, only a girl, and her name was Isobel but they all called her Issy and Issy was scared of just about everything but she just couldn't live with things the way they are any more. She wanted more than anything to do what was right so she could get some sleep when she put her head down on her pillow at night and that's why she joined the Sash.

She came into the Sash office one morning, as timid as a mouse but with her mind made up and my mother, who likes that type of thing, thought it was wonderful and she kept on telling Issy exactly how wonderful she thought it was and giving her advice and telling her that the more you acted brave the braver you actually got.

The trouble is that when it came to things Issy was scared of, her husband was right on top of the list. She was scared almost to death of him and to his mind that was exactly the way things should be.

He's the kind of man who likes people to be scared of him and he thought it was up to his wife to show the way to everyone else.

So Issy went around saying her husband wouldn't let her do this or would never allow that or even that he would kill her if she ever stepped out of line and she didn't really have to pretend because she truly was scared of him.

She was too scared to tell him about being in the Sash and that was a big mistake because someone was bound to see her in the end. The Sash don't hide away in doorways or anything like that. When they stand up for what they believe they stand where the world can see them.

That's what they were doing. They were standing right on the steps of Parliament with Queen Victoria sitting on the one side of them and half Cape Town on the other and policemen all over the show to keep everyone in their place when Issy's husband came past and according to what Dudda says that was no accident either.

'His friends brought him to see for himself what his wife was up to,' Dudda says. 'You could see on his face what a shock it was to him. He didn't like what he saw and because all his friends were with him he had to do something about it.'

They were a whole lot of men together and pushing this one man forward and saying he should have a look at what his supposed to be off her head, too scared to say boo to a goose wife, Issy, is doing, standing draped in a black sash saying she wants kaffirs for neighbours and Blacks prancing around the streets as if they're decent people and worth something, looking at white women like Issy and her friends with everyone knew what on their minds.

They said it would serve all those bitches right if they got what they deserved because that's what they were asking

279

for, but how would they like it when it actually came their way, that was what they wanted to know.

That's what Dudda told us they said and I believe him. For one thing he isn't Gus-Seep and for another his one good eye was as big as it could get and still stay in his head and he was shaking all over.

One thing I remember about Dudda is that he is a shy kind of boy and can't stand fights which is more than you can say for Issy's husband.

Seeing Issy, black sash and all, was too much for him and his friends were all watching and poor Issy was piggy in the middle which, in my opinion, serves her right for being such a barefaced liar and expecting never to get caught out.

It didn't matter how red in the face her husband went or how much he yelled, Issy couldn't just leave the protest and pack up her placard and go home. Not even if she wanted to. Those women may be high society and look as if butter wouldn't melt in their mouths but they're hard as nails when it comes to that kind of thing. Once you're there with your placard in your hand you can't change your mind. It's in for a penny in for a pound. Those are the rules.

You're supposed to suffer in silence except Gus-Seep whispered to me that they don't really expect to suffer at all, so this must have come as quite a shock to them although they couldn't show it.

The point is that once you have your sash on you become another person and you don't say anything, no matter what happens.

When we asked my mother about it when she first joined she told us the Sash wasn't a tea party and keeping quiet makes everything more dignified so I suppose in a way you have to take your hat off to Issy. At least she stuck to that part of it although there was nothing very dignified in what happened after that.

Maybe she didn't say anything but what was there to say with her husband going red in the face and yelling and stamping the ground like a mad bull and his friends shouting that it was his job as a husband to put his mad bitch of a wife in her place.

280

This is what Dudda said and I know it's true because I could see he was beyond lying and he said he could see then what was coming my mother's way and he knew it wasn't going to be good.

My mother says we can forget what people say about the Valley, after what she saw she wouldn't like to be a fly on the wall and see what goes on in high-society houses once their doors are closed for the night, not if a so-called educated man can go berserk in the middle of Adderley Street and attack a woman the way Issy's husband did with all those other men looking on and half of them police in uniform who were supposed to keep the peace and no-one doing anything.

'No-one lifted a finger to help her,' my mother says in her new small, terrible, full of pain voice. 'That's what I can't understand. There were so many people there and no-one even tried to help her.'

James, who's standing right at the back, makes with his hands as if to say she shouldn't try and speak any more when it hurts so much but I don't think there's anything more she wants to say. Just that she can't understand how people can leave Issy cringing on the ground trying to protect herself while she's being beaten black and blue by her husband and no-one willing to lift a finger to help her.

It's the kind of thing my mother just can't stand.

Dudda says it happened so fast no-one could actually believe it was happening at all.

'It was really terrible,' he says. 'The man was like a lunatic. He was screaming even louder than the woman and his friends were shouting as if they were at a prize fight and looking for blood.'

Issy's husband was kicking her something terrible and pulling her around by her black sash and, as if that wasn't enough, the police dogs started barking and pulling at their leads and all you saw was big teeth and mad eyes everywhere.

'I've never seen anything like it in my life,' Dudda says and I believe him because old Dudda has never been the bravest and even talking about it was making him shake like a leaf.

It was too much for my mother. She threw herself across Issy so Issy's husband kicked her a few times too just for good luck because she happened to be there and getting in his way and it's a wonder she didn't lose a few ribs in the process instead of just having them cracked and a lung punctured and then a policeman chipped in and tried to pull them all apart and my mother says what happened then was not his fault.

He was trying to break it up and things got out of hand and he lifted up his truncheon, no-one knows why, except that's what they're trained to do and they don't know how to do anything else and he brought it down as hard as he could and he was a very big man and it landed in my mother's face because she couldn't pull her arm out in time to stop it even though she saw what was coming and she did try.

I can't see the sense of it. I just sit there smelling the hospital smell and listening to them talking and telling their story, my mother and old Dudda One-Eye, the first-year medical student who none of the doctors or nurses treat with any respect, and I can't see the sense of it at all and this is not the end of the story because something happened before my mother got into hospital and it involved Katy van Breda.

'Can you believe this?' Katy says. 'They've taken that madman away and the police refuse to charge him.'

She's so furious that's the very first thing she says even before she asks if Gloria's all right and two other Sash women sitting with her who can see how bad it is and are trying to stop the blood can't even be bothered to listen to her.

'Issy?' Gloria wants to know and she's sitting on the hard ground which refuses to stay still underneath her and her face, her neck and her shoulder are ice-cold and burning at the same time. There are splashes of blood on her skirt and she can't turn her neck.

'Some of the Sash people are looking after Issy and I think she's doing better than you are. We need to get you to a hospital.'

'I'm sorry.' The words won't come out properly and it hurts when they try to help her up and what she really wants is to sit down again or even lie flat in the road while she waits for the pain to go away but she can't do either of those things and she can't think of anything else to say.

'It's that stupid bastard that should be sorry,' Katy says. 'He should be put away for what he did here today, but he won't be.'

There are four of them all squashed into Katy's little red car and Gloria is in the front holding Katy's hanky up to her face but it isn't enough and she can feel her own blood wet and sticky in her hands.

'Hold on,' Katy says and her foot is flat on the accelerator and the little car is roaring and going as fast as it can. 'You just hold on. They'll sort you out as soon as we get to the hospital.'

But when they get to the hospital it isn't like that.

Katy jumps out at the outpatients and runs inside and comes out and there's a nurse behind her and she's talking cool and calm and giving the story and instructions as if the world is about to stop for her and do exactly what she says it must.

'This woman's taken the most terrible beating,' she says. 'She was unconscious for at least ten minutes but no-one was willing to call an ambulance. She's lost some teeth. I think her cheekbone's smashed and we'll certainly need a wheelchair.'

'I can see it's nasty,' the nurse says and she has a young, open face and she's looking down into the open car and behind her an ambulance stops with its siren still scream-ing and its red light flashing and people come out quick-smart at the sound of it and they're opening ambulance doors and telling each other to get a move on.

'It's over to you now,' Katy says. 'We've done all we can. I'll sort out admission forms and that kind of thing but for God's sake get her some kind of painkiller and a doctor to have a look at her.'

'You'll have to go to Somerset Hospital,' the nurse says. 'We can't treat this here. Those are our rules.'

When my mother told us this she said it was obvious the three Black Sash women hadn't heard about these rules because they stood looking at each other and at the nurse and the nurse was very young and red in the face but she knew about rules and was standing her ground and my mother saw another fight coming and there was nothing she could do about it.

She sat in the car with the hanky on her face and tried to call out to them to tell them they mustn't worry so much because the blood all over the place probably made it look worse than it was and perhaps they had been wrong to think she needed a doctor. Once it was cleaned up maybe it wouldn't look so bad. Perhaps they could find a chemist somewhere and get some antiseptic and fix it up themselves but Katy seemed to have gone stone-deaf she just kept staring at the nurse.

'Have I made some terrible mistake?' she wants to know. Her face is white as snow with anger and her eyes are like two blue diamonds flashing in her head and you can hear in her voice she won't stand for people who get between her and what she knows is right.

'Is this a hospital or isn't it because that's what it claims to be. There's a sign at the front gate that says so.'

My mother felt sorry for the nurse because she looked as if she was going to burst into tears. She didn't make the rules and a woman like Katy when she was crossed was not a woman you would like to come up against even if you were a lot older and wiser than the little nurse was and you could see she'd said what she'd been told to say and had no idea what she could say next.

'It is a hospital but we can't treat this person here,' she

says and you can hear in her voice she isn't so sure of herself now.

'It isn't allowed and there's nothing I can do about it. I'd like to help you but I can't. If your friend was bleeding to death in front of me, I couldn't help you. You'd still have to take her to the Somerset.'

My mother thought Katy was going to have a heart attack. It was terrible but even so it was funny and although her head was aching and everything was swimming in front of her she couldn't help thinking how funny it was because if Katy did have a heart attack then at least one of them was in the right place because the nurse could take her in right there on the spot and see she was looked after. That was allowed.

'Get out of my way,' Katy says. 'I'm going to speak to the superintendent of this hospital and ask him if he's ever heard of such a thing as the Hippocratic oath.'

Then she pushes the nurse to one side and marches straight into the hospital and ten minutes later she comes marching out again with the hospital superintendent behind her.

One thing you can say about Miss Katy van Breda, the top-drawer lady who you can't believe would ever swear or raise her voice, when she tells someone their fortune they know exactly where they can get off and that's exactly what she did but it didn't help at all which my mother could have told her and had tried to tell her but she simply wouldn't listen.

No-one likes to say it when people are good to them and Katy would never admit it but women like Katy and her friends are so used to getting their own way they really believe the whole world has nothing better to do than be ready and waiting to jump when they snap their fingers but my mother knew this time Katy was in for a disappointment.

She'd seen the look on the hospital superintendent's face before. It was the same look she'd seen on the faces of the men in the Government offices and at Coloured Affairs and she knew if Katy kept putting her foot down and demanding her own way they would be in for a very long wait. It could take all night or even longer. She'd found that out when she sat on the steps at the Roeland Street jail.

So she just sat in the car watching what was going on and waiting for Katy to finish so they could go to the Somerset because by that time she knew she needed a doctor and that was the only place they'd find one willing to help her. Her face was beginning to get really sore and she was hot and cold all over and shaking like a leaf.

Katy gave them what for. She carried on as if she was going to take the hospital apart brick by brick with her bare hands. She called the hospital superintendent a racist moron right to his face and told him he had no right to call himself a doctor when he was nothing better than a pig's arse.

When he said he'd have her arrested for disturbing the peace she called him a bloody fool and an incompetent but in the end she came away without so much as an aspirin.

They drove away with everyone staring at them and saying they were those mad women from the Black Sash who made trouble wherever they went but they had the cheek to act surprised when they got what they'd been begging for and what they deserved.

Katy tried her best and put up a good show but in the end she knew how badly hurt my mother was and how sore it must be and she couldn't stay and fight any more.

She got back in the car and sat behind the wheel with a face like stone and went foot flat down all the way back to town to the Somerset Hospital.

She drove as if the devil was chasing her. She didn't even bother to hit her hooter to get other cars out of the way but they saw her coming and got out of the way anyway and it had been such a day that my mother thought all they were short of now was a traffic cop on a motorbike coming after them for speeding.

She would have felt sorry for him if he did because she could see Katy was just ready for someone to stop her and ask her what she was up to because she was in a mood to tell exactly what she was up to and why and a little bit more besides. So it was just as well it didn't happen.

My mother would have liked to say something to Katy to make her feel better but by that time her face was very sore and she was feeling really sick and was glad Katy was driving the way she was because she wanted something for the pain and she would be glad when they eventually got to any hospital that would take her.

I see them all sitting around her bed and I see myself too, standing there still in my school uniform listening to them talking and putting in their ten cents' worth and it still doesn't make any sense to me.

My mother's face is split right open. It's all swelled up and has stitches in it. Her eye is closed up and a terrible purple colour with just a few eyelashes like little wires sticking out of it.

Some of her teeth are broken and her arm sticks out from her body bandaged to a board so she can hardly move. She is sitting in a narrow hospital bed and my grandmother is sitting next to her wiping her eyes with her apron because although she keeps on saying how grateful she is that God saw fit to spare my mother and not to take her from us she can't stop crying and the tears are coming out of her face like a fountain and my mother is holding her hand, trying to tell her that it isn't the end of the world but I am not so sure.

When I look at her it hurts me in my heart as though I'm the one who's been kicked in the ribs and had my face all smashed up and I can see it hurts James too.

I know this because the whole time we are there and everyone is talking James stands behind the others and doesn't say anything at all but there are tears in his eyes and I can see them and what I want to do is stand a little bit backwards so I can take his hand and hold onto it but I don't do it because I don't know how to.

I stand where I am smelling the hospital smell and I turn to look behind me and we look at each other and don't say

287

anything but I know his heart aches because mine does too and there really is such a thing as two people having a heart to heart but it isn't the way we think it is because it's silent and has nothing to do with words.

James is a wonderful actor. He should have been on the stage. He goes to visit my mother every day. He takes her newspapers and books and asks her questions about what she's read in them.

She says it must be because he can't help himself. Once a teacher always a teacher but he says he's checking up on her. He wants to be sure she's still with us and knows what's going on.

He knows this kind of talk makes her cross. That's why he does it.

Sometimes being cross is what keeps my mother going and as soon as she has her fighting boots on and is getting one up on him again and ticking him off he'll know for sure she's her old self again.

He takes her flowers, purple gladioli, chrysanthemums the colour of gold, and red and yellow dahlias, so she always has something nice to look at and the weather is getting finer and sometimes they sit outside under the corrugated iron roof of the hospital stoep and take in the afternoon sun together.

They sit there when they can, each in his own chair and my mother with a blanket over her legs like an old lady and the table between them with my mother's glass on it with a straw so she can drink and she drinks very slowly because everything hurts her.

They sit there for hours, sometimes him talking and sometimes her, getting little words out through her sore teeth and jaw wire and because I know what my mother is really like I can't believe she can sit so still for such a very long time, with her hands in her lap and the sun on her sore face and just James for company.

The people going past, the doctors and nurses and the other patients, have given up on them. They don't even try and work out what it is they say to one another or why they want to tire themselves out with a lifetime of talk in just a few weeks of afternoons.

James likes to give my mother good news when he can and he always tells that first to cheer her up but he doesn't hide the bad news just because she's in hospital.

'You can't go on lying around here forever,' he says. 'There's still lots of work to be done and there isn't any place for slackers.'

She likes that kind of talk. It shows nothing's changed. The Government may be sitting back, congratulating themselves on getting rid of us and thinking they're winners but it's only just beginning and all they've won is the first round.

'You feeling ready to take them on again?' James wants to know. 'We're still waiting to see who the champion of the world will be and my money's on you and so is a lot of other people's.'

'You be the champion if that's what you want,' she says and he tells her he'd like to and he's willing but he can't do it without her.

My grandmother says James does my mother a world of good because he's so full of the kind of fighting talk that's always music to her ears. But he's only full of fighting talk once he gets inside the ward where she is. When he's standing outside in the corridor, it's a different story and sometimes he has to wait for a very long time before he gets up his courage and opens the door.

He stands with his back against the wall and his head down, holding his books and flowers in front of him and he stares at the ground. He's not so full of fighting talk then.

He doesn't see the nurses going up and down giving him funny looks, or the people in wheelchairs being pushed past by orderlies in a hurry and nearly knocking him over.

He just stands there for as long as it takes, with his presents in his hand and his thoughts locked in his head and the rest of the world goes by and he doesn't even notice it.

Once he's opened the door it is different. That's when he could put Laurence Olivier out of business.

My mother's face will never be right again and she knows it. She knew it when she was lying on the ground and couldn't lift her arm up in time to protect herself and the truncheon hit her.

She says she could hear it coming through the air and it made a funny sound as if it was singing. Imagine.

The doctors say if it had been her arm that was hit the bone would have been broken in a million places. That's how hard the hit was and my mother is really a funny kind of woman. When they tell her this she shrugs and doesn't say anything. She asks Stella to bring her a mirror, that's all, and Stella takes the silver-looking hand mirror my mother uses when she washes her hair and she looks at herself long and hard in it and it seems to me as if the good side of her face, the side that's still working, smiles a little bit.

I've seen her looking in that mirror, holding it quite still, turning her face from side to side and looking at herself as if it is some other person's face she sees.

I don't know what she's thinking. I don't even know if she's surprised at what she looks like now.

She must look at her face a lot because if she doesn't hear you coming that's what you'll find her doing, sitting by the window in the light with the mirror in her hand and James' books and papers lying closed on the table next to her bed and for a change Stella can't say she's looking at herself out of vanity because she isn't beautiful any more and she's never going to be again. Those days are over.

Katy van Breda came to the hospital to see my mother but she wasn't like the other visitors. She didn't bring books or flowers or bottles of cool drink. She had a briefcase with her and she meant business.

'Nothing can ever put right what's been done to you,' she

says. 'But you can sue these men and I hope you will and if that's what you decide to do, I'll help you.'

If you look at them you'd never think that was the kind of thing they were talking about. They look like two ordinary women together. They look as if they're being gentle and kind to one another and talking about ordinary things. You could even think they were best friends.

'I know how much has been taken from you but you still have some rights left. Why don't you use them? Surely after what's been done to you, you're not going to leave it at that?'

That's what Katy wants to know but my mother has seen women beaten by men before for things they have done and for things they have never done and her fight is not for herself alone and it's not with the two madmen who hit her, it's with the whole world and that's something Katy doesn't seem to understand.

'Give the law a chance,' she says. 'If you won't, I can't help you and if enough people won't then no-one will be able to help any of us. It's up to you.'

My mother shakes her head that she won't do it and you can see how cross Katy is, even though she's trying not to show it. She wants what she wants and as far as everything else is concerned she's like a doctor and she talks the way doctors do when they ask how you're feeling but they don't really want to know.

When my mother says thank you for what she's done and for getting her to a hospital that would take her she looks right through her as though she's talking about some other person and you can see real friends are not what Katy's after, because in a way she's like my mother and her argument is also with the whole world and real friends might try to stop her and would only get in the way.

At least she came to see if my mother was still in one piece before she got on with the job but we have the feeling we've seen the last of her and she won't be back in a hurry.

My mother says we mustn't mind what she's told us about Katy's visit. It's her way and as she can't do what Katy wants and they can't agree with each other perhaps from now on they will be going their separate ways and if that's the way it is, then that's the way it has to be but my mother can't change the way she feels.

One day Katy will realize that no matter how hard she tries, the world can never be made perfect under the law because the people in it aren't perfect. That's why they do the things they do to one another and just can't get anything right.

So, even though she's gone on her way we're still talking about Katy and my grandmother, who's seen her with her own eyes now, says you can see in her face she's a woman who likes her own way. That is the way God made her and she likes to walk alone.

Some people are like that and maybe they have the right idea. We're born alone and we die alone and if we choose to walk alone in the middle part of our journey you can understand that, and it's not such a bad thing really.

When my mother sits in her dressing-gown on the end of the hospital bed with James' flowers and books and the glass with a straw on the locker next to her and looks at me in that way she has, I can't look at her at all and then when she looks away I can't take my eyes off her.

She looks really horrible. There are big black stitches in her face and black and blue all around them, her eye is red and swollen to a tiny sticky slit with eyelashes poking out of it. Her lip is big and fat and split open and her two front teeth are broken. There's wire sticking out of the front of her face and she has a white neck brace on her neck. She looks just like Frankenstein.

I go to the hospital every day with my grandmother holding me by my hand and dragging me along and talking nicely to me but I don't talk to her at all. I don't even answer her if she asks me a question and she doesn't know what's in my heart. If I had my way I wouldn't turn in at the hospital gate. I would go right past it and just keep on walking.

I hate that hospital. I hate the way the nurses talk to my

mother asking her how she is and telling her she'll be going home before she knows it and saying how popular she is and how many visitors she has and how brave she is and how pleased all the doctors are with her because she never complains and is a real example to everyone.

I don't want to be there and I think my mother knows it although she never says anything to me.

What I hate most of all is seeing my mother looking in the mirror at her face and pushing her hair back the way she always does so that she can get a better view of it.

I can't understand how she can keep on looking at something so horrible as if it's the most interesting thing she ever saw in her life and it hurts me to see my grandmother sitting on a chair by the side of the bed so small and so quiet, not even trying to say that all of it is God's will and not for us to understand because my mother will never allow that kind of talk.

But some good things come out of it. These days my mother talks nicely to my grandmother and to Stella. She's not so impatient with them any more and she tells Gus-Seep it's fool talk to say he'll go after the policeman who hurt her with knives and with his gangster friends. That won't do any good and it's not what she wants in any case.

She wants her Seepie to be safe and not to run any risks because if her face wasn't so sore and she could smile, he's the one she would smile at because if he will bend closer she will whisper a secret to him and the secret is that he is her favourite and she has a soft spot for him.

She looks at me a lot. She thinks I don't see her but even when I pretend I don't, I do.

I can feel her eyes on me but all she does is look. She never has anything to say to me and that's all right with me because I don't have anything to say to her either.

Then one day it's different.

'You're always in such a hurry,' she says. 'But today I want you to stay and talk to me for a few minutes after the others go. Your granny will wait for you outside in the passage. She's not going to run away without you.'

This is not what I want and she knows it. I don't want to

be alone with her and whatever it is she has to say to me, I don't want to hear it and when we're alone and she's ready to speak I am standing as far away from her as I can get and my eyes are on the ground.

'Why can't you look at me, Lily?' she wants to know and she's sitting straight up in her bed like a queen, with pillows behind her back and her hair a black splash against them and sitting between all her beautiful hair is her truly horrible face.

There are just the two of us and she's waiting for me to answer and through my screwed-up eyes which I can hardly bear to lift off the floor so I can look up at her I can see she looks like Dudda One-Eye with her one eye still red and half-closed and the other one flashing.

'I asked you a question. I'm waiting for an answer,' she says and she sounds like Mr Christie when he's fed up with us and in a bad mood.

'Do you think what happened to me is the end of the world?'

That's the question and because I'm quiet and going red and the cat's got my tongue, she knows without my saying it that this is exactly what I think and she shakes her head as if she's angry but has just remembered it's no good being angry with me. I may be stupid and not the smart kind of child she likes to have around but like it or not, I'm all she has. I'm the cross she has to bear.

'If that's what you think, then you're very much mistaken,' she says. 'Worlds don't end that easily. Whether we're ready for it or not, tomorrow always comes, so we may as well get used to the idea.'

She says what happened to her is a part of life and that's all it is. One day I will find it all out for myself which, to be honest, I am not so keen to do as I once was.

There have been times lately when I think life is a bit like The Whip. You pay twenty cents so you can go round and round at the speed of light and feel the lights flashing in your head and hear the music playing and the people shouting after you while you fly around but after a while it makes you feel a bit sick and you want to get off but the lights are still flashing and the music's still playing and there's no-one to tell you feel sick and have had enough and you have to stay on until the end of the ride because that's what you paid for.

'You can do something for me in future,' my mother says. 'I want you to look at me and not keep turning your face away. It's not a big thing and I think you can do it if you really try but you must make me a promise.'

I say that I will because that's what I have to say but I'm not so sure.

'Promise me you'll always remember it's only my face that's broken and when you think about it, that's not such an important thing. A person's heart is the thing that counts and it would take more than two madmen and all of the Government to break my heart. Only the people I love can do that.'

I'm scared to look, but because of my mother being the way she is and quick to get cross, I'm more scared not to, and once I make up my mind and do it, it's not so bad really and my mother looks right back at me with her good eye flashing fire and I know what my grandmother says is true. Spirits are just the same as arms and legs. No matter what people tell you they can be broken. But not my mother's.

15

Temperance

In the middle of all these bad things, out of the blue, Carole-Amelia is back in my life. She's written me a special letter to say she found out what her mother did and she's sorry. She misses me and as far as she's concerned we're still best friends and will be to the end.

'Sorry's all well and good,' my grandmother says, 'but if it was a horse it wouldn't take you very far.'

She pulls up her nose and says that's something I should think about while I'm so anxious for Carole-Amelia not to stop liking me and to go on being my friend but I need something nice to happen to me and so I don't want to think about it right now.

Carole-Amelia says she's been thinking about me. She couldn't understand what happened when my letters suddenly went missing because she kept them in a special place in a chocolate box under the jerseys in her cupboard and when her mother said the maid must have thrown them out by mistake she never believed it.

Her mother's like that. She always blames everything on the maid. That's why no decent person will ever work for them.

She went on writing to me for a long time and her mother was always pretend-nice and said she would post the letters for her while she was in school so they could get the morning post and get to me quicker but no letters ever came back from me any more and she'd almost given up on me.

She was spending her life running backwards and

forwards to the letter box and moaning about it because there was never anything there for her any more and in the end, she got on everyone's nerves and they would like to have killed her but she wouldn't stop.

She made up her mind to get on a train and a bus and come and find me, or to ask her father to bring her one Sunday in one of his cars and he said he might and she begged and pleaded with him and nagged him so much to do it straightaway that in the end her mother had to tell her the whole story, which was that her letters had never been posted.

She told her straight out that she had torn them up and thrown them away and Carole-Amelia says there really were a lot of them. She doesn't know exactly how many but a whole pile, because she considers me her best friend and tells me everything and she doesn't care if we're different colours but that is something her mother just can't understand.

Her mother thought if she didn't hear from me for a long time, she'd forget all about me but she didn't, so for the sake of peace in the home, her mother said she could write me one last letter and explain things, and that's what she's doing and she hopes I understand.

Her mother is good for nothing these days and her father has found a full-time maid to look after them. She's a native girl and she has a maid's name because her real name is in native and too difficult to say.

Believe it or not, their girl's maid's name is Temperance and that was too much for her father. After he heard that, he knew she was the girl for them and he took her there and then and wouldn't even look at another girl although plenty of girls come to the gate looking for work these days. He said a bit of temperance was exactly what they needed in their house and Temperance would suit them just fine.

Carole-Amelia likes Temperance very much. She's black as the ace of spades but she's willing and she smiles a lot and everything is spick and span, so her mother can be in bed every day until twelve o'clock before she starts screaming for Temperance to bring her cold Coke and tea because she always wakes up thirsty in the morning and cold Coke and tea is what she wants and she won't stand up out of her bed until she gets it.

In the beginning her mother didn't see what was so funny about Temperance being Temperance and asked her father to let her in on the joke because if everyone was having such a good laugh about it maybe he should explain it to her so she could have a good laugh too because she'd lost count of how many years it was since last she'd had anything to laugh at.

So he told her. Only, when she heard what the joke was, she didn't think it was very funny and that's why in the beginning she gave Temperance such a hard time which was just to show who was the madam.

She told Temperance that if she liked the idea of working for them, she must call her madam and the master was master and Carole-Amelia was Miss Carole-Amelia.

Carole-Amelia says she liked that. She thought it would be like being called Miss Lillah or Aunty Lillah which is what I told her people in our house call me but it isn't the same.

Her mother finally got over the 'madam' business when she saw what a good worker Temperance was and things are back to normal now, except Carole-Amelia is not going to be an air hostess any more.

She says she has news for me but I mustn't tell anyone. Not a living soul and especially not her mother.

She knows I don't know her mother and have never clapped eyes on her but after her stupid letter to my school I must have learned a thing or two and all she'll say is that I don't know how lucky I am.

The news is that Carole-Amelia is learning to drive. Her father says you're never too young to learn and is teaching her.

They don't go out on the roads yet but as soon as she hurries up and looks a little bit older they'll be able to get away with roads as well.

So, you better watch out, she says, because I'm coming

for you in my Ford Thunderbird and we'll both look as old as the hills and we can ride around like two maniacs.

She has not forgotten.

On Sundays Temperance wears a uniform and badges and goes to the Church of Zion. All the maids in the garden suburbs do. They meet in one place and cluck away to each other in native and they look so happy you'd swear they hadn't seen another living soul for the whole week and if you go past them they don't even notice you. All you see are teeth and smiles and them having a good time.

The Sunday business doesn't really suit her mother but her father says she better keep her big mouth shut about it because there's nothing wrong with a maid who goes to church. It isn't like stealing or lying around drunk all day which is what some people do and anyway, good girls like Temperance are hard to find and he wants to hang onto her.

Her mother says if he believes the church story he'll believe anything and Temperance probably has ideas of her own and behind his back she's doing exactly what she likes.

Good-as-gold Temperance probably has a big, black boyfriend who sneaks in and out of her room every night just like all the other native girls do and the two of them are probably getting ready to murder them in their beds and steal their things.

She says she wouldn't be at all surprised but she doesn't care. She doesn't care about anything any more.

Carole-Amelia says she doesn't think it's true about Temperance murdering them in their beds. Her father told her he doesn't know why her mother is so worried about it. She wouldn't even know the difference.

On Sundays when Temperance has her day off and her mother wakes up shouting for cold Coke and tea, that's the signal for her and her father to make themselves scarce. They go out quietly and get in the car and her father puts in some potato chips and a six-pack for himself and a six-pack of baby Cokes for Carole-Amelia and they take a

drive out in whichever car is at their house for the week-
end.

Mostly they drive into the country to the old motor-
racing track. Hardly anyone goes there any more and grass
is growing everywhere but it's quiet and they like it and her
father takes the car for a burn just to get everything out of
his system and she sits on the grass and watches him and
when he's had enough he parks the car under a tree and
they put out a blanket and lie next to each other and drink
their six-packs and then she takes the car for a spin herself
with her father sitting next to her.

Round and round the track they go. As much as she likes.
Until it's time to go home but they never leave until she's
quite sure she's had enough and can't drive another inch
because her father says it's her day and they'll stay or go to
suit her and he won't budge until she tells him she's ready
to go home.

It is all up to her. If it was up to him she thinks they
could stay there and go round and round forever but even if
it has to end sometime and they have to go home at the end
of it, this is still what she would call a really good day.

Her father says there's no reason why she shouldn't be a
stock-car driver one day. It was what he wanted to be when
he was her age but then he grew up and met her mother
and that was the end of that.

If you start early enough the world can be your oyster
and you can end up with your name in lights and everyone
coming out to see you burning up the track at a zillion
miles an hour and that's what she's going to do. This is also
the reason why she's not going to be an air hostess any
more. Her plans have changed and she wants me to be the
first to know.

She says she meant all those things she wrote on the back
of her letters. H.O.L.L.A.N.D. and I.T.A.L.Y. and everything
else and she truly believes that when we are grown up and
she gets rid of her mother we will meet.

In the meantime she will never forget me and will make
it her business to find me one day and see me face to face
because that was the idea of 'Getting to Know You' in the

first place. She's sorry that in the end it all went wrong and fell flat on its face but never mind, H.O.L.L.A.N.D., for old times' sake.

It's a nice letter and I show it to my grandmother and Gus-Seep and Gus-Seep says he's sure Carole-Amelia is a good girl at heart and I mustn't hold what happened against her.

It is all her mother's fault, any fool can see that but at our age we have to do what our mothers tell us and I suppose that's true but Carole-Amelia's mother is one thing and my mother is a completely different story.

16

The Way It's Going To Be

Since my mother came out of hospital there have never been so many cars outside our house. Our best cups are out so often my grandmother says it's a waste of time putting them back into the display cabinet after they've been washed up. So they live in the kitchen now with the everyday things.

The Sash have been very nice. In the beginning we thought they were stuck up and snobs. We would never have believed when you got to know them they would turn out to be such nice women. We see a lot of them now and we've changed our minds for the better. It just goes to show we can be wrong the same as anyone else can.

They have a lot of time for my mother. When she was still in hospital they went to visit her every single day, just as if they were the ordinary people and she was the special one and Stella didn't even pull my mother's leg about it because, without their sashes on, they were just like ordinary people and not that different to us really.

They made a big fuss of my mother and brought her a garden full of flowers and soft things to eat and jelly in a hundred different colours so she wouldn't starve and wouldn't hurt herself even more while she was waiting for the doctor to take her wires out and the dentist to fix her teeth and they told her that Issy's husband had taken her away to give her a baby.

Being the kind of man he was it was the only thing he could think of to do to keep Issy in her place and they supposed that was one thing he was good for anyhow and they all laughed about it and my mother tried to laugh with them and she would have if she could.

My mother is nicer these days. She doesn't mind these smart women sitting at our kitchen table or offering to wash up their own teacups, which is a thing my grandmother would never allow them to do.

She tells them how welcome they are in our house and when they say what a nice house it is, she says it's small but we like it very much because it's a house full of memories for us.

'I grew up here with my sister and my brothers,' she says. 'And if these walls could speak they'd tell you a few stories. We spent our childhood here. My sister was married from this house and my father was buried from it.'

But we are part of the removals now. One of these days the house will be pulled down and we will be moving to the Flats and she's not quite sure what will happen to us after that. That is the next problem and that's what she's thinking about now.

The Sash women speak the same way James does. The removals are terrible and a disgrace but despite what is happening to us, we must keep our courage up because it is just one chapter and not the whole story.

'When you feel up to it, you must come back to us,' they say. 'There's a lot of work to do and we need you to work with us. We'll always have a place for you.'

My mother shakes her head and tells them she made up her mind when she was in hospital that instead of worrying about the whole world, it's her own family she must think about now and she thinks the world and the Sash will manage very well without her.

When she tells them this you can see they're really disappointed. They say they would be proud to have her stand with them and she could do it again, any time, any place, anywhere.

They mean it too. You can see it in their faces but when they ask her what her answer is she says she doesn't think so.

We are not blind and deaf and dumb. We can see for

ourselves that our world is getting smaller and soon it will vanish altogether.

My grandmother and Stella and I aren't fools but we should have been smarter and we shouldn't have let ourselves be fooled by my mother sitting so quiet waiting without a murmur for her broken face to get well.

She looked sad and as if butter wouldn't melt in her mouth and we all felt sorry for what happened to her but we could have saved our sorry. We couldn't see what was going on inside her head. We didn't know she already had her plans for us all worked out.

She knew what she was going to do and so did James but they kept it to themselves and we went on with our lives pretending that no matter how much things changed the important things would always stay the same.

Then one day, when they were good and ready, they told us what was coming next and we knew then why they'd had so many secrets and couldn't look us straight in the eye. What had happened before had not been easy but this was going to be the hardest thing of all.

James is the one to tell me.

It's winter school holidays. A Saturday afternoon and he's been visiting at our house and because it's what he wants we've stepped out together to take a breath of air.

We're walking in the rain dressed in our raincoats and I'm wearing red wellington boots and we're talking nicely to each other.

'Why don't I ever see you wearing the birthday locket I gave you?' he wants to know. 'I've been wanting to catch you out to see which boy's picture is inside it because I know you'll never tell me who your sweetheart is. I wanted to have a look for myself.'

I tell him, in case he doesn't know it, that locket is solid gold and too valuable for someone my age and my grandmother worries I might get careless and it might get lost, so it's put away in a box until I get older and grow into it.

'I think we must do something about that,' James says. 'You're not the kind of girl who loses things and that's not the kind of locket that should spend one more minute in a box but I'll buy you a safety chain if it makes your grandmother happy.'

They've almost finished with our Valley now. It's an empty place and because it's raining and not really a day for people to be walking, it feels as if James and I are the only people who are left.

It never used to be like this. Not ever. Not even if there was a tornado and the rain came down out of the sky like a river. But it's different now.

The people we know have gone away little by little so at first we hardly noticed, because it didn't seem so important. We were getting on with our lives and when we looked again there was hardly anyone left.

It's what my grandmother said. It's like bleeding to death a drop at a time but it all works out the same in the end. When you wake up you're dead. I see that now and I see it doesn't only happen to people, it happens to places too.

It's happened to our Valley but funnily enough it doesn't matter so much to me because I'm happy.

I don't care if we're the only people left. I wouldn't care if we were the only people left in the whole world. The empty streets are not so bad if you remember the people who were once in them and if you get sad because they're gone, you can always close your eyes and pretend they're still there and, in your mind, you can put them all right back there where they belong.

We're walking along talking about our lives and I'm doing a skip and a jump which is what I always do, to try and make our steps rhyme but James' walk is too big and I can't make it work.

We're telling about our lives and the things that have happened to us. A little bit him and then a little me. The way friends do. As though there's no difference between us at all.

He says I may have heard that because of the sit-in at the College he lost the chance of being made principal.

'It was something important to me,' he says. 'But when it turned out the way it did I found I didn't mind nearly as much as I thought I would and if I could do it over again, I'd do it the same way.'

There are worse things that can happen to you in this world and we both know that now.

'While we still have our voices left I think we must use them,' James says and he splashes puddles while he's saying it and doesn't even know he's doing it and although we're talking grown-up things, he's not like a grown-up at all.

'Are they going to take our voices away as well?' I want to know.

'I don't think so,' he says and he gives me a nice smile. 'I don't think so for a single minute but I wouldn't be surprised if they tried.'

We are together under his umbrella and the rain is coming down like anything and my red wellingtons are jumping in and out of puddles and James says we may as well walk down past the old graveyard towards the river where the weeping willows are, because the rain is making the river come down like Victoria Falls and it's a sight to see.

I tell him about the old lady gum trees and about Andries and how I used to like going to the old graveyard and how after Andries put his head under the train I used to light one of my birthday candles for him every night because Mr Asher told me that is what you do when you want to remember someone.

I tell him a little bit about Mr Asher and Miss Tebaldi and Mr Gigli. I tell him I still have the records Mr Asher gave me for my birthday. I haven't had time to play them lately but I will play them for him one day if he'd like me to and he says one day he would like that very much.

I tell him some other things too but I don't tell him everything and when it's his turn he tells me how all through his university days and even when he was still at school he used to come to our house and how my mother taught him to dance and Stella wound the gramophone and my grandmother sat like Queen Victoria in one of the Chesterfield chairs and how much she enjoyed herself.

He says he pushed himself into our family looking for a dancing partner and wanting to get to know my mother better, because she was the prettiest girl he'd ever seen and how he did get to know her and to know me too and the rest of our family and how he ended up as a friend of our house.

We walk along for a bit more and he tells me some other things too about how things used to be, but I don't think he tells me everything either.

It's nice by the river. We can't sit down because even though the rain has stopped and turned back into clouds everything is dripping and wet.

So we stand side by side under James' big umbrella which is so big it's like a little black house over our heads and my wellington boots look pretty, red on green in the wet grass and the river swirls by brown and foaming and ice-cold like beer and the bare willow branches are wet and weeping real rain tears into the water which they never do in summer and it's really nice there with James standing next to me and the old lady gum trees on the little slope behind us and the white wall of the graveyard behind them and something comes into my head.

I know I'm not ever going to be like my mother who's always running around looking for something more and if God stopped the world right there and then and asked me how I was getting along, I would be able to look Him straight in the eye and tell Him how happy I am but I don't think James is and so I ask him what's the matter.

'I asked you to come for a walk with me because there's something I want to say to you,' he says and I can see it's a serious thing because James has a look on his face I have never seen there before.

'You mustn't mind that it's me who's saying this. Your mother wanted to talk to you herself but I thought I should be the one. After all, I've known you for a very long time. I've known you for much longer than your mother has.'

He says he's been showing off to my mother and throwing his weight around as far as I'm concerned.

'I told her you'd grown up right in front of me,' he says. 'I don't know any other child as well as I know you and when I look at you now, I see you aren't going to be a child for very much longer and so we must make the most of you while we can.'

He says he never used to have much time for children but I'm a good advertisement for them and have turned out to be such a nice girl that he's begun to think differently and has gone so far as to tell my mother this and I can just imagine that. My being so nice must have come as news to her. She must nearly have fallen on her back.

'You don't always like your mother as much as you would like to, do you, Lily?' he says and I don't even have to answer him because he knows it's true.

'You don't have to feel guilty about it because it will change. You'll see. One day when you're older and know her better and understand her a little bit more, it will be different.'

He says if I don't mind him saying so and won't take it as an insult, he thinks in some ways he and I are a little bit alike and sometimes he looks at me and thinks he understands me and that's why he wants to be the one to say what has to be said.

'I think when I've told you what I have to say and you realize what a big thing it is, you'll go home and think about it. That's all I'm asking right now. Just think about it. Will you do that?'

I watch the river going by and I say I'll think about it but I know about 'think about it'. Grown-ups say that to children to make themselves feel better when it's not good news and everything is already decided and there's really nothing to think about at all.

James says nothing lasts for ever. Things change and that's what's happened to the Valley.

He realizes now there was nothing anyone could do to stop what was happening but he and my mother felt they had to try and they'd tried their best and although I needn't understand all of it now, he wants me to know they will always go on trying. Only, now, with no hope left for the Valley, they will try in other ways.

'The terrible thing that happened to your mother wasn't for nothing,' he says. 'I want you to remember that. One day people are going to talk about these times and ask what you remember about them and then you'll have a very special story to tell.'

My story will be that my mother was a woman of courage. When times were bad she stood up to be counted and didn't mind how much it cost her and we both know it cost her a very great deal, more than some other people, who were not as strong as my mother, might be willing to pay.

This is what James says while we stand by the river wrapped in the cold, clean air with the smell of the wet ground all around us.

'It's going to take more than one person to put things right,' he says. 'It's going to take all the energy and all the will of an awful lot of people. It may take a very long time, longer than anyone expects and it's going to be very, very hard.'

He says he and my mother, my grandmother and Stella have looked at the way things are changing and seen how different everything is these days from how it used to be.

He says because I am the youngest they have been worrying about me and what will become of me.

'We've talked about it a lot,' he says. 'We don't think what's happening here should be your battle. Once upon a time your mother thought it should be, but she changed her mind and your grandmother never agreed with it in the first place. You're not responsible for what grown-ups have made of the world, Lily, and you shouldn't be made to pay a price for it.'

He says I am the most precious thing in all the world to each and every one of them and when a person's house is burning down, it's always the most precious thing you want to save.

They have a plan which he is going to tell me.

That's why we're there facing each other with the smell

of rain around us and raindrops shining like diamonds in the grass and the little beer river rushing by and James' black umbrella over our heads because of the last drips of rain and he looks me right in the eyes and tells me that the plan is to send me away to England to live with my uncle, Errol, in Southampton.

He knows it's a big surprise to me and a long way to ask someone to go, even if it's for the best reasons in the world but it will only be until things get better at home and when I ask him when he thinks that will be, he can't say. He doesn't even try.

This is what they have sent him to tell me.

Gus-Seep's old carthorse has dropped dead, Frank Adams' medals and all, and because his heart is so tender Gus-Seep can't take it and has disappeared.

Just when I need him to tell my family that I'm not going anywhere, he's gone missing and so, on top of everything else, we have that to think about and we're all nearly dead with worry because we remember the day the police came to tell us about Royston.

Not even Philander or the girlies down at The Buildings know where Gus-Seep is. Stella has asked them. They say they aren't holding anything back and if they knew where to find him they'd tell us.

They used to know everything but that was only when Gus-Seep was there to tell them. Now he's missing they know as little as everyone else. All they can say is they hope he hurries up and finds his way back soon because The Buildings are coming down one of these days and they're all going to have to move on and they can't imagine going anywhere without taking Gus-Seep and his harmonica with them.

Life's very funny. In our family Gus-Seep is always pushed forward as the biggest storyteller in the history of the world but it seems to me that the rest of my family aren't so very far behind him.

My grandmother and Stella have always said when trouble comes knocking at the front door a family must stick together. They've said that at least a million times and now trouble has come and is right here inside our house and looking at us with its teeth bared, they've decided to send me away.

I can't understand it. Not unless they've been lying to me all my life.

At least with Gus-Seep you know where you stand. He tells stories but he doesn't hurt anyone. He doesn't look you right in the eye and tell you lies.

I keep thinking about my Uncle Errol living in Southampton which we always talked about as if it was a faraway place, about as far away as you can get but it's turned out that in the end it isn't far enough away because my mother managed to get hold of him.

You'd think he would have had a heart attack from shock getting a letter from her after all these years. He must have thought someone had died or we'd won the sweepstake and were coming to visit him. My mother is lucky he didn't keel over dead from a heart attack with her letter in his hand because then she would have had a death on her conscience.

Not that it would have worried her. Once she's made up her mind it wouldn't make any difference at all to her and it doesn't make any difference to me, because I'm not going anywhere and no-one is going to make me.

I have learned something from my own family that I didn't know before. People are funny. First they stab you in the heart and then they're nice to you and carry on as though nothing has happened.

'You must stop this nonsense and all this crying,' Stella says. 'Granny's worried to death about Gus-Seep and you're just making things worse. Every time we look at you, you've got a thousand questions and you blame us for things we can't even help and then you start crying all over again.'

She says I must pull myself together and stop upsetting people because in case I don't know it, other people in our house have their troubles too.

I know that but I don't care.

Gus-Seep's gone and Evie is back with her mother again and flat on her back in bed with nerves and disappointment and blaming us because James didn't get the principal's job after she bragged to all her friends that he would.

'Think about all the people who've already packed up and left the Valley and taken their broken hearts with them,' Stella says. 'Think how they feel trying to put roots down all over again out on the Flats.'

She asks me if I know that even old Dollie is gone now and when they took down his faraway-places pictures and put them on the back of the lorry they just fell to pieces because they were so old. 'By The Seaside' where I had my picture taken for a treat was lying in little pieces all over the road and people even trod on it by mistake and broke it up even more so that, in the end, it could never be put together again.

'I know it's hard for you but it isn't easy for any of us,' Stella says. 'Poor Granny has to pack up after a lifetime in this house. She doesn't know where she's going to land up. At least you know you're going to Errol.'

Everyone is fed up with me but I can't help it.

'Really, Lily, you must try and put yourself in other people's shoes. Everyone is doing the best they can and so must you. You must do your best to understand.'

What I understand is that everything is different at our house. It's not what it used to be. These days no-one can look in my eyes when they talk to me except my mother and that's because she doesn't care.

She has no heart. We all know that and trying to talk to her is like talking to the wall and your breath is wasted.

She lets you talk as much as you like and when you run out of words and have to catch your breath that's when she catches you and chips in and tries to make you listen.

She says Errol is a big success in Southampton. He's the manager of a clothes shop and although I may not know it that's exactly the right job for him because he was always a very smart dresser and one step ahead of any fashion that was ever invented. Everyone said so.

'Did you know, before he was a dancing teacher or a steward on Union Castle he was apprentice to Mr Bardien?'

I didn't know and I don't care. Mr Bardien is the Muslim tailor who used to be on the main street but he's gone away to Mitchell's Plain now and just thinking about that and how things used to be makes me start crying all over again.

'He could have gone far in that line if it was what he wanted. He never forgot the tricks of the trade old Bardien taught him and these are the kind of things which come in useful later in life.'

This is Stella chipping in and putting in her five cents' worth.

'That's often the way and you should remember that, Lily,' she says. 'Everything you learn in life can turn out to be useful to you later on.'

When I ask about Errol being a smart dresser Stella says she doesn't know about that. He certainly didn't dress like anyone else she knows and people on the street were always looking out for him to see what he was wearing and what he had to say for himself.

They could always see him coming and he always had something funny to say to them. It was the easiest thing in the world for him to make people laugh and although what he said was sometimes a little bit too naughty to suit my grandmother's tastes, when people said Errol was a bit of a card you had to agree with them.

When Errol went out he sometimes looked a bit too much like a Christmas tree for Stella's liking but my grandmother's ears have been out all the time and she doesn't like it when the conversation goes this way, so she chips in and says she doesn't know about that and that's not what really matters anyway.

'What matters is that he was always a good boy and people had a lot of time for him and so will you. You'll see if I'm not right.'

We all love Errol now. The way they are all going on, if my mother told me Errol could tango on water and never even get his feet wet I wouldn't be surprised and they'd expect me to believe that too.

People certainly get funny when they stab you in the heart.

I put my money on Gus-Seep because Gus-Seep understands things and has never let me down, but he's still missing. We keep hoping we'll wake up one morning and find him lying drunk on the floor of our front room like we used to but although I look every day and run there straightaway, first thing in the morning when I wake up, so far this hasn't happened.

Stella puts the blame squarely on the horse. The horse is the one who broke Gus-Seep's heart by dying and although it wasn't such a wonderful horse Gus-Seep thought it was and he always said that except for Flora Dora there was no other horse like it and he would never hear a word against it.

Gus-Seep couldn't have loved that horse more if it was the winner of the Durban July and had made him a millionaire. He and that horse understood one another and he treated it as if it was a baby and they went everywhere together.

If we ever wanted Gus-Seep we could send one of the children to look for him and if they could find the horse they knew Gus-Seep wouldn't be too far behind. But those days are also over and it's the police who bring Gus-Seep back and they hand him over to us with a warning.

The police haven't got much time for people with broken hearts and wandering ways and they tell us this straight.

'If a man can't find his own way home, it isn't a police problem,' they say. 'We'll help you out this time but there won't be a next time. If your son likes the gutter so much next time we'll leave him lying right where he is and when he sobers up properly, you make sure he knows that's what we said.'

Poor Gus-Seep. After the police have gone he stands in our kitchen with his face hanging down and my mother puts her arms around him and calls him her little Seepie and looks as if she's going to burst into tears any minute and Stella says he looks a picture of misery but he must cheer up because it's not the end of the world. It's nothing a few slices of bread and polony and a cup of coffee won't fix.

We're just glad to have him back in one piece because we were mad with worry about him but he's not himself. He eats up all his polony sandwich but even then he's not the Seepie we know. He doesn't even try to cheer us up and make it better with one of his lies. I think it's because it's hard even to lie when your heart is broken and so we just stand there and look at one another.

My grandmother says I must look on the bright side and keep my chin up and remember I'm going away but it's not for ever. It's only until they get settled in a new place and things change for the better but she can't say when that will be.

'Perhaps when I turn a hundred years old things will have changed for the better and then I can come home but everyone will have forgotten me by then.'

'Don't you talk like that,' my grandmother says getting hold of me. 'Do you think I'd ever let you go for such a long time? I could never spare you for that long and your mother and James both know where I stand. So you can pick your chin right up off the ground if you don't mind. We don't need any long faces around here.'

She says I mustn't think about the day I leave them, which is all anyone seems to be talking about these days. I must think of the day I'll be coming back because between ourselves, that's what she's doing and can't I just imagine what a red-letter day that will be.

'You'll come straight to our new place,' she says and I ask her how I'm supposed to do that when I don't even know where it will be and she tells me not to keep myself such a fool.

'I suppose it'll be somewhere in Athlone or Salt River or Lavender Hill. What difference does it make? You'll know straightaway which place it is because I'll have my nice

315

ginger cake baking in the oven and you'll smell it the minute you get out of the car.'

She says I'll give everyone a big surprise when I tell them I don't need anyone to show me which is my old granny's house because I can find it all by myself.

All our old friends and neighbours will be settled out on the Flats by then so when I arrive with my suitcase in my hand I'll think I'm right back where I started and will never know the difference.

That's what my grandmother says.

'If you think there was excitement the day your mother came walking down our road then you better think again because that's nothing compared to how it will be the day you come back.'

She says I can mark her words and must give her a big smile right now, straightaway before the clock strikes or the wind changes because she can see just by looking at me I'm not looking on the bright side and on that day, when I come home, I will feel a big fool for being so sad right now.

'You don't believe me but you'll see. Time will go quickly and it'll seem to you you've never been away at all. Time's like that. You blink and it's all behind you.'

She'll blink and I'll be back and grown up and speaking such lah-di-dah English no-one will understand a word I say. I'll be such a young lady they'll have to look twice to be sure it's really me because I'll be dressed to kill in all the latest fashions.

'Errol will make sure of that and money will be no object. That's something you can say about Errol. You'll be walking into the best shops and pointing out what you want and he'll have his wallet out before you can even open your mouth to say what you fancy.'

This is the way we talk because it makes us feel better. I haven't even gone yet and already we're thinking about all the things we'll talk about when I get back, so it isn't really so bad.

*   *   *

316

'James and I have something to tell you, Lily,' my mother says. 'It's something we could pretend about but we've never lied to you and we won't start now. We think you should know the truth.'

My mother has never pretended anything to me just to make it better and she has never lied. So, when the day comes when she and James sit down with me in the front room of my grandmother's house where we can close the door and be alone and no-one can hear us and my mother tells me the truth, I believe her.

The truth is that although they've filled in all the forms and done everything that was asked of them, I can't have a normal passport like other people.

'It's partly my fault,' my mother says. 'I won't pretend it isn't. It's one of the ways they have of punishing people for being what they call troublemakers. They think I need to be put in my place.'

She's been told she must learn her lesson once and for all and her lesson is that she can't do just as she pleases and expect the world to carry on as if it owes her a living.

These days passports are like the sweets you offer children. You can only have one if you behave yourself.

'All the arrangements have been made and you're still going to Errol just as we planned,' James says. 'So that hasn't changed at all.'

'What has changed then?' I want to know and I look at his face and I look at hers and I wonder which of them will be the one to tell me because I can see whatever it is, it is not good news and this time my mother is the one doing the talking.

Her eyes never leave my face and her voice is very serious and she tells me without mincing her words that I have to leave on something called an exit permit. It's the only way.

They explain it very carefully and tell me all the reasons why it is this way. They tell me exactly what they've been told themselves but they needn't have bothered. I know what an exit permit is and they can see on my face that I know.

James shows my mother that he wants to say something too and he does.

'We're not free to come and go as we please any more,' he says and he says it in that quiet way he has, so that even though he's telling you something really terrible, it doesn't seem quite so bad.

'It's another part of what's happening to all of us these days but what your mother says is true. We never thought you'd be punished for decisions we made and things we chose to do. I know it's unfair. We didn't want this to be your battle but now it is and that's not fair either.'

These are some of the truths we must all face these new days. So we sit in the front room of my grandmother's house where once my mother taught James to quickstep and to waltz and we face them together.

The truth is that it's all over. There's nothing left of our Valley. There is the graveyard and there are the old gum trees that have been there for ever but they stand by themselves now. There's no-one left to sit in their roots and crack their friar's balsam leaves and listen to them creak like old ladies in the wind.

The churches are still there and the little pink roses mosque with the silver star and the sickle moon like a hajji hat on its head but everywhere else the grass is already beginning to grow in the rubble where the houses once stood and not even the southeaster has any respect for us any more.

It roars off the mountain on its way to the bay as if it's angry with us. It sets the dust dancing so it gets in our eyes and stings our faces and we think it's having fun and games with us and doesn't mind if we get hurt in the process.

The Buildings have gone and their music has gone with them and Gus-Seep has taken to wandering again and Philander is sitting in some other place dreaming of long-gone Matilda with her sweet ways and her generous heart and there's no Gus-Seep to comfort him with a little tune on his harmonica.

The truth is that one of these days my grandmother's legs will carry her up our hill for the last time and there will be no Stella on her hopalong way home after work. They will be on their way and I will be on mine but we will be going in different directions and that is the hardest truth of all.

With an exit permit you can go but you cannot come back. So, that is the way it is to going to be.

When Gus-Seep hears I'm leaving he says if it was up to him he would have the Coons dancing on the docks even if it wasn't exactly New Year and I would have a send-off to remember.

In the old days he could have done it and he would have been there himself. He would have been playing a tune on his harmonica and dancing with the best of them and never mind if those days are past, he still has a surprise for me and the surprise is a big hanky Stella made out of a piece of Gus-Seep's old Dixie Darkies Coon suit.

It's rock and roll pink satin with emerald green stripes and there's black all around it.

Even if the Coons aren't there to give me a proper send-off and see me on my way at least I have a little bit of them to take with me, just for the memory and on the day that I leave even if he's the only one there who's danced in the New Year with the Coons in Roeland Street, he will still be there to wave me goodbye. He will come with his horse and cart and I can depend on it.

But things are different now and his horse is dead and in the end, on the day I leave Gus-Seep goes missing again. He hasn't even said goodbye to me. I haven't had the pleasure of looking on his face one last time, last look, just for old times' sake.

James comes in his friend's car to take us to the docks and although he makes a big thing about carrying my suitcase out ready to go in the car and saying how lucky I am and what a world traveller I'm becoming, I don't mind because I know he's only trying to cheer me up and make me feel better because there's been a terrible fight at our house and I can't even look at my mother.

It's about Stella's snap album.

'Don't you feel like giving me the snap album for a goodbye present?' I say. 'Just for old times' sake? Then I can show it to Errol and tell him all about the pictures and when he sees how you all look these days, we can have a good laugh together.'

Although I've been thinking about it, at first I didn't like to ask because I know how Stella loves that album, but I love it too and I really want it and this is the very last thing I ask for.

I'm ready to leave and am dressed in my new travelling clothes and look the smartest I've ever looked. Just the thing, Stella says and my grandmother says I'm a proper young lady and look the part and at least I'm not going to disgrace them when I get to the other side.

I'm wearing a navy-blue skirt and brass-button jacket to match. I have a white blouse and a lace collar and I have stockings on my legs like a grown-up lady for the first time in my life and their seams are straight as arrows and I know this because I nearly break my neck to keep on checking on them.

My hair is out of plaits and although everyone says it looks fine, it's nearly as wild as someone else's hair I know and I can feel it tickling around my face and at the back of my neck as if it knows going out in a grown-up hairdo for the first time is a serious occasion, but it will try and make me laugh anyway.

I'm wearing a red beret on my head because scarves are for working women and not young lady travellers and my grandmother has already kissed me a thousand times and straightened my clothes and I'm ready to go.

'No hard feelings if you don't want to give it,' I tell Stella. 'I'm only asking because I'm going such a long way, otherwise I wouldn't ask at all and I'll look after it, cross my heart. When I come back I'll give it back to you, right in your hands with a few snaps of my own in it.'

It isn't the whole truth. The truth is that I'm afraid if I don't take my life with me to look at whenever I like, I might not remember.

That's what I've been thinking and that's what's been worrying me but I needn't have worried because Stella says it's fine by her. She goes to fetch it and puts it right in my hands and says it's her pleasure to give it to me and I can have it with her love, even the picture of Frank Adams which I don't really want.

I kiss her and say thank you and hold it across my heart against my chest with our whole life in it and my mother says I must say thank you and give it back to Stella because I'm not allowed to take it.

'Stella doesn't mind,' I say. 'She said so. She knows I'll look after it.'

'You heard me, Lily,' my mother says. 'Give Stella her book back. We don't need a whole long song and a dance about it and say your goodbyes now once and for all. We have to be on our way.'

She's being spiteful. I know that. It's a small thing to ask and important to me and Stella knows how I feel but I can see on her face that she won't go against my mother and make a big fight just before I leave. So when I hold out the album, she takes it back and gives me a little smile to show if it was up to her, she would give me anything in the world I asked for, for old times' sake, and now our final goodbye is spoiled and I will never ever forgive my mother for that and I don't care if she knows it.

All that is left of the Valley now is open pieces of ground and houses with boards across their windows and broken-up steps and streets and still my heart is sore about leaving here, especially because of how it is now.

My grandmother knows how I feel and her heart is sore too but she tells me she's made up her mind about something in this time while my mother's been with us and for a goodbye present she will tell me what it is.

Our old Valley is exactly the same as my mother is. Its face is broken but not its heart and not its spirit. She says those are the things we carry inside us and the only things that really count and if I remember this and think about it this way, perhaps it will make me feel better about things when I am far away. But I am not so sure.

James says that for a treat I can sit in the front of the car with him but I don't want to.

'She can sit in front,' I say and I'm so cross I won't even look at her and I won't give her a name. 'I'd rather sit in the back.'

I have my suitcase next to me and I don't even care about my new stockings. When we pull away I kneel on the seat and look out through the back window and wave.

My grandmother and Stella are standing by our gate with their arms around each other and their cardigans over their summer overalls. The little bit of loquat tree is sticking over their heads like a sunshade and they wave back so hard you'd think their arms were going to fall off but in a blink they are gone.

As soon as we turn the corner they're out of sight and then I sit in the middle of the seat with my suitcase big and heavy on my lap and my hands folded on top of it and I look straight ahead between my mother's head and James' and I don't say anything and they don't say anything either and so it's a long drive to the docks.

The ship is very big. You don't get that idea when you look at pictures but up close you can see why it's called a Castle.

In real life the ship is like a floating building and not what I expected at all. There are cars all over the show on the dockside and people waving them on and showing them where they can stop and when they must move on.

There are native boys carrying so many suitcases you can't see them properly and people are calling out to each other and everyone is in a hurry except us and James is talking nicely all the time and my mother is smart as paint but if you'd paid me a hundred rand I wouldn't have been able to look in her face.

'When we get to the passport office, let me do the talking,' James says and he doesn't say please but it's right there in his voice.

He gives her a little sideways look but she's looking out straight ahead of her and you'd think she was deaf.

'I know how you feel but there's no turning back now. You just have to make peace with it. We agreed on that. You remember what we said? No matter how they treat us, let's just do what we have to do and get this over with as quickly as we can.'

James always speaks nicely to my mother, just the way he speaks to everyone, so it's hard to know what he's said wrong this time but when she turns her face to him, it doesn't matter about the scars, that look we all know is on it.

'We want a good send-off for Lily,' he says. 'We agreed on that. No matter how you may feel, we don't need any fireworks. Not today.'

We all know by now that fireworks when we least expect them are my mother's speciality but there should be no need for them this time because we know what we have to do. The passport men in the office in town have told us a hundred times and then told us all over again just in case we're stupid and don't understand, so we know exactly what we must do and we have plenty of time to do it in.

The passport shed is full of people standing in rows under their letter of the alphabet. Mine is D for Daniels and there's nothing my mother can do about that. I have to have a name and my grandmother gave me hers, free of charge and no questions asked and I'm proud to have it.

My mother had no other suggestions. No matter how many times my grandmother asked her, she made no offers and it's far too late now and in the passport shed my name is something my mother can be grateful to my grandmother for because the D queue is shorter than some of the others and moving fast.

The passport man is not so bad. He greets us nicely and asks for our papers and James hands them over and my mother's face is like thunder because he takes one look at them and one look at us and pulls up his eyebrows and holds up his hand to call someone else over.

One passport man is not enough for us and our exit permit, we have to have three and we also have to be taken to a separate table miles from anyone else.

We're the only people this is happening to but at least once we get there they ask if we would like to sit down and James puts my suitcase down and says thank you, we would like to sit down but he doesn't dare look at my mother.

There we sit. James and my mother on either side of me and me in the middle and the passport man opens up my passport and looks at my picture in which I am grinning like a fool and then he looks at me, just to make sure.

'So you're the one who's travelling,' he says and he looks at my book and he looks at me. 'And how old are you, may I ask?'

'Lily is eleven years old, nearly twelve,' James says. 'Her date of birth is in the passport.'

The man looks at me even harder because although I'm not small like my mother, despite my grown-up clothes, I still look young for my age and no-one would expect to see me riding a Ford Thunderbird. Not yet.

'The purser knows all about Lily,' James says. 'Special arrangements have been made for her with the Union Castle office in town.'

I will share a cabin with two older girls who are also travelling and a retired schoolteacher and they will keep an eye out for me.

The Government office in Cape Town have letters from my uncle in Southampton and from lawyers there, and my uncle who is a citizen of England now will fetch me from the purser's office once we reach the other end. It's all arranged and all in my file.

'Your arrangements with the Union Castle Line are your own business,' the passport man says. 'They've got nothing to do with me.'

He puts my passport down on the table and lifts a red stamp but he doesn't stamp it down at once like they do in the post office. He turns it around and shows it to us so we can read the upside down writing on it.

'An exit permit is a very serious thing,' he says. 'It's not something we see every day. Not even here. Do you understand what it means? Once I've stamped this passport and you leave the country, you'll never be able to come back. Do you understand that?'

He asks me if my mother and father have explained all this to me and I can feel my mother move as if she's going to say something but James speaks and in his nice voice says we understand. Everything has been explained to us many times over and they have discussed it with me.

I am a very bright girl, he says and I understand perfectly.

Then James tells the passport man how it is. He says this is not a thing they've done without thinking about it. The only reason they're doing it at all is because they have no option and because I am so precious to both of them they want me to have the very best in my life and when he says this he looks right at me and I can't help it. I have to go red and smile.

I knew James would answer for me but I can speak up for myself now. I am not afraid of this man or anyone else for that matter. I have realized something over these past weeks. My grandmother is right. God takes away something with one hand but he always gives back something else with the other. No-one need speak for me any more. Those days are past. I can answer for myself now.

'My family have explained everything to me,' I say and I look the passport man straight in the eye and don't look away. 'There's nothing about it I don't understand.'

In a way an exit permit is like Roeland Street. They lock the door behind you and throw away the key. You can't change your mind. There are no second chances.

The man says he has children of his own and asks again how old I am and if James is my father and James says he is an old friend of our family and they have entrusted him to speak on my behalf.

The passport man looks at us one at a time and shakes his head as if he's never seen people like us in his life before, then he bangs down the red stamp on my passport and he says as far as he's concerned, that's the end of the story and I'm free to go.

Inside, the ship is like a palace. You can't see the sun but it doesn't matter because there are electric lights everywhere and my grandmother would fall right over if she thought about how much that must be costing and thick carpets for your feet and everyone is so excited you would think we were going to a dance.

James has me by the hand although I am really too big for that now and my mother is walking behind us.

We know the name of the lady purser who will look after me and the names of the other girls and the schoolteacher in my cabin.

We know the name of the steward who takes my suitcase down a million corridors, with us walking behind and being greeted by people we've never seen in our lives before and they look at my mother in the way people look at her these days and pretend they don't notice what has happened to her face, as if it makes no difference to them at all and perhaps it doesn't.

Everyone is excited and willing to greet every person they clap eyes on even if they don't know them from a bar of soap.

James greets back but my mother won't and I don't want to look at her so I look down at the floor and my first-time stockings gleaming in the light and my shiny new shoes marching along.

I don't have to look at her. I know without looking that she has that look on her face and it's a look like thunder.

The steward is small as a jockey and he talks all the time and is nice to us. He says he has a special place on the deck for me from where I can wave goodbye to my mother and father when the ship moves out and no-one says anything because he means well.

'Your place is in a private part of the deck, as high up on the ship as you can go,' he says. 'It's supposed to be First Class and VIPs only but that's you, isn't it?'

I am the youngest person travelling alone on the ship and he says that makes me a VIP in his book and nothing is out of bounds to me.

'When you stand up there the people down below will look very small. When you wave to them you can pretend you're the Queen.'

Our arrangements are all made. James and my mother will say goodbye to me right there at my waving spot but that will not be the last I see of them. When the ship whistle blasts for all ashore they'll go down on the docks and I'll stand where I am so they know exactly where to see me and I can stand there as long as I like waving away.

There is a band. There will be music. The ship's siren will blow and there will be a lot of noise. The steward has explained all this to me and when I'm ready I know my way back as far as the purser's office and when I get that far someone will send for him and he will take me back to my cabin because he is at my service. It is his job and his pleasure. That is what he says, so that is how it will be.

When we are alone James calls me Aunty Lillah and says he has something for me and he takes a box out of his pocket and inside it is the gold sweetheart locket.

'You remember that day we talked about it?' he says. 'I wanted to give you something special to remember us by. I persuaded your granny to let you have this back.'

He's had a safety chain put on it, for 'in case', and he puts it around my neck himself and does up the clasp and the safety chain and says quietly in my ear I must remember it is his surprise for me and very, very special.

He asks me if I have a big kiss for him. He says I must make it the biggest kiss I can manage because it will have to last him for a little while and while he's thinking about it, perhaps I can spare him two kisses, a big kiss and then a last kiss and he asks if I can manage that and I say I think I can.

James is tall. He has to bend down so I can put my arms around his neck.

'Last kiss, Aunty Lillah,' he says right in my ear. Last kiss and then he stands up and turns away quickly and I give him last touch but his eyes are shining and he doesn't seem to notice.

'You say goodbye to your mother now,' he says. 'And I'll go and find a good place we can stand to wave you on your way.'

He says he hopes I'm not so grown-up these days that I've forgotten all our old games because we haven't finished yet. There's still last look and that can go on for a very long time and he, for one, has not forgotten about that and then he remembers and he gives me last touch quickly and I touch him back.

Sometimes when we play he turns back fast to catch me out because the one who gets last touch will be the lucky one. That's how the game works but this time James is going quickly as if he's in a big hurry and he doesn't touch back. So I suppose that makes me the lucky one.

Then there's just my mother and me.

She's very smart, my mother, just like she always is. Smart as paint, my grandmother would say.

She's tall in white high-heeled shoes and her legs are shimmering with nylon and she's wearing a blue dress with a big white collar.

'I know you're cross with me about the snap album,' she says and I say it doesn't really matter and I don't want to talk about it.

'I want to talk about it,' she says. 'And I want you to listen to me because what I have to say is important.'

She says the snap album belongs to Stella and even

though Stella will give it to me and it's hers to give, it's not really mine to take because the life in pictures in the snap album doesn't belong to me alone. I am only a small part of it and a latecomer.

My life isn't one bit like Stella's life in pictures.

'The big difference is that your life is all in front of you and you don't need to look behind.'

She asks me if I understand what she's saying to me but I don't really, so I don't answer her. I don't even look at her.

'When you love someone you want to give them the world. Stella would have given you that album and anything else you asked for but afterwards, when she and Granny are alone and want to have a look at those pictures of all of us, they're going to miss it like anything and she'll be sorry then for giving it away, even though she'll never tell you that.'

My mother says love makes fools of people. It makes them silly and over-generous and when this happens, if someone doesn't keep a sensible head on their shoulders and think for the others, the whole world will be given away and no-one would even have thought twice about it.

'You don't need Stella's pictures,' she says. 'You already have all the pictures you need. They're right inside your head and in your heart of hearts and you can look at them whenever you like. You probably have enough pictures inside you to last you for the rest of your life.'

She says they will jump into my head when I least expect them to. Mostly they will cheer me up but sometimes it will not work that way at all. Then they will pull at my heart and make me sad but I must expect that too, because that's life and something I will very soon find out for myself.

'Don't worry about the pictures, just write to Granny as often as you can and if you and Errol have new pictures you can slip one in with the letter for her to look at because she'd like that.'

She says my letters will be like gold to my grandmother and I must write neatly with all the spelling right and no crossing out, to show I am becoming an educated person and I must also write big to show I am kind, because no matter what she says, even with her glasses on her nose and right in the middle of her face, my grandmother doesn't see very well and that's the reason she reads so slowly.

'The one thing you never have to worry about is that your family will forget you or you will forget them. You never will. Not even if you want to, not even if a day comes when that's what you want more than anything else in the world.'

It's a very strange thing to say but this is the way my mother talks. A day like that will never come and my mother only talks like this because she says the kind of things no other person would ever think about saying and she hasn't found out yet that she isn't always right.

My mother stands there looking at me in my new grown-up lady clothes, in my smart coat and my first-time stockings and my red beret and my sweetheart locket shining in the sun and she carries on as if she has all the time in the world.

She isn't worried about the ship's siren going off or the band beginning to play because things like that don't worry her.

She says what she wants to say and she says it in her own good time and as far as she's concerned the world can go along in its own sweet way, it doesn't worry her at all.

'I don't want us to part with bad blood between us,' she says and she calls me Lily, which no-one else in our family does.

'I know when you saw me walking down the road that day you were expecting and maybe hoping for a very different kind of person. I know I'm not anyone's idea of a mother but there's not very much I can do about it.'

She stands with the wide-awake seagulls dancing in the air above her and the breeze pulling at her hair and she looks into my eyes and says she knows it will be no good saying she's sorry to have disappointed me because that's just the way things are. She's the kind of person she is and I'm the kind of person I am and it couldn't really have turned out any other way.

She has one last thing to tell me and she says if I will

listen carefully she will whisper it to me in my ear just the same way Gus-Seep does when he has special secrets to tell and she bends down and puts her mouth close to my ear as if she is kissing me goodbye and I can smell her scent and her skin is soft and warm against mine and she whispers to me and she says that no matter what I think of her, what she wants to tell me is that I am exactly the kind of person she would like me to be and she wouldn't want me any other way.

It takes some time for my mother to get off the ship. The band is playing and the people on the docks are throwing rainbows of paper streamers and they spin out fast and curl against the blue sky.

The docks are full of people and they're throwing their streamers one after the other and calling out people's names and blowing kisses and it's like Roeland Street at Coon time and the air is so hot with excitement I'm surprised you can't see it like the midday heat haze that shimmers like water on the streets in the Valley but disappears when you start chasing it.

I can see my mother's back. She's walking between people towards where James is standing in a good spot high up on the concrete block in front of the passport office.

She's walking in the same way she walked on that day when she walked down our hill back into our lives, only this time she's going the other way, walking on her white high heels and the bright colours of fallen paper streamers are all around her. They are lying in her path like flowers.

You can see she's a dancer because her back is so straight and her head is held so high and behind the combs that keep it in place her hair is flying out like a black cloud that wants to be up and off and fly away on its own private business and she walks so lightly it looks as if she isn't touching the ground at all.

I lean over the rail and look down and it's true what the steward said. The people on the dock look very small and I think, if she loves me she will stop and look back before she gets to James. It's what my grandmother would have done. My grandmother never left me anywhere without looking back at least twenty million times just to make sure I was still there. But my mother is not my grandmother. She doesn't stop. She doesn't hesitate. Not even for a minute. She doesn't turn her head. She just keeps on walking and by the time she reaches James the gangplank is up and the little green and yellow tugs are pushing at the big ship and tooting their hooters as if they're in a hurry and the band is playing and the ship is moving away from the docks.

It's a very strange feeling. For a ship as big as a floating palace our ship moves like a swan across the water so if you don't look down and see the bits of oil like rainbows drifting, getting bigger and then breaking up you would never think you were moving at all.

The band plays 'Now Is The Hour' and I think about Gus-Seep and the horse bible and how I came to know Carole-Amelia in the first place and the streamers stretch out further and further, bright pink and purple and blue and lime green, like the Muslim women's dresses at Labarang time and they are like reins and you'd think people were trying to hold the boat to the shore with them but they are only paper and they begin to break and fall into the water.

It's a funny feeling. It feels as if you're not moving at all. It is as if you are standing quite still and all the small people on the docks are the ones who are drifting away.

'Wish Me Luck As You Wave Me Goodbye' plays the band and I can see James' handkerchief waving. I have forgotten Gus-Seep's Dixie Darkies hanky, rock and roll pink satin and emerald green and black around the edges, and I pull it out of my skirt pocket and hold onto it tight so it won't fly away and I wave like mad.

Last look, James. I shout it out loud. I don't know if he can hear me but I don't care because I feel like shouting anyway. Last look, James. Wish me luck as you wave me goodbye.

My locket is gleaming gold in the sun and I lift it up to look at it, for the memory and for the joy of seeing it shine like fire in the sun and it springs open when I touch it and inside, cut out neatly, one in each side, are Dollie's ID pictures of my grandmother and of Stella and I know now this is James' surprise for me because he is not like my mother. He likes to be quite sure and does not trust to memory, and he knows me, because now that I am grown up in some ways we are alike. We are not people who take chances when it comes to remembering the people we love. He knows now I will have my people with me for always.

I can still see James and my mother but they are very small and my mother has a hanky out and is waving it and I am leaning on the rail watching them go further and further away and I am waving like a mad person and I am not cross about the snap album any more.

I think if I close my eyes and breathe in deep enough I will be able to smell my mother's scent coming to me across the water and I think it will be a smell that will follow me all the way around the world.

I hoped the wind would be blowing so old Van Hunks could blow me out and the white horses could dance next to our ship and pull it along to the big sea but it is a fine day and you can see the mountain against the sky and it looks as if someone has drawn it there with crayon.

It's funny about the mountain. It's so big you could never move it and it is always there. You know you won't wake up one morning and find out that it's packed up and left in the night like the people in Kitchener Terrace used to do.

But when you glide along like a swan on the sea the mountain looks different. You can't believe it is holding up a whole city at its feet. It looks as if it is made of light and in a very little while you can't see the city at all. Just the blue mountain floating between the blue sea and the blue sky and I like that. I like the idea of our house with my grandmother in the kitchen inside it floating carefree in a big blue as if they are already living in Heaven but they just do not know it.

The sea is big. You can't bring it home in a bottle like I used to think, but I know this now and I think about Joycie living in a maid's room on top of Mr Asher's flats in Sea Point and looking out at the big sea every day of her life.

I never got to Sea Point like I promised but I wish Mr Asher could see me now because you go right past Sea Point on the way to England and you can see the blocks of flats sticking up like little teeth with the maids' rooms on top. I can see them for myself and I still have my Coon hanky in my hand and I wave it. Goodbye, goodbye, Mr Asher and goodbye, Joycie, I call, even if they can't hear me. That is not the important thing. It is the thought that counts.

I think that if my ears were as big as my grandmother says they are, if they were only big enough, I would hear Miss Tebaldi and Mr Gigli singing in Mr Asher's flat and their singing would be like my mother's scent and follow me all around the world.

Then it is over and I listen to the hum of the engines and the swish of the sea and I dig into the inside pocket of my brass-button, going-away jacket to put the Coon hanky away and inside the pocket I feel something like paper and I think that in the rush Stella has left the price tag in my jacket and now it is stuck and won't come out and I pull again and I feel a safety pin and I dig deeper and I know what it is. It is not a price tag at all. I can feel it and I know. I know.

I undo the pin and pull the paper out and it is my old label with my name on it and my address at my grandmother's house and I know my grandmother must have come into my room when I was sleeping and put it there just like she always does and I know something else too. Although it is true that the world is a big place I know where I belong in it and so do the people who love me.

17

Last Lines

My Uncle Errol makes a big fuss of me. He and his friend, Tony, cannot do enough. They treat me like a queen.

They have a nice house with stairs. I can't get over the stairs. I have always wanted to live in a house with stairs right inside the house and not just going down into the backyard and now I am. So that is one good thing.

Errol was waiting for me when my ship came in and although I was wearing my label because I knew it was what my grandmother would have wanted, I needn't have bothered. We would easily have found each other.

'You're your mother to a T,' Errol says. 'I would have known you anywhere. Every time I look at you I see your mother. I keep wanting to call you Gloria all the time.'

It's funny. When Gus-Seep talks about his ship coming in he means it in a different way but my ship really did come in and it needed two tugs to show it the way because there's no mountain in Southampton so there's no way of knowing for sure you really are at the end of the line.

Errol and his friend, Tony, were waiting for me and waving like mad from the docks and holding up a big board with my name on it so I would be sure to see them.

I'm lucky. I have my own room and everything in it is pink. The sheets, the blankets, the curtains, the carpet and the eiderdown.

'We've always wanted a pink room in our house,' Errol says. 'But so far it's only been us two lads living here and we didn't want people to give us funny looks but now you're here with us, at last we can have our way.'

They have me to thank for that, or at least that's what Errol says.

I like Errol. In a way he reminds me of Gus-Seep. It's his way of talking I think. He always looks for nice things to say and stories that will make people laugh but he isn't such a liar as Gus-Seep is. At least I don't think so but it's still early days and time will tell.

He cannot do enough for me. There are clothes in my cupboard. Skirts and jerseys and a coat with a velvet collar and every kind of shoe you can think of.

I have a Dolly Varden dressing table with a pink frill and a hairbrush and comb and even pink rose soap still in its paper, with a label on it and it smells to high Heaven. There is nothing they haven't thought about.

There's a framed picture on the wall. It's meant to look like embroidery but it isn't. I stood on the bed to touch it and see. It's of a small house with lots of flowers in the garden and butterflies and little birds all over the show. There's a neat path and the blue smoke coming out of the chimney in supposed-to-be cross stitches. It's like no house I ever saw but then it's only a picture. Underneath it says 'Home Is Where The Heart Is' and that part's true.

'I hope you like it,' Errol says. 'Because it's yours, just like everything else in this house is because this is your home now and it's share and share alike here just like it was in Constitution Street.'

I don't have much to share but I gave Errol the picture of himself as Carmen Miranda. Old Dollie sent it to me when he heard I was going to live with my Uncle Errol and Errol looked at it, at himself in the skirt and the sequin bust bodice and the big gold earrings swinging all over the place and the red lipstick mouth and the painted eyes and the basket of fruit on his head and he couldn't believe his eyes.

He laughed so much he had to sit down.

'Come and have a look at this,' he said and he handed the picture over to Tony but he was laughing so much he was shaking and the picture nearly fell on the floor and when Tony saw it, he laughed too.

'Show us a leg then,' he said and Errol pretended to

dance and swung his hips a bit just for old times' sake and I shouted, 'Swing your hips, sugar lips!' just like they do at Coon time and Errol did his best but you really need all of Roeland Street and the open road to do it properly but Tony didn't know that so he laughed anyway.

We all laughed until we got tears in our eyes and Errol kept saying those were the days and imagine old Dollie keeping the picture all these years and when I write to Granny I must tell her she should go to old Dollie and tell him Errol can still shake a leg with the best of them and I can tell my granny this is true and no fibs because I've seen it with my own eyes and that's the message Dollie can pass on to anyone who will still remember him.

People here are very nice and polite but they keep themselves to themselves and live very quietly.

Errol tells everyone I'm his sister's child from sunny South Africa and am living at their house now.

'This is Miss Lily of the Valley,' he says. 'And you better mind your p's and q's with her because she's a proper little madam and knows her own mind.'

He winks at me when he says it and doesn't tell anyone else why he calls me that. He says it's our little secret but even when I go to the shops without him the shopkeepers say what can they do for Miss Lily of the Valley today. So it looks like this is my name here but I don't mind.

Errol's house is not too far from the docks and sometimes we take a walk and sit there and watch the ships come and go and if there's a lavender lady of the Union Castle Line, we look to see if there's anyone we know on board so we can go up to them and ask them if they've seen our people in Cape Town and perhaps have some news for us but so far there hasn't been.

Errol says we may just strike it lucky because the world is a small place. It's much smaller than we think and so you never know and one day we're almost sure to see someone who knows us.

Sometimes we sit there for quite a long time and the

world comes and goes and there's always a lot to see. It's a bit like a poor man's bioscope but it's not the same and I like it best on the days the lavender ladies are there because they're nice ships and like best friends to me because I've been in one and I know them now and we don't have any secrets from each other.

I watch them being unloaded and I know where they've come from and where they're going back to and in my mind I ask them to take messages back and little kisses and to say that Aunty Lillah, Miss Lily of the Valley, remembers everything and everyone and sends her love.

Then Errol looks at his watch and says it's home time and time for a nice cup of tea and then we go back the same way we came.

At first he used to hold my hand but I told him it was silly. There's no need for that type of thing now. I'm too old to have my hand held. I won't get lost. I'm old enough to walk alone and he gives me a funny look but I think he understands.

Epilogue

I did not see my grandmother again. She went to Salt River with Stella and died there two years later. Stella telephoned to tell me.

They wanted me to come home for the funeral and James went to the passport people and talked about exit permits and special circumstances and asked if I could come back even if it was only for a single day but they looked at him as if he was mad and told him that old people die every day and my grandmother's death was not a special circumstance.

They told James people like us are amazing because we want our cake and we want to eat it too. Has no-one ever told us an exit permit is a one-way ticket and one-way means you can't go running backwards and forwards for funerals or for any other story you feel like cooking up. You can forget about it. It doesn't work like that.

If we didn't know it before, we know it now.

Stella says I mustn't mind. They hadn't built their hopes too high and, in the end, when they realized I wasn't coming they went ahead and buried my granny without me being there to touch her face one last time and kiss her goodbye and wish her well on her way.

It was a very nice funeral but Stella was the only child there. Errol and I were together, my mother was long gone and Gus-Seep had gone missing the way he was always doing these days.

A lot of people came from the Flats all the way to the cemetery at Maitland out of respect for my grandmother who was a woman they all knew. There were all kinds of faces there from the old days, even poor old Mrs Elias put in an appearance although there was no sign of Portia.

They sang 'Rock Of Ages' which was what my grandmother had always wanted and they sang their hearts out and she would have been pleased about that.

Afterwards they went back to the little Salt River house where my grandmother had seen out her days with Stella to look after her and there was curry and funeral rice, yellow with turmeric and sweet with sugar and raisins and plenty for everyone.

The Muslim women sent their husbands all the way by car with little Labarang cakes all colours of the rainbow, even though it wasn't Labarang, just for old times' sake and enough for everyone to have one or two to remember them by the sweetness and all in all it was a very good send-off.

Stella kept expecting my mother to make an appearance, prancing along on her high-heeled shoes, smart as paint and dressed up to the nines but she didn't and everyone who was there was too polite to mention it or to ask any questions. It was exactly like old times but it didn't spoil anything. It was a very nice affair anyway.

Stella writes to me. After my grandmother died, she married Frank Adams. He came back from the whalers with money in his pocket just like he said he would and he came looking for her.

He decided his days of being a rolling stone were over and he was on the lookout for a nice, old-fashioned girl who knew where a woman's place was and wasn't too full of herself.

Stella was of the same mind and had been for years so nothing could suit her better.

They have no children but in a way they have Royston and the way Stella is carrying on these days you'd think he was a saint.

There's no family either side for them to have Sunday lunch with so they go to the Maitland Cemetery Extension instead and spend Sunday at Royston's grave.

At first, Stella says, they used to take flowers but that

didn't work out. The Extension is new and there's no water trough like in the old graveyard in the Valley.

At Maitland there are only hosepipes and these keep getting stolen, so they've put some nice everlastings on Royston's grave instead of fresh. Really nice. Under glass. Violets and roses and daffodils. If you didn't know, from far you would never tell the difference. At least that's what Stella says.

My mother was killed in a car accident outside Johannesburg and one of her friends, a man she was in business with, got word to our family.

James went up by aeroplane to see to things and he wrote to me about it and said he knew exactly what to do because they'd talked once about how she would like everything done if she died one day and he did exactly what she asked, in the same way he always did.

When she left the Valley the last time, she told him she'd made up her mind that after all that had happened there, she would never come back again and James made sure she never had to.

We all knew how my mother was when she made up her mind about something and it would take a braver man than James to try and do things differently. This is what he wrote to me.

She was cremated in Johannesburg and he took her ashes and threw them to the wind. He said he liked to think of the wind blowing wherever it pleased and my mother riding high and free on it and having a bird's-eye view of our little world and seeing for herself how small it actually is when you're free at last and can see what it looks like when you have the sun and the moon and the stars and all eternity for company.

That was how he liked to think of her and how he thought about her now and he thought it was the kind of thing she would like too.

It is hard to find a high place in Johannesburg. Everything there is as flat as a pancake but in the end he managed to find a little hill and that's where he could do

341

my mother a small service, at last, after all these years. It was all he'd wanted to do all his life and a pleasure she'd always denied him.

When it was over, he sat on the ground for a long time and thought about her and while he sat there, he realized nothing had really changed at all.

She walked through his head just the same as she always did, stamping her way along through his thoughts as though she owned them, with her eyes flashing fire and her face all in one piece again with her beautiful smile right in the middle of it and her hair flying out behind her as if it had a life of its own and wanted to fly off free all by itself.

He wasn't sad. He said it was all right and he was happy, happier than he had been for a very long time.

He was sitting there thinking his thoughts when he heard a sound like an express train coming fast and it was one of those flash summer storms that come rolling in from the veld in the late afternoons.

There was the sound of thunder and the sky boiling with clouds and it sounded as if God had his fighting boots on and was pushing his furniture around Heaven and there was lightning everywhere and thunder cracking and it began pouring with rain and in two minutes flat he was soaked to the skin and the world was going mad around him and it served him right for sitting out in the veld by himself, lost to the world in his daydreams.

He said it was funny. It reminded him of my mother who'd always liked fireworks and he stood there in the rain remembering that and laughing like a lunatic in his grey suit with the black mourning band around the arm and the rain streaming down his face.

After my mother died James wrote me a long letter. He said there was some unfinished business between us and some things he'd wanted to speak to me about for a long time.

While my mother was alive he never thought it his place to speak, but now she was no longer in this world with us, he'd like to say what he felt must be said.

He wrote about my mother the way he'd known her when

she was young and the way it was between them. He said she had more energy and ambition than any girl he'd ever known and more brains too and if she'd had her chances, the very same chances she'd made sure he had, things would have turned out very differently for her.

He put onto paper the things she'd told him and the things he knew about her later life. The shameful shebeen things my grandmother and Stella would never even talk about which in the end were not so shameful after all.

He said I mustn't judge her because I'd never been called upon to walk in her shoes or endure the things she'd had to endure.

He said in many ways hers had been the hardest life of all because she was a strong and intelligent woman who'd lived in a very bad time. He called it a time of lost opportunity.

He wrote about how hard she'd tried for a better life and how often she'd suffered the humiliation of being sent on her way and having doors slammed in her face.

He said there were a great many things it was not possible for her to do and he wrote with great tenderness about her pain, her loneliness and frustration and her deepening sense of disillusionment.

'She was hindered in every possible way. Everywhere she turned her path was blocked because of her colour so that in the end she became angry and disheartened and went in another direction.'

He said if things had been different, her life would not have turned out the way it had and when I think of her this is what he would ask me to remember.

Despite everything she always knew what the right things in life were. Those were the things she'd stood up for and would be remembered for and they were the things she'd wanted for me.

He wrote very beautifully and he was generous. He gave me all he could spare of the things they had talked about in their time together, although I knew they were the most precious things in the world to him.

It was the best and kindest letter I ever had and I read it

343

again and again and never showed it to anyone else and then one day I took it out into the backyard of Errol's house in Southampton and I made a small fire in a concrete fireplace that stands there for burning autumn leaves and I struck a match and set the letter alight and watched it burn and it burned very beautifully in yellow and blue flame that reminded me of Royston dancing under the streetlights on that last New Year a long time ago and it gave off a small heat and the smell of burning paper and then it was gone.

I had learned my lesson about letters and learned it the hard way and I didn't need a letter from James to tell me that he thought my mother was the sun and the moon rolled into one and if she'd asked him to pull down the stars for her, he would have plucked them out of the sky one by one and given them to her on a plate.

I knew that. James told me other things too but he had nothing to tell I didn't already know and had not known for a very long time and because in many ways we were like one another, we understood these things and there was no more that needed to be said about it.

James stays my friend and a friend of any house where I am, just as he's always been and he writes to me sometimes and tells me the things that have happened to the people we know and I write back to him and tell him about my life as it is now and I tell him everything and hold nothing back.

Dudda Dollie became a doctor just as he always wanted. We didn't know it then but one day he would find his way into the newspaper when he became head of a big children's hospital in Sydney, Australia. When we heard it we were glad because this is the type of thing that happens to a genius and he deserved it.

Something strange happened to Jack Hoxie. One day when she wasn't looking out for herself God got hold of her and changed her back into Portia Elias again.

These days Portia works in Athlone at a centre for saving gangster girls from the street and I know what my grandmother would have said. She would have said that putting Portia Elias in charge of gangster girls is like putting the wolf in charge of the sheep, but that's what happened and my grandmother would have laughed about it and understood it and said that life is like that.

Katy van Breda died in a police cell in solitary confinement. She was arrested for unspecified crimes against the security of the state. It said in the newspaper she hanged herself but nobody believed it. She was thirty-three years old.

Once Revd Rainbird started walking he couldn't stop. He spent his last years as a fearless walker for justice. From the day he knew what he must do he never turned back and in a way it just goes to show that God is a bit like James and my mother.

He has different voices for different people but when He wants them to do something for Him he knows exactly how to tell them.

Old Humphrey died and Revd Rainbird had a small statue of a bulldog in its heyday put up in the side aisle of St Peter's Church in his memory. Underneath it is a little plaque and it says that Humphrey was a much loved dog, a true friend to man and faithful unto death.

I lived for a long time with Errol and his friend, Tony, and I came to like Southampton. Errol said he chose it because he liked to be close to the ships. It reminded him of Cape Town and made him feel at home.

He isn't crazy like my mother but he's funny and kind. He has a nice nature and he makes people laugh. In a way he's like Gus-Seep and sometimes he disappears too but we always know where to find him.

He goes down to the docks because he likes to see the ships come and go and he kept on going there long after I'd outgrown going with him and people knew him there and liked him and he didn't get in anyone's way.

It's funny. My grandmother was right about Errol in very many ways but in some ways she was wrong. If she could have seen him and Tony together she would have known it wasn't only the faraway places he fell in love with.

Sometimes at New Year we tell Tony about the Coons and Carmen Miranda and the Queens-for-a-Day and Errol dances a little bit and throws his hips just for fun and for old times' sake but it isn't the same.

I suppose it was different when he wore his costume, the satin and beads and the big gold earrings and the bananas and oranges and pineapples and grapes in a basket on his head and he was young with the music all around him and people cheering him on but Tony and I do our best.

James and Evie went to Canada and he studied there and then they went home again and now he teaches at the university. They have no children.

Even now, with everything changed, some things are still the same. No matter how hard she wishes it, poor old Evie can't get rid of our family.

She won't allow our name to be spoken in her house. James keeps my letters in his desk at the university and there are strict instructions to his lawyer that if anything happens to him they must be burned unread.

Although he does not live there any more James sometimes goes to the Valley and the first time he went back, after he had just got back from Canada, he wrote and told me about it.

He said I would fall on my back if I saw how things had changed.

The houses that were left standing, which were the good solid ones, were sold to white people in the end and tarted up so you would hardly know them. Our house was one of them.

He went to look for himself. He couldn't believe what he saw and he doesn't think I would either.

Our hill was just the same and hard on his legs these days and when he got to what had been our front gate he was only really sure he was in the right place when he saw the same old bit of loquat tree sticking out from over the top of a high wall.

He stood outside just staring through the gate at the house and in the end a very smart woman came out and asked what his business was and did he have a problem and he told her he had no problem at all. He'd known the people who lived there once upon a time and that was us.

He says she was a bit cross at first but the new owner looked a nice enough woman and in the end she was apologetic. She'd had a few frights lately, she told him. There was an undesirable hanging around their neighbourhood and you could never be too careful these days. Then she invited him to come in and have a look around at all they'd done inside, if that was what he wanted.

James said he couldn't help thinking the invitation was because she'd made up her mind by that time that he was quite respectable-looking for a coloured man and would probably stop short of knocking her over the head or raping her or running off with her family silver.

He couldn't go inside. He couldn't bring himself to do it because his heart was so full of all of us and all that had happened in that house and my mother was in his mind where she always was and his head was full of all the things that were between them, those things he'd written to me about.

Did I remember the old loquat tree in the front? No-one had ever seen a tree like it. It was always so generous with fruit. There was always enough and to spare and he was there in loquat time and through the smart new gate he could see that the tree was hanging heavy with fruit, so at least that hadn't changed and, while he was looking at the tree, for some reason he still hasn't been able to work out the woman asked if he would like to come in as far as the front yard and help himself to as many loquats as he liked.

She didn't mind how many. She would give him a bag and he could help himself.

He doesn't know why she did that but he said no, thank you. He'd just stand there for a moment or two if she had no objection and then he'd be on his way and that was what he did.

Gus-Seep is a problem.

James says Gus-Seep keeps hanging around the house. It

turned out he was the 'undesirable' the woman had been talking about and, although she didn't know him from a bar of soap, she was frightened of him and kept complaining to the police about the dangerous vagrant man in their respectable neighbourhood and the police kept telling her not to worry about it.

They knew who Gus-Seep was. Everyone did and he was harmless enough. All he was was a some-time hawker and some-time vagrant and always around there and he wouldn't harm a fly.

They'd chased him away often enough in the past. They'd even thrown him in the back of their van and dumped him miles away in the middle of the bush out in the *bundu* far beyond the Flats but he always found his way back and they were fed up with him by now. They realized they would never get rid of him so they'd decided they might just as well let him be.

Still, in the end, they had to pick him up and take him in and when they asked him who his family was he gave James' name and the police telephoned James and James who hadn't heard from Gus-Seep for a very long time went at once to see him, to find out what was going on.

When he got to the police station Gus-Seep was there, although not in a cell. He was standing out in the main charge office, very much under the weather and crying and telling terrible stories and in between the stories and the tears he played a tune on his old harmonica and then he cried some more and the way he was carrying on made the policemen laugh at him, although James says he doesn't think they were laughing at him to be unkind. They just couldn't help themselves.

Gus-Seep has gone very old and James says if I saw him I would hardly recognize him and once he'd got over the shock of seeing James there and calmed down, they sat together and had a talk and Gus-Seep whispered to James the things that were on his mind.

He said he felt death coming and was afraid, although it was not the dying itself that he minded. He was quite ready for that and it couldn't come fast enough as far as he was

348

concerned. All the people he cared about had gone away or been taken from him, so when death did come it would find him waiting and willing and, in any case, he looked on the bright side.

He didn't have much time for this world any more but he had high hopes of finding a better kind of life on the other side.

The trouble was that he missed his mother. That was why he kept hanging around her house. The thing he was afraid of was that if he was not in his place at his mother's house when the moment finally came how would she know where to find him?

James says he felt terribly sorry for poor Gus-Seep then because you could see in his eyes he was old and tired and the world had not been good to him. He had lost his way in life.

James says he couldn't have cared less about Gus-Seep's condition or the policemen being there and looking at them. He took Gus-Seep's hand and held onto it for a very long time because at that moment his heart was too full to speak and then he put his arm around Gus-Seep's shoulders as if he was his own brother and he could not have loved him more than he did in that moment. He told him not to worry.

Everyone who knew his mother knew she was nobody's fool. You had to get up very early in the morning to catch her out and here he was, her own son, telling stories behind her back and carrying on as if she had no sense at all.

James told Gus-Seep he had nothing in the world to worry about. His mother was a wise old bird. When the moment came she would always know where to come and fetch the people she loved, no matter where in the world they happened to be.

FRIEDA AND MIN
by Pamela Jooste

A moving novel about the friendship between two women against the backdrop of South Africa under Apartheid.

When Frieda first met Min, with her golden hair and ivory bones, what struck her most was that Min was wearing a pair of African sandals, the sort made out of old car tyres. She was a silent, unhappy girl, dumped on Frieda's exuberant family in Johannesburg for the summer of 1964 so that her flighty mother could go off with her new husband. In a way, Min and Frieda were both outsiders – Min, raised in the bush by her idealistic doctor father, and Frieda, daughter of a poor Jewish saxophone player who lived almost on top of a native neighborhood. The two girls, thrown together – the 'white kaffir' and the poor Jewish girl, formed a strange but loyal friendship that was to last even though Frieda chose to follow the conventional path that was expected of her, while Min felt compelled to devote herself to a clinic in the bush, leading to terrible years of oppression and betrayal.

0 385 40912 5

NOW AVAILABLE AS A DOUBLEDAY HARDBACK

HUMAN CROQUET
Kate Atkinson

'VIVID AND INTRIGUING . . . FIZZLES AND CRACKLES
ALONG . . . A COMPELLING STORY WITH EXCURSIONS
INTO FANTASY, EXPERIMENT AND OUTRAGEOUS
GRAND GUIGNOL . . . A *TOUR DE FORCE*'
Penelope Lively, *Independent*

Once it had been the great forest of Lythe – a vast and
impenetrable thicket of green with a mystery in the very
heart of the trees. And here, in the beginning, lived the
Fairfaxes, grandly, at Fairfax Manor, visited once by the
great Gloriana herself.

But over the centuries the forest had been destroyed,
replaced by Streets of Trees. The Fairfaxes had dwindled
too; now they lived in 'Arden' at the end of Hawthorne
Close and were hardly a family at all.

There was Vinny (the Aunt from Hell) – with her cats and
her crab-apple face. And Gordon, who had forgotten them
for seven years and, when he remembered, came back with
fat Debbie, who shared her one brain cell with a poodle.
And then there were Charles and Isobel, the children.
Charles, the acne-scarred Lost Boy, passed his life awaiting
visits from aliens and the return of his mother. But it is
Isobel to whom the story belongs – Isobel, born on the
Streets of Trees, who drops into pockets of time and out
again. Isobel is sixteen and she too is waiting for the return
of her mother – the thin, dangerous Eliza with her scent of
nicotine, Arpège and sex, whose disappearance is part of the
mystery that still remains at the heart of the forest.

'IT READS LIKE A DARKER SHENA MACKAY OR A
FUNNIER, MORE LITERARY BARBARA VINE. VIVID,
RICHLY IMAGINATIVE, HILARIOUS AND FRIGHTENING
BY TURNS'
Cressida Connolly, *Observer*

0 552 99619 X

BLACK SWAN

A SELECTED LIST OF FINE WRITING
AVAILABLE FROM BLACK SWAN

99313	1	OF LOVE AND SHADOWS	*Isabel Allende*	£6.99
99619	X	HUMAN CROQUET	*Kate Atkinson*	£6.99
99670	X	THE MISTRESS OF SPICES	*Chitra Banerjee Divakaruni*	£6.99
99587	8	LIKE WATER FOR CHOCOLATE	*Laura Esquivel*	£6.99
99602	5	THE LAST GIRL	*Penelope Evans*	£5.99
99721	8	BEFORE WOMEN HAD WINGS	*Connie May Fowler*	£6.99
99731	5	BLUEPRINT FOR A PROPHET	*Carl Gibeily*	£6.99
99760	9	THE DRESS CIRCLE	*Laurie Graham*	£6.99
99774	9	THE CUCKOO'S PARTING CRY	*Anthea Halliwell*	£5.99
99681	5	A MAP OF THE WORLD	*Jane Hamilton*	£6.99
99637	8	MISS McKIRDY'S DAUGHTERS WILL NOW DANCE THE HIGHLAND FLING	*Barbara Kinghorn*	£6.99
99748	X	THE BEAR WENT OVER THE MOUNTAIN	*William Kotzwinkle*	£6.99
99736	6	KISS AND KIN	*Angela Lambert*	£6.99
99807	9	MONTENEGRO	*Starling Lawrence*	£6.99
99711	0	THE VILLA MARINI	*Gloria Montero*	£6.99
99709	9	THEORY OF MIND	*Sanjida O'Connell*	£6.99
99536	3	IN THE PLACE OF FALLEN LEAVES	*Tim Pears*	£5.99
99733	1	MR BRIGHTLY'S EVENING OFF	*Kathleen Rowntree*	£6.99
99777	3	THE SPARROW	*Mary Doria Russell*	£6.99
99749	8	PORTOFINO	*Frank Schaeffer*	£6.99
99753	6	AN ACCIDENTAL LIFE	*Titia Sutherland*	£6.99
99700	5	NEXT OF KIN	*Joanna Trollope*	£6.99
99780	3	KNOWLEDGE OF ANGELS	*Jill Paton Walsh*	£6.99
99673	4	DINA'S BOOK	*Herbjørg Wassmo*	£6.99
99723	4	PART OF THE FURNITURE	*Mary Wesley*	£6.99
99761	7	THE GATECRASHER	*Madeleine Wickham*	£6.99